A GAME OF MASQUERADE

SHANI COSSINS

Content Warning Note:
Whilst the individual historically known as Jack the Ripper did exist, all other characters and events depicted in this novel are entirely fictitious. Any resemblance to actual persons, living or deceased, or to real events, is purely coincidental and unintended.

The content is semi-graphic with no extreme depictions of violence nor on-page sex scenes. It does, however, contain elements that include:

Underage prostitution and indentured servitude
Assault and sexual assault
Murder
Disembowelment
Prejudice—antisemitism
Lynching
Kidnapping

Publisher:
Australian Self Publishing Group, Pty. Ltd. / Inspiring Publishers
PO Box 159, Calwell, ACT 2905, Australia.
Phone: 61-(0) 2 6291-2904
http://australianselfpublishinggroup.com

A catalogue record for this book is available from the National Library of Australia

National Library of Australia Prepublication Data Service

Author: Shani Cossins

Title: **A GAME OF MASQUERADE**

ISBN: 978-1-923250-95-6 (Print)
ISBN: 978-1-923250-97-0 (ePub2)
ISBN: 978-1-923250-96-3 (eBook)

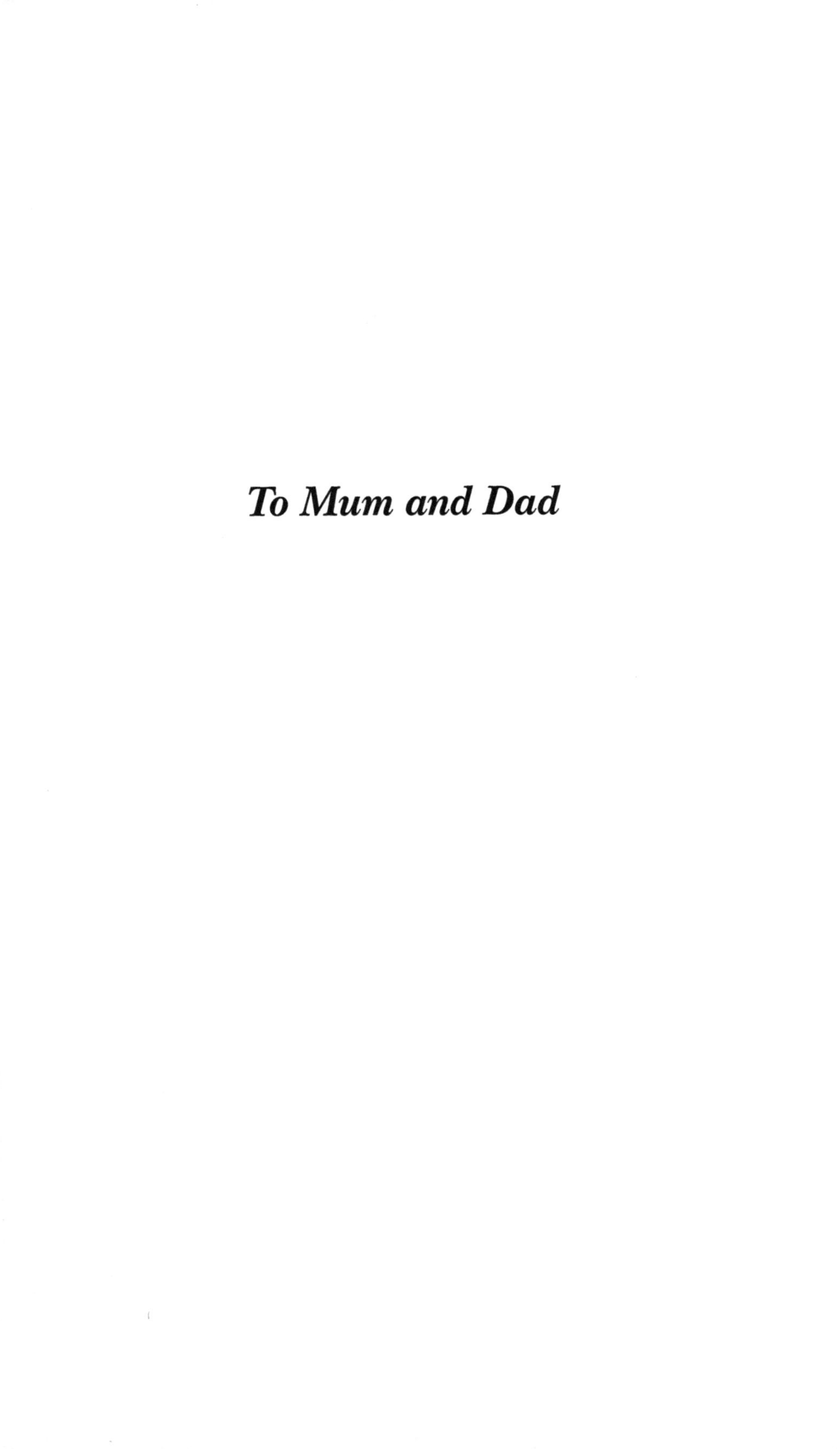

To Mum and Dad

CHAPTER 1

Martha stood in the darkening street, her once vibrant blue eyes now devoid of emotion. She had no dreams left.

She could no longer smile and barely raised her head to meet anyone's gaze. When men walked by, they looked at her with contempt and even the lowest among them kept their distance. Did she think she could charm them with her pale cheeks, marked by tell-tale red spots and her convulsive cough?

Another spasm tore through her chest and she doubled over, coughing violently. Once the spasm subsided, she wiped the flecks of blood from her chin and stood there shivering from the pain. How long could she keep going on like this? Would anyone care when she died? If she fell down now would anyone even notice an unwanted creature of the streets? Oliver certainly wouldn't but then Oliver only cared about himself and his filthy business. But what about Elsie? The woman who had found Martha crying at the water's edge all those months ago— the night Georgie had breathed his last. Would she care when Martha breathed her last? Martha clearly remembered the first time she encountered the woman. It was dark and she thought she was alone. Finally drumming up the courage to walk into the water, she kissed the lifeless bundle in her arms and stepped away from the shore.

A woman cautiously approached asking what she was doing. Martha jumped, startled by the other's presence. 'Leave me alone.'

The woman took a step back and held out her hands, palms raised. 'Is awlright, I ain't tryin' to do nothin'. Yer jus' look right upset.' She glanced at the bundle cradled in Martha's arms. 'Wos in the shawl?'

Martha pressed the bundle to her chest and took a step closer towards the water. 'Nothin'. Leave me alone.'

Elsie shrugged. 'Then if it's nothin' then wotcha got to hide?'

Martha steeled herself wondering if the woman was going to try to take her little boy from her. She took another step towards the water; the waves gently lapping over her worn boots.

'Get outta the water, you'll only catch cold.'

'I said, Leave. Me. Alone!'

Elsie remained silent for a few moments. A ship in the distance announced its presence by blasting its horn. 'New limeys'll be in town fer a bit.'

Martha didn't care; Georgie was dead and she was going to join him.

'Why don't yer come with me, I'll buy yer a drink?'

Martha couldn't see the woman very well in the darkness but she could hear the kindness in her voice. Or at least what appeared to be kindness.

The woman took Martha's silence as encouragement and slowly took a step forward. 'Was it your little'un?'

Martha gripped the bundle and whimpered a soft 'yes'.

'Boy or girl?'

'Boy.'

'Wos 'is name?'

Martha frowned. Why was she talking to this stranger? She had no business asking her the name of her little boy. Why couldn't she just go away and let her get on with the rightful business of drowning herself?

'I never 'ad kiddies meself,' the woman remarked when Martha said nothing. 'I always said I would 'ave liked to 'ave 'ad a boy but my ol' man died at sea.' She snorted. 'Hardly ever saw 'im and when I did 'e was always too bloomin' drunk to get a decent conversation out of 'im or anythin' else for that matter.'

Martha remained silent wondering if this woman was going to stay much longer.

'An' then I finds out 'e dies of some disease I ain't never even 'eard of.' The woman took a step forward and folded her arms in front of her. Martha could see her ample silhouette now that she was closer.

'Georgie George,' Martha muttered.

Elsie frowned then smiled. Martha could hear the smile in her voice. 'Now that is a proper, nice name. Do you know that George was the name of my father, Gord rest his soul. An' wot's yours then, love?'

Martha didn't want to say.

'Mine's Elsie. Only first names 'ere we use.' She lowered her voice conspiratorially, 'and it don't matter who you were before.'

Martha looked at the bundle in her arms and stepped away from the water. Her boots had leaked and her feet were cold. 'Martha.'

'Now that's a nice name too Martha I like that. Now why don't you come with me, Martha as I wager you could do with a friend.'

Tears stung in Martha's eyes and she hugged the bundle to her chest. 'I can't Georgie's dead I can't'.

Elsie stepped forward and placed a comforting arm around the woman. 'Georgie is alwright now, you don't 'ave to worry about him no more. But we do 'ave to worry about you.'

Martha looked at the woman and could smell gin on her breath.

'I know a man that takes care of me and a whole lot of other … ladies like me. The business ain't pretty but it will put food and drink in yer mouth, as long as you do as yer told.'

Martha swallowed. She knew what Elsie was and didn't think she could do that.

'You are on yer own I take it?'

Martha nodded. 'Me 'usband ran off with some trollop.' She blushed realising she shouldn't have said that. 'Sorry. I didn't mean … '

'Say no more,' the woman waved her hand dismissively. 'I know wot I am but don't make it my business to steal other women's 'usbands. Hope the cow gets wot she deserves!'

Martha smiled despite herself. Strangely, she was warming to this woman.

'Will ya come then?'

Martha hesitated. Could she really accept this woman's proposition? A moment ago she was going to do herself in but all of a sudden she had a friend where she didn't before.

Elsie took her silence as an agreement. 'Then you 'ave to let the little 'un go. Come on love, I'll help you.'

Martha sobbed on the woman's shoulder and Elsie cradled both the bundle and Martha in her arms. 'We'll do it nice and gently. E's asleep now, bless 'im an' 'e won't feel a thing.'

Elsie very gently took the bundle from Martha and placed it at the water's edge before giving it a gentle push. The bundle travelled several feet across the surface before submerging and disappearing. Martha gasped and wanted to run in after it but Elsie held her back. 'You need to come with me. Oliver will be waitin.'

And Oliver was waiting; standing outside The Ten Bells, cigar clenched between his teeth, and the veins in his neck bulging, furious that Elsie's return was long overdue. He glowered as he saw the woman trudging up the street with another in tow. 'And just where the bleedin' 'ell 'ave you been? Unless you've been 'umpin the entire Queen's Guard you better 'ave a good excuse!'

Elsie gave him a withering look. 'I did awlright t'night as I always do *and*,' she emphasised the word, jutting out her chin. 'I would like to introduce you to Martha.'

Oliver cast a blood shot eye over the woman and Martha cringed. 'So?'

'So, this 'ere lady needs a job and a place to stay.'

'Does she now?'

'And I thought if you put 'er under your protection she'd be safe.'

Oliver took the cigar out of his mouth and flicked some grit from his fingers. 'Martha is it?'

Martha gulped and nodded.

'You've been plucked, I take it?'

Elsie rolled her eyes and Martha looked down, her cheeks burning.

'Well a'course she 'as.' Elsie placed a comforting arm around her. 'I wouldn't a brung her otherwise.'

Oliver breathed a heavy sigh. Why was Elsie always bringing in unwanted strays?

'So can she stay?'

'Dunno.'

Elsie smiled, looking hopeful. 'Is that a yes?'

He stabbed the cigar at her face. 'Now I didn't say that. But,' he smiled, leering at the frightened woman. 'As it so 'appens we do 'ave an opening for a new girl.' Oliver regarded Martha. 'Course she don't look that young.' He glanced at Elsie. 'Yer couldn't 'ave gorn an' picked up someone say about ten or eleven instead? I got a few customers who likes 'em young and fresh.'

There was a roar of laughter from within the tavern and through a window a bearded, ugly brute with broken teeth banged on the windowpane, blowing kisses at the two women and flapping his tongue at them. Elsie ignored him and Martha felt ill.

Oliver shook his head at her reaction. 'I dunno Martha. You don't look as if your 'eart's in it.'

'Er heart don't 'ave to be in it,' Elsie replied simply. 'But it's better than starvin' to death.'

Martha looked at Elsie and then at Oliver smiling weakly. 'I was married to a swine who ran orf an' left me. I ain't got no place to go now.'

Oliver took another puff of his cigar and shrugged. 'Awlright. You prove yourself t'night and you can stay.' He pushed open the door to the tavern and ushered the women inside.

The only thing left for Martha to look forward to was the thought that she would soon be joining Georgie in the next life. A small flicker of a smile crept across her face before her thoughts were interrupted by the sound of horses clip-clopping down the street. She turned to see a coach loom into view and automatically straightened her dress and hat attempting a seductive stance which was barely convincing. The coachman, however, spotted her and the carriage came to a halt.

Martha eyed the fine carriage with some interest and sauntered over to the driver. He wore a long, black coat and his hat obscured his face.

'Good evenin' Sir,' she greeted politely. 'A lovely night, ain't it?'

The coachman remained silent, not moving.

'Would you care for some company Sir?'

Again he did not answer.

She nodded towards the carriage door. 'Then per'aps your gentleman passenger would like some company?'

For the third time he did not reply and this made Martha nervous. She glanced back up the street imagining the warmth and security of the tavern. She could go back. If the man didn't want anything then she'd simply go back. But what would Oliver say? *You let a toff slip right through your fingers? You dumb, stupid whore!* Then there would be the rest—a beating, perhaps something worse. No, she had to do business tonight.

The carriage door swung open. The passenger, dressed just like the coachman sat calmly looking at her.

'Good evenin' Sir ... '

He struck like lightning, dragging her into the carriage and slamming the door shut. Her terrified screams were silenced almost immediately, as a hot spray of blood spewed from a crevice in the carriage floor onto the cobblestones below.

The coach vanished into the night.

The sole occupant of a laboratory starship tossed his data-hexagon across the room in frustration. It had taken Jackard Menz, his former student, precisely three timing signatures to introduce a virus that erased every parcel of data with no hope of retrieval. Due to this wanton vandalism and the occupant's anxiety over his own narrow escape, he had inadvertently drifted off whilst manually operating the navigation controls. Did the controls develop a fault during his lapse of concentration? Or was there a tremor in the vortex that nudged him off course?

He glanced at his reflection on the panel before him. His receding fair hair was peppered with grey, and his sharp, angular features and hollow cheeks spoke of years of weary experience.

He smiled ruefully at the face before him before turning his attention to his present location. Earth, London, 1888. He had had no intention of visiting this world but perhaps it was a blessing in disguise as it would be unlikely that anyone would be looking for him here; particularly as the homing device lay smashed on the floor.

He downloaded a notebook and pencil into real-time circa 1888 and began briefly jotting down some thoughts. Handwriting was tedious but at least tamper-proof from viruses.

> ***Diary Extract 1.0***
> *I start my new life and new journal entry and immediately find myself at a loose end. I may as well take the opportunity to look around. I've only ever observed the human species from the safety of my lab; it will be an interesting experiment to view them firsthand.*
> ***Diary Extract End - 1.0***

Professor Orlando Delbrotman activated the dimension controls as a kaleidoscope of colours strobed across his face. It was past midnight, local time, and he could detect many life-forms scurrying about in the immediate vicinity. He queried the ship's database for currency requirements and suitable suggestions of attire circa 1888 electing a grey, three-piece suit with matching grey boots. Once the garments and funds had been downloaded, he dispensed with his Lecturer's Robe and replaced it with the outfit that the ship's computer had generated.

He briefly observed himself in the mirrored glass of the observation deck and straightened his tie; it would suffice. After setting the exterior shell of the ship out of phase rendering it invisible to the naked eye, he activated the door mechanism and cautiously stepped outside into the night. Dirt, stench and decay overwhelmed his senses briefly making him think twice about continuing his venture. Two prostitutes walking by spotted the visitor standing alone and quickly altered their aimless wandering to good purpose. They greeted him with big, friendly smiles giving him saucy winks, ensuring he had a clear view of their barely concealed chests. He smiled, returning their pleasantries, completely oblivious to their advances.

'Are you looking for company Sir?' one of them asked. Her words were slurred from cheap rum.

The Professor smelt the fermented brew on her breath which gave him an idea. 'I was looking for a local … public house, I think that's the right word for it. Perhaps you could recommend one.'

She gestured towards the main street. 'The Ten Bells is close by.' She looked him up and down. 'Yer new around, 'ere, ain't yer? Don't think I've seen your face before.'

He gave her a guarded look. 'I suspect not.'

Both women sniggered.

'Don't say much, does he?' one said brashly. 'Well tell us yer name then!'

'Yeah, wos your name? Mine's Maggie,' the older woman said and nudged the younger, 'an' this 'ere's Victoria.'

'Watcha doin' in an alley all by yeself?'

'I bet 'e was waitin' jus' for us!'

'That 'e was! An' now 'e's gonna get two at once!' Both women burst into fits of laughter cackling at a shared joke the alien barely understood. He knew these women were only human and meant him no harm but he couldn't shake the feeling that he was being cross-examined. It was a silly feeling but after living in a place where every action or word was scrutinised, it was hard not to be continually on one's guard.

'I walked down a blind alley by mistake,' he lied, 'which is where you now find me.' He took a step towards the street.

Maggie quickly hooked her arm through his. 'I'll show you where to go.'

'Thank you but no, I'll find my own way.' He shook his arm free and hurried along leaving the two girls disgruntled.

'Maybe 'e don't like women?' suggested Victoria. 'I 'ad an uncle like that once. 'E was more keen on little boys.'

Maggie grabbed hold of her friend's hand and scowled, 'come on let's look somewhere else. I ain't wastin' my time on 'im.'

Arnold Backer, the barman of The Ten Bells had made two shillings so far and it was barely morning. He had successfully beaten every hopeful who had idiotically challenged him to an arm wrestle without so much as working up a sweat. The losers by contrast were cradling their injured arms and being consoled by Oliver's girls; their sympathy was true and meaningful—until the money ran out.

Oliver stood on a table shouting above the frenzy. 'I'm now gonna offer yer three!' He stabbed three fingers in the air. 'Three free visits to my girls if any of you scum can beat the Emperor of Arm Wrestling: Arnold J Backer!'

Immediately the regulars who had been hesitating whether to give Backer a try dropped what they were doing and began jostling with each other to get in line while Backer obligingly finished them off one by one.

Elsie sat scowling in the corner beside Molly, Oliver's latest acquisition; she was not at all amused with the pimp's cavalier proposition. 'Who the 'ell does 'e think 'e is offerin' free ones. I've got a right mind to kick him off 'is bleedin' perch. Bastard!'

Molly took a sip of beer before replying, 'the boss; ain't 'e? 'E can do wot he likes.'

Her companion snorted. 'Well I'm not gonna be a party to it. It's bad enough being paid so little let alone nothin' at all.'

Molly grinned. 'Yeah but Backer's winning.'

Amidst the shouting, agony and sweat of the game, the door opened and in walked a stranger, unnoticed.

The Professor's senses swam with the smell of cheap liquor, heat and unwashed, reeking bodies. He grimaced and turned to leave when Oliver spotted the solitary stranger. He nodded approvingly, noting the Professor's expensive clothes and jumped off the table and approached him.

'Good evenin' to you, Sir. Care for a drink? A whore? Or an arm wrestle with Backer 'ere?'

The Professor examined the gorilla seated at a nearby table and smiled weakly. 'Perhaps a drink.'

Oliver slapped him on the back and ushered him over to the bar. 'Awl right the game's over! All you lot can bugger orf!'

The contenders grumbled and grouched but Backer stood up and gave them a warning look before returning to his place behind the bar. When the crowd disbursed one sailor was left holding a coin in his fist and he slammed it down challengingly in front of Oliver. 'I want my fill of flesh.'

'Then why don't you go ask Elsie?' another sailor yelled out. 'She's got plenty for the takin'!'

The revellers burst into fits of laughter while Elsie damned them all to hell but the sailor was not satisfied. He wanted his turn with Backer.

'I said I'm 'avin' a go and I'm not leavin' until I do.'

Oliver's smile faded and the tavern mob grew silent, sensing the friction in the air.

'You know there's really no need for this,' said the Professor politely, attempting to dispel the tense atmosphere. 'I'm sure Mr Backer here would be happy to oblige you at another time.'

The barman stared at the Professor then gave a quick nod of assent.

'Did I ask for your opinion?' The sailor walked over to the stranger, standing so close that the Professor could smell his sour breath.

'Leave it alone Skinner, like the gentleman said, you can 'ave your go another time.'

Skinner turned towards his fellow shipmate, his face as black as thunder; the room froze and Oliver rolled his eyes and nodded at Backer. Just as Skinner took a swing at the other man, Backer leapt around the bar, scattering glasses and grabbed hold of the attacker's arm.

'Yer want an arm wrestle, I'll give yer an arm wrestle.' Backer twisted Skinner's arm behind him almost to breaking point then smashed his head into the table, splintering wood. He then picked up the bloody mess before it could protest and threw it bodily out of the door. Backer was greeted with whistles and cheers while the Professor stared in disgust at the pooling blood on the floor.

'It's not a pretty sight,' Oliver told the stranger. 'But some-one's got to keep discipline around 'ere. 'E's a troublemaker that Skinner is, awl right.' He pointed at Backer. 'See that 'e's banned 'ere for a week. That'll teach 'im to start a punch up.'

Backer nodded and returned to his place behind the bar. He smiled stupidly at the Professor, happy to be serving a toff now that everything was back to normal. 'A drink I can offer you Sir?'

The Professor didn't reply, his eyes were still fixed upon the blood staining the floor, memories of the past taunting him. He shuddered and tried stepping towards the exit but Oliver was not about to let a rich toff slip through his fingers that easily. 'Now we can't 'ave our gentleman 'ere drinking in the middle of all this mess, can we? Go and fetch Billy t' clean it all up.'

Backer bobbed down then lifted a trapdoor in the floor and bellowed for Billy. Moments later the barman reappeared holding the ear of a dirty youth dressed in rags. He handed the boy a mop and told him to get to work. Billy limped over to the mess on the floor grumbling that not only was he hungry but his ear was hurting. Backer told him to shut his trap while Oliver steered the Professor out of the way.

'Now Sir, I must insist that you 'ave a drink. What'll it be? We 'ave the finest range of ales and spirits in all of London.'

The Professor seriously doubted that but had the feeling he wouldn't be allowed to leave until he spent some money. Perhaps one drink wouldn't hurt—hopefully. 'Do you have any light beer?'

Backer had never heard of light beer so he looked to Oliver for guidance but Oliver seemed to be studiously studying the ceiling. That often happened when Backer needed help, particularly when the pimp had no idea himself but wasn't about to admit it.

'Well we've got beer but it's sort of dark. Like a copper colour.'

This amused the Professor. 'Then a half pint will do nicely.'

Skinner groaned in pain and frustration, spitting up blood. He felt for the damage done to his face and sucked in his breath. His nose wobbled and he could feel the bone shift. Coughing up more blood he managed a muted curse in the direction of the tavern and slowly tried to stand up. He had barely adjusted to this mean feat when a figure rounded a corner colliding with him. The man was dressed in black with a black woollen scarf obscuring his face. He was about to yell at this man to get out of his way but something made him stop and think.

'Pardon Guv'ner.'

The man said nothing and hurried away, hastily wiping the few specs of blood from his coat courtesy of Skinner. The sailor stumbled along for several more paces then passed out on a pile of rubbish.

Oliver beamed at the Professor after some mutual introductions. 'So yer a professor?'

The visitor nodded.

Oliver nodded sagely then frowned, obviously unsure what a professor did. 'Wot do you do then?'

'I'm a teacher. I teach science, history and languages.'

Oliver nodded again, waiting for him to continue but the alien had answered his question and was not disposed to be any chattier than was absolutely necessary. Oliver however was determined to keep this man ... potentially a rich man entertained which naturally meant companionship of the opposite sex.

'I always say we should learn from each other. You teach me,' he touched his hand to his chest, 'an' I teach you. Or to be more precise ... ' He spied Molly chatting to Elsie at the table in the corner; time for the girl to earn her keep. 'Molly!'

Molly jumped when she heard her name bellowed and cringed assuming she had done something wrong. Oliver invited her over, patting the empty seat between himself and the Professor and the girl slowly walked over sitting stiffly between them.

'This 'ere's Molly. She just started a coupla weeks ago, didncha Molls?'

Molly nodded timidly.

'An this 'ere is a professor wot's gonna teach yer—so you make sure you teach 'im a few things in return!' Oliver guffawed then lit a cigar, throwing the match on the floor.

The girl blushed and held out her hand towards the stranger. 'Pleased to met yer.' He gave her a sad look wondering how old the little creature was and gently shook her hand.

'Very nice to meet you too.'

Oliver looked from one to the other, wondering if he left them to it would anything actually happen. Molly, he had to admit, was at least trying her best. She was a shy girl to start with, but a lot of blokes liked it that way, particularly at her age; made it feel as if they were in control.

'So where d'ya come from?' Molly asked politely.

The Professor raised an eyebrow but answered honestly. 'Oh, a very long way away.'

Oliver drew back on his cigar then spoke, puffing out smoke rings. 'So yer on 'olliday or jus' travellin' around?'

The visitor smiled, displaying a set of perfect white teeth. Oliver wondered if they were false. 'Er yes,' he replied evasively, 'and as such I thank you for your hospitality but it's time I was on my way.'

Molly's face fell. 'Oh Sir, must ya go?'

He stood up and placed a few coppers on the table for the untouched beer. 'Yes well I'm a busy man.'

Molly was about to protest when Oliver kicked her ankle under the table. The girl grumbled. 'Ow! That hurt!'

The Professor gave her a puzzled look while Oliver placed a finger to his lips, trying to shut the girl up. She blushed. 'Oops, aren't I clumsy? I must 'ave kicked the table leg by mistake.'

'Well Professor,' declared Oliver standing up and extending a hand. 'Ave a pleasant journey wherever the road takes yer.'

'Thank you,' he shook hands with the man, hoping that he wouldn't catch anything.

'Yer be careful out there now. There are thieves and rogues everywhere.'

The Professor strode to the door and waved. 'I'll heed the advice. Goodnight.'

Just as he left the tavern, Oliver grabbed hold of Molly's arm and dragged her over to him. 'Oliver wot the bleedin' 'ell ...'

'Shut up and listen good. I want yer to follow that Professor fella.'

She gave him a baffled look. 'Why? 'e says 'e's gotta go.'

He shook his head despairingly. 'Yer stupid tart, ain't yer ever 'eard that line before?'

'Wot?'

With barely restrained patience he explained. 'When a piece of quality like that wants a whore like you, 'e doesn't want the whole world to know about it. So 'e says 'e's leaving and that's your cue to go after 'im and change 'is mind for 'im. That way it's kept all private like and it doesn't muck up 'is pride.'

'Oh.' She allowed the information to sink in then thinking better of it added. 'Wait a minute I'm not goin' after 'im alone.'

He tightened his grip on her arm. 'And why not?'

She winced. 'I'll do business with 'im up stairs 'ere in the tavern but I'm not goin' out there now.'

'You'll do as you're told!'

Molly bit back tears. 'I can't go out alone. Wot if 'e's the Kipper?'

The tavern grew silent with the mention of *that* name. Oliver growled and struck her across the face; she fell to the floor and started crying.

'E's not the bloody Kipper, cos 'e wants to 'ram ya, not gut ya! Didn't yer listen to wot I jus' said? Now yer get out there and earn yer living!'

She stood up with as much dignity as she could muster and headed for the door. Elsie, still at her corner table muttered a curse towards the pimp.

The Professor walked down the street narrowly avoiding the drunks and vagrants that stumbled across his path. Why did he have such an uneasy feeling about this location? Had there really been a vortex tremor or had he only imagined it? Why should it trouble him this way? And why, for that matter, should a pool of blood belonging to the sailor who had been unceremoniously thrown out, torment him? Hadn't he gone over it a million times in his head before? If there had been anything he could have done to stop Menz he would have done so. He was not responsible for the student's death no matter what the wardens said ...

He came to an abrupt halt and pulled out a handkerchief from his breast pocket, dabbing at his forehead. The sound of Menz's maniacal laughter echoed in his mind as the events of the last few days played out in his head. Menz alone in the lab; Menz erasing the data-hexagon; Menz tampering with his university scores; the Professor discovering the student. Then arguments; accusations; screaming; a weapon raised; a struggle ...

He looked up at the night sky and put his hands over his ears. He did not want to think about it—he couldn't.

Slowly the image receded and with a clearer mind the alien realised he had overshot the blind alley. He had reached a wharf. There was a factory up ahead and all was silent except for the scuttling of rodents scurrying up and down near the water's edge.

Molly, in the meantime, had been secretly following the Professor, ducking in doorways and behind corners of alleyways whenever he appeared to look back. She spotted him looking over the edge of the wharf, and then watched as he wandered over to some shipping crates stacked alongside the factory wall. She stepped forward and was about to call out to him when a hand clamped over her mouth and tried to drag her away. The terrified girl struggled violently as a knife came towards her throat. With strength she didn't realise she possessed, Molly wrenched her mouth open and bit down as hard as she could. The attacker lost his grip and howled in pain, alerting the Professor.

'Elp me! Somebody 'elp me!' She screamed frantically.

The Professor ran towards the cry as her attacker fled, disappearing into the night. Molly rushed over to him, screaming hysterically.

'It was 'im! It was Jack the Ripper! 'e wos gonna spill me guts!' She shook in terror, wailing loudly.

'Calm down, it's all right he's gone now,' the Professor replied firmly. 'I won't let anything happen to you. You're safe now.'

She wept uncontrollably against the alien's chest. He placed a protective arm around her shoulder whilst staring in the direction of where her attacker had fled. He had heard of this Jack the Ripper before whilst studying as a boy on his home world. Numerous monsters littered Earth's history and he had developed a thesis based not only on *their* insane minds but on others who were accordingly infected by the insanity either by choice or by fear. He recalled he received a perfect mark for the thesis but then promptly sentenced to one day's penance as the work was twelve data-streams too long and focussed far too much emphasis on ape behaviour. That, he thought, was the whole point of the exercise but the university thought otherwise.

The Professor looked down at the girl and gently brushed a strand of hair from her forehead. 'Calm down and tell me why you were down here alone.'

'Oliver made me come,' she hiccuped. 'E thought yer wanted to do business quiet like so 'e 'ad me follow yer.'

The Professor grimaced. 'I can assure you that was not my intention.'

Molly held her sleeve to her runny nose but the Professor quickly whipped out his handkerchief and handed it to her.

'Oh Sir I can't use this, it's too nice.'

'Nonsense, you use it and you keep it.'

Molly's tear-stained eyes lit up. 'Yer very kind Sir.' She gave him an uncertain look. 'Yer won't leave me now will yer?'

He shook his head, reached into his pocket and produced a small tin, then opened it. 'Would you care for a crème sphere?'

'A wot?'

'A crème sphere. It's a little like toffee.' He took a piece from the tin and popped it in his mouth. Molly slowly took a piece then slid it onto her tongue and let the delicious creamy layers melt across her taste buds.

'Nice, isn't it?' He smiled at her.

His warmth and kindness touched Molly visibly calming her shaken nerves. But the talk of food reminded her of the yawning pit in her stomach.

'Would it be too much Sir if I asked yer for another one?'

He looked at her with concern. 'How long is it since you've eaten?'

'Last night.'

'Then it's time you ate something better than sweets. Come along, follow me.'

The one room squalor with its dirty, brown walls and rotting wooden frame was almost waiting for the day when it would crumble and gratefully collapse in a heap. Inside, a simple wooden bed against the wall contained the sleeping form of Molly, while the Professor sat on an old rickety chair with his feet on the table and his diary in hand.

Diary Extract 1.1

I believe I just caught a glimpse of Jack the Ripper himself. Unfortunately, it was dark, and I was too far away to pick out anything more than a figure in a black coat carrying a bag. Luckily, I happened to be in the vicinity otherwise he would have taken the life of a young girl I met only minutes earlier in The Ten Bells. Needless to say: lucky for her too.

The girl, Molly, was understandably in a complete state of shock when I rescued her. I stayed by her side and when I realised the poor soul was hungry, I suggested we find somewhere to eat to try and take her mind off things. Before we set off, I placed an hypnotic suggestion telling her mind to sleep and forget, then instructed her to walk with me to where my ship lay hidden. Once we had ascended to the dormitory level, I activated the food synthesiser producing bread, cake and sausages. I thought it best to allow her to eat in familiar territory so after descending, and once outside in the alley I informed her sub-conscious that we had just visited a local inn and purchased some food. She was so excited over the plain fare that she completely forgot her anxieties, grabbed me by the hand and ran all the way back to her lodgings. When we reached her one room hovel in Whitechapel, she invited me inside then without ceremony, fell upon the food voraciously. I feel such pity for the poor little creature.

And now it is daylight and I am still concerned whether the fault within the navigational controls actually occurred when I dozed off, or whether the tremor in the vortex caused it. And another thing that's now added to my list of concerns—Jack the Ripper. The authorities never caught him, and people have been pondering his identity for centuries. There are so many theories that I can't help wondering where fact ends and fiction begins. However, the question is, should I interfere? If history is changed, would it really matter? Could the vortex tremor have anything to do with it? Or is that just coincidence? Too many questions and not enough answers. Would the police have any information about the murders that have already occurred? Undoubtedly some. Perhaps I should pay the local constabulary a visit; find out what I can, then perhaps see if I should offer my assistance.

Diary Extract End - 1.1

The Professor removed his feet from the table and checked on Molly. The girl was sleeping peacefully, then sensing his presence she opened her eyes and gave him a groggy grin.

'Is it mornin'?'

'Afternoon actually,' he replied. 'No need for you to get up though. I'm just going out for a while.'

She sat bolt upright in bed. 'Yer not leaving me?'

He regarded her for a moment. 'Well, you could come along but then you'd have to agree to help me.'

She shrugged her shoulders. 'What are ya doin?'

'I need to speak to the police. I want to look into their progress concerning the Ripper murders.'

The previous night's images came flooding back to her and she shivered. 'Ow could I 'elp?'

'Well, you could describe what you saw of the man. It might help them in their investigation.'

She gave him a dubious look but swung her legs over the side of the bed and reached for a pair of torn stockings. The Professor politely turned his head away and pulled back the sacking curtain of the window.

'Wot if they want to put me away?'

'And why would they want to do that?'

'Cos.' She shrugged, there was no need to say more. It was clear to Molly why the police wouldn't like her.

The Professor shook his head in response. 'The police don't care what you do. They're too busy looking for murderers. People who deserve to be locked up.'

She stood up and slipped her feet into a pair of tattered boots. 'Well I ain't a good girl, y'know.'

He looked at her and wondered at the degradation of humanity. 'You won't be put in prison. I'll see to that.'

She twirled her long, curly brown hair into a bun, pinned it in place then grabbed a piece of leftover bread. 'Awl right I'll come with yer.'

It had been two weeks since Detective Inspector Jonathan Brett and his partner, Detective Inspector Sydney Wainwright had been sent from Scotland Yard on assignment to the East End. Their task was to work alongside the local police to solve the case of Jack the Ripper, even though uniformed officers had already been sent from London to assist. Public opinion was divided as to the merit of this act. Shouldn't the designated police of the East End deal with this East End problem?

Surely a single murderer could easily be caught by trained law enforcers native to the area. And yet there were influential members of the public who weren't impressed with the skills these supposed trained officers were displaying and so after consultation with the Police Commissioner and Home Secretary, Scotland Yard's best and finest were brought in on the matter.

The two detectives in question however, had reached something of a stumbling block themselves. They had pored over the coroner's reports several times and had studied the photographic evidence of the victims thoroughly. But what had they learnt? Or more importantly, what had they missed? What type of person could have committed such a crime? A doctor? A butcher? Was it the work of an insane mind? Or the mind of a coldblooded calculated killer? These unanswered questions kept buzzing around Brett's head, as he sat within the tiny confines of the Police House office, his partner beside him in a similar state of unrest.

'Maybe we should get Doctor Waitley to go over the details again. There could be something that's been overlooked.'

Wainwright took a sip of lukewarm coffee before replying, 'I don't think there's anything more he can tell us. It's up to us now.'

Brett picked up one of the photographs then tossed it back on the table, clearly angered. 'Well just what the hell have we come up with so far? Virtually nothing. And if we don't nail him soon, the commissioner will be after our necks.'

'You think? I'd say it'd more likely be the uniformed lot around here.'

Brett sighed, exasperated. 'Yeah, you're probably right. They seem to loathe us, intruding on their miserable territory.'

A knock at the door interrupted their discussion.

'Come in!' called Brett.

A young constable entered, his face twitching irritably at an inflamed boil on the side of his nose.

'Yes Briggs?'

'Sorry to intrude Sir, but there's a gentleman wishing to see you.'

Wainwright leaned forward. 'Oh?'

'Yes Sir, he's with a young lady and he says that she was attacked by the Ripper early this morning.'

Brett and Wainwright barely allowed the young PC to finish his sentence before charging out of their office to find a tall well-dressed gent standing beside a Limehouse district female at the front desk.

'Good afternoon,' said the Professor politely. 'I take it you are the gentlemen concerned with the Ripper murders?'

Wainwright gave the Professor a wary look then nodded. 'Yes Sir, I am Detective Inspector Sydney Wainwright, and this is Detective Inspector Jonathan Brett.' He gestured towards the other man.

'I'm very pleased to meet you, gentlemen.' The Professor shook hands with both men, leaving them slightly bemused.

'And you say this young lady was attacked early this morning?' asked Brett.

'That's correct,' he stepped closer and lowered his voice. 'Is there somewhere private we could speak?'

Brett nodded. 'Certainly, this way Sir.'

The inspectors returned to their office with the Professor in tow. Molly hesitated for a moment then hurried after them.

'And your names are ...?' Wainwright looked at the visitors expectantly.

'I am Professor Orlando Delbrotman and this young lady is Molly.'

Brett gave Wainwright a sceptical look at such an unusual name. 'A Professor you say? In what field may I ask?'

'History, science, language … '

'I see,' Brett replied not quite sure what to make of this stranger. 'And could you tell us exactly what happened?'

The Professor recounted what had occurred in the early hours of the morning.

'So you didn't actually get a look at his face?'

'It was a bit bleedin' 'ard when he 'ad a knife at me throat,' replied Molly curtly.

The alien winced at her brash tone. 'Yes well I can tell you he wore a dark coat and he was carrying some sort of bag.'

Wainwright gave him an interested look. 'Could you tell what kind of bag it was?'

The Professor frowned thoughtfully. 'Unfortunately, no. As my companion was extremely upset at the time, my immediate concern was for her safety therefore, I only caught a glimpse.' He glanced at the table, scanning the photographs. 'Do you mind if I take a look at these?' He reached out a hand but Wainwright scooped them up.

'I'm sorry Sir but you're not permitted to look at any evidence.' He glanced at Molly. 'Especially with the er … young lady present.'

The Professor turned around and placed an arm around the girl. 'Would you like some tea? Of course you would.' He looked at the detectives. 'Could we get her a cup of tea?'

Brett nodded. 'Er yes, I'll get Constable Briggs to make you a cup. Would you care to come with me?'

She glanced at the Professor for reassurance.

He smiled. 'Don't worry, you'll be all right. You just go with the gentleman, and he'll get you a nice brew.'

'Do yer 'ave any biscuits?' she asked tentatively.

'I'm sure we can find you something,' replied Brett. He turned to Wainwright. 'Be back in a moment.'

The inspector ushered Molly out, leaving the Professor and Wainwright alone.

'May I have a look at those photographs now?'

Wainwright hesitated. 'Very well but I must warn you, they're not a pretty sight.'

The Professor spread them out and examined each one.

'The first was Martha Turner,' explained the inspector. 'She was found at 5 am on 7th of August. She was left on the landing of a tenement block in Whitechapel. The second was Mary Ann Nichols, known as Pretty Polly, found twenty-four days later. And the latest was found on the 7th of this month near Spitalfields market. She was known as "Dark Annie" Chapman.'

The alien remained silent for several long moments. He mentally probed the pictures, as if willing the cadavers to tell their gruesome story. He could see one of them wandering the dark, empty streets searching for anyone interested in her personal wares. But wait; a single individual catches her eye, and she affects a cheeky, knowing smile and saunters over to him, asking if he requires the company of a lonely lady. He nods his head and holds out his hand, and as she grasps it, he leads her further down the alley, away from any possible prying eyes. She expects that he wishes to do business in the street, perhaps against a wall? She resignedly waits for him to make up his mind when suddenly she sees a flash of metal and then a feeling of burning agony sears across her throat. She instinctively claps a hand over her neck as blood pours from the wound. Simultaneously her knees give way, and she sinks to the ground in a terrified dream-like state. The man kneels down and cuts through her shawl and dress, and as she gurgles in a death throe of terror, he slits her torso open. He then cuts through her steaming organs and lifts them out one by one then arranges them beside the dead woman, along with her possessions. He looks up as he hears a movement in the distance but the Professor cannot see his face, and as this creature runs away into the night, the alien is left feeling disgusted and angered: who is this? *What* is this?

'All were easy targets as all of them were prostitutes.'

The alien breathed a jagged sigh, glancing at the inspector, his momentary trance broken. 'Where are the bodies now?'

'In the hospital morgue. They'll remain there until the case is closed.'

The Professor picked up the photographs, his face grim and set. 'I will need to examine them.'

'Sir?' Questioned Wainwright surprised. 'I'm sorry but that's not possible.'

The Professor frowned then tapped the side of his nose. 'You don't understand Inspector Wainwright. I've been sent here to assist you.'

'From Scotland Yard?'

'In a manner of speaking.'

'We weren't notified.'

'It's top secret,' he whispered. 'Hush-hush, if you know what I mean.'

Wainwright hesitated, uncertain whether to believe him or not. He glanced at the Professor's intense expression and immediately became privy to someone intelligent, earnest and constant. 'Very well then. We can arrange to go now if you wish.'

'Good.' The Professor returned the photographs then opened the door to see Molly chatting happily with the young policeman, Briggs. She looked up and placed her empty cup on the desk.

'Are we goin' now Professor?'

'Ah, well I have some business to do first with these good gentlemen here.'

She frowned. 'But I 'ave to be back in the tavern soon otherwise Oliver will get mad.'

'I'll take you back there, Miss,' said Briggs, trying to be helpful. 'I mean with your permission Sir.'

Wainwright nodded and the Professor smiled. 'Good lad.'

'Will yer come to the tavern t'night then?' asked Molly.

The Professor nodded although Molly had the feeling that his mind was on other things. She tapped him impatiently on the arm and he looked down at her and smiled promising to return to see her that night.

▲

CHAPTER 2

The Professor and detectives followed the mortuary attendant down the dimly lit hallway, and into the autopsy room. A middle-aged man with dark hair greying at the temples was scrubbing his hands in a sink. He looked up as the visitors entered, shaking his hands dry.

'Afternoon gentlemen. Back so soon?'

'This is Professor Delbrotman,' explained Wainwright. 'He is assisting us with the Ripper murders and wishes to see the bodies.'

The surgeon nodded and wiped his hands on a towel. 'I'm Doctor Waitley.'

The two men shook hands then Waitley picked up a container of metal instruments and handed them to the attendant. 'That's all for now. Now gentlemen if you would care to follow me?'

He led them down the corridor to a room at the far end and ushered them inside. It was cold and bare except for the remains of three women laid out on three separate tables. On closer inspection it was clear that they had their throats cut, their torsos slit open and their organs carefully removed, leaving a ghastly pink cavity. The Professor looked at the three victims with a mixture of pity and disgust.

The surgeon broke the silence. 'Whoever did it must have medical knowledge. As you can see, the flesh was not ripped haphazardly.'

'And the organs were placed neatly in a row beside each victim together with any belongings they happened to have with them at the time,' commented Wainwright.

'Obviously the work of some lunatic,' concluded Waitley.

The Professor looked at the doctor. 'Yes—an extremely orderly and clever one.'

Wainwright frowned. 'Orderly?'

'Yes well as you, yourself said. He takes his time and enjoys precision, almost as if taking a pride in what he does.'

The detective considered the Professor's comment of the murderer's achievements; what type of twisted mind could find satisfaction in such viciousness?

'So you agree that it is more than likely he is a surgeon?'

'Undoubtedly,' replied the Professor. 'The method of murder speaks for itself and as Doctor Waitley has confirmed: the incisions are not random.'

'I'm sure Doctor Grantley would agree with you there,' remarked Brett before shrugging. 'If he could ever make the time to see us.'

The Professor frowned. 'Doctor Grantley? Now that name is vaguely familiar ... '

This surprised the detective. 'Surely you jest. Doctor Grantley—*familiar*?'

The alien sighed inwardly; obviously this Grantley was someone significant. Had he heard of him before? Wasn't he some physician of note in this time period? It was a pity that he did not have a copy of his thesis to reference. He was sure there were several doctors consulted regarding the Ripper affair but could not recall all their names; this Grantley must have been one of them. The Professor looked at the detective's expression and thought he had better explain himself—even if it was a bluff. 'Well Inspector Brett, Scotland Yard is not confined to the borders of England. Its affairs extend to quite a number of other countries and since I have been assigned elsewhere for some time, you must permit me to reacquaint myself with all those of note.'

Brett carefully digested the words then nodded. 'Understandable. Well Doctor Grantley has the prestige of being one of the most important surgeons in England. He lectures at universities, has rooms in Harley Street and is Her Majesty's own personal physician.'

This jogged the Professor's memory, recalling the section of his thesis where he had made mention of the man. 'But surely Doctor Waitley's findings should be more than sufficient for the coroner's report. Why do you need Grantley's opinion?'

Waitley cleared his throat in mute embarrassment. 'Well a second opinion can sometimes appear useful.'

'To translate: I'm afraid to say that it comes down to politics,' explained Wainwright with a trace of irony. 'Scotland Yard needs to be seen to be speaking with the *right* people.'

The Professor understood; politics could be found in every walk of life. 'It's always the way. Well why don't we all pay the good doctor a visit in person?'

'There's no way without an appointment.'

'Nonsense, you're ... we are the police. We have every right to interview the man. We'll just have to wait at his surgery until he makes time for us. Tomorrow morning convenient?'

'Wait for him?' Echoed Wainwright doubtfully. 'We'd be wasting our time.'

'Indeed? Well we don't have anything better to do. Do we gentlemen?'

Oliver scrutinised the regulars filing into the tavern for the night, whilst Backer busied himself behind the bar. Molly sat alone, impatiently waiting for the Professor, fending off the crude advances of a hopeful customer.

'Bugger off Joshua, I ain't for sale!'

Joshua mopped the beer from his grubby shirtfront, gave her a whiskery kiss then trotted off to another table, seating himself between two girls sitting there.

Observing her frosty display, Oliver sauntered over and gave her an accusing look.

'Wot is it now?' she asked, her eyes fixed firmly on the door.

'Why ain't ya workin'?'

'I'm waitin' for the Professor.'

Oliver grinned smugly and sat down next to her. 'See I told yer 'e was too proud to ask you for it last night in front of everyone.' He held out his hand. 'So where's my money?'

'Wot money?'

'Well I 'ope yer didn't do it for nothin'.'

Molly scowled. 'We didn't do it.'

Oliver looked shocked. 'Yer wot? Then wot the bleedin' 'ell were yer doin'?'

The girl looked down and shook her head. 'Nothin' except for when the Professor just 'appened to save me life.'

'Wot?' Oliver gave her an incredulous look.

'I don' want to talk about it.'

He held up a warning finger. 'Yer will or else ...'

A uniformed policeman entered the tavern and made his way over to the bar. The customers and girls glanced suspiciously at this unwelcome stranger and all idle chatter was reduced to a whisper.

'We'll finish this later!' Oliver muttered venomously.

The policeman nodded at Backer, gaining his undivided attention. 'I'll have a pint of beer.'

'Yes Sir,' replied Backer. He filled a glass and slid it across the bar.

'Good evening Officer,' said Oliver, full of nervous charm. 'There'll be no charge for that one. Is that all right with you Mr Backer?'

Backer nodded his head enthusiastically until it looked as if it was about to tumble from his shoulders.

'Why thank you gentlemen,' replied the policeman. He took his beer and sat down alone in the corner. Everyone looked at each other but mostly at the blue uniform. The stranger stared back, the corners of his mouth twitching in amusement. 'Please, ladies and gentlemen do not stop your revelry on my account. I am here only to drink my beer, nothing else.'

The customers did not entirely trust his words and it took a few minutes for the atmosphere to relax ... somewhat. Oliver rapped his fingers nervously on the bar while watching the sailors and ruffians treating his girls with the utmost respect. That was definitely a new angle.

The Professor walked up to the door of The Ten Bells surprised by the lack of noise coming from within, then entered. Everyone stopped what they were doing and stared at the newcomer.

He smiled and nodded. 'Good evening!'

'Professor,' called Molly, hurrying over to him. 'I thought yer'd never get 'ere.'

'Oh Professor,' said Oliver, relieved that the attention aimed at the policeman had been diverted elsewhere. 'We was just wonderin' when yer was comin', weren't we Backer?'

Backer gave him a blank look. 'Eh?'

'Y'know, when the Professor was comin' to visit us again.' Oliver gave him a pointed look and it took no more than an extended half a minute for Backer to realise his cue.

'Oh yeah.' He picked up an empty glass. 'A glass of copper beer, Professor?'

'Why you remembered. That would be most welcome.'

Molly took the Professor's arm and ushered him over to a spare table.

'I'm so glad yer 'ere,' she said in a low voice. 'That peeler's put a damper on everythin'.' She pointed at the man seated at the back of the room.

The policeman finished his beer then walked over to where the Professor was seated.

'I haven't seen you around here before Sir.' His voice was thick and it grated on the alien's sensitive hearing.

'I'm a visitor to this area,' explained the Professor.

'Yes,' added Molly proudly. 'E's with Scotland Yard. I 'eard 'im say so to those two fellas at the Police House.'

Oliver swore under his breath at that piece of *welcome* news and made a mental note to ask Molly afterwards just how she happened to know so much.

'Scotland Yard?' the policeman echoed approvingly—almost. 'Well we must have a little chat afterwards about matters.'

'Certainly, I look forward to it Officer ... your name, Sir?'

The policeman looked jealously at the visitor's fine clothes having taken an instant dislike to him. 'I do indeed have a name as we all have one, don't we? It's Greensworth. Superintendent Robert Greensworth. Goodnight.' Before the Professor could reply, the man exited the tavern, leaving the alien wondering at the man's rudeness. The atmosphere lifted almost immediately and the sailors, ruffians and drunks returned to their normal behaviour.

'So wot happened after yer left me?' asked Molly importantly, looking around to ensure everyone was listening. She felt rather pleased at being the centre of attention.

'Well, the inspectors and I will try to see a Doctor Grantley tomorrow morning.'

Molly's eyes lit up. 'Cor blimey. 'E gets to see the Queen!'

The Professor raised both eyebrows, surprised that she should know such a thing. She shrugged her shoulders, 'some toff's talk all sortsa things in between their snorin'.'

The Professor betrayed nothing of the sadness that he felt for his newly acquired young friend; she was far too young to have lived so much. Molly frowned at his expression then gave him a cheeky grin. Broken out of his reverie he observed Oliver placing a glass of beer before him on the table. The Professor thanked him.

'My pleasure,' the other replied through clenched, decaying teeth. He gave Molly a narrow glance. 'I didn't realise that yer was a copper.'

'Inspector!' corrected Molly.

Oliver glowered at her sharp tone.

'More an advisor really,' explained the Professor. 'I'm here to assist with some important investigation.'

Oliver was about to question precisely what sort of investigation when the door was flung open by a portly gentleman, wearing a long cape, top hat, and carrying a black bag. He spread his arms theatrically gaining the attention of the room.

'My dear friends, I am arrived!'

When the regulars realised that the newcomer was the second-rate actor who had been hanging around Elsie for the last few weeks, they quickly returned their attentions to the girls and their drink.

'Douglas!' squealed Elsie, straightening her corsets. She flew over to him and flung her arms around his neck making up for the lukewarm reception he had just received.

'Ah my dear, you are even more beautiful than I recall the last time we met!'

She giggled and planted a kiss on his powdered cheek.

'Bloody 'ell,' breathed Oliver. 'If it ain't the great thespian 'imself.'

Douglas doffed his hat and bowed. 'Oliver.' He went over to Molly and lifted her hand and kissed it. 'Good evening Molly.'

The girl wiped her hand on her skirt and managed a reluctant smile. 'Allo Dougie.'

He winced at the words. 'Douglas my dear lady. The name is Douglas.'

The Professor gave the man a bemused look as the actor removed his threadbare cape with a flourish, successfully getting it twisted around one of the sailor's heads behind him.

'Ay watch it, fat arse!' The sailor spat, throwing the cloak back at him.

Douglas rose to his full height of five foot six inches and gasped. 'I do not converse with verbal cripples.'

'Yer wot?' The sailor was obviously itching for a fight.

'Leave it alone, Bernie,' said one of the other sailors at the table. 'It's just Cyril.'

Douglas glared at the man. 'My name is Douglas.'

The sailor rolled his eyes. 'Whatever.'

'Oi Douglas,' called Oliver. 'Come over and meet the Professor.'

Douglas turned around and raised an eyebrow. 'Pardon?'

'Say allo to the Pro-fess-or,' he enunciated each syllable.

Douglas looked the alien up and down and shook his head. 'I cannot speak to a man to whom I have not been properly introduced.'

Oliver swore under his breath, then with barely concealed impatience, stood up. 'Douglas, may I present yer to the Professor. Professor this is Douglas.'

The Professor stood and the two men shook hands.

'Douglas Forbes-Montague the Second to be precise.' He pulled up two chairs and seated Elsie, then himself, placing his black bag beside him on the floor.

'So you are a Professor? Of medicine perhaps? Do you know that I have had a dreadful back complaint for years.' He pointed to the lower part of his spine and looked suitably distressed. 'I would be ever so grateful if you would have a look ...'

'I'm sorry,' apologised the Professor reseating himself. 'I have many skills, but sadly, that of a physician is not one of them.'

'Oh.' Douglas was disappointed.

'And what line of business are you in Mr Forbes-Montague?'

He smiled. 'Douglas, my friends call me Douglas. Well you know Professor ... please forgive me, what is your full name?'

The alien opted for the human translation as his name in his native tongue had ninety-eight characters, not counting the clicks and punctuation. 'Professor Orlando Delbrotman but I prefer simply *Professor* when speaking with friends.'

Douglas beamed. 'Well *Professor*,' he spoke the word with pride, 'I have been an actor for many years.'

'Oh really?' The alien replied, with marked surprise.

'Oh yes. I have worked with all the greats you know.'

The Professor leaned forward; his eyes full of enthusiasm. He was beginning to warm to this character. 'Who?'

Douglas looked intently at the Professor, enjoying the moment of retelling an old story. 'Do you know of Tree?'

Molly frowned. 'Wot, yer mean like an apple tree?'

He gave her an impatient look. 'Not a tree dear girl, I mean Tree. Herbert Beerbohm Tree. One of the greatest actors this century has produced.' His voice burst with pride. 'And I worked with the man.'

Oliver, having heard the story a good two hundred times before, lit a cigar and excused himself from the table to join another group. Douglas's face fell.

'Oh do go on,' urged the Professor not wanting to disappoint the actor. 'I do so enjoy a good story.'

'Well,' he continued, regaining his cheerful state. 'Picture this. It was one minute before the second act. I was waiting for my cue to go on stage and lo and behold, the great Tree himself walked over to me.' He stared at the Professor, hoping that the man could grasp the wonder of the miracle that *he* had experienced. 'I was thunderstruck, and I nodded my head for no words would spring from my lips. The great Tree looked nervously around then spoke to me. To no one else you understand but to me.' He tapped himself on the chest with pride.

'And what did he say?' asked the Professor.

Elsie and Molly leaned forward waiting for Douglas to continue. He savoured the moment by not replying immediately thus heightening the tension.

'The time,' he grinned hugely. 'Tree asked me for the time.'

Everyone waited for him to go on but the story had ended.

'So what do you think of that?' Douglas was enjoying the moment; this memory was so precious to him.

'Well did you give him the time?' asked the Professor, stifling a grin.

'Yes,' Douglas breathed. 'I had my fob watch on so I was able to give him the time. What do you think of that then eh?'

The Professor leaned back and sighed. 'You are indeed a lucky man to have had such an honour.' His eyes wandered to the black bag at Douglas's feet and his expression clouded.

Standing near a horse trough outside The Ten Bells, Superintendent Greensworth walked away from the tavern, noting the time that Douglas Forbes-Montague II had entered.

Douglas took a healthy swig of beer and hugged Elsie to him. 'You know my dear, if I had the money, I would pour diamonds and pearls into your lap.'

Elsie held her stomach, laughing. 'Yer a sweet talker, aren't yer?'

He kissed her cheek three times in quick succession, then finished what was left of the beer. The Professor remained silent, observing the rowdy display; in particular, the girls, some he judged to be no more than eleven or twelve years old being herded upstairs by their excited, anxious clients. Oliver winked at them proudly, patting his breast pocket bulging with coins before lighting another cigar. The Professor's face remained an enigmatic mask revealing nothing of his opinion of the pimp.

Drumming up courage, Molly leaned towards the alien and tapped him on the shoulder. 'Professor.'

'Hmm?'

'Do ya wanna stay with me t'night?'

He looked at her. 'Are you still frightened to be alone?'

She nodded, ashamed. 'But do yer want to stay?'

Elsie shrieked and playfully slapped Douglas's wandering hands.

'Very well, if it makes you feel better.'

Molly hesitated for a moment before continuing, 'but wot I mean is do yer want to …' Her voice trailed off. 'I mean I'd prefer a kind gent like you than any of the rest.' She gestured towards the drunken horde.

The Professor frowned at the girl. 'If you're implying regarding your line of employment, then I must decline.'

Molly bit her lip. 'Please Professor, if I don't bring in any money soon, Oliver will beat it out of me.'

The Professor stared at the pimp dealing out cards to a group of sailors. His quick actions did not hide the fact that several of the cards found their way up the man's dirty sleeve; the sailors however, were obviously too drunk to notice.

The alien reached into his pocket and produced three shillings which he handed to the surprised girl.

'Here, this should keep Oliver happy.'

She took the coins and lovingly turned them between her fingers. 'I knew today would end up being a good one.'

The alien raised his eyebrows. 'Really? Why?'

'Well,' she continued shyly. 'It's me birthday.'

'Indeed? How old are you?'

'Fifteen!'

'Only fifteen?'

She beamed at him proudly and he turned towards the thespian with a sudden idea. 'Douglas.'

The actor disentangled himself from Elsie's grasp and looked up. 'Yes Professor?'

'What is the name of your play?'

'Ah!' His eyes glittered with pride. 'It is called *The Maiden's Dilemma.*'

'Where is it playing?'

'At The Ivory Palace,' he replied grandly.

'And who do you portray?'

Pleased that someone other than himself was so interested in his favourite subject, his chest filled with pride. 'I play the butler.'

'I see.'

'It is an extremely important part.'

The Professor nodded politely. 'I'm sure it is.'

'But do you in fact know why?'

The Professor smiled. 'Not really. Why?'

Douglas smiled triumphantly. 'Because in act one, I must open the door to the first suitor, and if I wasn't there to do it, then the play could not continue.'

The Professor clapped his hands in delight. 'That sounds quite fascinating. Douglas, would you be able to secure two seats in a box for tomorrow night's performance.'

'Why certainly, Professor!' he replied happily. 'I will leave them at the door and then all you have to do is pay for them when you arrive.' He frowned. 'But tell me Professor, who is to accompany you?'

The Professor turned to Molly who had been hanging on every word of the conversation. 'Well Molly, how would you like to go to the theatre to celebrate your birthday?'

'Me?' she squealed. 'Cor blimey, I've never been to the theatre in me life!' Her delight faltered and she looked down at her dress. 'But I ain't got no fancy clobber to wear.'

'No need to worry about that my girl,' said Elsie. 'I've got that toffy dress that 'Arold swiped ... er that is I mean ...' She gave the Professor a guilty look, afraid that her loose tongue would lead her into trouble. The Professor merely raised an eyebrow.

'Harold?' Snorted Douglas. 'Who is Harold?'

'E was a limey wot found a dress in some shipment from Paris or somewhere. 'E gave me that dress five years ago but I've never 'ad the nerve to wear it.'

Douglas sniffed. 'And do you still see this Harold?'

'Nah, he died of consumption about two or three years ago now. Anyway,' she grasped Molly's hand. 'Yer can wear it love. It's made of green satin and velvet.'

'Satin and velvet,' Molly echoed dumbfounded. 'But will it fit?'

'It'll fit perfect like. I'm a bit too old and fat for it now.' She looked down at her waistline and sighed. Molly threw her arms around her friend and then turned to the Professor who stood up, once again leaving his beer untouched.

'Would you care to finish this?' he asked, fully aware that Douglas's attention was focussed on the glass.

'You are a true gentleman Sir!' Douglas gushed. He rummaged inside his coat pocket, handing the alien a small card. 'And here is the address of the theatre for your convenience.'

The Professor thanked the thespian before pocketing the card, then strode to the door and waited while Molly dropped a shilling into Oliver's expectant hands.

'Ere. 'appy now?'

Making no reply Oliver blew a puff of smoke in her face. She glared at him, turned on her heels and followed the Professor out into the night.

'It's a bit cold,' she said, chafing her arms.

A small child ran passed them, his face and torn clothes as dark and as dirty as the night. The Professor and Molly walked up the cobblestoned street when suddenly a black carriage came hurtling out of nowhere, heading straight for them. The Professor swivelled around and pushed Molly out of the way just before it crossed their path. They both fell face down onto the street as the carriage disappeared into the distance. The Professor looked up, his face flecked with rainwater and mud.

'Are you all right?'

Molly sat up, shaking with fear. 'Bleedin' 'ell, we could've been killed.'

'You're not hurt?'

'No,' she grumbled. 'But look at the state of me dress. It's ruined.'

The Professor helped the girl to her feet. He stared in the direction that the carriage had taken. Couldn't the carriage driver have pulled on the reigns instead of whipping the horses? Didn't he realise that they both could have been killed?

'Let's go 'ome Professor.'

He nodded absently. 'Yes, I must get to Harley Street early tomorrow morning.'

A

CHAPTER 3

The morning light placed the squalor of the East End under a harsh microscope, exposing every visible sign of filth, depravity and hopelessness. Confronted with this tangible misery, the alien was forced to accept that this was the norm for the creatures who lived here; and the remaining tomorrows would bleed into each other, played out repeatedly. He took no pleasure in this pessimistic view but faced with such a stark reality, what other conclusion could be reached?

The Professor navigated the crowds, ensuring he made eye contact with no one. He walked past a dilapidated dwelling abutting the street and nearly tripped over a woman sitting on the porch, her legs stretched out and her back leaning against the front door. The woman rocked the baby back and forth smiling as she did so, then looked up at the Professor with a scowl. 'Watch where yer goin'!' She dragged her feet back then lifted a dirty shawl to reveal a sleeping baby, blissfully unaware of its future.

'Pardon me,' apologised the Professor. He hesitated then reached into a pocket and took out several pennies then gently dropped them beside the woman. She looked down then hurriedly scooped them up mumbling her thanks.

Dodging a muddy pool on the street, the Professor walked into Spitalfields market observing the stallholders tempting passers' by with their wares; their loud voices drowning each other out in an attempt to attract business. One enterprising fishmonger stuck a haddock under his nose and the alien, shocked, explained that he could never consider eating anything that reminded him of a Marin.

The fishmonger gave him an odd look. 'Wos that?'

The Professor stepped back, replying, 'It's more of a *who* than a *what.*' As he turned, he noticed a child gently tugging at his trouser pocket. The boy hoped to find money but instead discovered a small cube the size of a die. Snatching the cube back, the Professor felt angered by the attempted theft. However, upon seeing how painfully thin the child was, his heart softened. He handed the boy several coins. The child's face, a mixture of puzzlement and suspicion, brightened as he quickly raced off before the Professor could change his mind.

The alien replaced the cube (this time in his breast pocket) and continued through the market finally reaching the Police House. Within, the superintendent was busily pacing the floor, dictating notes to his assistant but came to an abrupt halt when the door opened, revealing an intruder on the threshold.

The alien nodded politely. 'Good morning Superintendent Greensworth. I'm here to see Detective Inspectors Brett and Wainwright.' He closed the door and walked towards the detectives' tiny office. 'Are they available?'

Greensworth had taken an instant dislike to the stranger the first time he had set eyes on him and his opinion had not changed. He gave the man a look of superiority mixed with contempt before replying. 'What is it you wish to see them about?'

'We planned to meet this morning to discuss the Ripper murders.'

'Oh the Ripper murders,' Greensworth replied with more than a hint of derision. 'All you fellows from the *Yard* seem to do is discuss the Ripper murders. Your talk is endless whilst we, who have the proper authority are doing all the foot work.'

The Professor considered this, sensing Greensworth's frustration and resentment. He had obviously been forced to accept that the local police needed help but the help given turned out to be of a higher station than his own. Not something that would sit well with the likes of Greensworth. 'As you well know Superintendent it's a difficult case and we need all the help on offer. I'm sure you understand that.'

Greensworth propped himself up on the side of his assistant's desk, folding his arms. 'Oh I can understand a number of things. What my assistant and I cannot understand is why we were sent not only two but now three inspectors from Scotland Yard, who seem to run around in circles achieving absolutely nothing, whilst we are out on the streets twenty-four hours a day, combing the East End for this man.' His face had turned red and his jaw visibly clenched.

The Professor raised an eyebrow. 'And how goes your investigation?'

'Satisfactory.'

'Then perhaps we could assist each other?'

The superintendent sneered. 'When the Ripper has been sentenced and hanged, I shall take great pleasure in seeing you and your two colleagues return to Scotland Yard, where you will be forced to explain away your incompetence.'

The Professor cleared his throat then turned and opened the inner office door. 'We'll see Superintendent. Good morning.'

Constable Briggs stepped away from the other side of the door as it opened, trying not so successfully to hide the fact that he had been eavesdropping on the conversation. 'Excuse me Sir, I wasn't listening ... well not really; I swear I wasn't doing anything!'

'It's all right,' replied the Professor, closing the door. He leaned towards the PC and whispered. 'Neither was I, according to Mr Greensworth.'

A flicker of confusion crossed Briggs's face, clearly missing his new inspector's quip. He then returned to more important matters, gathering up various newspaper cuttings on the desk and handed them to the alien. 'I thought these might be helpful to you Sir.' The Professor quickly scanned and returned them to the surprised constable. Had he actually been able to read each article so quickly?

'When are the detectives due? Do you know?'

'Any time Sir,' Briggs replied. He glanced around nervously before continuing. 'Watch out for the superintendent Sir, and his assistant. I think he wants to cause trouble because he doesn't want anyone from the Yard down here. He barely even tolerates the other police sent down from central London.'

'And you don't share his views?'

Briggs shook his head adamantly. 'No Sir. I say any help that can bring a cold-blooded murderer to justice is worth it.'

The Professor nodded, approvingly. 'You're a good man, Briggs.'

The office door opened once again, and the two detectives entered greeting the Professor.

He smiled. 'Ah good, you're both here. I think we should head off immediately and leave the superintendent to his *important* work.'

The inspectors shared a knowing look. 'I see you've met Greensworth then?'

'Not the friendliest of fellows.'

'Neither's his assistant, PC Hugh Barker,' agreed Brett. 'They're dying to see us fail.'

Briggs shook his head. 'They're nowhere closer to catching Jack than you are Sir.'

Wainwright laughed. 'The Yard thanks you for your vote of confidence.'

'Oh I meant no disrespect Sir!'

'We know that Briggs,' said Wainwright. 'Off you go, you've got work to do I'm sure.'

The young constable took his leave and the Professor and the two inspectors left soon after. Greensworth waited a few moments then turned to his assistant.

'Follow 'em Barker. I want to see what they're up to.'

The younger man frowned. 'But what about our lead ...'

'That can wait, now I've given you an order so get to it.'

Barker nodded, collected his hat and left the Police House.

The Professor and the inspectors walked to the end of the street corner and Brett hailed a cab. He gave the driver the address in Harley Street, the three men climbed into the carriage.

The Professor looked out of the window observing the changing view; once out of the squalor of the East End, London was transformed into bright, pristine buildings, clean streets and tailored gardens. A world away from where he had walked that very morning.

'Quite a contrast, isn't it?' commented Wainwright, noting the Professor's sombre expression.

'Quite so,' the alien gravely replied.

The cab entered a street where a row of freshly elegant buildings stood. Brett tapped the side of the carriage, and the driver brought the horses to a halt. The three men alighted, and Brett paid the cabby.

'Here we are then,' declared Wainwright. 'We'll be lucky if we can catch him though.'

'All we can do is try,' replied the Professor.

They walked up to the doctor's surgery; outside was a plate bearing the Royal Coat of Arms proclaiming:

DOCTOR ANDREW L GRANTLEY
PHYSICIAN AND SURGEON

BY APPOINTMENT TO HER MAJESTY
QUEEN VICTORIA

Wainwright rang the doorbell and moments later, a homely looking woman with grey hair tucked under a mob cap opened the door.

'Inspector Wainwright,' she said not entirely surprised.

'Good morning Mrs Craven, we are here to see Doctor Grantley. Is he available?'

She looked at the Professor wondering who the third man was, and Wainwright introduced him. 'Mrs Craven, this is Professor Delbrotman who has recently joined our investigation and you already know Inspector Brett.' His colleague nodded.

The three men, looking suitably pleased with that piece of welcome news, entered the hallway of the Victorian house and looked around. There was a waiting room and brightly lit consulting room leading off from the left of a corridor and a set of stairs beyond. Opposite was another set of rooms, with their doors closed. 'I didn't realise that the surgery would have a housekeeper,' commented the Professor. 'Do you work here full-time?'

'Oh yes Sir,' she replied thinking it a little strange to be asked such a question. You either worked all the time or you didn't. 'Someone still has to keep this place clean and with Doctor Grantley's odd working hours, someone has to prepare his meals.'

She led them through the consulting room then ushered them into an office. 'Would you care for some tea?'

'Not for me thank you,' replied the Professor, Wainwright and Brett also declined.

Mrs Craven turned to a side-table, picked up two trays with empty dishes stacked on them and politely excused herself.

The Professor wandered casually around the room, glancing at several framed pen-drawings of human anatomy, and a number of heavy leather-bound volumes on diseases and practical medicines in the bookcase behind the desk. A second door caught his eye and he reached for the doorknob; it was locked.

'Professor Delbrotman!' rebuked Brett. 'That's obviously a private area. I don't think Doctor Grantley would approve.'

'I daresay.' The Professor released the knob and sat down behind the desk.

Brett gave him a disapproving look, unable to understand why the Professor would be so bold. 'And you're sitting in Doctor Grantley's chair.'

'And a very comfortable one it is too ... It's just such a shame that Doctor Waitley couldn't be here to enjoy the benefit of Doctor Grantley's *superior* expertise.'

The detectives shared a moment of awkward silence before the door to the office opened, revealing a middle-aged man who appeared startled to find occupants in his room. The man, tall and just over six feet, was clean-shaven with thinning grey hair and a network of fine lines etched across his forehead and beneath his eyes. His gaze settled on the Professor, who was seated at his desk.

'Doctor Grantley, I presume?' enquired the Professor.

'Yes.' His voice sounded puzzled. Who were these people and why was one of them seated at his desk?

Wainwright stepped forward. 'I am Detective Inspector Wainwright, and this is Detective Inspector Brett ...'

'Oh, of course, of course,' replied Grantley, the names jogging his memory.

'Didn't Mrs Craven tell you we were waiting?' asked the Professor. He stood up and wandered to the window.

'No, I let myself in this morning.'

The Professor regarded him, his expression unreadable.

'So gentlemen,' the surgeon began, walking around behind his desk', I must apologise that I have been unable to see you before today but I have been extremely busy.'

'We understand,' replied Wainwright,' but now that you are here, we would appreciate it if you could give us your medical opinion on the Ripper murders.'

'Certainly gentlemen, I would be glad to.' He looked at the Professor who was staring out of the window. 'Forgive me Sir but I thought that Scotland Yard had assigned only two investigators to the case.'

The Professor turned around. 'Well the Yard thought that more assistance was due so I was sent down as well.'

'I see.'

Wainwright agreed. 'Yes indeed. Oh forgive me for not introducing you before. Permit me, Doctor Grantley; Professor Orlando Delbrotman.'

'Professor?' echoed Grantley thoughtfully. 'May I ask what field Sir?'

'Oh, science, history, language ... criminology of course but if we may let's get down to business.' He walked over to the doctor as Wainwright took out the photographs of each of the victims, then placed them in front of the surgeon. 'What can you tell us about these?'

Grantley picked up the photos and examined them. 'Well for one thing the bodies were not mutilated haphazardly.'

'The work of someone who knew what he was doing?' concluded the Professor.

Grantley scrutinised the pictures. 'Precisely. The murderer must have knowledge of human anatomy.'

'Like a surgeon?' asked the Professor.

Grantley frowned. 'Yes, or perhaps a butcher.'

'But what motive?' asked Brett. 'Why target prostitutes in this way?'

Grantley weighed up the possibilities. 'For one thing they are easy targets.'

The Professor plunged his hands into his pockets. 'That is obvious but why kill in this manner? What is the purpose of it?'

Grantley stared blankly at him.

'I mean to say there are quicker ways to despatch a human being, why do it that way?'

The surgeon rubbed his forehead thoughtfully. 'Perhaps he was *with* each of the women and became angry with them for some reason.' He looked at Wainwright. 'Did the autopsies reveal that intercourse had taken place?'

'Well that's the strange part of it,' replied the inspector. 'According to the reports no sexual relations took place just before the girls were murdered.'

'Nothing at all?' he asked surprised. 'How odd.'

'So there must be another reason,' concluded Brett.

Grantley looked at the photographs again. 'Well, I am afraid that I can offer no explanations regarding that, however, I can safely say after examining these pictures that whoever the murderer is, he is left-handed.'

Brett and Wainwright looked at each other then stared at the photo that the surgeon was holding.

'Are you certain?' asked Wainwright.

'Quite certain,' he assured the inspector. 'Let me show you.' He opened one of the desk drawers and took out a small knife from a leather pouch holding it in his left hand. 'Now watch carefully,' he instructed. He ran the knife gently down a finger of his right hand drawing blood. The Professor flinched.

The surgeon smiled at the alien. 'Surely you're not afraid of a little blood after witnessing such ghastly butchery, Professor Delbrotman?'

The alien frowned. 'No but it's something you should never get used to.'

'Indeed,' the surgeon agreed. He looked at each of the inspectors. 'Now look at this minor wound and see if you cannot see similarities with those vicious cuts on the victims.'

Both men frowned with concentration while the Professor stared at the cut on the surgeon's finger.

'Of course,' breathed Brett in wonder. 'From right to left.'

'Very good, Detective.' Grantley nodded approvingly. He took out a handkerchief and wound it around his finger. 'Now then gentlemen, can I help you with anything else?'

'Not for the present,' replied Wainwright. 'But if there is ...'

'Then by all means return.' He collected the photos then handed them to the inspector and opened the door. 'I wish you success in catching the criminal.'

'Thank you, Doctor,' replied Brett. 'We appreciate your time and we will see ourselves out.'

Grantley smiled then, after closing the door behind them, unlocked the inner door to his office and disappeared inside.

'I am very glad we took your advice by coming today,' said Brett.

The Professor was forced to agree as Waitley had obviously failed to pick up on the fact that the murderer was left-handed;

a piece of evidence that could, in the end, be vital in catching the criminal.

As the three men walked through the hallway, Mrs Craven appeared pushing a trolley with a tray carrying a large leg of roast lamb, ten roast potatoes, four pieces of pumpkin, fresh rolls and an entire cherry pie. The detectives' jaws dropped open in surprise as the grandfather clock near the staircase struck ten.

'Good lord,' exclaimed Brett. 'Who is that for? The doctor? And at this time of day?'

'As per usual,' grumbled Mrs Craven. 'Not that I mind cooking for him but I have to say that it is quite a lot for one man to eat for morning tea.'

'Morning tea?' The Professor was surprised. 'What an immensely healthy appetite, does he always like to eat like this?'

'Pretty much Sir. Sometimes it may be fish, or the dessert may be pudding ...'

'I mean the volume,' interrupted the Professor. 'Does he always eat this much?'

Glad of a little gossip, the woman nodded. 'Oh yes Sir. He has for some time now.'

'It's a wonder that he doesn't make himself ill,' replied Wainwright in disbelief.

'Well he works very hard you see, long hours and all.' She smiled politely then glanced down at the trolley. 'Excuse me but I must get on before this all gets cold and we can't have that, can we?' She hurried over to the front door and opened it for them. 'Good morning gentlemen.'

The three men thanked the housekeeper then walked out onto the street.

Hugh Barker ran down Harley Street observing the two inspectors and the Professor hailing a cab. Once the cab had passed, he hailed another and told the driver to follow the first.

The Professor opened the door to the Police House to find Greensworth in a mood darker than what it had been earlier that morning.

'Good morning,' said Wainwright following the Professor inside.

'It's far from being a good one,' the superintendent hissed.

'What's happened?'

Hugh Barker entered the main office from an inner door and Greensworth gave him a warning look to keep quiet.

'Just after you left this morning a reporter from the Central News Agency came to give me a copy of this.' He held up a piece of paper.

Without a word the Professor snatched the paper away and read the contents.

'What is it? What does it say?' asked Wainwright.

'He's showing off,' dismissed the Professor. 'This letter is apparently from Jack the Ripper himself telling us that he thoroughly enjoyed killing those girls and that he will be sending the ears of his next victim to us.'

Brett took the letter, reading it for himself and swore under his breath. 'I can't believe it. The bloody nerve ... '

'Oh, it's very common,' replied the Professor matter-of-factly. 'Most criminals feel a need to boast of their exploits, otherwise who would appreciate their diabolical work?'

'And so, do we wait until we are sent body parts of his next victim?' exploded Brett. 'He's toying with us, taking delight in the knowledge that we are getting nowhere!'

'Some would call that incompetence ... Inspector,' sneered Greensworth.

Brett glowered and rounded on the superintendent. 'And just tell me what the hell have you been doing all this time? I don't see you catching him!'

'Brett,' cautioned Wainwright.

He jabbed a finger towards Greensworth, glancing at his colleague. 'No! This has to be said. From day one you have been doing everything in your power to be obstructive ...'

'I?' Interrupted Greensworth sarcastically.

Brett continued, his anger and frustration escalating. 'And whilst I am the first to admit this case is baffling, I expected something better from our uniform enforcement who apparently couldn't find any criminal unless it jumped up and bit 'em in the arse ... and even then I don't know!'

'Oi!' Barker butted in, angry at the attack on his superior.

The Professor rolled his eyes as the argument escalated, each man unwilling to back down, or concede that the other was trying his hardest under extremely difficult circumstances. Wainwright looked from one to the other, trying to placate matters but it finally took the Professor who grabbed a truncheon and slammed it down on the table to silence both men. 'That's enough! Has it ever occurred to you that while you argue like idiotic children, a man somewhere out there is slaughtering human beings wherever and whenever he feels like it? He would be so pleased to know that the police cannot work together. So while you are distracted in a petty battle of egos, he freely terrorises London with perhaps no possibility of being caught. You are supposed to be on the same side so whether you like it or not, deal with it!'

Greensworth and Brett looked suitably abashed.

'You are of course quite right Professor,' agreed Brett. 'We should try to put our differences aside and concentrate on what is important.'

'Agreed,' said Greensworth grudgingly.

'Good,' approved the Professor. 'Now let's try collaboration and see what that can bring.'

Greensworth nodded but glanced slyly at his assistant. Barker returned a knowing smile.

▲

CHAPTER 4

Molly and Elsie peered through the dirty window outside The Ten Bells to see Oliver yelling at Billy, who was cowering behind Arnold Backer, a mop held in the young lad's quivering hand.

'I took yer in, didn' I?' Yelled Oliver, the obligatory cigar clenched between his teeth. He took it out and stabbed it in the boy's direction. 'No one wanted a brat with one leg shorter than the other an' one lookin' like a pig's trotter. Coulda sold you to the circus, but did I?'

Billy wailed, shivering in fear.

'No,' Oliver grunted, 'I didn't cos I looks after me own and so when Backer tells yer to do summink yer bloody well do it!'

Backer flinched at the mention of his name. 'Yes … well … Billy didn't really mean no 'arm, Oliver. 'E's only nine years old and it's 'ard for 'im.'

Oliver grabbed the child by the ear and dragged him out from behind the barman's protection. 'Yer wanna live to see ten?'

Billy sobbed, nodding.

'Then mop the bleedin' floor before I give yer a good thrashin!'

Oliver released him, and the boy wiped away the tears staining his dirty face and busied himself with mopping a patch of floor that would always look dirty no matter how hard it was cleaned. Elsie groaned and shook her head. The day she saw Oliver in a good mood would be the day he left this world in a wooden box. The woman clutched the papier mâché box she held in her arms firmly to her chest and steeled herself.

'Yer open the door Moll and go straight upstairs without a word. I'll be right behind yer.'

Molly nodded, understanding what Elsie meant. She too hoped that Oliver would simply ignore what they were doing. But Oliver had a shrewd sense of distrust, and he never liked his girls to have any secrets, particularly when they came in large, suspicious looking papier mâché boxes.

Molly opened the door and hurried inside followed by Elsie; Oliver naturally noticed them.

'Why the big 'urry ladies?'

The two women turned around and Elsie laid a supportive hand on Molly's arm. 'Old the box, I'll 'andle this.' Then facing Oliver she explained, 'I'm just goin' up to help Molly.'

Oliver raised an eyebrow. 'I didn' think a big girl like that needed any 'elp.'

She gave him a withering look. 'Very funny. I mean she's needs to get dolled up an' she needs my 'elp.'

Oliver sauntered over to where Elsie stood, his cigar in his hand and motioned towards the box. 'And wot's Molly got there?'

'A dress.'

Oliver gave her an incredulous look. 'A dress? What for? Wot yer both up to?'

'I'm goin' to the theatre with the Professor t'night,' explained Molly.

'You? The theatre? Since when 'ave you started having lah-di-dah ideas about such things?'

'It's Douglas's play,' defended Elsie sharply.

Oliver looked amused. 'Oh yeah? Should be a 'oot then,' he paused. 'Or then again maybe it won't.' He reached out and lifted the lid of the box before Molly could snatch it away. Inside, the green satin and velvet dress stood out vividly against the drab, smoky surroundings.

Oliver's eyes popped open in amazement. 'Where'd yer get summink like that?'

'From a limey,' Elsie replied simply.

'And yer didn't tell me about it?' He reached for the dress but Elsie grabbed the box from Molly, clutching it to herself.

'Go away, yer ain't takin' it.'

'I'll take wot I like. Don't forget I own yer, so therefore, I own everything you 'ave!'

Elsie backed away. 'Yer always takin', Oliver! Well yer ain't 'avin' this cos it's all I got, yer miserable pig!'

Oliver threw down his cigar, ground it underfoot then stalked over snatching the box with one hand and grabbing hold of Elsie's chin with the other, digging his fingers into her flesh. 'Molly ain't goin' nowhere! And if I ever 'ear another word like that comin' from your stinkin' 'ole then it won't be the Kipper wot yer got to be worried about!'

With the mention of *that* name, Backer grunted anxiously and Billy stopped his mopping staring at the pimp.

'And wot yer starin' at?' spat Oliver. 'Yer got nothin' to stare at, yer little bastard—yer nothin' but a son of a whore!'

The boy burst out sobbing; he dropped the mop then quickly disappeared down the cellar trapdoor behind the bar, slamming it shut.

'Yer shouldn't 'ave said that Oliver,' Backer said hesitantly. 'That ain't fair!'

'Shut up!'

The tavern door opened and Constable Briggs, stepped inside. Everyone looked in his direction and it was instantly clear to the young policeman that the friction in the air was as thick as treacle.

'Good afternoon,' he said tentatively.

No one replied.

'I hope I haven't interrupted anything.'

Oliver clenched his jaw and gave a strained smile. 'No Constable, we was just 'avin' a nice, quiet chat.'

Briggs nodded but from the looks of the others and the muffled howls coming from beneath the bar, he did not believe a single word of it. He looked at Molly and gave the pale-faced girl an encouraging smile. 'Miss, Professor Delbrotman told me that he will pick you up here at 6 pm tonight.'

'I dunno whether I can come now.' She glanced nervously at the pimp who stood there glowering.

'Oh?' Briggs turned to Oliver who was awkwardly holding onto the box. Sensing the constable's reproof, he reluctantly handed it to the girl.

'Ere, and don't yer get it dirty.'

Molly carefully took it from him. 'Thank yer.' She smiled at Briggs. 'Tell the Professor I'll be ready.'

The constable nodded then asked Backer for a glass of water. Backer obliged as the policeman sat down at the bar.

Oliver glared at Molly as the girl helped Elsie up the stairs. She gave the woman a worried look and gently brushed a tear from her cheek. 'Els' are yer awl right?'

'Always.' Her voice was edged with bitterness.

The room contained a bed and a rickety side table; a candle, now burnt down to the wick, sat perched in a recess in the wall. Elsie carefully set the box on the bed and lifted the dress out, holding it in front of her. Molly marvelled at its beauty and craftsmanship, wishing she had learned to sew such a lovely gown.

Elsie pushed aside her sadness and beamed at the girl. 'Come on, time we got yer cleaned up.'

'Wot yer mean?'

'Well yer gonna 'ave to wash yer face and neck before I letcha wear this dress, my girl.' She put the dress down on the bed and headed to the door. I'll go get Backer to fetch us some water.'

'I'll go,' Molly suggested helpfully. 'Oliver ain't as mad at me.'

Elsie sighed reluctantly agreeing with her. Within a few minutes, thanks to PC Briggs's calming presence, and Oliver's *magnanimous* approval, Backer had fetched some water in a vaguely clean jug and carried it upstairs, before handing it to Elsie.

Elsie peered into the jug with a disappointed look. 'There ain't much water there.'

'All Oliver can spare,' Backer grunted.

'Well,' she sighed, 'I s'pose it'll have to do. Thanks Backer,' Elsie smiled before closing the door in his face.

Downstairs Briggs finished his water (or what he could stomach) and thanked Oliver for his hospitality. The pimp gave him a greasy grin and invited him to come back soon. As soon as the constable had gone, Oliver grunted then angrily bit the end off another cigar before spitting it onto the floor. 'I don't like this at all. Molly 'igh tailin' it about with a peeler.'

'Why not? 'E pays well, don't 'e?'

'But that's it, in it?' He lowered his voice. 'I don't think they've actually done it yet.'

Backer shrugged. 'So maybe tonight's the night. Maybe 'e likes it when it's all toffed up.'

Not having thought of that possibility but not wanting to appear stupid, Oliver growled. 'Well of course 'e wants her toffed up! Wot do yer take me for? An idiot?'

'No Oliver.'

'*No Oliver,*' the pimp mimicked sarcastically. Shaking his head, as if the weight of the world was on his shoulders, he perched himself on a stool at the bar resting his head in his hands. Backer bit his lip, unsure whether he should stay still or move, then deciding that safety behind the bar was a better option.

'Wanna drink?'

Oliver looked up and sniffed. 'Yer paying fer a drink f'me?'

Backer was unsure but Oliver took his hesitation as a yes.

'Good. I need summink to soothe the nerves,' Oliver considered his selection. 'A double gin—and make sure yer pay up first!'

Backer reluctantly took a coin out of his pocket and placed it in a box before pouring the drink. Oliver took it holding the glass up to the light. 'The finest in London.' He grinned, 'wot should we drink to?'

To no more coins in me pocket, Backer miserably thought to himself.

'To business!' Oliver declared, 'and to me!' He laughed then swallowed the liquid down in one gulp. 'And stick that box away, idiot!'

Elsie smiled and rested both hands on the girl's shoulders. 'Yer are a very pretty girl an' very lucky to 'ave a gentleman who looks after 'er so well.'

'I know.' She wriggled out of her ragged dress, throwing it on the bed beside the box. 'But wot about Oliver?'

'As long as Oliver gets paid 'e'll be 'appy.'

Molly loosened her hair and it spilled out over her shoulders. 'I am sorry about wot 'appened before.'

'Don't even think about it, it's all over now. But with your Professor and my Cyril, we're doin' awl right.'

'Cyril?'

'Yes,' Elsie replied nervously. 'That's Douglas's real name.'

'Cyril!' cried Molly. 'Cor blimey, no wonder 'e changed it. Cyril's an 'orrible name!'

Elsie smiled uneasily. 'Well it's Douglas to everyone that knows 'im, except me on occasions, so don't yer get no ideas about calling 'im that, understand?'

'Sorry I didn't mean anythin' by it.'

'I know yer didn't.' Elsie patted the girl's cheek, and all was forgiven. Taking Molly's chin gently in her hand she sprinkled water onto her face and rubbed her skin until it was pink. Molly gasped and spluttered. 'Not so 'ard!'

'Stop yer complainin'. Yer ain't goin' out with a dirty face.' Elsie finished her scrubbing then set to work on the girl's neck and arms. When she was done, she scrutinised her work and nodded approvingly.

Molly rubbed her arms wondering if there was any skin left, then picked up the dress and stepped into it. 'So where did the limey get this dress?'

'Dunno,' replied Elsie, 'best not to know these things sometimes.' Elsie turned the girl around to face the wall then tightened the laces of the bodice. 'I ain't got stockings unfortunately but there are boots. No one'll know cos they do up well past the ankle.'

'Won't me feet 'urt?

'Yer'll 'ave to put up with it. Now let me look at yer.' Elsie stepped back to get a good view and smiled in satisfaction. The gown clung to the girl's slender curves with soft lace trimming the edges of the puff sleeves and a satin ribbon finishing in a bow beneath her bust. Elsie's eyes misted over.

'Wos wrong'?' Molly asked.

'Nothin',' Elsie dismissed. 'I was just seein' someone else for a moment a long time ago.' She puffed up the sleeves then ran her fingers through the girl's hair. 'I've got just the thing.' She swept Molly's hair up over her head, then grabbed the green feather from the box and pinned it in place. Molly looked down at herself and blushed.

'Is that really me?'

Elsie smiled sadly. 'It is my dear.'

Diary Extract 1.2

I haven't been particularly active this afternoon, so I thought I'd add another entry as it does give me something vaguely constructive to do.

I have been sitting for several hours, listening to the absurd bickering between Scotland Yard's finest, and the local police. I foolishly thought that after my rebuke I might see everyone working together but I was wrong. I do however, understand that everyone is tired and stressed and feels the pressure of being unproductive. The crux of the matter is that it is 1888, hardly the era of forensic science. There is no finger printing, or blood grouping—not much at all, except for wits. I know I have such skills that could lend themselves to aid the police but I must be very careful as history must not be tampered with unless absolutely necessary. And yet at the same time I also feel a sense of powerlessness, as if there is something trying to prevent me from being of any use at all.

I feel a barrier.

Diary Extract End - 1.2

The alien stared at the notebook in front of him, lost in thought. Constable Briggs entered the Police House and walking over to the Professor, cleared his throat trying to attract his attention.

'Excuse me Sir.'

'Yes Briggs?'

'You told me to remind you when it was half five and it's just on that now.'

'What? Already?'

Briggs stepped out of the way just in time to avoid colliding with the Professor as he bolted from his chair, heading for the door.

Wainwright looked surprised at this sudden display of animation. 'Where are you off to?'

'I have an appointment at the theatre with young Molly. I nearly forgot the time.' Within seconds, he was out the door, bounding down the street.

Turning to his assistant, Greensworth gave a quick nod and Barker slipped out after him. His sudden disappearance did not go unnoticed however, and Brett gave the superintendent an accusing look. 'Afraid that the Professor will find out something new before you do? Or do you have suspicions about him as well?'

Greensworth smiled enigmatically. 'We're all on the same the side Inspector, or have you forgotten?'

The Professor hurried through the marketplace until reaching the blind alley where his ship lay hidden. Still invisible to the naked eye, the alien unlocked the door and disappeared inside.

Barker, who had followed the Professor, cursed loudly with this unexpected vanishing act. Stamping his foot in frustration, he doubled back and opted down another street.

The database spun into life announcing that it had several suggestions for theatre attire circa 1888. The Professor ran a finger down the options then making his selection, downloaded to real-time. A moment passed and a recess appeared in the wall opposite, displaying a dinner suit, top hat, cape and silver-tipped cane. He took custody of the attire holding the outfit at arm's length suitably impressed.

Having changed, he stepped out into the alley, closing the invisible door behind him and strolled down the street, swinging his silver-tipped cane.

Barker who had been previously walking around in circles, couldn't believe his luck when he spotted his quarry sauntering by, looking like something out of a best-dressed advertisement for rich gents. Barker rubbed his hands in glee then hurried along ensuring that he remained several paces behind. The Professor slowed down to a halt and looked up at the sky then listened for nearby sounds: a cat growling; children yelling at each other; a heated argument down a nearby street; and something else. Footsteps—two; belonging to one person. He glanced out of the corner of his eye and grinned. Setting off once again, he tapped his cane on the ground and called out: 'Come along PC Barker! I always say there's no point in dawdling if there's someone you wish to follow!'

The policeman stopped in his tracks and blushed furiously, cursing the Professor's impertinence.

Backer poured a glass of gin and banged it down pointedly on the bar in front of Skinner. 'Think yerself lucky that Oliver let yer come back so early.'

The sailor smiled, the scar on his cheek twitching. 'Well money's money, ain't it?'

'Wot yer mean?'

'Just wot I said. You an' Oliver are 'ere to make money, so why begrudge me a gin or two when yer can make money out of it?'

Backer frowned, and Skinner dropped a few coppers onto the bar.

'I'm 'ere to 'ave me drink then 'ave a whore, nothin' else.'

Backer scooped up the coins then placed them in a box under the counter. 'Well I'm tellin' yer now, if yer start another fight like yer did last time and the time before that, I 'ave permission from Oliver to smash yer bloody face in.'

Skinner swallowed nervously although his face remained stubborn; he decided to change the subject. 'Wot about a tune eh Backer?' He got up from the bar and seated himself in front of a dilapidated piano and struck a key. A prostitute with a limp red feather entwined in her matted black hair sat down beside him and struck another key. He laughed, and with his right hand began playing a tune, while his left hand wandered down the tart's open blouse.

Oliver glanced around the bar from his vantage point at the top of the stairs before stomping down in a haze of cigar smoke. He started coughing and thumped his chest noisily, before hawking up a lump of phlegm onto the floor. 'Shit, I'm think I'm dyin'.'

Elsie flounced down after him, stepping over the disgusting mess. 'We live in 'ope.'

He shot her a filthy look, which she ignored.

'Get to work.'

She turned and gave him a mocking curtsy, then collected her usual tot of gin from Backer and joined a group of labourers who had just entered the tavern.

A few moments later the Professor opened the door gaining the attention of the drinkers, especially since he was now decked out in extremely elegant evening wear. He looked at the sea of greedy faces and could tell that most would have obligingly robbed him if they had half a chance.

Elsie hurried over to him, giving him a wink and a click of her tongue. 'Why Professor, don't yer scrub up nice. I'll just go an' get Molly for yer.'

'Thank you.'

'Evenin' Professor,' called Oliver expansively. 'Takin' my Molly out on the town I see.'

The Professor mentally scoffed at the pimp's audacity but nevertheless smiled pleasantly. 'Well, it was her birthday yesterday, so I think she deserves a treat.'

Oliver returned a reptilian grin. 'I trust it will be worth my while just as much as 'ers?'

The Professor nodded stiffly in acknowledgement, hiding his utter contempt for the man. Oliver slapped him on the back as if they were old friends.

'Good. I'm glad we understan' one another.'

Elsie came halfway down the stairs and cleared her throat. 'Professor, are yer ready?'

He nodded.

'Right.' She turned around and gestured to Molly to come down. The girl walked slowly down the stairs and stopped at the bottom looking very self-conscious. The sailors and locals whistled and cat-called, and even Backer fingered his dirty collar. This caused Oliver to beam proudly as if taking full credit for the girl's transformation. He placed his cigar in his mouth and chewed it triumphantly.

Molly gave the Professor a timid look. 'Well?'

The alien struggled to find the right words. He recognised the skilful craftsmanship of the dress; he was sure it was hand-sewn. He noted that she had washed her face and hands and neatly tied her hair. Without any cosmetics, her cheeks and lips appeared naturally pink, likely from pinching and biting to bring colour to her face. Her posture had improved as well. All these details were apparent but summarising their significance into a few words was challenging. He was a teacher, not a poet, yet he knew she deserved a compliment for her efforts.

Molly's expectant face started to show signs of disappointment when no reply was forthcoming, so he smiled warmly, carefully choosing the words: 'Most becoming and very ladylike.'

Her worried expression melted away. 'Really?'

'I will be proud to escort you to dinner and the theatre.'

'Cor blimey! Dinner as well?' Her ladylike demeanour slipped and the Professor hid an amused smile and took her by the arm.

'Now yer mind 'ow yer speak,' warned Elsie. 'No cursin' or nothin'.'

Molly frowned at her in annoyance. 'I won't.'

'Enjoy my Douglas's play!' Elsie waved through the window as the Professor and Molly disappeared down the street.

The Professor held up his hand as a carriage approached but the driver ignored him and continued on his way. Another came in quick succession and pulled up alongside him.

'Cab Sir?'

'Thank you,' the alien replied.

The driver climbed down and opened the door, offering to help Molly inside.

'Thank you.'

He nodded. 'Miss.'

The Professor gave the cabbie the directions to the hotel and sat down next to his young companion. Molly gazed out of the window in wonder, as the harsh, impoverished world she lived in transformed itself into the prosperous, refined world she had only ever dreamed about.

'Where we gonna eat?' She leaned forward eagerly, waiting for him to reply.

'It's a surprise.'

The driver took them to their destination then assisted his passengers out of the cab. The Professor paid the cabby as Molly stood transfixed, mesmerised by the throng of gorgeously dressed women being escorted by their elegantly attired escorts into the hotel. She took the Professor's arm and gave him a nervous look.

'I'm not a toff like them; they won't want me in there.'

'Nonsense. Money speaks all languages Molly, believe me I know.'

She looked up at the indecipherable squiggle over the door and squinted. 'Wot does that say?'

'The name of the hotel,' he replied. 'It's called 'The Grand Tower' and they have a rather elegant restaurant inside.'

The Professor escorted her through the double doors and into a foyer where a glittering chandelier hung from the ceiling and an imposing floral carpeted staircase led to a balcony above. Several couples stood chatting near the stairs: one couple in particular caught Molly's attention. The young woman was dressed in a midnight blue satin gown and wore a dazzling pearl choker, with a large sparkling sapphire at its centre that twinkled under the chandelier's lights. She looked adoringly at her escort and held out her left hand to an elderly couple displaying the magnificent diamond ring on her finger. Molly could hear their congratulatory words, and her heart fluttered with romantic notions.

'Isn't she beautiful?'

The Professor glanced in her direction and grunted. 'Quite, now come along.' They walked over to the entrance of the restaurant, where a tall thin man half strangled in a tight collar, stiff dicky and dinner suit stood in front of a desk, scrutinising an open book filled with names. He fiddled with his waxed moustache and gave the Professor a supercilious look.

'May I help you Sir?'

'I have a booking under the name of Delbrotman.'

The maître d' raised a sceptical eyebrow. Whoever heard of such a ridiculous name? The young girl on the gentleman's arm smiled brightly, giving him a wink. He shuddered imperceptibly at her lack of decorum.

'Delbrotman, you say Sir?' He turned several pages over and ran a finger down the page until he reached the name. 'May I have your full name Sir?'

'Certainly.' The Professor smiled, knowing full well there would have been only one Delbrotman listed. 'I am Professor Orlando Delbrotman.' He leaned forward conspiratorially and whispered into the man's ear.,'of Scotland Yard.'

The maître d' gave him a haughty look. 'I see.'

'I'm on a case, hush-hush you know.' He motioned towards Molly. 'This is my assistant.'

'Is 'The Grand Tower' in any danger?'

The Professor shook his head. 'Oh dear me no. I'm investigating elsewhere but even investigators must stop and eat sometime.' He stared earnestly at the maître d' trying not to laugh. The other man felt uncomfortable under such close scrutiny and cleared his throat.

'Delbrotman. Of course Sir.' He tapped the name on the page. 'If you would please wait one moment.'

The Professor thanked him.

The maître d' disappeared and clicked his fingers at a waiter. 'Giles, would you please show Professor Delbrotman and company to table thirty-seven.'

A young waiter with a starched, white cloth over his arm hurried over to the Professor. 'If you would walk this way Sir?'

The maître d' watched them walk into the restaurant and his permanently disdainful expression turned even more disdainful. 'Scotland Yard indeed!'

The Ten Bells was alive with boisterous singing and laughter accompanied by Skinner as he hammered away at the worn, old ivories, trying to keep up with Oliver, who was busy leading his congregation in the final verse of *The Farmer's Daughter*.

'And when 'er old father,'
'Caught 'em both in the barn!'
'E shot off the gent's two instead!'
'Ole`!'

Oliver clapped and cheered, and the drunks howled in delight then gradually the din died down, and the revellers staggered back to their gin and beer. The girls followed sporting saucy grins, shrieking and squealing. Skinner finished off the last of his beer and staggered over to a girl wearing a red dress and a matching red feather in her frizzy hair. Her flushed face and heaving bosom looked delicious to the half-drunk sailor.

He leaned against her and kissed her neck. 'Let's go upstairs.'

The whore giggled. 'Awlright.' She grabbed hold of his arm and guided him up the steps.

The noise from the bar below subsided as she made her way along the corridor while playfully fending off Skinner's wandering hands. She grabbed hold of one of his wrists to stop him tickling her and knocked on a door to see if it was occupied.

When no one answered, she opened the door and ordered him to get on the bed. Like an obedient dog waiting for his reward, Skinner did as he was told and collapsed, sinking into the lumpy mattress. The woman gave him a saucy wink then dispensed with her skirt, blouse and boots and climbed up beside him in her underwear; he didn't move.

'Well? Are yer just gonna sit there? Or do I 'ave to do it all by meself?'

He looked at her and grinned giddily. 'ang on, I'm comin'.'

The woman cackled and dragged off his shirt, revealing several tattoos on his muscular shoulders.

'Did that 'urt?' She ran a finger over one, a cobra wrapped around a sword.

'Nah.' He shook his head. He took off his boots and wriggled out of his bell bottoms. 'Big boys don't cry.'

She grinned leaning towards him. 'Come on then big boy.'

Instead of smiling back at her, he frowned, getting a good look at her raddled, sweaty face. She was obviously older than him, perhaps as old as his mother, if his mother had still been alive. Her face paint had run between the crow's feet around her eyes, and her powder had sunk into her cheeks. But it wasn't her face that he was interested in, was it? After all, he'd be leaving England soon; he wasn't even sure when he'd have another opportunity like this for some time. She took the feather out of her hair and tickled him under the chin. He gave her a wolfish grin and grabbed her.

Oliver collapsed in a chair beside Elsie who was being entertained with stories by a labourer who claimed to be a relative of Prince Albert.

'Really? Oh do go on,' Elsie tried not to sound bored. ''Ave yer really been to Buckingham Palace?'

The pimp gave Elsie an incredulous look. 'That's a good one. 'e's even more full of it than old Dougie.'

Elsie shot him a warning look. 'Yer want me to work so I'm workin'.'

He nodded. 'Well as long as e's got the money to pay up, 'e can call himself the Queen of Sheba fer all I care.'

The labourer glared at Oliver and the pimp bowed his head. 'Pardon me yer lordship, I was just checkin' to see if Elsie knew where one of me girl's 'as got to.'

'Which one?' She asked.

'Isabelle.'

She shrugged. 'Upstairs I think. I think she's with that Skinner but she might be finished by now.'

Oliver nodded, got up from the table and wandered over to the bar.

✧ ✧ ✧

Isabelle sighed deeply at Skinner's thunderous expression. 'Don't worry yerself about it. It 'appens sometimes.'

'Not ter me!'

She rolled over onto her side and ran a hand down his chest. 'We'll try again later. Just maybe ...'

He gave her a hard look. 'Wot?'

She tried to smile. 'Maybe just relax a bit more. I'm told that 'elps.'

'Relax?' he spat back. 'I'm about as relaxed as I can flamin' well get! Wot do yer think the problem is, yer stupid bitch!'

Isabelle sat up and grabbed hold of her bloomers. 'I was only tryin' to 'elp. There's no need to talk to me like that.'

He sat up and hissed at her. 'I can talk to yer any bloody way I want. I'm a payin' customer remember? So don't yer start takin' that tone wi' me.'

The woman scowled and slid off the bed, hastily pulling on her underwear. 'Right!' She picked up her skirt. 'Yer can go and find someone else to put up with yer floppy rooster.'

Skinner's eyes flashed with rage and he jumped off the bed, grabbing hold of her; she swore and tried to wriggle free from his grasp.

'Bugger orf! Lemme go!'

He seized her flailing arms and shoved them behind her, digging his fingers into her soft flesh. 'I ain't got no problem, see? It's *you* that 'as! How can a man get it up when 'e's got to look at some bleedin' ol' 'ag while doin' it?!'

The woman shot him a look of pure venom and spat in his face; he jerked his head away then she kicked him in the leg which caused him to lose his grip on her. She saw her opportunity and ran for the door but he charged after her, knocking her over. She came crashing to the floor with an enormous thud, bellowing and thrashing until Skinner flipped her onto her back, pinning her down.

'Well, well, well,' he said threateningly. 'Who's got problems now then eh?' She stopped yelling and stared at him, terrified. He traced a finger over her forehead, nose and lips then down her throat. She flinched. He slapped her hard across the face then clamped both hands around her neck and squeezed.

Backer looked up from spit polishing a glass and frowned at the noise from above. He put the glass down and walked over to Oliver who was smoking at the end of the bar.

'I'm gonna check upstairs.'

Oliver gave him a questioning look. 'Wot's up?'

'I 'eard a bangin' sound.'

The pimp grinned. 'Course yer did Backer, wot do yer think they do up there?'

'No.' The barman shook his head. 'I mean like somethin' being 'it 'ard.'

Elsie nonchalantly wandered closer to the bar accompanied by her labourer as she had heard the loud thump too and was worried. While she appeared to take an interest in his inane chatter, she was in fact trying to eavesdrop on the conversation between the barman and pimp.

Oliver exhaled some smoke thoughtfully then nodded. 'Awl right, I'll follow yer up and we'll take a look.' Then added, 'make sure yer lock the takings up first though. We don't want any scum 'elpin' 'emselves, while we're up there.'

Backer did as he was told and after the money was secured, the two men made their way upstairs and walked along the corridor. A muffled sound came from within one of the rooms and Oliver nodded to Backer.

'Open the door. If there ain't somethin' wrong then close it quick.'

Backer threw the door open.

Isabelle was spread out on the floor, her face rapidly turning purple and her hands helplessly clawing at Skinner's face. When the sailor saw Backer, he released the woman and rushed to the window and tried to open it.

Backer smiled wolfishly. 'I'm glad yer've done this. Now I can smash yer bloody face in, yer bastard!' He lumbered over and grabbed hold of Skinner's arm. The sailor tried to punch him but Backer head butted him, knocking him senseless.

Oliver bent over the injured woman just as Elsie raced into the room, gasping at the scene that lay before her.

'I knew there was somethin' up. Isabelle, oh Gord, are yer awl right?'

The other woman burst into tears and Elsie bent down and cradled her in her arms. She winced at the swollen red weals around her friend's neck.

'It's awl right now,' Elsie crooned. 'Skinner ain't gonna 'urt anyone again. Backer'll see to that.'

'Yer damn right Backer will,' replied Oliver angrily. 'Isabelle pulls in a good trade, and if that arsehole 'ad killed her, I'd be down money that's rightfully mine!'

'Should I take 'im downstairs?' asked Backer.

Oliver nodded. 'In the cellar but wake 'im up first. I want 'im to know it when yer kick the shit out of 'im.'

Backer grinned and slung the unconscious figure over his shoulder.

Molly sank back in her seat and smiled contentedly. Never had she eaten so much and so well. There had been minestrone soup, followed by pheasant under glass and then there was dessert still to follow.

'More champagne Miss?' asked a waiter, taking the bottle from the ice bucket.

'Later,' replied the Professor before she could answer. 'We'll have the dessert first.'

The waiter smiled pompously. 'Very good Sir.'

Molly frowned at her half empty glass then shrugged and polished off the rest.

'Steady,' warned her companion. 'Don't overdo it now.'

'But this is my birthday present.'

'But there's still more to come, remember? Don't forget about the play.'

She laughed. 'Ow could I forget? Dougie's always on about 'is acting.'

A waiter wheeled a gleaming silver trolley up to their table, as three other waiters deftly placed fresh napery before them.

'Your dessert Miss.'

Molly had chosen Cherries Jubilee from what her companion had read out to her from the menu. The Professor had chosen soufflé as he had read about it once during his Earth studies as a boy. It certainly lived up to its reputation.

Molly followed the Professor's example by picking up her napkin, shaking it and then dropping it onto her lap. She then spooned up a small piece of pie and placed it delicately in her mouth, conscious not to gulp it.

As the alien picked lightly at his soufflé, he noticed the maître d' personally escorting a couple to a table close to where a chamber orchestra was playing. The lady was seated first, then the gentleman, whose chair faced the Professor. The man gave him a rather worried look however, the Professor smiled warmly in his direction.

'Who's that yer smilin' at?' Asked Molly, wiping the crumbs from her mouth with the back of her hand. Then quickly recovering her etiquette, she grabbed her napkin and brought it to her mouth. A monocled fop at a neighbouring looked aghast at her.

'Doctor Grantley.'

Molly's face lit up and she twisted in her seat to get a good look at him. 'Cor, fancy seein' 'im wot goes to 'er Majesty all the time.'

The monocled fop's wife, upholstered in purple lace and pink feathers, paled at the girl's words and began fanning herself while glaring at the Professor. 'Society is in the decline Henry,' she hotly murmured to her husband.

Henry sniffed in disdainful agreement. 'Indeed.'

After staring at the Grantleys for a few more seconds, Molly turned around and polished off the last of her dessert. The Professor pressed the forefingers of both hands together thoughtfully, as he observed two roast chickens and accompanying vegetables being served to the physician, while his wife gave embarrassed smiles to several couples who looked nonplussed at the man's voracious appetite.

Molly stole another glance. ''E sure likes his Lilley and Skinner. Wot an appetite eh?'

The Professor frowned at her. 'Lilley and what?'

'Skinner. Lilley and Skinner—dinner. Ain't yer ever 'eard that before?'

His eyes widened. 'Ah! Rhyming slang of course. I have heard of it; quite prevalent in this time period, I believe.'

'Eh?'

He gave her a guarded look and reached out a hand as the waiter presented the bill on a small silver tray.

▲

CHAPTER 5

Skinner slowly opened his eyes trying to focus on his surroundings instead of the intense pain that drummed in his head. He could hear voices and laughter echoing from above, and figured he was still in the pub; probably dumped somewhere in the cellar. He sat up and gingerly felt for his face. His nose was smashed worse than last time, and lumps of clotted blood came away in his dirty hands. Shivering in the cold, he wrapped his arms around himself, realising that he was in fact stark naked sitting on a pile of old straw. Just what the hell had happened to his clothes? And more importantly what the hell had happened to him? Confusion started clouding his mind and his head began to spin like a child's top. Now what was it he was supposed to remember again? Something about a dirty, old whore ... that's right—she was the one that started it all. The events of the past hour came charging back with a vengeance and the adrenaline burned through his bloodstream, overpowering any sense of pain or weakness. It was payback time. So who deserved it first? The bitch? Oliver? Backer? Backer. It was time that miserable piece of scum was taught a lesson.

As if on cue the old wooden door to the cellar opened and the barman wandered in and gave the sailor a look that spoke volumes. 'So we're finally awake, are we?'

Skinner regarded him before speaking. 'Ow long 'ave I been 'ere?'

Backer scratched his chin thoughtfully. 'Oh, fer well over an 'our.'

'Where are me clothes?'

Backer walked over to one of the barrels and picked up a sailor's uniform. 'They're safe 'ere.'

Skinner experimented with standing unaided, before opting to crawl over to a nearby barrel and lean against it for support. 'I don't feel so good.'

Backer looked at him with mock concern. 'Aw, poor Skinny Winny. Yer should 'ave thought of that before messin' with Isabelle. Oliver ain't happy about that y'know. She can't work tonight 'cosa you.'

'She insulted me.'

Backer's eyes wandered down the sailor's naked body and he grinned. 'Can't say as I blame 'er. There's not much there, is there?'

The sailor met Backer's gaze before roaring in outrage and rushing at the barman repeatedly punching him in the face and neck. Backer wasn't expecting such a sudden attack and weathered a handful of vicious blows. He stumbled backwards and dabbed at a nostril registering with surprise his own blood on his hand. He stared at his fingers in disbelief then frowned as Skinner laughed hysterically. Calmly stepping forward, Backer swung back and punched Skinner in the stomach-the sailor doubled over coughing and spluttering. Then Backer kicked him sharply in the chest. Without another word, the barman collected Skinner's clothes, grabbed hold of the sailor in a headlock and dragged him up the cellar stairs and into the bar above. Skinner spat and growled, trying to cover himself up but it proved impossible, and he was greeted with shrieks of laughter and cat calls from the girls and their clients. As Backer flung open the door and threw the sailor and his clothes into the street, Skinner screamed in frustration and pain demanding blood but the barman ignored all threats and slammed the door shut. Skinner hastily grabbed hold of his clothes and stumbled down a nearby alley away from prying eyes. He'd be back to settle that bastard's hash. But first he had to have a plan.

The Ivory Palace Theatre was in a state of faded glory; or perhaps it had always been that way. From a distance it looked bright and opulent but on closer inspection, the gold paint had chipped away from the theatre sign, the carpet was worn in several places, the red velvet curtains had small holes left by industrious moths and the seats were cracked. Still, it was a proper theatre and to Molly who had never been inside one before, it couldn't get any better than this.

The Professor had purchased a program and was casually perusing it while Molly gazed incomprehensibly at the words.

'Wot does this say?' She pointed at the page.

'It lists the actors' names and the parts they play.'

She smiled excitedly. 'Where's Dougie then?'

The Professor scanned the page and found the butler at the second last entry on the list. 'There he is.'

Molly nodded approvingly. 'Well 'e ain't last on the list. Who is last then?'

He smiled before replying. 'A dog named Truffles.'

A gentleman in a dinner suit and powdered face walked into the foyer and clapped his hands to gain the attention of the crowd. 'Ladies and gentlemen, act one commences in five minutes. Would you please take your seats.'

The Professor took Molly by the arm and ushered her through the crowd and up to their box. An attendant checked their tickets before seating them and closed the door. Molly's eyes lit up as she watched the people below being seated, then her mouth dropped open at the modest chandelier hanging above them.

'Oh Professor this is so beautiful.'

The alien smiled at her in reserved judgement. He closed the program, studying the cover. *The Maiden's Dilemma* had been printed beneath the name of the theatre together with a pen-drawing of a blushing girl surrounded by a series of heavily lip-rouged young men.

The lights dimmed in the theatre and the audience chatter fell to a whisper. An elderly man with a waxed moustache and hair parted in the centre, rose out of the orchestra pit and bowed to the patrons. They clapped politely. As the velvet curtains opened to reveal a young woman pacing up and down in a drawing room set, the orchestra began to play. The actress fanned herself theatrically, until there was a knock at the scenery door which sent the backdrop gently swaying. The *maiden* cried aloud 'enter' and none other than Douglas himself appeared, looking as butler-like as he could manage, in an ill-fitting stiff dinner suit, powdered wig, and enough rouge on his cheeks and lips to outdo the powder and paint worn by the actress.

Molly elbowed the Professor lightly on the arm and gestured towards the stage. 'Dougie,' she whispered gleefully.

The Professor placed a finger to his lips and nodded.

Billy held a boiled fish head in his hand. It was plump and round and had a permanently stunned expression across its sticky head. Billy sniffed the head and sucked on it. It definitely tasted good, and it made him feel proud. He had bought that fish head all by himself from the fish monger, and with his own money too.

The prostitutes sauntering passed him, either ignored him or gave his matted nest of hair an affectionate tousle. He smiled at one, showing his dirty brown teeth.

'Allo.' He waved at the woman.

She turned around and strolled back over to him. 'Lo, Billy. Watcha doin' 'ere all by yerself?'

'I bought a fish 'ead,' he said proudly.

The tart nodded approvingly and giggled. 'Well ain't we Lord Muck then eh?' She gave him a wink then started to walk away, but the boy followed after her as anyone who gave Billy the time of day instantly became his best friend. The woman however, didn't want any kid with a limp and a crooked hand tagging along after her, so she turned around and patted him on the cheek. 'Why don't yer go back to the tavern. It's gettin' cold out now.'

Billy frowned and looked away. 'I wanna eat me fish outside. I can be out 'ere if I want! I'm all big now!'

She grinned cheekily. 'Don't tell me old Oliver's got yer an' your fish 'ead doin' business now too?'

He gave her a puzzled look, then smiled inanely not understanding what she meant.

'Well I can't stay talkin' to yer all night. I've gotta get at least another two in if I can.' She laughed heartily, realising her unintended pun. 'Double meaning in that eh Billy! I didn't mean two at once—I ain't that wide!'

He laughed at her joke though it was clear he didn't understand her *double entendre* and waved as she disappeared down the street. 'Bye bye Big Liz!'

'That's Long Liz, my love!' she called back. 'I likes 'em long and lean!'

He nodded and mouthed her name correctly then limped up the alley into the gloom and emptiness of Whitechapel. He looked around suddenly feeling unsure of himself, wishing that Big ... no, no ... *Long* Liz was with him. Or anyone. He didn't want to be alone anymore. It was too quiet. Still, he did have his boiled fish head, and oh, there was a carriage up ahead. A nice big black one with ... wait. A carriage? What was a toff's carriage doing here? Visiting the girls? He hobbled over and crouched behind a mound of rubbish, keeping his eye trained on the coach. The door to the tenement block across the street opened and out of the gloom appeared a man dressed in black. He closed the door and rested his weight against it, making Billy think the man must be tired or ill. Then the man seemingly regained strength and rushed over to the coach and propped his foot on the carriage step and Billy's blood froze because for a split second the man in black shimmered out of shape, before leaping into the carriage. The coachman whipped the horses which made them rear from the blow before racing away into the night.

Billy's mouth went dry and his fingers loosened on the fish head.

'Gotcha!' cried a street urchin and snatched the fish away before running down the street.

'Stop!' yelled Billy, stumbling after him, promptly forgetting about the coach. He finally caught up with the boy only to find a group of children who laughed and jeered at him.

Billy growled, 'guv it back!'

The ragged urchin held the fish head up and waved it around. 'Make me.'

The coachman assisted Molly to alight then the Professor paid the fare and the man went on his way. The girl twirled around, her face glowing.

'I loved the play! I thought Cynthia was beautiful and I am so glad she got it off with Edgar and not that idiot, Charles, or the other one, yer know, Rupert.'

The Professor smiled indulgently. 'Agreed but I think the correct way of putting it is that Cynthia ended up *marrying* Edgar.'

Molly grinned. 'Oh yeah that's wot I meant.' She took his arm, and they walked up the street heading for her home. 'Yer will stay tonight, won't yer?'

The Professor avoided walking in a muddy puddle. 'If it pleases you.'

'It does.' She hesitated before continuing, 'Professor this was the best time I've ever 'ad.' She reached up and gave him a kiss on the cheek. He withdrew embarrassed.

'Did I do somethin' wrong?'

The Professor shook his head. 'No. I'm just not used to young ladies kissing the cheek, that's all!'

Molly smiled sensing that he was joking with her. But she also had the strange feeling that there was a deeper reason why he didn't want her to get any closer to him. She wondered what that could be but never got the chance to ask as a loud shrieking sound shattered the calm followed by cruel laughter. Without a moment's hesitation, the Professor bolted down the street towards the noise, pulling Molly along with him and found a gang of street urchins who were tossing a fish head to one another while Billy tried in vain to snatch it back.

'Come and get it!' shrieked a young girl, her dirty face twisted into a sneer. She lifted her torn dress above her knees and dangled the fish between her legs. When Billy hobbled over, she tossed it to a small boy who reached out but dropped it. The others dived for it, but the Professor barged in between them and picked the fish up between his thumb and forefinger. The group instantly froze, looking nervously at the Professor and then at Molly while Billy howled in frustration.

'What is going on here?'

The children glanced at one another before pushing the youngest to be the spokesman. They shoved him forward and he gaped at the man towering over him.

'Nuffink Guv'ner.'

'Oh? Then what were you doing with this?' He held the fish head up and gave it a distasteful look. 'Well? Isn't anyone going to answer me?'

Billy limped over, his eyes streaming with tears. 'It's mine. They took it from me.'

The alien looked at the boy with pity, then returned the fish head to him. He then pointed his cane accusingly, glaring at the urchins. 'If I ever see any of you doing this sort of thing again, you will all be arrested.'

The children looked dubiously at the stranger, then the boy who had stolen the fish in the first place stepped boldly over and stuck out his chin. 'Yer ain't got nuffink on us!'

The Professor glared at the boy then tapped his cane on the ground. The tip of the cane flipped open on a hinge and the boy's expression turned from curiosity to fear as a burst of fire sprung from the opening, landing at the child's feet. The boy jumped back in terror as the flames licked at his bare legs. Molly looked aghast and jumped out of the way then the boy bolted out of sight, followed by the rest of the terrified group. The Professor gave a self-satisfied nod then ran the tip of the cane over the flame extinguishing it.

Molly gulped. 'Wo ... wot is that thing?'

The Professor could have told her it was a *survival stick* disguised as a cane; very useful when finding yourself at the mercy of the elements with no heat to keep you warm, instead opting for a more palatable lie. 'It's a top-secret piece of equipment from Scotland Yard. You're not to say anything about it to anyone, understand?'

She nodded then turned to Billy who had curled himself up into a tight ball on the ground, whimpering pitifully.

'Billy, wot were yer doin' out 'ere by yerself?'

The Professor bent down to the boy, glancing at Molly. 'He's the young lad from The Ten Bells, isn't he?'

'Yeah, 'e 'elps Backer out with the cleanin' an' all.'

The Professor raised an eyebrow, wondering how such a child could become entangled with the likes of Backer or worse still, Oliver. He looked down at the boy and gave him an encouraging smile then gently helped him to his feet. 'There now Billy, everything's going to be all right.'

The boy gave him an uncertain look. 'Yer do magic like the other man.'

'What do you mean?'

'The other man. The man in black!'

Molly shrugged her shoulders giving him an incredulous look. 'Go back to Oliver before 'e skins yer alive. Go on now.'

Billy pouted at her then ran off.

'Magic?' Thought the Professor aloud. 'Very curious ... '

It had been a dull night for Hugh Barker. He had followed the Professor and his tart from the tavern to the hotel and then to the theatre. He then had to wait outside in the rain, dreaming longingly of his wife's pork pie going to waste whilst imagining Greensworth settling in to enjoy a nice roast with his family in front of a roaring fire. It also hadn't helped matters that Professor whats-his-name, had not attempted any solo investigation of the Ripper murders. What was he to tell the superintendent? *Ah,*

well he had a nice meal then went to the theatre then returned the girl home. At least he could have booked a room in the hotel for a rendezvous with the whore but he didn't even do that. Why? Greensworth would not be pleased.

As Barker trudged up the street, he spotted a bulky, muscular sailor sitting up against a brick wall repeatedly punching his fist into his other hand. The man's face was covered with bruises and dried blood, and his nose was too flat for his face with an odd lump bulging at the bridge. This man however, was of interest to the superintendent's greater plan … perhaps it wouldn't be a wasted evening after all.

'Good evening to you Sir,' he ventured.

The sailor gave him a sour look. 'I ain't disturbin' the peace. There's nothin' wrong with sittin' 'ere.'

'Of course not.' The policeman bobbed down on his haunches. 'Now let me see, you do look so familiar. May I enquire as to your name, Sir?'

'Me mates call me Skinner,' the other replied suspiciously. 'Why d'yer wanna know, Copper?'

'Mr Skinner! Of course, I thought I recognised you. It's been a while since you've graced us with your presence down the lockup.' He gave the sailor a calculating smile. 'My name's Hugh Barker. And I have a proposition for you.'

The other looked at him distrustfully. 'Oh yeah?'

'Well Skinner,' continued the officer, his tone laced with sarcasm, 'I think we'll drop the *Mr*, don't you? Now I'm sure you've heard about a nasty piece of work called Jack the Ripper.'

The sailor gave him a venomous look. 'I ain't 'im.'

Barker shook his head pleasantly. 'No, no, perish the thought. But you see, Scotland Yard has entered into the affair and my superintendent and I agree that the whole business should be down to us to sort. I mean, it is our area and there are three detectives from the Yard that really have nothing to do with the East End.'

'So what?'

'Well Skinner, the superintendent and I know how you operate. You know a lot of people. A lot of tough ones, if I may say so. I think it would be useful if you were to rustle up some of them to help us hunt down the Ripper before Scotland Yard does.'

Sensing a negotiation at hand, the sailor gave the policeman a calculating look. 'And why should I 'elp you?'

'Because even if the local police catch him, the Yard will take all the credit.'

The sailor's face twisted into a grin. 'Why should I care about that?'

Barker reached into his pocket and dropped a handful of coins into the man's lap. 'Does this change your mind?'

Molly leaned against the doorway of her hovel, lazily regarding the Professor. 'Yer comin' in?'

'I will if you can you tell me something about Billy?'

She shrugged, opened the door and walked inside. The Professor followed her, bending his head to accommodate the low doorway.

'I dunno a lot.' She closed the door then crossed the room to her bed and flopped down on it. 'I ain't been workin' for Oliver that long but one thing I do know is that Billy works for 'im and 'as for a long time.'

The Professor placed his cane on the table then changing his mind, picked it up and turned towards the door. Molly leaped up after him. 'Yer jus' came in. Where yer goin' now?'

'I have some pressing things I need to do.'

'Well let me come with yer.'

'Alone Molly,' he replied firmly.

'But I don' want to be left 'ere all by meself.'

He gave her an encouraging smile. 'You'll be all right, just lock the door and don't open it to anyone except me.'

She pulled a pouting expression before relenting. 'Awl right. But if I'm gone by the time yer get back, yer will come by the tavern, won't yer?'

He smiled at her. 'I promise.'

She closed the door after him then slid an old rickety chair up against it and sat on her bed, waiting for morning.

▲

CHAPTER 6

Dawn was creeping over the horizon and Spitalfields market was slowly showing signs of life ready for the morning's trade. The Professor ignored this activity, steering his way through the steadily building throng, his aim to return to the ship and change out of his evening attire before meeting the detectives at the Police House. Almost within sight of the blind alley, the Professor turned a sharp corner and promptly collided with a policeman, accidentally knocking him to the ground. The alien reached out to assist the young man, only to recognise the constable's face.

'Briggs? I do apologise, are you all right?'

The constable ignored the question but took the Professor's proffered hand. 'Oh Professor Delbrotman, thank God! I was coming to look for you.'

'What is it?'

'There's been another murder, Sir.'

'Where?'

Briggs signalled the alien to follow. 'Follow me, I'll show you.'

The Professor hurried after the constable winding his way through street after street until it was almost impossible to tell how far he had come. The houses and buildings all looked so similar; stooped over on an angle like menacing giants in the half-light of dawn. A large factory with its chimney charred black from smoke loomed into view and Briggs ushered the alien through its iron gates. He pointed out the gruesome discovery and the Professor bent down examining the remains of a woman; her dress was torn and there were two deep gashes across her chest.

'It must be the Ripper again Sir,' stated Briggs. 'She's not been done like the others though.'

'No but it was enough to rob her of her life, whoever she was.' The Professor rose then looked around checking to see if there were any passersby; so far no one paid them any attention. 'Can you please go and fetch Brett and Wainwright and tell them to arrange for a carriage to take the body away. I will wait here until they arrive.'

The constable nodded then turning away from the poor woman's remains, bolted through the gates and down the street.

The Professor paced up and down, impatient for the arrival of the detectives. It concerned him that if matters took too long then the workers would arrive at the factory gates only to be met with the hideous discovery—then panic would ensue. Fortunately, within half an hour a police carriage rolled down the street coming to a stop at the gates. The inspectors leapt out as two other officers loaded the body into the back of the coach, the Professor assisting.

'We'll follow in a cab to the hospital,' said Brett directly. 'Doctor Waitley will proceed from there.'

Once the carriage departed, the detectives hailed a cab just as the factory workers began trudging through the gates. The alien breathed a sigh of relief that none of the workers were aware of the grisly discovery, then climbed into the awaiting cab and shut the door. As the cab set off, the three men sat in silence, each lost in thought. Wainwright observed the alien's preoccupied expression and wondered if they, or anyone for that matter, were capable of catching the murderer before he did more harm. The Professor noticed the detective's contemplative look and raised his eyebrows, almost as if he could read the other man's mind.

'He's not giving up, but neither will we,' replied the alien simply.

Wainwright looked mildly surprised but nodded in agreement; the Professor was right. The hunt had to continue until the criminal was swinging from the end of a rope.

The carriage finally came to a halt at the hospital steps, then the Professor and the detectives alighted after paying the cabbie, who had been instructed to drive around the back of the building, where the woman's body was received by two attendants. The three men followed on foot to be greeted by Doctor Waitley who ushered them inside and into the autopsy room. An attendant pulled back two bloodied sheets revealing another two mutilated prostitutes.

'I'm afraid gentlemen, that your newest discovery was not the only victim from last night,' the Doctor stated gravely.

Wainwright swallowed in disgust at the sight of the butchered bodies, particularly the one who had had her ears severed. He pointed towards the dead woman's head. 'When was this one found?'

'About five this morning so I've been told,' replied the Doctor stepping aside to allow another stretcher to be brought in—that of the newly slashed woman.

'He was busy last night then, wasn't he?' Brett rubbed the bridge of his nose wearily. 'So busy that he must have run out of time to finish the third.'

'And I believe the *third* was Elizabeth Stride.' Wainwright turned to his colleague. 'Remember when we tried interviewing the locals when we were first assigned here? She was one of many who was none too willing to talk,' the detective shook his head at the waste of a life. 'They used to call her *Long Liz*.'

'Have you made a positive identification of the others?' the Professor asked, circling each table slowly.

'Only Catherine Eddowes so far,' replied Waitley. 'The one with the severed ears.'

The Professor examined the cadaver's head and the bloodied holes of what was left of the ears; a shadow passed over his face. 'Do you recall the letter from the Ripper stating that he would send the ears of one of his victims to the police?'

The detectives shared a look of disgust then headed straight for the door. 'We'll head back to the Police House,' said Brett. 'Professor you stay here with Doctor Waitley while he does the autopsy.'

The door closed with a bang that echoed eerily. Waitley took a fresh sheet of paper from a new file and began writing down details as the Professor pondered his next move.

For once Greensworth had no snide remarks to make. Not even a hint of derision crept into his voice when he saw Brett and Wainwright return to the Police House. His greeting was grave and brief. Fearing the worst, Wainwright gave the superintendent a questioning look before speaking. 'Have there been any unwanted deliveries?'

Greensworth pointed to a small wooden box sitting on his desk.

Brett glanced at his partner then hesitantly reached out a hand and lifted the lid. Beneath was a piece of paper with the wording *my compliments to you gentlemen, Yours truly, Jack.* It had been written in blood. He lifted the paper to reveal two neatly severed ears.

'When did this arrive?' Asked Wainwright.

'My assistant found it on the door step this morning.'

The inspector turned to Hugh Barker. 'Was there anyone suspicious looking hanging around who may have delivered it?'

Barker gave him a patronising sneer. '*Suspicious looking*? Is there anyone from around here who is *not* suspicious looking?'

Wainwright glared, even in desperate circumstances, Barker could never manage to be anything other than condescending. 'I meant—did you see who left the box?'

The policeman gave the detective a hard look. 'No.'

'I see.' He turned to the superintendent. 'This piece of evidence needs to be taken to Waitley immediately, which I will do so myself now.' Wainwright closed the box with a snap. 'Brett, start asking around if anyone was seen dropping off this parcel. Perhaps offering them a few coins might loosen a few tongues.'

Brett nodded. 'Good idea.'

Wainwright opened the door addressing the superintendent. 'I'll let you know of any further developments when they arise.'

Greensworth nodded and waited until the detectives had left before signalling his assistant to follow him into the inner office.

'I want you to go and find Skinner to see what he's up to. I don't want you coming and telling me that he's run off with all that money for nothing.'

Barker shook his head. 'He won't have, I promised him more where that came from when the job's done. Wonder if he'll be in that tavern now? Probably sleeping it off somewhere in the arms of some whore.'

'I don't care!' Greensworth thumped the desk in frustration. 'Find him! And keep your eyes on Forbes-Montague! That swine will hang for it yet! Mark my words.'

'It certainly can't just be coincidence,' Barker agreed smugly. 'I'll see what I can do.'

'Discreetly,' the other man warned. 'And when that *Professor* and Wainwright have finished with Waitley, I am going to put my second plan to the test.'

Hugh Barker grinned, he could hardly wait.

Skinner had been dutifully wandering the streets for hours, looking for the right sort of people to join a lynching mob as per strict instructions received from PC Hugh Barker. He thought it rather amusing that the police had given him free reign to do so—that is—break the law, but the Peelers had never been known to play it straight unless it suited them, and it apparently suited them now to catch a murderer using highly unorthodox methods.

Skinner had managed to talk to a few interested parties along the way but it was hard going as even the most crooked were highly suspicious of a Peeler-sanctioned execution. Even with the offer of payment, Skinner received so many spits in the eye and threats to do interesting things with his mother that he eventually concluded that if the job was to be done properly, then you had to go to the one person who had his finger on the pulse of the East End. The one person who could get anyone to do anything (for a fee of course) was to be found in, or rather under Chin-Lee's Laundry.

Skinner turned down The East India Dock Road and entered the laundry to find three ancient Chinese gentlemen conversing near the front counter. He walked past, ignoring their chatter and pushed open a partition to reveal more Chinese, their long hair tied neatly in plaits and their loose-fitting trousers and shirts, damp from the steamy air. They were loading dirty washing into huge tubs of hot, soapy water and the vapour rising from the tubs turned the air acrid. Skinner sniffed in derision; he hated wash houses and particularly the people who ran them.

One of the old men shuffled up to him and grinned ingratiatingly. 'You got washing?'

Skinner looked at him with contempt. 'It's down below I want.'

The little man returned to his friends and chattered something quickly in Chinese before returning to the sailor.

'You got money?'

Skinner fished out a coin and dangled it in front of the man. A wrinkled hand reached out for it, but Skinner snatched it away. 'Uh, uh.' He shook his head. 'I know 'ow yer Chinamen operate. Take me down first then yer can 'ave yer reward.'

The man twittered an obscenity then giving Skinner a toothless grin, beckoned him to follow. They walked through the laundry, then a lad moved a basket of clothes away to reveal a trap door in the floor. The boy lifted it open, and Skinner handed the coin to the man before climbing down a ladder.

His senses were instantly assailed with the strong smell of opium and when the child had closed the trap door it took him a few minutes for his eyes to adjust to the hazy semi-darkness.

Jumping from the second last rung, he peered at several figures propped up against the mildewed walls, smoking opium pipes. A single lantern flickered in the corner.

'I thought this stuff was supposed to make yer feel better.'

A man, young in years but with a wasted, yellow face looked up and squinted at the intruder. His parched, dry skin stretched into a smile, and he coughed. 'I know that voice.'

'So yer should. I thought I'd find yer down 'ere, yer tosser.'

His friend chuckled then slowly stood up, the effort exhausting him. It was clear he was in a great deal of pain. He hobbled over to where the sailor stood. 'Well, well, well, Skinner. It's been a long time.'

Skinner snorted. 'Yeah well I work for a livin', don't I? I don't go round beggin' then snuffin' it up.'

The other man's eyes welled with tears of self-pity. 'Yer know I can't afford a doctor. This stuff helps.'

Skinner shrugged and helped the addicted cripple to return to his spot on the floor. He sat down next to him who hungrily sucked on the pipe, then relaxed.

'Danny I might as well tell yer this ain't a social call. I gotta proposition.'

The others in the room registered vague interest.

Danny nodded. 'I'm listenin'.'

'This place gets quite a lot of activity in the night and that's when I want yer to start exercisin' yer influence.'

Danny gave him a puzzled look. 'I don't sell the stuff anymore, I just smoke it.'

'I know that, that's not wot I meant.' He leaned closer to the addict and lowered his voice to a whisper. 'Yer hear about the Kipper, don't yer?'

Danny frowned. 'I don't wanna know.'

'I'll make it worth yer while, so shut up an' listen. It's high time that bastard's put out of the way an' since the Peelers can't get out of their own stinkin' road, an' do something about it, I've been told it's up to us.'

Danny gave him a ludicrous stare. 'Are yer the Angel bleedin' Gabriel? Wot do yer care if a bunch of old tarts get it? They ain't worth nothin'.'

'Danny,' warned Skinner trying to keep his temper in check. ''E ain't just some loser wot's knockin 'em off. Gord knows there's enough of those about. It's 'is sick methods wot's got this place shaken up. And it ain't just that neither.'

Danny inhaled the last of his opium and gave the sailor a vague look.

'Im wot's doin' it ain't one of us. 'E's a toff, or at the very least some cracked up doctor, and he don't belong 'ere.'

Danny grinned. 'I'd like to meet him. Maybe he can fix me lungs or me legs.'

Skinner punched the wall in frustration triggering the other figures in the gloom to moan and shift uneasily. 'Jesus Danny I oughta knock some sense into ya.'

The addict groaned painfully and licked his lips in the hope of tasting the last drop of the narcotic. 'Awl right Skinner, keep yer shirt on. There's plenty that come down 'ere, and they in turn can spread the word.'

'Tell 'em that we're organising a lynching party. That should encourage their taste for blood.'

Danny smiled knowingly. 'And yours too no doubt.' He looked at the other addicts in the den and gave Skinner an agitated glance. The sailor reached into his pocket and gave the man three gold coins. 'Tell the lot of 'em to meet me at The 'Orse's Saddle the next two nights.'

'Will do.'

Skinner jumped up quickly, leaving Danny dismayed at the display of agility. 'Make sure yer do it Danny before yer finish yerself off.'

Danny smiled sadly. 'I can 'ardly wait.'

Diary Extract 1.3

Just a quick note whilst Doctor Waitley finishes the autopsy reports. There have been more murders committed and I am extremely angry. I'm angry with myself and I'm disgusted with that Jack the Ripper creature—a prime example of human abomination. But I have no leads other than the fact that he possesses medical knowledge and that he's left-handed. Well that certainly narrows the field, doesn't it? How many left-handed surgeons are there in London? We can't convict them all in the blind hope that one of them could be the Ripper. Why do I keep drawing a blank? What is this barrier I sense?

Again and again I keep staring at the remains of Catherine Eddowes. Her body is the most mutilated. She barely looks like a person anymore; as if both her essence and physical being have been stolen, doomed never to be whole. Tragic and yet oddly interesting. Have I just inadvertently stumbled onto something here? Could there be a reason that not only renders these women dead but leaves them without an identity? Are they no longer entitled to be called a human being?

Perhaps I am onto something here.
Diary Extract End - 1.3

Waitley dropped the pile of used instruments into a bucket then drew the sheets over the two bodies.

'I stated on the report just as you suggested that the Ripper was likely disturbed by a passer-by when he murdered Elizabeth Stride.'

'Well it would explain his unfinished ... task,' replied the Professor, pocketing his diary. 'Tell me, do you know much about Doctor Grantley?'

Waitley looked mildly surprised at the sudden question. 'He's a fine surgeon. He tends to Her Majesty ...'

'Yes, yes I know that but what do you know of him?'

Waitley considered the question and handed the bucket to an attendant who took it away. 'To speak truth Professor, very little. I know Scotland Yard desired his medical opinion on the matter of the Ripper murders, because he is one of the most respected and knowledgeable surgeons this country has today.'

The Professor slid his hands into his pockets, regarding the doctor. 'I didn't ask you whether he was a good doctor, I want to know what sort of man he is.'

Waitley felt nervous under the Professor's intense scrutiny and stepped back as two attendants took away the cadavers on stretchers. He cleared his throat. 'Well Professor, I do understand that he is close to retirement age.'

The alien nodded encouragingly. 'Go on.'

'I've read in the papers that his tireless workload is beginning to take its toll. One cannot work like a thirty-year-old when one is nearing sixty.'

'I agree.' The alien looked up searching for inspiration before continuing. 'Tell me, has his *tiredness* appeared suddenly?'

Waitley frowned. 'Well, I couldn't say for sure as I do not know the man personally but from what the papers say his age has appeared to have caught up with him recently. It is understandable, I certainly feel it myself these past few weeks.'

'I see. Thank you so much, you've been a great help. Good day Doctor.' The alien vanished through the door, his footsteps receding in the distance. Waitley shook his head, puzzled. 'Odd chap.'

Within seconds of the Professor leaving, Greensworth arrived at the hospital calling out for the doctor. He entered the autopsy room to find him standing alone.

The surgeon greeted the superintendent. 'Just in time. I've completed the reports and can confirm that the severed ears do belong to one of the victims as shown here.'

'Very good,' replied Greensworth, taking the report and scanning it. 'I just saw Delbrotman in the hall, he seemed in a great hurry. Do you know if he'll be returning any time soon?'

Waitley shrugged. 'I don't know. I don't think so. I think he may be off to see Doctor Grantley.'

Greensworth snorted in amusement. 'Good. Now if you have an hour to spare I should like your assistance.'

'Certainly. How may I be of help?'

Greensworth gave the surgeon a look of triumph. 'Go and get a clean scalpel and I'll tell you.'

The Professor returned to his ship and changed out of his evening attire, replacing it with his original grey suit. Before leaving, he checked the controls for any tracking echoes that might have arisen during the last few hours. Satisfied that his whereabouts remained obscured, he exited the ship and hailed a passing cab. After a short trip, he arrived at Doctor Grantley's surgery and rang the doorbell. The housekeeper answered and informed him that the doctor was consulting at Buckingham Palace due to His Royal Highness the Duke of Clarence's persistent earache.

'Will he be back soon?' the Professor asked, peering over the housekeeper's shoulder into the hallway.

'Not until late this afternoon Sir.'

'Do you happen to know what time?'

She shook her head. 'I'm sorry Sir, all I know is that he won't be in for lunch.' She sighed gratefully then added, 'which will allow me to get some cleaning done for a change.'

'Ah yes,' replied the Professor thoughtfully. 'The good doctor's healthy appetite.'

Mrs Craven nodded in agreement. 'Do you want me to inform Doctor Grantley that you came to see him today?'

'Please,' replied the alien. 'You may also tell him that I'd appreciate another audience with him. That is of course, when he has a few minutes to spare.'

The housekeeper nodded and the Professor walked away, then on an impulse, he turned around just as the door was about to close.

'Oh Mrs Craven.'

'Yes Sir?'

'Does Doctor Grantley use a private carriage when he attends Buckingham Palace?'

'Yes indeed Sir. Her Majesty generously bestowed upon him one of her own personal coaches.'

'Thank you, Mrs Craven.' The Professor walked away, then paused at the corner of the street to buy a newspaper from a young boy shouting about the latest victims of Jack the Ripper. The local gentry were completely ignoring the boy's alarming cries, effectively pretending the problem did not exist. The Professor noted their indifference while skimming through the paper. 'Tell me, lad, do you sell your papers here every day?'

'Yus Guv'ner.'

'What time?'

'Mornin' an' night.'

The Professor tucked the paper under his arm. 'So you would see people coming and going all the time.'

The boy nodded.

'Do you know a Doctor Grantley?'

'Yeah, 'e sometimes buys the paper from me.'

'Really? Trade seems to be a bit slow today though, doesn't it?'

The boy shrugged giving the Professor a suspicious look. 'S'pose.' He wasn't too sure about this gent and if he kept hanging around asking questions then the papers wouldn't be sold, and he'd be the one getting into trouble for it. 'Do yer want any more papers cos if yer don't I got work to do.'

'No but I was wondering if you could help me?'

The word *help* echoed in the boy's mind and he quickly turned it to his advantage. 'It'll cost yer!'

The alien casually tossed the boy some coins, which were quickly stashed away.

'Now I want you to think very, very carefully about this. Have you ever seen anything oddly suspicious or out of the ordinary when you've come to sell your papers here? Perhaps at night, when there are not too many people about.'

The boy frowned in concentration then looked nervously at the alien. 'Well there is summink ...'

The Professor bent down to the boy. 'Go on.'

'Yer ain't gonna believe me Guv.'

The alien dropped his voice to a whisper, 'if it's the truth then I will.'

The lad hesitated. 'Well, a few weeks ago I saw this thing for the first time. It was down the street a bit. I'd just finished up when I saw this ... thing.'

'What?'

He gave the Professor an anxious look and swallowed hard. 'I ain't a kid anymore. I'm nearly thirteen. I don't scare easily, an' I don't believe in ghosts.' He looked away. 'Well I never used ta'.'

The Professor was silent allowing the boy to continue.

'See I thought I saw this geezer who was dressed up in dark clothes though it was a bit 'ard to tell 'cos it was nearly night, yer know, anyway I was walkin' up the street an' I 'eard a door open and for some reason, I don't know, I 'id behind the gate of a 'ouse.

I then took a butchers over the top and wot I saw made me think I saw a ghost.' He waited for the Professor to scoff but instead the alien gazed at him intently, willing him to proceed.

'Can you describe the ghost?'

'Like I said,' continued the boy,' 'e 'ad dark clothes on then all of a sudden 'e kind of went out of shape. Sort of went wobbly and shiny.' He smiled weakly. 'Sounds daft, don't it?'

The Professor gave him a thoughtful look. 'Not necessarily. Have you seen him since?'

'No.'

'Do you remember the house where you saw it?'

'I weren't lookin' that 'ard at the time if yer know wot I mean.'

'Thank you, your help has been most valuable.' The Professor reached into his pocket and handed the boy another coin.

'If there's anythin' else yer wanna know Guv, y'know where yer can find me!'

The Professor thanked the lad then hailed a hansom cab. 'Buckingham Palace, if you please,' he told the driver.

▲

CHAPTER 7

Waitley leaned over the body of Catherine Eddowes studying the dead woman's face. Greensworth in turn, leaned over to see what the doctor was doing, eager to learn if his experiment was possible.

'There's no apparent damage to her eye cavities so far as I can see,' concluded Waitley. 'However, I can't be sure unless I make an internal examination.'

'Then do so,' replied Greensworth.

Waitley shook his head. 'I don't think anything more of the cadaver should be disturbed.'

The superintendent sighed. 'Then we're back to where we started. There's no way of knowing for sure if her eyes are intact, therefore no absolute certainty if the print remains.'

Waitley gave him a doubtful look. 'That is if your theory is correct.'

Greensworth bristled in annoyance but made no reply. This so-called specialist obviously didn't know as much as he seemed to think he did. 'Just open her eye lids again and keep them open until I am done, *Doctor Waitley.*'

The surgeon pointedly ignored the superintendent's sharp tone but did as he was instructed. Greensworth adjusted the tripod, ducked under the black cloth and focussed the camera lens on the dead woman's eyes.

'The identity of Jack the Ripper is ...' He left the remainder of the sentence unspoken as a blinding flash lit up the mortuary room, and the smell of burnt powder wafted into the air.

'Got it!' he exclaimed. Waitley nodded politely though not at all confident despite Greensworth's conviction.

The superintendent retrieved the slate and picked up his equipment. 'Once the photograph has been developed, I'm sure you will be interested to know the identity of the blackguard.'

'Indeed,' replied the doctor politely, ushering him out. Once Greensworth had left, Waitley pulled the sheet over the corpse and dimmed the light. For the sake of those poor women and the hideous secret that they kept, he hoped, deep down, that it might just work.

The Professor alighted from the cab as it reached Buckingham Palace and made his way along the perimeter until he found a closed gate flanked by two royal guards. A black coach adorned with the royal standard stood nearby. When the Professor attempted to approach it, he was met with stern looks from the guards and a warning glance from a third individual standing by the coach. The guards, evidently used to the man, ignored him but continued to glare at the Professor. The Professor noted the man's dishevelled appearance: he was without a jacket, wore a food-stained vest over a tattered, dirty shirt, and his trousers were frayed at the edges. His thick sideburns and thinning hair looked greasy and unkempt. He was not the sort of fellow the Professor, or anyone else, would expect to see guarding a carriage belonging to the Queen of England.

The man scowled at the Professor while nervously fingering a small scrap of paper in his dirty hands. When the Professor tried to speak, the man backed away gradually and then, with an abrupt burst of energy, ran off down the street. The Professor dashed after him, unwilling to let the stranger out of his sight, calling out as he chased him.

The man glanced back every so often to check on his pursuer who was slowly gaining on him. Another glance almost cost him the race however, when he collided with a middle-aged gentleman strolling by.

'If you please Sir!' the man bellowed at being knocked over. The scrap of paper that the stranger had been clutching dropped and when he frantically reached for it, the note tore in two. The stranger swore and leapt up, barrelling through the crowded street up ahead.

The Professor came to a halt to help the gentleman; unfortunately, this act of kindness allowed the stranger to disappear into the throng. 'Are you all right?'

The gentleman grunted in assent, grateful for the assistance. 'Well I might not be as young as I used to be but I am born of strong stock. Comes from my youth being spent on the Punjab, what?'

Amused, the Professor allowed himself a small smile. 'Glad to hear it.'

'I say did that man pick your pocket?'

'No.'

'Then why may I ask were you chasing after him?'

The Professor stared into the crowd, as if willing the stranger to reappear. 'That's a rather difficult question to answer.'

'Look there's no need to feel any pity for these lawbreakers who attempt to steal from good honest men like yourself,' the man stated resolutely, observing the Professor's uneasy manner and assuming it to be guilt over class privilege. 'Why, those sorts are always complaining that they're given no chance in life, that it's merely because of class distinction that sets them on a path of crime but when good men like you and I offer assistance, they throw it right back in our faces! Steal the food from a baby if given half the chance!'

The Professor nodded politely then something caught his attention and he looked down at the ground.

'I'm a magistrate y'see,' continued the gentleman, smoothing his waxed moustache. 'So I know all about it. Don't you concern yourself about his welfare because prison is the only thing that ruffians like that deserve!'

The magistrate stopped talking when he realised the Professor was no longer listening to his diatribe and he too looked down, wondering what the fellow was looking at. 'Something the matter?'

'Your foot,' replied the Professor quietly. 'Would you please lift your left foot.'

Curious, the man did as he was asked and the alien bent down and picked up a torn piece of paper.

'Goodness me, what's that?'

The Professor studied it. It was a fragment of a message written neatly in black ink. The magistrate pulled out his monocle and read the paper aloud.

'"tonight and the morrow at Whistler's Inn. Leave coach, same time. J."' He looked at the alien. 'I wonder what the top half said.'

The Professor tapped the paper thoughtfully then pocketed it.

'Should we contact the authorities? Or perhaps I can be of service?'

'Your name Sir?' the Professor asked, ignoring his questions.

'Sir Archibald Darnley,' was the proud reply.

The Professor looked at Sir Archibald's hopeful expression then shook his head. 'There is nothing more you can do but I must say your help has been invaluable.'

'It has?'

'It has indeed. Good day Sir Archibald!' The Professor shook his hand then rushed off, leaving the magistrate to ponder just what he'd done to be so helpful. 'Damn shame I couldn't do more,' he murmured to himself. 'Whatever he's up to seems a lot more interesting than anything I've done in a long time.' He sighed wistfully then climbed the steps of The Vanderbury Gentlemen's Club and disappeared inside.

Simmering with frustration, Brett trudged up the path, back towards the Police House, after having returned home for a bath and a change of clothes. His enquiries had gotten him nowhere since the locals were too frightened, too drunk, or too indignant to answer any of his questions. Asking any of them for information was akin to getting blood out of a stone.

'Did you see anyone deliver a box to the Police House madam?'

'I ain't seen nuffin and I know nuffin.'

'A small box Sir ...'

'Was it small?'

'Yes, that's what I just said.' Brett bent down to an old man who sat wedged between an empty fire drum and a one-eyed pit bull terrier. The dog growled a warning at the detective not to come too close.

'Well I might've seen sumfin', then again I might not've.'

Brett reached into his pocket and took out a chunk of bread. 'You're hungry, old man. Try eating something then perhaps you'll remember more.'

The old man stared at the bread his eyes widening in surprise. His surprise quickly turned into a fit of coughing, which sent the pit bull terrier into a barking frenzy. Brett dropped the bread and took a step back, keeping his gaze locked on the growling dog. Suddenly with no further warning the dog leaped at the inspector, who bolted down the street to get away. Fortunately, a hind paw limp hampered the animal and after a few short minutes, it gave up, hobbling back to its master.

Brett did not look over his shoulder until he could run no further. He collapsed in the doorway of a house to catch his breath only to receive the contents of a chamber pot dumped on his head from the window above.

He bellowed in outrage and glared up at the window. 'You there! I'll arrest you for this!'

A fat red-faced woman thumbed her nose at him and closed the window with a bang. Brett thumped on the door. 'Open up I say in the name of the law!'

A painfully thin child opened the door and wiped her runny nose with the back of her sleeve. She gave the inspector a curious look and pointed to his head. 'You've got *ukkel* on ya.'

'What!' he roared, infuriated. 'Let me through, I'm charging whoever's responsible for this!'

The fat woman waddled over and screamed, dragging the child back inside, then a stubbly faced man in a pair of dirty long johns pushed both of them aside and pointed a rusty sword at the inspector's nose.

'Get out or ya dead!' his voice snarled.

'Look at what your wife did to me!'

The man edged forward, and Brett stepped back. 'She ain't me wife but if yer don't want yer 'ead bouncin' to the ground then get outta me 'ouse.'

Brett glanced at the locals gathering, waiting for the fight to begin. He backed away, leaving the group disappointed.

'An' stay out!' the man shouted after him.

INTERLUDE

Aurelia sorted her way through several credits until finding the right amount. The molecular energy bars had been costing her a small fortune, and now, yet again, they had risen in price. She handed the store vender a fifty-credit disc and received a mere five bars in change. She sighed deeply, hoping that the doctor would soon be able to prescribe a less potent and certainly less expensive alternative for her son's medical condition.

She thanked the spiny canine vendor, and he returned the pleasantry, hoping her boy's health would improve. Aurelia smiled then walked out of the shop and into the bright morning sunshine. The sky was gold and ivory, with bold strokes of pink and magenta. It was a beautiful day, such as she hadn't noticed in a long time. Of course, there was never enough time to enjoy such a vision as her priority was to be home looking after her treasured only child. Since losing her husband, the boy was all she had, and she rarely chose to spend time anywhere else.

She hurried through the bustling city, populated with every kind of life form that had ever been encountered, and some yet to be encountered. This was quite the norm since few of the population chose to exist in their natural state; it was preferable and sensible to transform into something that would assist them in carrying out their daily activities, whatever they may be.

A Law-Enforcer standing eleven feet tall, with muscles bulging through his armoured body suit politely greeted the woman as she passed him.

'Good morning, Ma'am. And how has your son been keeping lately?'

She stopped to catch her breath before replying. 'I think a little improved. He's certainly developing his father's bold attitude.'

The Law-Enforcer laughed. 'Indeed? Well if he's anything like his father was, then you should be very proud.'

Aurelia thanked the enforcer then left him to break up an argument between a large bird and something that resembled a lizard covered in fur.

After passing through the two crystal spires that marked the entrance to the city, she hurried on, finally reaching her home at the foot of a mountain range. The shutters to her house had been sealed across the frosted plasty-glass windows, and a force field lock had been coded across the front door for maximum security. With the recent crime levels on the rise, she had made certain that the entire house was something of a strong hold. She pushed her violet curls over her shoulder and quietly concentrated on the lock. When the mechanism registered the telepathic message, it scanned her organs for identification then deactivated, satisfied that the intruder's vital prints matched the owner of the house.

The door opened and a servo-bot trundled up to her, extending a wiry arm. 'Shall I take your burden?' Its voice was hollow and metallic.

The woman looked at the metal box on wheels and sighed at the double-edged words. 'Take the food and put it in the kitchen.' The bot took the parcel, reversed, then stopped when she questioned it. 'Is Kyeldsen awake yet?'

'Yes,' the machine replied. 'He wanted to know your location.'

The woman nodded then the metal box trundled out of sight, leaving her alone in the shadows. 'Shutters open!' She commanded. The shutters obeyed and slid back from the windows, allowing bars of sunlight to flood the room. Closing the front door behind her, she walked through the bare hallway and onto the revolving ramp, stepping off at the second level. She could hear the constant rapping her son made against the containment cube. She entered his room and he let out a blood-curdling cry and launched himself at the walls of his prison.

'Mother! I demand to be released now!'

Aurelia glanced at the micro-controls on the side of the cube and sighed with relief that he hadn't yet found a way to switch them off.

'You know what Elder says. You must remain in a decontaminated area for a sixth of a cycle each day.' She smiled at him, her violet eyes pleading. 'It is for your own good.'

Kyeldsen shook convulsively and fell onto the floor of the glass cube in a tantrum. 'I cannot endure this torture. I am well Mother! I am well! Please let me out!' He gave his best, most earnest pleading look, and then scowled when he registered what life form she had transformed into. 'Why do you look like this?'

Aurelia walked over to the controls and his expression turned to hope. 'It is easier when I need to carry supplies. My time is cut in half when I possess two strong arms and two long legs.' She deactivated the cube and an opening appeared. He quickly scrambled out and breathed a sigh of relief.

'What are you supposed to be?'

She looked down at herself. 'A humanoid.'

He nodded, digesting the information then reached out for her to pick him up.

'Kyeldsen it's time for breakfast, then some remedial exercise and I want you to go down to the kitchen by yourself.'

He scowled once again, baring his teeth. 'I cannot.'

'Why?'

'I'm too tired.'

Aurelia placed her hands on her hips. 'Then back you go to your cube.'

This ghastly prospect was all the impetus the boy needed, and he trotted out of his room and onto the ramp, scurrying all the way down, ignoring the fact that it would have brought him to the bottom level. Aurelia joined him, highly amused by his sudden burst of energy. 'Servo!' she demanded. The bot trundled up to her and waited, giving some sort of impression of expectancy. 'Prepare breakfast for Kyeldsen and bring me an open packet of Mol-Ener Bars.'

The boy's face wrinkled in frustration. 'I don't want one. They taste funny.'

'Then I daresay you will find it *hilarious* to finish a whole one this time.'

Kyeldsen was unamused at his mother's quip. 'But they don't taste like real food and they smell like mine-waste.'

Aurelia placed a hand across her son's back and ushered him into the kitchen. She lifted him onto his favourite anti-gravity seat and watched him suspended in front of her. 'I know it doesn't taste the best but it is rich in molecular energy and can provide you with an enormous boost so that you can practice learning to transform.' She took a single bar and proffered it to her son. He reluctantly took it from her and nibbled on one corner.

Kyeldsen instructed his seat to shift him to the kitchen window and he gazed wistfully at the other children running up and down changing into all sorts of nonsensical life forms. His mother caught the boy's expression and gently stroked his forehead. 'You will be able to join in with them soon.'

'I don't want to be different anymore,' he replied gravely. 'I know I can be better than any of them.'

Aurelia kissed his cheek. 'In time we'll show the world what you can do.'

CHAPTER 8

Doctor Grantley was in no mood for Lady Edith as he knew it would take at least an hour of his time if not more, listening to more complaints about her aching hips, her palpating heart, her gammy knees or whatever ailed her *that* day. Surely the woman could see that if she lost thirty pounds and actually found herself something else to do other than eat and whinge about her phantom ailments, then it would be better all round.

The day hadn't started out so irritating. He'd left home early leaving instructions for the staff not to bother preparing him any breakfast. He'd looked in on his wife who was snoring gently and pulled the blankets which had slipped down over her shoulder. Hailing a hansom, he arrived at the surgery then proceeded to tuck into a hearty breakfast of steak, bacon and eggs prepared by Mrs Craven. Dear Mrs Craven, did she ever wonder why her duties involved preparing such huge meals for him too? Perhaps her generous salary quelled any uncertainties there.

He poured himself a strong cup of coffee and contentedly breathed in its aroma. 'Mrs Craven!'

Straightening her mob cap, the housekeeper hurried in. 'Yes Sir?'

'I have an appointment at Buckingham Palace at 10 am and I don't expect to return until later this afternoon. I have no other appointments this morning as I need to catch up on some paperwork.'

The woman nodded. 'Very good Sir. Is there anything else I can get you?'

'No thank you Mrs Craven. As usual you have excelled yourself. Your breakfast was most satisfactory.'

She bowed her head in acknowledgement.

'You may go and please remember I do not wish to be disturbed by anyone. If there are any callers, you may tell them that the surgery will open at 4 pm today.'

Mrs Craven curtsied then left his office, closing the door behind her. He waited for a few seconds before unlocking the door to his private quarters then vanished inside, re-locking the door from within.

After administering to Prince Albert's earache (*some warm oil, Your Highness then suspend the offending ear over a basin of hot water. Take care to cover your head when you venture outside*) he waited for his driver to bring the carriage up to the palace side entrance to return him to Harley Street. The man however, did not show up, so Her Majesty graciously allowed one of her own personal drivers to take him back to his surgery instead. That had worried the doctor, and he made a mental note to admonish his driver as he had already paid the man handsomely to take care of the royal coach.

When he returned, Mrs Craven informed him that that Scotland Yard fellow, Professor Delbrotman, had inquired of his whereabouts and that he hoped to see him as soon as possible. Grantley was tired of the Yard constantly asking for his aid. He had given the detectives as much help as was humanly possible and could not imagine what they would want now. On top of that his first patient at 4 pm was Lady Edith Bloomsbury —the one woman who had more aches and ills than an entire hospital ward.

Grantley removed his hat and coat and handed them to Mrs Craven who opened the door to the surgery. Lady Edith twisted around in her chair appearing suitably agitated.

'Why Lady Bloomsbury,' he exclaimed cheerfully. 'Back so soon? How is the corn on your little toe?'

She shook her lace handkerchief dismissively. 'A little better Doctor.'

'And your elbow?'

She frowned trying to recall the affliction. 'Oh yes,' she tentatively massaged her arm. 'The ointment, I believe has relieved the pain somewhat.'

'Well, I'm glad to hear it.' He sat down at his desk then opened up her medical file and dated the top of the page; the file was twice the size of all his other patients. 'Now what seems to be the problem?' Or more to the point: what seems to be the problem, *now*?

She swallowed dramatically and dabbed her cheek delicately with her handkerchief. 'It's my appetite.'

'*Yes?*' He dipped the nib of his pen in the ink well and readied himself to commence writing.

She bit her lip and leaned forward in her chair. 'I believe that my appetite is diminishing.'

Grantley looked at her in amazement, wryly thinking of the time when she tripped over in her own home, and it had taken at least three stable boys, not to mention the butler to help her up. By contrast, her skinny, miserable excuse for a husband stood by unable to do anything but did manage to take her to see the doctor as soon as she had regained her dignity. Bruised buttocks and an equally bruised ego were all that she had suffered.

'My dear Lady Bloomsbury I think a reduction in appetite could only be of benefit.'

Her double chin trembled in annoyance. 'What are you implying, Doctor? That I eat too much?'

Grantley jotted down some notes before replying. 'Perish the thought, dear lady. I was merely stating that a plainer diet would be more beneficial for your heart.'

She placed a hand to her bosom and her cheeks paled. 'Is there something you're trying to tell me Doctor? I must know.'

He gave her a distracted look then cleared his throat. 'I, er, only meant that from your family history, the women appear to have a problem with weak hearts, therefore, it is sensible to be aware of such things and take extra care.'

Lady Bloomsbury sighed deeply and dabbed at her face with the handkerchief. 'You are of course right Doctor.' She patted her ample bosom. 'I fear I am afflicted with a weak heart.'

And enjoying very bad health exceptionally well, he mused. 'Well then, I suggest you tell me when you began to lose your appetite and anything else that might be relevant.'

With such an open invitation she began prattling with added vigour. Doctor Grantley instantly regretted his last statement and made a mental note never to word it quite like that again.

Greensworth felt a chill run up and down his spine and his heart started pumping wildly. He had won. He had finally won. And now he could send Wainwright, Brett and that meddling Professor Delbrotman back to Scotland Yard requesting that next time, should there be a next time, not to bother sending anyone as their help was about as useful as a midwife in a nunnery. Or perhaps an even better idea, Greensworth thought with glee, would be to force the detectives into an early retirement in light of their public failure. They'd be sent packing leaving the proper authorities to do their work in peace. And then finally he would be recognised for all his diligent efforts in catching the culprit single-handed. The prospect made the superintendent thirsty for power. After all, he wouldn't be staying in this foul pit forever. Perhaps he would be promoted for his grand accomplishment. He could see the newspaper headlines:

EAST END SUPERINTENDENT SUCCEEDS WHERE SCOTLAND YARD COULD NOT

Or:

JACK THE RIPPER MYSTERY SOLVED AN OPEN INVITATION TO SCOTLAND YARD GIVEN TO OUR MAN GREENSWORTH

His picture would be in the paper. Perhaps there would be an invitation to Buckingham Palace. His imagination transported him to a brightly lit palace room where huge oil paintings hung from the walls and ornate, priceless ornaments stood proudly on polished tables. He would kneel before his monarch, this tiny woman dressed in black; her greying hair tied in a bun under a white lace veil.

'Your Majesty,' he would whisper, not daring to look up.

'Rise,' would come the reply, her voice quiet, though with an underlying tone of steel.

He would slowly reach his full height towering over his monarch. Her large, round eyes and usually disagreeable mouth would then twitch into a smile.

'You have done well Superintendent Greensworth. We are pleased.'

He would be speechless, not able to utter a single word to this great lady.

He imagined her frowning. 'You say nothing?'

'No Your Majesty,' he would suddenly blurt out, not wishing to offend her. 'I simply wish to thank you, Ma'am.'

'Thank us?' she would echo. 'It is we who should be thanking you. You have restored our faith in the good of our people. Now that that common criminal is disposed of, we shall sleep safer than we have in some time.'

That would be a day he would never forget; and the story would be told, and retold, repeatedly to his children and then to his future grandchildren.

Now the possibilities were limitless. The slime of the East End would crawl back into its pit when his name was mentioned, and every woman would be jealous of his most fortunate wife. There may even be a knighthood …

The door slammed shut cutting short his glorious daydream.

'Mr Greensworth, you look so elated, makes for a nice change.' The Professor walked towards the superintendent noting his ecstatic expression. 'Anything you care to share?'

The superintendent gave the alien a look of superiority.

'Well don't keep me in suspense.'

Greensworth burst out laughing and the Professor gave him a surprised look. He was certain he hadn't delivered anything witty that would warrant such a reaction. He was also certain that Greensworth's sanity was walking a fine line.

'Ha!' he retorted, his solemn demeanour snapping back to attention. He picked up a large brown envelope, brandishing it like a sword. 'This is the beginning for me and the end for you!'

The Professor nodded slowly, recognising the signs: he had been wrong. Greensworth's sanity was not walking a fine line after all. He had obviously passed that point long ago but had been rather adept at hiding it.

'What is it you're trying to tell me, Superintendent?'

Greensworth didn't reply, savouring the moment. *His* moment. 'What I have here is the evidence needed to send you and your two colleagues back to Scotland Yard empty-handed.' The superintendent gave a self-satisfied smile.

As if on cue Wainwright and Brett entered the Police House and looked from the Professor to Greensworth, sensing there was something wrong.

'Good afternoon.'

'Shh!' hissed the Professor. 'Mr Greensworth is about to reveal something very important.'

Greensworth smirked unaware that the alien was humouring him. 'I am glad you have both returned to see this too.'

'Well we've got something to show you as well,' replied Wainwright. 'But,' he glanced at his colleague for confirmation, 'I suppose it can wait.'

The superintendent held up the envelope in the air as if testing its weight. 'Inside is a photograph of the eyes belonging to one Catherine Eddowes.'

The detectives shared a puzzled look.

'Why take a photograph of the eyes of a dead woman?' asked Brett.

'Isn't it obvious?' replied Greensworth curtly. 'The image of her assailant has been recorded on her retinas. The photograph will therefore show the identity of Jack the Ripper.'

Wainwright's first instinct was to dismiss the superintendent's theory outright, as Greensworth had been a significant thorn in their side from the beginning. However, what if Greensworth had actually cracked the case? Though Scotland Yard would be far from pleased that its two most respected detectives, along with Delbrotman, had failed miserably, catching the Ripper would bring closure to the case and ensure that the foul villain received his due punishment. Brett, on the other hand, remained entirely sceptical. He made a mental note to include Greensworth and his assistant, Hugh Barker, in his final report, suggesting that enforced resignation might be the most merciful conclusion for both.

The superintendent smiled triumphantly relishing the moment. 'Well gentlemen? You say nothing?'

'Impossible.'

Greensworth glared at the Professor. 'I beg your pardon?'

'I'm sorry but it's impossible.'

The superintendent's face turned red with rage. 'How dare you insult me!'

The Professor raised both hands in a placating gesture. 'Mr Greensworth your motivation of testing all possibilities is admirable but I am afraid that it is a medical impossibility to record retinal print of the human eye after death.' The alien tactfully left out the part about it not coming into the realms of possibility until late in the 23rd century.

'But I have the evidence!'

Brett shrugged his shoulders. 'Well let's settle it. Show us.'

The superintendent tore open the envelope and with thumb and forefinger slid the photograph out.

'I take it you've already seen the picture?' Asked Wainwright.

Greensworth faltered almost imperceptibly before regaining control. 'I ... I was not present when it was being developed. There was no need.'

The Professor studied the black and white photograph. The eyes of the dead woman were clearly shown, but no retinal recording of the murderer was revealed. While the inspectors examined the picture confirming this fact, Greensworth remained frozen on the spot, his hopes, dreams and revenge dashed in one single moment.

'Well then,' said Brett, breaking the silence. 'Here's something else for you to have a look at.' He reached into his pocket and unfolded a large piece of paper with a cartoon drawn on it. 'We found it rolled up in a newspaper left at the front door.'

Greensworth made no move, so the Professor took the paper, glanced at it, and showed it to the superintendent. It was a pen sketch drawing of a police officer with a cloth tied over his face blindly stumbling around in the dark. A group of ugly looking rogues were laughing and taunting him and behind the police officer, on a broken fence was a poster offering a reward for the capture of Jack the Ripper.

It was obvious to the Professor and his colleagues that what little faith the public had in them had been sorely tested and would only worsen in time.

The Whistler's Inn had been standing since the reign of Charles II and looked as if it hadn't been cleaned since then. The Tuttle family had inherited the establishment several years before under somewhat curious circumstances—the previous owner had generously given it to them free of charge then promptly left for Australia. That was the official version. There was however talk, that the Tuttles had taken a shine to the inn and didn't see any reason why they should shell out a penny to a common thief who had already cheated the premises out from under its previous owner. So, they arranged for negotiations to take place at the Thames then one watery accident later, promptly took over the inn. The previous owner was never heard from again.

Time had marched on and the Tuttles had become quite content with their *investment*; the bar was always filled to capacity and the bedrooms were seldom without activity. With this kind of success, they had hired several bar maids and stable boys who all enjoyed the Tuttles hospitality.

'More swill Annie!' bellowed Mr Tuttle from the kitchen. His face was drenched in sweat from tending a huge cauldron filled with stew over a crackling fire.

His wife poured a tumbler of ale and slid it across the bar to a customer before replying. 'I'm comin'!' She slapped a young girl on the backside ordering her to take over serving then waddled off into the kitchen. 'Well my love? 'Ow is it?'

'See for yerself.'

She leaned over the boiling mess, sniffing its aroma. 'Smells good. Gimme a spoon.' Her husband handed her one and she took a measured sip. 'It'll do.'

'Wos that supposed to mean?'

She smiled seductively at her husband and licked her lips. 'I'd gobble it up all meself if it weren't for the customers.'

He gave her a wet kiss on the cheek and patted her backside. 'That's my Annie.'

A roar from the crowded bar prompted the landlady to waddle back out to the bar. One of the serving girls had just tipped a jug of beer over a sailor's head after he had dragged her onto his knee.

'Wot's goin' on 'ere?'

'The bitch tipped it on me!'

'Yer bleedin' well deserved it, yer dirty swine!'

The landlady cuffed the girl across the head. 'Get out the back. I'll deal with yer later. And *you*,' she pointed to the sailor. 'I'll have yer guts minced for my stew if you ever touch one of my girls again!'

The crowd roared with laughter and the sailor stood up towering over the diminutive woman. 'I'd like to see yer try Mrs.'

The noise subdued and Annie Tuttle smiled, showing decayed teeth. Her husband wiped his hands down the front of his shirt and came out to see what was going on. He was just in time to witness his wife knee a burly looking sailor firmly in the groin. The man collapsed onto the floor in shock, groaning in agony. The crowd applauded as Mrs Tuttle theatrically brushed a few strands of hair away from her face then adjusted her corset. 'All in a day's work.' Mr Tuttle whistled at his wife then picked up the sailor by the collar and dragged him out the door. 'An' don' come back!'

The sailor crawled away, his hand protectively cradling his crotch; the pain was bad, and he wondered how much damage had been done to his family jewels. He glanced up miserably to find a tall gentleman in a fine grey suit standing over him. The stranger gave him a sympathetic look. 'Looks like you've been in the wars.'

The sailor mumbled something unintelligibly.

'Let me help you up.' He bent down and placed an arm around the sailor's shoulder, smelling cheap liquor. 'You should really try taking a bath in water. I believe beer's only good for the hair.' The sailor slowly stood, still half-bent over from the pain in his groin. The Professor smiled encouragingly. 'Are you right to walk or do you need some extra help?'

The sailor made no reply but within seconds the door to the inn was flung open and a fat, red-faced woman waddled purposefully out, hands on hips. 'Are yer still 'ere? I thought I told ya to get!'

The Professor looked dismayed wondering if she was referring to him or the sailor. 'Well I've only just arrived.'

Mrs Tuttle glared at the stranger. 'Is this scum a friend of yours?'

'No, we've only just met.'

'Oh.' This naturally changed everything. 'Well I do apologise to you Sir. My 'usband just threw this swine out 'cos he was messin' around with my girls.' She stabbed a finger towards the sailor. 'When I say get, I mean get! Or would yer like another knee up yer?' She promptly swivelled about and bellowed to one of the stable boys, and a dark haired lad with a pock-marked face ran over to the sailor and dragged him away.

'Was that really necessary?' the Professor gently rebuked. 'He did look to be in quite a lot of discomfort.'

Annie Tuttle grinned. 'You would be too if your *little essentials* 'ad taken a beatin'.' She waggled her eyebrows up and down suggestively. 'Now Sir, would yer be wantin' some refreshment?'

'Thank you, Mrs ...?'

'Tuttle. And you are ...?'

'Delbrotman. Professor Orlando Delbrotman but to my friends, I prefer *Professor*.' He gave her a charming smile and she blushed girlishly. 'I'm actually looking for someone who makes regularly visits here, so I shall take up your kind offer and wait for him inside.'

Still bemused by the elegant stranger, she ventured, 'And somethin' to eat per'aps? A basin of stew? Me 'usband makes it fresh.'

The stable boy returned catching the last of the conversation. 'Yeah, smells just like donkey shit an' tastes like that too!'

'Wot!' the woman screeched. She swung at the boy, but he dodged her, running back to the stables making braying noises and laughing. The Professor smiled. 'I'm sure Mr Tuttle is an exquisite chef, par excellence.'

Annie Tuttle nodded slowly, not quite grasping the alien's refined words but evidently pacified by them. She opened the door to the tavern and politely invited him to enter.

The Whistler's Inn was larger than The Ten Bells but was equally smoky, dark, sweaty and stinking. Fortunately, the Professor's sense of smell had grown accustomed to stench; he supposed that it was possible to get used to anything if you put your mind to it.

'A fine establishment you have here,' the alien commented. He regarded the basin of stew she pushed in front of him with detached curiosity.

'We like it,' replied Mrs Tuttle cheerfully. 'And we like it all the better when fine quality such as yerself comes to visit.'

The Professor smiled politely, and she self-consciously smoothed her lank hair behind her ears. His smile however froze when he observed the visible sweat rings encircling the armpits of her grubby dress. She grabbed a tumbler from beneath the bar and filled it with beer then placed it beside the basin. The alien could imagine the bacteria leaping from her dirty dress to the beer and back again.

'Annie!'

'Wot?'

'Get yer arse in 'ere!'

She cleared her throat. 'My 'usband. 'If ya'll jus' excuse me.' She waddled into the kitchen allowing the Professor just enough time to pour his stew into the basin of the drunk beside him. He seemed to be asleep, so the alien nudged him awake. 'You haven't finished your dinner yet.'

The drunk gave him a giddy grin, picked up his spoon and began shovelling the greasy mess into his mouth.

A few minutes later Annie Tuttle hurried back and to her delight, witnessed an almost empty bowl. 'Finished already? Would ya like some more?'

The Professor patted his stomach comfortably. 'Thank you but no. It was delicious but one bowl of your husband's stew will do me for a very long time.'

The drunk pushed his cleared basin forward. 'I'll 'ave some more.'

'Where's yer money first?'

The Professor dropped a few copper coins onto the bar. 'His stew's on me.'

Another drinker seated a few spaces away wheezed with laughter. 'I'd watch meself if I was you, or yer may live to regret those words.'

The Professor gave the man a curious look.

'E eats another 'elpin' an' the swill will really be on yer—one basin's enough to make a man spew fer a month!'

Annie Tuttle looked suitably insulted and scooped up the coins in irritation. 'This gentleman is just being kindly and I'll 'ave no words against my 'usband's cookin'!'

The Professor smiled once again at the woman then checking to ensure no one was paying any attention, he leaned forward lowering his voice. 'I was wondering, if you're not too busy if I could have a word.'

'Oh?'

'In private if possible?'

Mrs Tuttle blushed then stuffed the coins down her ample bosom. 'Right you are. This way Sir.'

The drunk looked dismayed. 'Oi! Wot about me stew?'

The landlady grabbed hold of a serving girl and told her to tend to the brute. She then ushered the Professor through the smoky kitchen and towards the back alley. Mr Tuttle gave the alien a distrustful look while chewing on his pipe. His wife winked at her husband and rubbed her fingers together with one hand, implying the smell of money. This did not go unnoticed, however, the Professor tactfully decided to ignore it.

'Well Sir?'

He slid both hands into his pockets, regarding her. 'I daresay your inn is always very busy?'

'Indeed Sir. As yer can see, we have a full 'ouse as usual.'

'Do many gentlemen come here?'

'Yer mean as 'igh a quality as you, Sir?'

'Yes.'

'A few. But those that do like to keep to 'emselves.'

The Professor retrieved the fragment of the note belonging to the ruffian who had run away and re-read it. 'I am supposed to meet someone here. A man about, oh, six foot, dark wavy hair, small deep-set eyes, usually accompanies another gentleman. Would you know him?'

Annie Tuttle's sigh was long and weary. 'Dearie yer could mean anyone. Wot's 'is name?'

The Professor glanced at the note. 'I'm not sure as he is merely an acquaintance of a friend. But my particular friend likes to be known as J.'

The landlady frowned. 'Jay?'

The Professor read the landlady's sceptical expression explaining that 'J' was a nick name. 'We always used to call each other letters of the alphabet when we were at school. A bit of fun really.'

Mrs Tuttle wasn't entirely certain whether to believe such a story but suddenly it didn't seem so important compared with the ten-pound note that she saw being taken out of the gentleman's breast pocket. He casually toyed with it between his fingers.

'Perhaps you may have seen him and his friend?'

The woman gazed hungrily at the money and a sly grin spread across her face. 'Now that yer mention it, there is a fella that often comes in, always showing orf that he drives a carriage for some special toff.' she cackled. 'The idiot says 'e drives one of the Queen's coaches!'

The Professor's eyes opened wide, and Annie Tuttle felt herself being drawn towards the hypnotic orbs. 'What does he look like?'

'Well, 'e's tall, beefy and 'as black little beady eyes that stare out at yer like a pig.'

'Does he ever come here with another man?'

'P'raps. I ain't never noticed much.'

'Is he here today?'

She shook her head firmly. 'Yer always know when 'e's 'ere by 'is loud voice and 'is showin' off. If 'e's 'ere then 'is coach will be in the stables. If not, then 'e may be up at The Ten Bells or The 'Orse's Saddle.'

'How do you know he'd be in either of those places?'

The woman shrugged her shoulders. 'The likes of 'im is either whorin' or dealin' with scum like 'i'self. He's always flappin' his tongue about both joints.'

The Professor gave Annie Tuttle a smile and she grinned back displaying two rows of dirty brown teeth.

'Thank you, dear lady, you have been most helpful.' He handed her the ten pound note which she quickly tucked it into her bosom.

'Thank yer, Professor. And if there's anythin' else I can ever do for yer ...'

'I shall indeed let you know. Now I must take my leave.'

'Wait, ain't yer gonna wait for yer friend?'

The Professor evaded the question with another smile. 'Good evening Mrs Tuttle!' He strode off, leaving her feeling perplexed and yet jubilant at the same time—fancy such quality speaking with her as if they were old friends.

Mr Tuttle ventured outside and gave his wife an accusing look. 'Wot's been goin' on 'ere?'

'Look at this.' She pulled out the ten-pound note and waved it in front of his face. He grabbed hold of her arm and dragged her towards him. 'Wot did yer do to get that?'

'I merely chatted with the gent.' She bristled refusing to be bullied. 'And don' you get no ideas about 'ow far I went George Tuttle, yer 'ear?'

'But a tenner?'

'I am a respectable married woman an' I don' do those things no more!'

Her husband gave a guttural chuckle and tried to kiss her; she was still his Annie! She playfully pushed him away with one of her meaty arms. 'Oh bugger orf.'

The Professor walked through the back alley and across to the stables where several stable hands busied themselves pitching feed into the horses' pens. He looked around and casually wandered over to where the coaches were standing.

'Can I 'elp yer Sir?' a stable boy looked up from shifting hay into the stalls and asked the stranger. 'Are yer after ya carriage?'

'Not mine, no. I'm waiting for a friend. I was just wondering if his coach had arrived yet. Perhaps his driver is waiting here for him?'

The boy shook his head. 'Na. Nobody's waitin' 'ere. Sorry Guv.'

The alien's eyes flickered over the carriages. 'Never mind, I might pop back later. Thank you.'

The boy leaned on his pitchfork watching the Professor leave. Once he was gone a figure in a dark coat and coarsely woven trousers came out from behind one of the stalls. He walked past the stable boy and threw him a coin.

'Was that the toff yer meant? The one wot's been followin' yer?'

The man didn't answer but turned his deep-set, piggy eyes towards the inn then hurried inside.

Diary Extract 1.4

I'm in a hansom heading back to The Ten Bells and I have some important news to disclose: I tried to see Doctor Grantley today but as he was absent, I thought I would wait for him outside Buckingham Palace. I did not get the chance to see him but I did happen to find a ruffian who dropped a fragment of a note after running away from me. This is vital evidence regarding the Ripper case as I'm sure he is in league with the murderer himself.

I still have concerns over the possible vortex tremor but as yet I'm no closer to any conclusions. I also have concerns over how much I am interfering with Earth's history. Would it be better to leave Brett and Wainwright to continue the investigation on their own? And yet without me, Molly would have been brutally murdered. But if memory serves me correctly there is no record of her being a statistic. So have I tampered with history or done its bidding? One thing I do know is that no further murders take place. Why? Why would Jack the Ripper stop now?

Diary Extract End - 1.4

Professor Delbrotman opened the door to The Ten Bells to find Oliver playing cards with a group of sailors, while several girls were doing their best to entertain the rest of the evening regulars. If he had entered the next day, next week or next year, the scene would have been the same. 'As usual, beer, women and cards.'

Oliver looked up and chuckled. 'Well you've come to the right place Professor, come on in. I was meanin' to catch up with yer.' He stood up and spread out five cards on the table. 'Full 'ouse gentlemen, now pay up.' The gamblers grumbled while reluctantly handing over their money. 'Backer, fill these 'ere gentlemen's glasses while I speak with the Professor 'ere.'

Backer poured their drinks then nodded at the alien. 'I'll get yer a copper beer.'

'Thank you.'

Oliver invited the Professor to sit down at the corner table, near the piano. He whipped out a cigar and offered it to the alien. 'No thank you. I don't smoke.'

'Don't smoke? Why not?'

'I promised my mother I wouldn't.'

Oliver grunted. He pointedly lit up another cigar in the certainty that the Professor had no idea just what he was missing. 'Look, I'd like to know whether this is true or not. I 'eard that you're from Scotland Yard. Am I right?'

'Unofficially.'

'Is that a yes?'

'You could say that.'

'Yer not lookin' to close me down for any reason, are yer?'

The Professor smiled disarmingly. 'Now why would I want to close such a charming establishment as this?'

Oliver shrugged. 'Could 'ave yer reasons. On the other 'and you are seein' Molly. I bet the Peelers wouldn't be too impressed to know somethin' like that was goin' on.' He sniffed triumphantly. 'By the way, 'ow was your little outing last night? Did she behave 'erself?'

'Molly is a very sweet young lady,' replied the Professor truthfully. 'But to resort to blackmail is a very low thing indeed. It disappoints me greatly.'

Oliver grunted contemptuously, 'oh yeah?'

Yes,' the Professor continued his voice hardening. 'It makes one think of prison cells, and hard labour and long and lengthy sentences with no hope for appeal ...'

Oliver turned visibly pale and gulped. 'Well of course ... I mean yer 'ave ta see it from my point of view ... I got a business to run and ... '

'Then I'll leave your business to you, and you leave mine to me.'

Oliver laughed nervously, 'then it's settled.' He took out a cigar and offered it to the alien magnanimously. 'Ave a cigar.'

'I told you, I don't smoke.'

'Ave one anyway, it's on the 'ouse.'

The Professor reluctantly took the proffered cigar and slid it into his pocket. Molly who had been listening to the heated exchange from the top of the stairs, skipped lightly down and hurried over, attempting to wrap her arms around the alien's neck. Embarrassed, he disentangled himself and gently chided, 'now Molly, a lady doesn't strangle her friends.'

She giggled and seating herself beside him, grasped his hand. This caused Oliver to smirk and suggestively lick his lips. The Professor glared at him, then without further ado, Oliver rose and went to rejoin his gambling cronies whilst barking, 'Backer, get the Professor 'is beer.'

'So wot yer been up to?'

'I went for a long walk.'

'I could 'ave kept yer company.'

'No I had some thinking to do.'

'About, y'know?' She gave him a worried look; the Ripper was always there, like a hovering storm cloud.

He squeezed her hand reassuringly then looked up to see Douglas descending the stairs, leaning heavily on Elsie for support. They came over to the table and she eased him gently into a chair opposite the Professor.

'Profesher,' he slurred. 'How nishe it is to shee you again.'

'Ow much 'as 'e 'ad?' asked Molly.

'Three bottles of straight gut-rot,' replied Elsie matter-of-factly. 'I can't do a thing with 'im. He staggered upstairs then passed out on me bed.'

'Why'd 'e 'ave so much?'

Elsie rolled her eyes at Molly. 'Douglas's play finished last night—the performance yer saw. He was so 'eartbroken that he got 'imself blind stinkin' drunk.'

The Professor shook his head. 'Surely you have more great roles to perform in other plays?'

Douglas hiccuped and gave him a giddy grin.

'Well 'e is part of the company but yer know 'ow it is.' Elsie whisked a glass away from Douglas's grasp. 'E's always afraid they won't give 'im any new parts.'

'I am an actor's actor!' Douglas wailed in reply. 'The theatre beckonsh!' He jumped up and swung his arms about dramatically. 'It is in my blood to perform!'

'Sit down and shut up!' bellowed a bearded man at a nearby table.

Douglas staggered over to him and hiccupped. 'Is that you Joshua?'

'Yeah Dougie, now go sit back with yer whore or I'll nail yer big mouth shut.'

Douglas flung his arms over the man's shoulders and wept uncontrollably. By this time the regulars had stopped what they were doing and watched the spectacle in fascination. The Professor, however, did not find it at all amusing but felt pity for the poor drunken creature.

'Get orf me yer idiot!' spat Joshua; he pushed Douglas away. 'Now if yer sit down quiet like, I'll get yer a drink.'

Elsie winced but said nothing. The last thing he needed was another drink. Douglas however digested this piece of good news then theatrically spread his arms, announcing: 'Joshua, you have the soul of a poet! I am but a humble player who bows to your most blessed offer! If only the world could be as generous as Joshua ... '

The ditch digger shook his head in disbelief then stood and grabbed hold of the actor. 'If yer want yer arse kicked rather than a drink then I can arrange it!' Douglas hiccupped then staggered back to his seat unaware that he had made a fool of himself as well as Joshua. The ditch digger grabbed his own pot of beer and slammed it down in front of the actor before returning to his mates who were laughing like hysterical pigs. The actor eagerly gulped the liquor before dropping the pot on the floor.

'Well, yer made a spectacle of yerself, didn't yer?' scolded Elsie, wiping Douglas's beer-flecked chin with her handkerchief. 'I don' know what I see in yer.'

'Well I've got a surprise for you in my little black bag upstairs.' Douglas then leaned forward and whispered in her ear, and she giggled despite herself. 'But you'll have to help me back up there to show you.' He winked at her.

Elsie cleared her throat, stood up and helped Douglas to his feet.

'Until we meet again Professhor!'

The alien nodded then watched Elsie half carry him back up the stairs.

'Do yer know Douglas Forbes-Montague II isn't 'is real name?'

The Professor smiled at Molly. 'Now why does that not sur-prise me.'

'Don't tell anyone this 'cos I'm sworn to secrecy by Elsie but it's really Cyril.'

'Really?'

'Yeah, dunno where 'e got the Douglas from.'

The Professor smiled sadly. 'Well, we all have masks to wear in this world and Douglas looks as if he needs his.'

INTERLUDE

Today I am a robot in a bright yellow vest
Then I am an insect, flowers growing from my chest
Should I be a spaceship swinging all around the stars?
Or perhaps a big red monster with razor sharp claws?
I know I can be anything,
I won't be just the same.
Change now! Change now!
Who will win the game?

When the last line of the rhyme had been recited, the children shimmered out of shape transforming into a wild array of peculiar, abstract creatures. The game proceeded the same way each time, and by process of elimination, the slowest child to transform would be 'out.'

The group turned to the slowest who had transformed into a bear-like creature with multiple hooves springing from its hind legs.

'You're out,' one said to the slowest.

The child grunted. 'I am not.'

'Yes you are, Arnuu. We'd all finished, and your legs were still half-formed.'

Arnuu growled and bared razor-sharp fangs. 'That's not fair! You said the end of the rhyme too quickly! I wasn't ready!'

A rainbow-coloured biped shook several tentacles at the boy. 'You're always saying that, you'll just have to be patient until a new game is started.'

Arnuu glared at Tox; she was always the most popular and fair-minded in the group and to his annoyance, usually the winner of this stupid game. 'Fine, just hurry up then, will you? I've got to go home soon.'

Jogih sniggered which was no mean feat since his mouth now appeared beneath his left heel. He lifted his foot and spat out the dirt he had accidentally licked up.

Arnuu bucked and snorted at him. 'And what's with you, Jogih?'

'Arnuu must run home soon. Arnuu's has to obey mummy!' His voice dripped with childish sarcasm.

Arnuu stuck out a forked tongue. 'Look who's talking, mine-waste-for-brains.'

The group watched and waited for Arnuu to reply, then Jogih to match his insults for nastier ones. That was always the fun part. Would they just yell at each other? Or would the insults turn into a fist/tentacle/dimensional brawl until an adult intervened to break up the fight? Once, Arnuu had shoved Jogih so hard in a fit of frenzy, he had wedged him between the third and sixth dimensions and had to be mathematically extricated by one of the Elders. Arnuu had been severely punished but had always maintained it was worth seeing Jogih stuck headfirst in Dimension-6 for three whole cycles with no food, and no one to hear him complain. That was worth any punishment!

'What did you call me? Mine-waste? You stinking ... '

'Oh why don't you shut your foul, little mouth before you put your foot in it.' Arnuu burst out laughing, realising what he had just said. 'Did you hear that? Foot in mouth? Get it? Jogih's mouth is on his foot!'

His friends started cackling and Jogih stamped his foot angrily, accidentally receiving another mouthful of dirt.

Kyeldsen swallowed the last of his Mole-Ener Bar while hovering in front of the window watching the other children play.

Jogih was such a fool, and Arnuu was no better but at least they could manage to play the game.

Aurelia followed her son's gaze and sighed heavily. He just wanted to be an ordinary little boy, playing with the other children instead of being cooped up in that infernal decontamination cube, cycle-in, cycle-out. The servo-bot extended an arm and handed her a plate, which she passed to her son.

'Now make sure you eat every morsel.'

Kyeldsen looked at the food, then gazed out through the window again. 'I want to go outside and play.'

'Not yet. You're not strong enough.'

Kyeldsen began shovelling the food into his mouth and with two quick gulps had swallowed the lot. 'I've eaten my Mol-Ener Bar and now my breakfast.' He turned around and looked at her imploringly. 'Please let me go. If I get tired, I can just sit and watch them.'

Her heart twisted in silent agony, tears prickled her violet eyes. Her little boy just wanted to be normal. Was that too much to ask? 'All right. But you must return in one segment, or if you start to feel weak, earlier. Do you promise?'

Kyeldsen nodded enthusiastically so Aurelia lifted him from the anti-gravity seat and set him on the floor. He looked so little and fragile beside the towering servo-bot, but what he lacked in physical strength, he made up for with an iron will. Just like his father.

'Door open,' Aurelia commanded. The door dutifully swung on its hinges and Kyeldsen made his first step outside into the world, alone.

The Determiners returned from their quarter-cycle recess and took their seats within the court. The squat, pale faced Determiner seated in the centre rose and stood on the dais so all the court could see him deliver the verdict.

A robed humanoid with six arms cleared his throat and struck a metal gong. 'You have listened to the defence and prosecution of the accused—Den Taln Marg.'

'We have,' replied the standing Determiner.

'You have taken into account his plea of insanity at the time of the murders.'

The Determiner acknowledged with a nod of his head.

'And what is your verdict Determiner-one-of-nine?'

The Determiner glanced at his fellow jury before replying. 'Bearing in mind the accused's plea of insanity, and the manner of each murder, together with the prosecution and defence ...'

Den Taln Marg leaned forward in his seat and itched ferociously at a sore through his fur. His Defence Counsellor smiled encouragingly, displaying gold teeth.

'... we, the Determiners find Den Taln Marg guilty of the seven murders committed fifty cycles ago. We further press for the extraction penalty.'

The Judge struck the gong once again. 'Den Taln Marg, your sentence has been passed. You are to be taken from this courtroom and prepared for extraction. Due to your callous removal of seven fellow Phymordans, and the fact that you show no remorse, your execution will be open to the public. Furthermore, you will not be given the luxury of sedation. Court adjourned.'

Marg dug his long nails into his flesh drawing blood and glowered at his Defence. The Phymordan coughed apologetically then closed his file. 'I'm sorry.'

'Indeed?' He stood up, towering over him menacingly. 'You're not the one who's going to be extracted.'

Two court guards resembling massive Herculean figures, seized the accused and bound his paws in chains.

'Such a fuss over little old me.' He sneered at the two Phymordan guards. 'Who'd have thought I could command such attention.'

'You are not authorised to speak.' The guards dragged him from the stand and through double doors. The Defence slipped his data-pad into a silver case and snapped it shut, while the families of the murdered victims hugged each other in relief. They were not going to miss Den Taln Marg's execution for all the Phymordan tea-juice in the cosmos.

The Prosecution and Defence nodded respectfully to one another then left the courtroom, heading for their chambers.

'Arnuu, Jogih! Look!'

The two children stopped in mid fight to see what Tox was pointing at. Arnuu took his hoof out of Jogih's mouth and stared at the stranger standing a few paces away. Jogih closed his mouth and quickly re-morphed it back onto his face. They both looked at the newcomer suspiciously.

The figure shivered in the cool breeze then meekly stepped forward.

'You're Kyeldsen, aren't you?' asked Tox.

The child nodded. 'I would like to join in your game.'

Several of the other children shrugged whatever represented their shoulders whilst staring at the little Phymordan in his natural state: a short, pale silhouette of a figure. Translucent milky eyes, a flat nose and a slit for a mouth, with spindly arms and legs. Kyeldsen could hear them whisper *who is he?* and *why does he want to walk around in his natural state? Can't he change?*

'I remember seeing a story about you and your mother on the News-cast,' said Tox. 'Your father was killed, wasn't he?'

Kyeldsen's heart twisted but his milky eyes remained impassive. 'He was an overseer at the mine. He died trying to save some miners from a fire.'

The other children looked pityingly at him and Tox beckoned the little boy over. 'Of course you can come and play with us. Do you know the rules?'

'Yes, I watch you all the time from my window.' He pointed to his house a short distance away.

'Then why didn't you come out before?' asked Arnuu.

Kyeldsen shrugged defensively. 'Maybe I didn't feel like it before.'

Arnuu whispered something to Jogih but Kyeldsen didn't hear what he said.

'Come then,' announced Tox, sensing that Arnuu and Jogih would like nothing better than to pick a fight with their new playmate, 'we shall start a fresh game with everyone involved.'

The children stood in a close group then sang the rhyme afresh.

'... *Change now, change now'*
'Who will win the game?'

Immediately the group shimmered and transformed into bizarre creatures with nonsensical protrusions. Kyeldsen's skin turned red with determination but all he could manage was a single, limp feather hanging loosely from his finger.

'You're supposed to change,' protested one of the other Phymordan children. 'You're supposed to morph, that's the point of the game.'

Kyeldsen bit back tears of frustration and thrust the feather on his finger into the other's two faces, 'I did! Look!'

The child shook its twin heads in despair. 'No you *non*. All of you has to change, not just one little part of a finger.'

The other children, except for Tox laughed out loud and pointed cruelly at him. He couldn't transform! He was hopeless! What was the point of being a Phymordan if you couldn't do that?

Kyeldsen's frame shook with rage. How dare they laugh at him? He'd proven with a feather on his finger that he could change. He didn't need to change his state any further. He'd show them not to laugh at him! He charged suddenly, knocking the twin-headed child to the ground. Tox looked outraged at the display and morphed into a mini hurricane and blew them away from each other.

'Hey!' shouted Arnuu angrily. 'You're only allowed to morph into something you can touch and hold!'

'We're not playing the game now!' Tox yelled back. She shimmered and re-morphed as a humanoid. 'I will have no more fighting in this group!'

Kyeldsen, sporting a bruised head buried his face in his hands, shutting out the world, while the other child dabbed at his bloodied nostrils and growled angrily. 'He can't be in the group anymore.'

'Yeah!' cried Jogih.

The others agreed and threw dirt at the boy prompting Tox to cuff her playmates across their heads. 'I am the oldest so I say who can and can't be included.'

Arnuu rubbed his leathery chest thoughtfully, then a smile spread across his face. 'Yeah, Kyeldsen can stay.'

'What?' spluttered Jogih.

He raised a finger. 'On one condition; an initiation.'

Tox was about to protest but was silenced by the rest; deep down she knew when the word initiation was uttered, it was out of her hands. Despite his anger, Kyeldsen gave Arnuu a questioning look.

'I heard my parents talking about that murderer Den Taln Marg early this morning.'

Jogih shivered. 'You mean that one who killed all those people?'

Arnuu nodded. 'There's to be a public execution at the Court-Chamber this very afternoon. I say if Kyeldsen wants to be in our group then he has to go witness it first. All we'll have to do is decide who goes with him to make sure he does go, that is if he's got the stomach for it.'

'This is madness,' interrupted Tox. 'Children aren't allowed to see those sorts of things, only adults.'

'Not if we morph.' Arnuu grinned smugly.

Jogih shook his head. 'My father is a court guard and he says that everyone attending executions must be in their natural state. They even scan you to make sure you're not hiding your identity.'

Arnuu's scowled then another idea sprang forth. 'So, what if we come when the execution is already underway? And even if it isn't, who will notice short looking adults? Remember it is to be a public execution. There'll be so many people there they won't be able to scan everybody.'

'It's too dangerous,' argued Tox. 'You could get into an awful lot of trouble.'

Kyeldsen slowly stood up. 'I'm not afraid. I'll tell my mother that we are going for a walk to Arnuu's house for lunch. She won't suspect anything.'

Arnuu nodded. 'Good. Then let's go.'

CHAPTER 9

Nettie Wickins, the landlady of The Horse's Saddle turned her sour face towards where Skinner had seated himself. She picked up a tray laden with glasses and a jug of beer then shuffled over, plonking it down in front of him. Skinner reached for the jug but Nettie pulled the tray towards her. 'Not until yer pay up first Mr Skinner.'

He gave her a wounded look that was entirely unconvincing. 'Ain't I always good for it?'

She grunted. 'On the odd occasion.'

'Well this must be your lucky day.' He produced a gold coin from his pocket and waved it seductively in front of her hungry eyes before she snatched it from him.

'Oi manners, Mrs,' he chided. 'Coulda taken me fingers.'

The landlady gave him a withering look, then flounced back behind the bar with a self-satisfied smirk. Skinner chuckled and poured himself a drink. Money was the one thing that made everybody feel happy and in control but the old dame needn't think she was getting any more of it on this day. And if she tried, well, she'd soon find out who did have control.

Skinner took a swig of beer then noticed three burly strangers, wharfies he surmised, entering the pub. They milled around the doorway and looked around suspiciously before spotting him seated in the corner. The sailor raised his glass invitingly and they walked over to him.

'Take a seat gentlemen,' Skinner offered. 'There's plenty of beer and I've ordered some kidney pie.'

'I don' like kidney pie,' one stated. His voice crackled from smoking cheap tobacco.

'Then all the more for your two friends. There's mutton stew on the way as well. P'rhaps that'll please yer better.'

The wharfie gave him a dubious look. 'Mutton stew?'

Skinner nodded. 'Yeah, gotta eat to keep yer strength up, don't yer?'

The man looked challengingly at Skinner. 'Yer sounded just like my ol' mother then.'

Skinner gave him a surprised look.

'I never liked my ol' mother.' With that vital piece of information out in the open, he sat down and the other two followed suit. Skinner couldn't help wondering if this brute was quite right in the head.

'Well I bet your dear, ol' mother was never paid to knock the stuffin' outta someone. I daresay you've been in contact with Danny?'

The wharfie bit off the end of his thumbnail and spat it onto the table. 'We've 'eard from Danny. And by the way, don' say nothin' 'bout my mother again, understand?'

'I didn't say nothin' and yer jus' said yer didn't like 'er.' Skinner did not like the way this conversation was heading.

'I didn't but my little brother 'ere loved 'er better than a pet dog.' The man jerked his head towards the boy beside him. Skinner gave the pimply youth an incredulous look. His expression changed however when the boy plunged a knife he had been toying with into the table, splitting the wood and narrowly missing Skinner's hand. The sailor was pleased—this kid was good. Perhaps Danny picked the right ones to do the job after all.

The Professor took a measured sip of beer as Molly inched her chair closer, sending a clear message to the other girls that he belonged to her *so keep yer hands orf or else!* This however, did not stop Rosie from sauntering over and draping herself across the table trying to block the Professor's view of Molly, so the only one he could see was Rosie. Molly scowled; she wasn't sure how long the stupid old cow had been working in The Ten Bells but she'd been told that Rosie was Tommy's girl, long before Oliver had taken over the tavern. Tommy had run The Ten Bells for years before they found his body one morning, face down in a ditch. Molly was only a nipper at the time but she could still remember Rosie screaming her head off in anguish as they took him away. No one ever found out how Tommy died but as quick as you like, Oliver paid off all of Tommy's debts and took over the tavern, and naturally all its contents—namely the girls. Rosie was now fat and old and had to wear a wig because most of her hair had fallen out. Elsie once told Molly that they used to tease her by hiding her wig; Molly wished she could snatch it off her now while the old hag was busy trying to make eyes at her gentleman.

'Why don't yer bugger orf?'

Rosie batted her eyelashes innocently. 'Weren't doin' nothin', dearie. Just seein' if the gentleman would like another glass of beer.'

'I haven't finished this one yet,' replied the Professor politely, 'but thank you for asking.'

She took this as an open invitation and grabbed a chair drawing it up beside the alien, ignoring the thunderous expression on the other girl's face.

155

'Ain't yer got work somewhere?' asked Molly pointedly.

The woman shrugged her shoulders. 'No.'

The Professor felt decidedly fenced in between the women. He cleared his throat trying to give them the message that he felt uncomfortable under such close scrutiny then spied a young lad holding a broom coming out from behind the bar. Oliver called to him and the boy limped over.

'Billy,' the alien murmured to himself. The boy who had his fish stolen; the boy who saw something strange in the night. What was it he thought he saw? Magic? Perhaps like the paper boy in Harley Street? The Professor suddenly felt a sinking feeling in the pit of stomach. Why hadn't he asked to talk to Billy before? Yes, he had been preoccupied with the discovery of more murders, the Buckingham Palace stranger and The Whistler's Inn but somehow, he had completely forgotten about the boy in the process. Surely his memory wasn't that bad? How could he have just simply forgotten?

The Professor rose from his seat and Molly gave him a puzzled look. 'Are yer goin?'

'No. I just want to have a word with Billy.' The Professor walked over to the boy and tapped him on the shoulder, startling him.

'Wot!' Billy cried.

The boy tried hobbling away but Oliver leaned over and grabbed him by the arm. 'Wot's goin' on?'

'I was just wondering if I could have a word with Billy.' The Professor pulled up a chair beside Oliver.

The pimp gave him a wary look. 'Why?'

The Professor replied with a disarming smile. 'I promise I won't take up too much of his time.'

Oliver reluctantly agreed and told the boy to sit down. The Professor looked pointedly at the pimp, hoping that he would move to another table but he stubbornly lit another cigar, waiting for the alien to start talking. The Professor sighed then smiled in encouragement, trying to make the boy feel as comfortable as he could despite Oliver's presence.

'Now Billy, remember when those nasty children stole your fish?'

He nodded slowly.

'Remember what you said to me after I gave your fish back to you?'

The boy thought hard, then nodded again.

The alien's eyes opened wide, resembling huge shining orbs. Billy was drawn in, blinking at the light within. 'I said a man do magic.'

'That's right,' replied the Professor approvingly. 'Now I want you to describe to me what the magic man looked like.'

Oliver nonchalantly puffed out a ring of smoke, feigning disinterest whilst trying to follow the conversation.

'Um,' Billy murmured. 'I only saw 'im from far away.'

'That's all right. Just tell me what you saw.'

''E 'ad a black coat and 'at, and 'e 'ad a scarf.'

The Professor nodded encouragingly. 'Right. Were you able to see his face?'

The boy shook his head.

'Could you see anything else?'

Billy nodded. ''E was climbin' into 'is carriage.'

'And what did the carriage look like?'

'It was black and 'ad gold on the door.'

The Professor smiled grimly. 'I see.'

'But before 'e stepped into 'is carriage, he did some magic.'

Oliver raised an eyebrow. 'Magic?'

The Professor silenced the pimp with a hard look. 'Describe the magic to me Billy.'

Billy tried to find words to describe what he had seen but he shook his head in frustration.

'Did he shimmer?' suggested the alien, helpfully. 'As if he went out of shape.'

The boy looked excited, nodding vehemently. 'Yes, yes!'

Oliver coughed incredulously. 'Oh come on, wot a load of rubbish.'

The Professor gave him an annoyed look.

'Look, Billy wouldn't know wot bleedin' day it is at the best of time, an' yer startin' to sound just as dim.'

The Professor scowled. 'I beg your pardon?'

Oliver rolled his eyes theatrically. 'My *dear* Professor, no one sees someone shimmer out of shape unless they've knocked back a few too many.' He looked at the child. 'Billy, were yer drunk?'

'No,' the boy replied.

Oliver shook his head sadly. 'Now why don't I believe that?'

'I wasn't drinkin',' insisted Billy.

'Oh yeah? And I'm sure if the Professor asked whether this geezer yer saw was paradin' around in a pair of French lacy bloomers yer would have said *yes*.'

The Professor grunted and glared at Oliver, incensed at the pimp's flippancy.

'Now keep yer shirt on Professor,' said Oliver, suddenly wondering if he had gone too far because after all, this man was from Scotland Yard, and he could easily close him down and put him, not to mention his girls in the lockup, and what would happen to all the barrels of liquor in the cellar? 'I'm sure even the boys down in Scotland Yard 'ave a drink or two occasionally, it's just that even if Billy wasn't drunk, I wouldn't put too much into wot he says.' He tapped his head. 'E's simple yer see.'

The boy's eyes filled with tears and he quickly hobbled away hiding behind the safety of the bar. The Professor continued glaring at Oliver.

'People like Billy have feelings too, you know.'

'Yeah,' added Molly. She had been casually listening in to the conversation from the table nearby. Oliver turned around and gave her a murderous look, which silenced her immediately.

'I 'ave been good to Billy,' Oliver replied defensively, turning back to the Professor. 'E's nearly ten years old and 'e's been 'ere since 'e was born.'

'So Molly said.' At the mention of her name Molly sidled over to the alien and stood behind him, one hand on his shoulder.

'Is mother used to work 'ere til she died.' Oliver pictured the faded prettiness of the blousy woman who had given birth to Billy. He smiled, reminiscing. 'She originally worked for Tommy, the geezer wot owned this fine place before me.'

Molly bit back an incredulous cough.

'Fat Daisy was 'er name. She 'ad this butcher friend named Ben who used to come round 'ere a lot. A good customer, 'e was.' Oliver puffed on his cigar before continuing. 'Is old lady and 'im didn't get on but Fat Daisy doted on him, so 'e promised Fat Daisy that 'e'd move out and they'd shack up together.' He laughed shrewdly. 'And Fat Daisy believed him too.'

'So wot 'appened?' asked Molly.

Oliver sighed heavily. 'Well, Fat Daisy caught him with someone else in the back room of 'is butcher shop.'

The Professor raised both eyebrows.

'I'll never forget it!' He slapped his thigh heartily. 'I'd just taken over this place and I was comin' in to open up and I 'eard a scream that would 'ave woken the bleedin' dead!'

Oliver's voice had risen in pitch and the tavern grew silent, eager to hear who he was talking about and what happened.

Oliver stood up, pleased with being the centre of attention, and pointed towards the front door.

'Down that street I saw Ben come runnin', squealin' like a pig. And then I saw Fat Daisy after 'im with a meat cleaver, ready to do him in for being unfaithful!'

Backer laughed loudly. 'I remember that too Oliver.'

Oliver gave him a warning look. *This* was his story, so Backer could just keep his mouth shut. The barman got the message and continued to spit polish the glasses.

'Poor ol' Ben! When 'is old lady got wind of wot happened, she threw 'im out. And then 'e came crawlin' back to Fat Daisy but she would have none of it. By this time her belly was big, and she was feeling crook. Poor old Dais' then crawled inside a gin bottle and never got back out.'

'So wot 'appened to 'er?' asked Molly, voicing everyone's curiosity.

Oliver sat down again and spat out his cigar stub on the floor. 'Fell down those stairs in a drunken stupor, didn't she?' He jerked his thumb towards the stairs. 'Some say that's why Billy ain't normal, cos she fell down on 'er belly. The next thing, we 'elped her up, dragged her upstairs and after a while she 'ad the brat.'

Molly looked away sadly and Rosie shook her head, remembering that terrible night.

'She was screamin' 'er guts out,' continued Oliver, 'then she suddenly stopped, then we heard the brat screamin' instead. That's when I knew that was the end of Fat Daisy.' The story finished abruptly; Oliver lit up another cigar. 'And the brat's been 'ere ever since,' he added unnecessarily.

The Professor couldn't help but think that Oliver was one of the most contemptible individuals he had ever encountered, with his cruel humour and equally harsh temper. It was a wonder to him that Billy had stayed all this time; perhaps a spiteful word from a surrogate father was better than nothing at all. After all, where could Billy have gone? Most likely, he would have ended up in the Poor House, where life was barely tolerable except when one was asleep. The Professor shuddered as he recalled texts from his childhood on the subject. The Poor House was one of the most dreadful prisons, second only to the flame-pits of Kagila, where orphaned natives were forced to mine precious gems while evading the ice-flames that constantly erupted from the gem veins. Their life expectancy ranged from six days to a month. Fortunately for Kagila, there were plenty of expendable orphans; unfortunately for the orphans, their lives were grim and short.

The Professor sighed, discarding the unhappy thought bringing him back to the present and the situation at hand. What of the beady-eyed stranger from Buckingham Palace who dropped the note? He knew this ruffian could not be Jack the Ripper himself as the note signed with the letter J had to have been given to him by the writer. He therefore must be Jack's eyes and ears of the East End, and his coach driver from what the fragment of the note confirmed. Whoever Jack the Ripper was, he was not a native of the East End. Instead, he was most likely a well-to-do surgeon and had hired this person to find suitable victims and help keep his identity a secret. But the biggest secret of all was not only who this murderer was but whether he was in fact a human being. Didn't Billy's story and the paper boy's correlate? Could a human being fail to maintain a solid form? It seemed impossible unless this unwelcome visitor was from another world.

Skinner watched the three wharfies, joined by a dozen others, swarm over the food and drink like rats in a sewer.

'There's more where that came from,' said Skinner, leaning back in his seat, glass in hand.

'Not bad swill,' approved one of the ruffians and belched loudly.

'Well gentlemen, as I was sayin', our mutual contact, Danny, has been spreadin' the word about the Kipper. Y'see what we 'ave 'ere is a situation that's now up to us t'deal with.'

'Why?' one asked, snout down in his basin of stew. Everyone else had the same question on their minds.

Skinner plonked his glass down on the table loudly, demanding their full attention. 'This, my friends, is a situation that affects all of us. We all know that there's plenty of thievin' and murderin' around these parts, that's always been a fact of life.'

There were a murmurs of agreement from the group.

'It's just this one man, this one stinkin' little nobody wot's shakin' this place up. The whores don' wanta go out on the streets no more, afraid that they'll be next on the menu for the ... ' he glanced around and leaned forward, 'the Kipper. Consequently, we are forced to go to them which means that there's no way we can get outta payin' for it.'

This group understood and Skinner continued. 'I mean, wasn't it easy before, eh? Yer could go along to a tavern and dutifully pay for services if yer wanted to, or if yer couldn't scrounge a few coppers, yer could 'ave 'er in a ware'ouse alley then dump the bitch before she could 'oller for 'elp.'

Fists thumped the tables with exclamations of *yeah* and *it was good in them days*; Skinner knew he finally had them eating out of his hand.

'An' another thing, this geezer ain't one of us. I mean it ain't the first time we 'ear of whores being knocked off, it's just 'is methods. They're not the methods of the likes of us. E's got to have knowledge.' Skinner tapped the side of his head 'Expert knowledge like a doctor so 'e can delicately carve up the girls.'

'So is 'e a doctor or a butcher like?' asked one of the wharfies.

Skinner grinned viciously. 'In more ways than one mate. E's a mad bastard who 'as knives to cut 'em all up fancy like.' He paused for the climax. 'And I just 'appen to know who 'e is.'

'Wot?'

'Then who is 'e?'

'Yeah! We'll kill 'im!'

'Cuttin' up our girls like that!'

Skinner savoured the thrill of his vast knowledge; he was enjoying this. 'I 'ave been speakin' with the local Peelers.'

The climax plummeted, and the men groaned dismissively. 'They don't know nothin!'

Skinner struck the table with his fist. 'Oh yes they do. They've been observin' one man who just 'appened to be close by when the murders took place. 'E was even seen runnin' from the one that 'e 'adn't finished guttin.'

'Awlright then,' replied the pimply youth, fingering his knife, 'if the Peelers know who 'e is, then why 'aven't they nabbed 'im?'

Skinner smiled, ready for the question. 'Scotland Yard 'ave been a right pain in the arse for them, always 'amperin' their investigations, consequently the Peelers 'aven't been able to catch 'im. And anyway, yer try to catch a Kipper that's as slippery as an old codfish in a stinkin' 'ole like this wearing a policeman's getup. You'll see 'ow 'ard it is.'

'Which comes back to us,' said the youth's brother. 'Wot exactly do yer want us to do?'

'Oh somethin' that's right up your alley,' Skinner replied casually. 'We're gonna lynch the bastard.' Skinner reached into his pocket and tossed several gold coins onto the table. Complete attention focussed on the glittering pile. 'There's more where that came from if we do the job right. When 'e's dead, we'll get more of the lolly, and the Peelers'll get their pretty faces printed in the mornin' paper. Is it a deal?'

One of the men smiled, revealing decayed teeth. 'I say you've gotta deal Skinner. Now wot's the Kipper's name?'

'It's ... '

'Cyril!' Screeched Elsie, cackling. She jumped on the bed, discarding her skirt. 'Yer are a naughty boy then, aren't ya?'

Douglas hiccupped and took out some lip-rouge from his bag and smeared it over his white, flabby chest. 'I draw a heart on my chest because you have utterly stolen mine!' He snorted and almost tripped over his own feet. Elsie collapsed in a fit of giggles and laid on her back.

'But you really do love me, don't you?' he suddenly asked, all trace of humour gone.

She rolled over to face him, supporting her head with one hand. 'Course not, yer just a plaything to me.' She expected him to laugh but all he gave her was a hurt look. 'Silly! Wot's the matter with yer? I was only jokin'.'

Douglas's bottom lip trembled and he sat down on the bed beside her, staring at his feet. 'I wouldn't blame you if you meant it.' He turned to look at her. 'After all I'm just a washed up old has been. No!' He struck the bed with his fist and Elsie sat up with a start. 'How can I be a *has been* when I was never anything to start with?'

'Cyril,' she replied soothingly.' Now don' start goin' all maudlin again. You'll get some more work in the theatre.'

He sighed wearily. 'I don't mean just that, I mean,' he turned around and took hold of her hands, 'what have I ever achieved? My father was a respectable doctor. What have I become in this infernal pit I call home?'

She squeezed his hands reassuringly. 'You're my Cyril. My Douglas Forbes-Montague II—the king of the theatre.'

He smiled sadly. 'You'd never leave me, my dear, would you?'

Elsie shook her head. 'As long as I'm still 'ere, I'll be with yer.'

Douglas glanced at his bag on the floor and his eyes clouded in sorrow. 'Because if you ever did, I would be forced to ...'

'Wot?'

He flung open his bag and seized a knife, brandishing it in front of Elsie's horrified eyes.

The Professor was in a pensive mood; he drummed his fingers on the table and said, 'I think it's time I found the detectives.'

'I'll come with ya,' replied Molly helpfully.

'No I think it may be safer for you to remain here.'

She frowned. 'But who'll look after ya?'

'Look after me? I don't need any looking after.'

'Then wot about me? Aren't yer gonna at least walk me back 'ome?'

'Of course.' Just as they stood up together, a blood curdling scream followed by cries for help ripped through the air, silencing everyone in the tavern. Oliver and Backer stared at each other then the barman ran out from the counter and rushed upstairs with Oliver close behind him. The Professor hurried after them just as police whistles were heard nearby.

Hugh Barker had been biding his time in The Horse's Saddle, discreetly observing Skinner rallying the local rabble in preparation for the Ripper's *purge*. Superintendent Greensworth may not have had concrete evidence from the photograph supporting his theory that it would show who the murderer was but they both had strong suspicions as to the identity, regardless. Although Skinner had explained that it was indeed hard to catch the culprit in a conspicuous uniform, close observation had led the two officers to several conclusions: number one, the Ripper had medical knowledge; and number two, he knew the East End well and could come and go without too many heads turning. Barker was also certain that many of the public house locals probably knew him well, and the thought wouldn't have entered their tiny minds that he was a cold-blooded killer. Another point was the fact that the girls were easy targets, perhaps to vent his rage because of some sort of inadequacy? Hugh Barker grudgingly had to agree with Brett and Wainwright: perhaps he was forbidden for some reason to practise medicine. That would explain a lot, especially since the man Barker and Greensworth thought was Jack the Ripper was now a second-rate actor, instead of a doctor.

Barker left some coins on the table after finishing his beer then walked out of the pub, heading for The Ten Bells, enroute to the Police House. He greeted several police officers on the way, then looked around, eyes peeled as he heard the familiar frenzied police whistle from another officer up ahead, followed by running footsteps. He took up the hunt and followed the sound to none other than The Ten Bells.

Oliver and Backer followed by the Professor burst through the door of Elsie's bedroom and found her screaming on the bed, wrestling with Douglas.

'Bloody 'ell!' swore Oliver, registering the knife in the actor's hand.

The alien rushed over to Douglas and grappled with him while a flood of police officers stormed into the tavern and charged upstairs, following the muffled howling sounds. The Professor, by this time, had managed to wrench the knife from Douglas's grip while Elsie wailed in anguish. Oliver picked up the knife from the floor but was quickly relieved of it as Barker rushed in and looked around, assessing the situation.

He smiled triumphantly. 'You're coming for a little trip down the Police House.'

'No!' screamed Elsie. 'Don't let 'em take 'im!' She collapsed on the floor as Molly charged in, weaving her way through the crowd, to put her arms around her friend. ''E wasn't trying to kill me!' She hiccuped hysterically. 'It wasn't me!'

'It's awlright Els', calm down,' Molly replied gently. She glanced up at the Professor and gave him a helpless look.

The Professor looked at Douglas's quivering form being dragged away. Then at Oliver and Backer shouting at the police officers that they couldn't just barge in here unannounced, then at Elsie's hysterics. It was time to silence the madness.

'Quiet!' he shouted above the noise. His power silenced them, except for Douglas who was murmuring something incomprehensible to himself, his eyes glazed over.

Satisfied that he had their attention, he knelt down in front of Elsie and spoke quietly to her. 'Was Douglas trying to hurt you?'

'No!' she whispered fiercely. 'E said that if I didn't really love 'im, life wasn't worth livin'.' She grabbed hold of the Professor's hands in desperation. 'E was drunk and maudlin and no matter 'ow much I told 'im I would always stay with 'im, 'e wouldn't believe me. 'E was gonna kill 'imself! I was trying to stop 'im but if it wasn't for yer coming when yer did ...' Tears spilled from her eyes and she buried her head in Molly's shoulder for comfort.

The alien looked at her with pity and nodded, satisfied with her explanation. He walked over to the two officers who were holding Douglas. 'Gentlemen, I am attached to Scotland Yard and if you will release this man into my custody, we will all be able to sort out this misunderstanding.'

Barker smiled and shook his head. 'Not this time Professor Delbrotman. You, and Inspectors Brett and Wainwright have no jurisdiction in this circumstance.' He gestured towards Douglas. 'He's gonna come with us to the lockup, it's all over now.'

The Professor narrowed his eyes at the man. 'What are you implying?'

'This whore doesn't know what she's talking about.' He gestured contemptuously towards Elsie. 'Today was the final nail in the coffin,' he grinned, 'no pun intended.' He glanced at his fellow officers approvingly. 'Well lads, we've finally caught him.' He leaned forward, his face inches from Douglas's. 'It's Douglas, isn't it? Or should I say Jack the Ripper?'

▲

CHAPTER 10

Detective Inspector Brett signed the report bound for Scotland Yard then placed it in a large brown envelope, addressing the document *private and confidential*. He knew his superior, Chief Inspector Godfrey was waiting impatiently to hear of any progress about the Ripper case, and though there had been little development, he did take time to mention Superintendent Greensworth's *astonishing* method of using retinal photography to reveal the killer. Brett reflected that there had to be some form of humour to counteract the whole ghastly affair.

The inspector sealed the envelope then gave it to the waiting courier. 'This must be hand delivered to Chief Inspector Godfrey alone, and no one else. Is that clear?'

The young man nodded. 'Yes Sir.'

'Good. You may go.'

The lack of success in finding the murderer had led to many sleepless nights which weighed heavily on Brett's shoulders. He slumped in his chair and rubbed his dry, weary eyes; he could almost feel the sensation of sleep overcoming his senses when a cacophony of cries, shouts and whistles brought him rapidly back from the brink. His eyes snapped open, and he bounded out of the office to witness a flood of police officers dragging a half-naked, portly individual by force. A moment later, the Professor rushed in bellowing at PC Barker who roared right back at him, in between hollering for Greensworth. The superintendent meanwhile had been licking his wounds in his office. He was still furious that his *methods* had come to naught. He slumped down his chair but on hearing the commotion, he rushed out to see what was happening.

'Help me!' wailed the prisoner. 'I'm innocent, I never meant to do anything wrong!'

Brett was dumbfounded with all the confusion then Wainwright, returning from an errand, pushed his way through the mob and bellowed, 'what the blazes is going on?'

Greensworth shoved Wainwright out of the way then grabbed a clump of the prisoner's hair, cruelly dragging his head back at an odd angle. 'I've got you now!' He looked at Barker and gave a triumphant nod. 'Well done Mr Barker, well done!' He gave a fierce grin then realised that somehow, he had lost his grip on the prisoner but was in turn being held firmly by that meddling Delbrotman. Both the Professor's grip and expression stopped the superintendent in his tracks.

'What is the meaning of this? Unhand me at once!'

'Mr Greensworth!' The Professor growled with such force that the man visibly flinched.

'Professor Delbrotman,' whimpered Douglas. 'Help me, please.' He gazed imploringly at the alien then promptly passed out, collapsing against three of the police officers, before sliding to the floor.

'What are you playing at?'

The alien waited and the question was simple enough but Greensworth hesitated before replying. 'My duty, Professor Delbrotman, gentlemen,' he acknowledged the two inspectors.

Brett raised an eyebrow. 'What? Arresting harmless fools for sport?'

The superintendent clenched his jaw and cast a contemptuous glance towards the detective. 'My patience has finally paid off.' He shared a secretive smile with Barker. 'And I no longer have to employ other ... methods.' Barker nodded, thinking momentarily of Skinner's crusade. 'I now possess what I have been seeking.' He gestured at the semi-naked actor. 'I have my Jack the Ripper, and now my Police House returned to me.' He looked pointedly at Wainwright, Brett and the Professor. 'You are no longer required here. You may return to Scotland Yard forthwith.'

'What are you talking about?' demanded Wainwright. 'You're expecting me to believe that *this*,' he stabbed a finger at Douglas, 'is what's been eluding us all this time? *This* is our murderer?'

The superintendent nodded self-righteously but the Professor shook his head.

'Greensworth, you've got the wrong man.'

'Really? And what makes you think so?'

'Because it is impossible to catch the real offender—for you at least.'

Greensworth snorted in contempt. 'Impossible you say? Not at all, unless ...'

The Professor was tired of the games this human was playing. 'Well?'

'Unless,' Greensworth paused, heightening the anticipation of the moment, 'you know more of this affair than meets the eye.'

The alien couldn't have agreed more, bearing in mind what he had discovered, and his knowledge of 1888 but instead placed an arm around a surprised Barker, changing tack. 'Absolutely astounding, isn't he?'

The PC cringed, repulsed by the alien's close proximity and suspicious of his sarcastic tone.

'Indeed he is!' The Professor continued, 'Superintendent Greensworth, I congratulate you!' He stepped towards Greensworth who automatically took a step back just in case the Professor tried to put an arm around his shoulder as well. 'I just had to be completely sure that you were sure. After all there's no point in locking someone up if you've got the wrong person, is there? Therefore, the villain would still be at large while an innocent man would be found guilty. You know I'm extremely satisfied that my confidence in your abilities has proven correct.'

The superintendent looked cynically at the alien. 'Indeed?'

'Why yes! Now you'll be able to extract the confession you want from Douglas. And as for us,' he gestured towards the detectives, 'we can all go back to Scotland Yard where we belong, telling all and sundry of your grand accomplishment in catching the *right* man.'

Greensworth gave him a withering look. He knew the Professor was being sarcastic but he was not going to *cast pearl before swine*, instead ordering that the unconscious actor be put under lock and key until he was sensible enough to be interrogated. The inspectors were unhappy about this but sensed that Delbrotman was up to something, so they remained silent, following him into their tiny office just as Douglas was taken away.

'I don't like this at all,' said Brett, propping himself on the side of the desk. 'Greensworth's trying to find an easy answer and it's impossible to do so.'

Wainwright frowned. 'He can't be right. I mean that man can't possibly be Jack the Ripper, can he?'

'Absolutely not,' snapped the Professor. 'Douglas Forbes-Montague is a third-rate actor with great aspirations in both name and status. Unfortunately, the poor devil has neither.'

Wainwright shrugged. 'All right. But then how does a third-rate actor get to be a cold-blooded murderer? Or more importantly, why does Greensworth think he is?'

The Professor planted his hands in his pockets and heaved a laborious sigh. 'Well, a bit of deduction. And a good deal of twisting the evidence to fit the facts, much like wedging a square peg in a round hole.'

'Such as?' asked the inspectors at the same time.

'One black bag for instance.'

Brett raised both eyebrows. 'Yes, and?'

The Professor walked around the other side of the desk and flopped into a chair. 'Think about it. Douglas is an actor, and actors usually leave their greasepaint and paraphernalia at the theatre.'

'Right,' replied Brett.

'However, Douglas always carries the same black bag with him at all times, filled with I presume, his theatrical kit.'

'A lot of people carry bags,' reasoned Wainwright. 'I mean granted, we are searching for someone who carries a bag with them but what should make his so different?'

'The difference, gentlemen is *that* type of bag is only ever used by the medical fraternity. It is standard whenever you see a doctor.'

'Is he a doctor as well?' Asked Brett.

The Professor shook his head.

'Unless he's lying,' hazarded Wainwright. 'I mean look at what we have here: a man who I daresay frequents practically every den of iniquity known to man, which would make him well known in these parts. Why then would anyone be suspicious of some-one like that? He appears to be merely an actor but carries a medical bag which,' he snapped his fingers and pointed at Brett, connecting the dots in his mind, 'is always with him, and from the description given by the Professor and the girl seems to be pretty damn close in fitting the bill.'

Brett looked incredulous. 'So what you're saying is that he's actually a doctor, whilst pretending to be an actor so he can commit murder?'

Wainwright pursed his lips. 'Don't make a joke about it. I mean I hate to admit it but what if Greensworth is right?'

'It just doesn't make enough sense,' replied Brett. He looked at the Professor for reassurance. The alien smiled thinly.

'Our murderer is a doctor but it's not Douglas.'

'How can you be so sure?'

The Professor knew that Douglas was not an alien and therefore innocent. The alien who seemed to have a problem retaining a solid humanoid appearance was the real killer. He couldn't reveal that to the inspectors but replied, 'because if we can find the right carriage driver then in turn, we can find our murderer.'

Elsie feverishly trembled as Molly patiently stroked her friend's hair trying to calm her down. Every time she tried to rush out of the room, Molly crooned and cajoled the woman back to bed. She was really worried about her friend. Obviously, Douglas meant much more to her than any another customer.

'I can't bear it,' Elsie whimpered. 'Wot are they gonna do to my Douglas?'

'Nothin', 'e'll be awlright,' assured Molly. 'The Professor's with 'im. 'E'll know wot to do.'

Elsie let out a miserable wail. 'No, 'e'll hang for this, I know 'e will.'

Molly's hand faltered on the woman's, hair. 'Wot are ya on about?'

'Well yer 'eard the Peelers, didn't yer? They think that my Douglas is the Kipper.'

Molly shook her head. 'Ow could 'e be? 'Es had the opportunity for years if 'e wanted to commit murder. Douglas wouldn't 'arm a flea.'

Elsie gave the girl a sad look. 'But wot about Martha?'

'Wot about 'er?'

''E used to visit 'er. 'E even used to go back to 'er if I was busy with someone else.'

Molly shrugged not liking where this conversation was heading. 'So?'

'So?! She was the first one that got done in, and my Douglas found 'er dead. And then 'e found Polly and "Dark Annie". I'm sure the Peelers were suspicious of 'im always turnin' up when someone died.'

'But that doesn't mean 'e 'ad anythin' to do with it,' suggested Molly helpfully. 'I mean, it could've been anyone that found 'em.'

'Found 'em carryin' that bloody medical bag 'e's so fond of?' Elsie replied bitterly. 'I wish 'e'd thrown that thing in the river. I warned 'im people'd get suspicious.'

Molly clasped the woman's trembling hand. 'Wot bag? Yer mean the one that 'e takes to the theatre?'

Elsie sat up, gripping the girl's hand tightly. 'Yes that bag. It belonged to Douglas's father who was a doctor. It was left to 'im on 'is old man's death bed as a promise.'

Molly looked worried. 'A promise to wot?'

'That Douglas would follow in 'is father's footsteps and become a doctor.' Her voice had dropped to a whisper. 'Douglas went to medical school but ended up failin'.'

Molly shook her head, not grasping the implications.

'Oh Molly!' Elsie exclaimed wretchedly. 'Don' yer understand? The Peeler's are after a murderer who is a doctor.'

'How do yer know?'

Elsie flopped back on the pillow listlessly. 'Cos Douglas told me the way the girls were killed, it could only 'ave been a surgeon wot done it. An' Douglas was nearly a doctor which means 'e'll make the drop for sure.'

Douglas stared miserably at a cockroach undertaking a cross-country trek across the prison cell floor near his outstretched feet. He hated the dark, and the lockup was depressingly gloomy. There was a tiny window, high in a recess on the cell wall opposite but it only allowed a dismal ribbon of light to enter, just enough to observe the bug's progress. He had been in prison for only an hour but it seemed like a month. He had woken from semi-consciousness to find himself being hurled unceremoniously into a cell, along with a coat to wear. Thank Heaven the British constabulary had a measure of decency because the cell was cold and dank and all he was wearing was the bottom half of his long underwear. After a few minutes he heard shouts from above and he wondered if the Professor was attempting to convince everyone that it had all been a horrid mistake. Him, the Ripper? Absolutely not. He loved women, all women. And just because he had discovered several of the poor victims didn't mean that he was responsible for their deaths. Oh Father, he reflected wretchedly, what would you think of me now? I squandered the opportunity to pass the medical exams by throwing my inherence away on futile pleasures and now I am a cheap actor, living in cheap squalor, and being entertained by cheap women. And just when I thought I could stoop no lower, I am accused of murder and thrown into prison. He sneezed miserably, wiping his nose across his coat sleeve. And what will Elsie be thinking right now of my stupid attempt at suicide? I wouldn't really have killed myself and certainly not with that knife. It was only an old prop left over from Julius Caesar. Congratulations Douglas Forbes-Montague II—He groaned angrily. Oh, what's the use? I am nothing but a flea in England's luxurious fur! Congratulations plain old Cyril Cohen. Your father Joseph Cohen is probably turning in his grave right now.

The Professor had recounted his experiences concerning the mysterious stranger, the note that had been signed with a J, and The Whistler's Inn. Brett demanded why he had not been informed of this before but as the Professor pointed out, the events of the last couple of hours had sidetracked matters.

'But it doesn't help if you keep things from us,' complained the inspector. 'We are supposed to be working together, remember?'

'I know,' replied the Professor apologetically. 'You must forgive me but certain circumstances have forbidden me from including you both.'

'Is it anything to do with Greensworth?' asked Wainwright. 'Because if we find he's been interfering more than usual then Scotland Yard has every right in charging him with obstructing the law.'

Brett snorted contemptuously. 'Obstructing the law? He's a bloody walking obstruction.'

Wainwright tut-tutted. 'Don't say that too loud. The *obstruction* will try and put us both on report. He's very good at finding fault in others.'

Brett smiled. 'What? And then throw us in the lockup alongside Douglas?'

'I wouldn't put it passed him.'

The Professor studied both men, considering what to do next. Could he trust them? As decent, law-abiding citizens? Certainly.

But could he trust them with the truth? There was an alien influence, which he knew with absolute certainty. Could they handle such information? Or would they dismiss him as a lunatic and laugh in his face?

'Gentlemen,' the Professor said solemnly. 'There is something more ... I have a case to put before you.'

Jonathan Brett raised an eyebrow. 'This sounds serious. What else have you found out?' He glanced at his partner before returning his attention to the alien. 'But you'd better get a move on before Greensworth personally puts the noose around Douglas's neck.'

The Professor agreed then asked that both men listen very carefully to what he had to say. 'I admit that I had little realisation of what was at stake here when I first arrived. Certainly, I knew that an horrific crime against humanity had been committed, and I assumed that the person responsible was, shall we say, a man.'

Brett snorted. 'Surely you're not about to tell us that Jack the Ripper is female?'

'No,' replied the Professor. 'I meant that I thought he was human. But now I don't think he is.'

Wainwright gave the Professor an incredulous look. 'Pardon?'

The Professor swallowed. 'I don't believe that Jack the Ripper is a human being. I believe he is disguised as a human and has the full run of the East End with the help of a human lackey, the ruffian who drives him around in a carriage. That carriage will most certainly be at The Whistler's Inn tonight. Therefore, all we need do is apprehend the coachman. Then he will lead us to our murderer.'

'The one who isn't human?' completed Brett, sceptically.

'Correct.'

'Professor, when this case has been closed, you should take a rest cure. I think the strain is finally getting to you.'

The Professor knew this was not going to be easy. 'Look I do understand that this is extremely hard for you to comprehend but I can prove it.'

'And how do you propose to do that?' Wainwright was baffled.

'I will show you something that I have concealed near The Ten Bells which will give you ample proof but first I think another more important matter is at hand.'

Brett shook his head in disbelief; was the man joking? If so, then it was indeed in poor taste.

The Professor smiled knowingly, almost as if he had read the other man's thoughts. 'Before you commit me to an asylum, we have to have Douglas released then I promise you all will be revealed.' He held out his hand in a gesture of friendship. 'I honestly do need your help in this matter. Please give me the benefit of the doubt.'

Brett looked into the Professor's eyes and suddenly felt an overwhelming sense of purpose and comfort and his doubts were swept aside. He shrugged his shoulders and shook hands with the alien. 'I don't know why Professor but I'll try.'

'I too,' added Wainwright, looking into the alien's compelling eyes.

The Professor smiled and secretly breathed a sigh of relief. He loathed placing anyone under his will unless it was for a very good reason. However, a minor hypnotic suggestion was required if the detectives were to accept the Professor's conclusions. It would also cushion the blow when they saw his ship for the first time.

Skinner stepped outside The Horse's Saddle and lit a cigarette. He inhaled with satisfaction and turned to the group.

'Right then,' he announced. 'We need to split up and spread the word further. We need more men, and we also need weapons and torches and such like.'

Jake O'Regan, with his mean pock-marked face and sadistic reputation—he'd beaten his own sister viciously because she wouldn't give him the money she earned on the streets—offered to supply some knives and clubs. 'I can get some of these from, ah, clients of mine that owe me certain … favours.' He remained silent on the details leaving the rest up to the imagination.

Skinner nodded approvingly. 'Good. We need clubs. I know Danny can also 'elp us there with 'is contacts but it'll 'elp the cause if everyone can pitch in.'

The sailor waited for the murmurs of agreement.

'Awlright, that's all for the business side of things. Now I need to find that scumbag, see wot 'e's up to and keep an eye on 'im until we're ready. We need to do the job in the night, see. We don't need any of the Peelers interfering, so we'll meet back 'ere, same time, tomorra night.'

One of the ruffians, Charlie Fry scratched at the lice in his hair. 'I thought yer said the Peeler's are with us on this one.'

The sailor nervously looked around, shushing the thief. 'Keep yer voice down yer stupid bugger! We don't want the 'ole bleedin' world to 'ear.'

Charlie scowled. 'Well answer the bloody question then!'

Skinner held up both hands, placating him. He could feel the growing restlessness. 'Awlright, awlight. Keep yer shirt on. You've already got some of the gold as payment but that's from the uniformed coppers. Scotland Yard are being kept out of this, remember, 'cos they don't understand 'ow things work down 'ere. Got it?'

It took several long seconds for that piece of information to be processed. Once understood, the tension in the air relaxed.

'Now I'll need some 'elp lookin' around for 'im so who's with me? I only need one or two of yers.'

Several feet shuffled about uncomfortably, and all eyes avoided the sailor's hard gaze.

Skinner growled angrily. 'Oh come on! Yer actin' like a pack of bleedin' school girls! Wot are yer afraid of? Yer all fired up about bashin' 'im dead when yer together but yer backbones go to mush when I ask for volunteers. 'E ain't gonna try an' kill yer! 'E only goes for whores, and unless yer do 'umpin' for a rum tottie in yer spare time, I don't think yer gonna be in any particular danger.'

The thugs looked suitably embarrassed, then Charlie warily put his hand up. 'I'll go with yer, Skinner.'

The sailor nodded, clearly annoyed with the rest. 'Good. At least one of yers ain't afraid.' He looked Charlie square in the eye. 'Ow are ya at lock pickin' by the way?'

The other man wiggled his fingers in front of Skinner and cackled. 'Well they don't call me Charlie *the light fingered* for nothin'.'

It was the first quiet night old Nigel Frobisher had had in several weeks. It was peaceful, and Nigel almost felt that he was king of this fine establishment. After hanging up the costumes and locking the props away, he idly shuffled across the stage of The Ivory Palace and stopped in front of the prompter's box. The air was thick with dust motes and the empty rows of seats gave the theatre an eerie appearance. There had been talk by several of the actors that there was a ghost haunting the theatre. Apparently, he preferred to appear in the off season, when the out-of-work actors returned to collect their belongings. Horace and Douglas swore blue, black and yellow that they had witnessed an apparition appear in their dressing room after the last play had finished. It bowed low at their feet then asked for a swig of gin. Unfortunately, the actors had just finished their last bottle so there was none to spare, so the ghost simply shrugged and disappeared. Douglas and Horace then passed out. Nigel chuckled to himself. The only spirits there that night was of the intoxicating kind.

Nigel continued to shuffle through the wings and along a narrow corridor until he found his favourite nook and sat down. He placed both feet upon the table near the stage door and picked up a newspaper.

Several paragraphs in, he had cause to look up and listen. He was certain he could hear a scratching sound near the door. Could it be that infernal stray cat that kept hanging around? He thought it would've gotten bored by now and wandered off as no one paid it much attention. The scratching stopped and Nigel returned to his reading. He reached for his coffee cup and brought it to his lips, then the scratching started again.

'Bloody cat,' he muttered and plonked the cup back down on the table then stood up. He shuffled over to the door and bent down, trying to hear any meowing. Perhaps a saucer of milk might shut it up? It worked the last time even though he promised Mr Grimble, the theatre owner that he wouldn't encourage the flea-ridden thing.

He reached into his pocket and pulled out a bunch of keys on a metal ring. He found the correct key and opened the door, expecting to find little Ginger—well he had to give it a name, didn't he?—instead finding two thugs, a sailor and his ruffian companion. The second man was holding a long piece of wire.

'Hey, what are you doing with that thing?' demanded Nigel.

'Now 'ang on a minute,' placated Skinner.

'Get out!'

'Look we was just tryin' to ...'

'I know what you was tryin'!' Nigel quickly grabbed the first thing at hand and waved it threateningly. 'Now get out!'

Skinner cleared his throat and grinned at Charlie who responded in kind.

'And wot do yer propose yer gonna do with that?' Skinner pointed at the pink parasol being brandished like a sword.

Nigel glanced at it and his cheeks went red. 'Try and step over this threshold and I'll show yer.'

Skinner held up his hands and shivered with mock fear. 'Ooh dearie me. 'E's gonna keep the sun orf me if it kills 'im.'

Charlie laughed out loud, and Nigel caught a whiff of his fetid breath. He turned his face away scowling, which prompted Skinner to push through the door. Nigel tried hitting the sailor with the parasol but he brushed it aside while Charlie walked in and shut the door behind him.

'Now sit-down and shut up!' Skinner was tired of playing games.

Nigel gulped and promptly sat back down again.

'Now if yer can stop playin' 'eroes for one second, I want to ask yer somethin'.'

Nigel crossed his arms defiantly. 'Well I can tell you for certain that Mr Grimble keeps none of the takings here on the premises.'

Skinner looked up Charlie as the thief wound the wire around his fingers threateningly. 'Did ya 'ear that my friend? 'E thinks we want money.'

Charlie grinned at the possibility.

'No my good *Sir*,' he spat the last word in Nigel's face. 'We don't want yer money. All we want is some information.'

Nigel looked at him suspiciously.

'Y'have a certain Douglas Forbes-Montague wot works 'ere.'

Nigel frowned.

'We just want to know where 'is lodgings are, thas all.'

CHAPTER 11

The news was spreading.

Jack the Ripper's identity was no longer secret, and armed with this newfound knowledge, a hunt was on to bring him down once and for all. Rumours had been rife as to the identity of the murderer but now there was no more doubt as to who this monster was; and to think he had been under everyone's nose brazenly thinking he could get away with it all this time! It was so plainly obvious: he was a doctor; a regular customer of the whores; he thought no one would suspect him because everybody knew him. Like hell they wouldn't! The people were going to reclaim their territory and arm themselves ready for when Skinner would summon them to battle. Then they'd show *him* who was afraid!

Skinner and Charlie Fry, in the meantime, had been busily following the directions of Nigel Frobisher which brought them to a tenement block in Whitechapel, and the location of Douglas's lodgings. They entered the building and stepped over a drunk huddled near the foot of the stairs; a half-empty bottle of gin lay next to him. Charlie reached for the bottle but the old man opened one eye, cursed, and snatched it away. Skinner halfway up the stairs, turned around to see what the thief was doing.

'Leave it, come on, we gotta a job to do.'

Charlie scowled and scurried up the steps after his partner, ignoring the drunk's verbal abuse. Once the two men had reached the floor above, the drunk closed his eyes and settled back for another extended snooze.

Upon reaching the corridor, Skinner walked up and down until he found Douglas's rooms. 'Ere we go, number 12, just wot ol' Nigel said.'

Charlie grinned. 'And 'e only 'ad to lose two teeth before 'e remembered the address. 'E'll wanta answer your questions a bit quicker next time, won't 'e?'

Skinner looked at the thief contemptuously. 'Wot would I go back and see that ol' fool for? We've already got the information we need. Do yer think I got nothin' better t'do with me time?'

'No, I mean yes.' Charlie gave him a weak smile. He didn't want to anger the sailor again so he adopted a casual air. 'It's just that Nigel's learnt an important lesson, 'asn't 'e? No one who wants to keep 'is teeth will try messin' about with ya, Skinner.' He winked trying to be ingratiating.

Skinner grunted and an ugly smile spread across his face. 'I like yer, Charlie. You're a useful little mongrel when yer wanna be.'

Charlie beamed, assuming Skinner had paid him a compliment.

'Now get yer wire an' open the door.'

Charlie fished out the single tool of his trade and placed one end into the lock. He leaned his ear against the door and crooned to it, trying to convince the lock to open.

Skinner crossed his arms impatiently. 'Come on, 'urry up.'

'Ssh!' hissed Charlie. 'This is a delicate operation.' A moment later the lock clicked and the door swung open. Charlie straightened up and pocketed the wire, immensely pleased with himself. He looked at Skinner waiting for thanks for a job well done; Skinner ignored him and walked inside.

Douglas's home was a cramped two room affair consisting of a tiny parlour and connecting bedroom. The two men stood in the former looking around with mild interest. The place was spartan with very little furnishings and what there was, showed signs of wear and tear. A table had a dip in its centre with the veneer peeling off and two dining chairs had sagging seats from years of use. There was a couch that might have been nice when it was new, but the cherubs woven into the design had been attacked by insects, leaving a honeycomb effect. Skinner grunted in mock approval. '*Very nice*. Everythin' neat 'n tidy, even if it is a dump with nothin' much to look at.'

Charlie rubbed his hands together and headed for the bedroom door. 'Let me be the judge of that.'

The bedroom was musty and dank not that it bothered Charlie as he felt quite comfortable in airless, dirty surroundings. Skinner on the other hand, although accustomed to being cooped up below decks on his ship, much preferred fresh air, and the invigorating tang of the ocean and he wasn't going to stay put while Charlie scurried around like a rat, searching for treasure.

'This bedroom stinks. I'll wait for yer out 'ere.'

Charlie looked up and cackled. 'It ain't so bad.' He spied a small chest of drawers beside the bed, and opened the top drawer and began rummaging around, peering at the contents. 'I'll give yer a yell if I'm onto somethin'.'

Skinner scowled at the thief then walked back into the parlour. The little tosser may have been a good thief but he acted like a sewer rat, and he smelt like one too.

This was what Charlie enjoyed doing best; just him by himself, running his grubby fingers through someone else's possessions —and being paid for it too. He affectionately patted the two gold coins, that sat comfortably in his pocket, and mentally crowed with excitement at the prospect of more to follow.

He could hear Skinner in the other room, pacing up and down impatiently, so not wishing to incur his wrath he set to work exploring Douglas's belongings. He pulled out two shirts once white but now faded to a pale grey. Charlie dropped them on the floor. Next: a pair of braces with silver buckles. He tried to tear the buckles off but the elastic in the braces snapped him painfully across the chin and he howled in pain, causing Skinner to come rushing in.

'Wot are yer doin'?'

Charlie swivelled around with a guilty expression on his face. 'Er nothin'...'

'I can see that, now 'urry up and get on with it.'

Once Skinner had stalked out, Charlie, feeling particularly brave now that the sailor could no longer see him, stabbed two irate fingers in the air in his direction then tossed the braces onto the bed. Muttering under his breath he knelt and opened the bottom drawer and found a bundle of theatre scripts tied with string. In sheer frustration he tore at the string and tossed the sheets of paper into the air. Didn't Douglas have anything better than this? He growled in annoyance then pulled the drawer out and thumped it into the side of the bed in frustration. Assuming that the bed was nailed to the floor so that no one could try and steal it, he was surprised to find that knocking it made it shift. This revealed a section of the floorboard which had been cut out then replaced—a secret compartment!

He licked his lips with excitement then pushed one end of the loose floorboard causing it to pop out. Charlie peered into the gap.

Skinner was contemplating kicking Charlie firmly up the backside if he didn't get a move on, when suddenly the thief called out to him that he had found something.

'Well? Wot 'ave yer found?'

Charlie jumped up and waved him over. 'Come quick. See for yerself.'

Skinner felt a slight rise of anticipation but was certainly not going to show it so he allowed a long moment to elapse before walking in and bending down beside the thief. Charlie had managed to drag out three leather bound books, wrapped in material and was busily trying to tear the cloth away. Skinner grabbed the books from him and scanned the spines of each. He said nothing and glanced at Charlie who looked fit to burst with excitement.

'Well, wot yer think?' the thief pleaded with the sailor.

Skinner opened the first book and read the inscription written on the page. '"To my dear son Cyril, may these volumes assist you in your medical studies as they helped me in mine. Your loving father, Joseph".' He handed two of the books to Charlie. 'These are books for a doctor.'

Charlie snatched the volumes back and flicked through several pages; he stared in horrified fascination at a diagram in *Gray's Anatomy*. 'Do I really look like that inside meself?'

Skinner shrugged, not looking up, clearly more interested in the third book. Charlie made a face and muttered a disgusted *ugh* before slamming the book he was holding shut.

'Found it!' Skinner was grinning.

The thief looked at the book in the sailor's hands uncomprehendingly. 'Wot?'

'This,' he tapped the page smugly, is a Bible but not just any Bible. It is the Bible of the Old Testament.'

Charlie nodded knowledgeably but it was as plain as day that he didn't understand what Skinner was driving at.

'I thought I 'eard some of me shipmates say that old Douglas was really called Cyril.' He grinned viciously. 'Yer can run but yer can't 'ide.'

'Wot yer talkin' about?'

He held up the book. 'This is a Jews' Bible. And this,' he held up the cloth that had protected the books, 'is a prayer shawl. That Peeler, Barker 'ad heard from listenin' around that Dougie was really a Jew called Cyril, Cyril Cohen to be exact, and some of my shipmates knew 'im by that name too, before passin' 'imself off as *Douglas* the actor.'

Charlie frowned. 'Ow'd they know that?'

Skinner shrugged. 'Yer live down 'ere long enough, people get to know yer. Apparently 'e was gonna become a doctor but somethin' went wrong. That's accordin' to the Peelers.' Skinner placed the books and the shawl back in the gap in the floor. 'Somethin' went wrong awlright. 'E's been carvin' up our girls and wot's more 'e's a stinkin' Jew.'

Charlie nodded sagely in agreement. 'Well that explains everythin' then, dunnit? The Jews are not men to be blamed for nothin'.'

Skinner couldn't have agreed more but chose not to bother answering the thief. He ordered Charlie to replace everything properly so Douglas would be none the wiser when he returned home. Charlie complained as it was in his nature to steal whatever had been found but a warning fist in his face ensured he did as he was told.

A bar of light stabbed at the darkness surrounding Douglas and he shielded his eyes with his hand. He heard footsteps then quickly stood up and rushed over to the iron door.

'Hello? Is anyone there? Please let me out! I am innocent!'

'That's for the Bailiff to decide,' was the reply. Hugh Barker walked over to the cell door and placed the lantern at his feet before taking out a set of keys.

'Where is the Professor?' whimpered Douglas. 'Please, I must see him.'

'The Professor is indisposed,' replied Barker coldly. 'You are to come with me.'

Douglas took a step back from the jail door and accidentally squashed the cockroach that had made its final journey.

Greensworth swallowed the last drop of milk in his glass then set it down on the table before him. He wholeheartedly wished there was a cure for ulcers but the only thing the doctor had prescribed was milk and plenty of it to soothe the afflicted area. He massaged his stomach absent-mindedly whilst reflecting that he should really seek a second opinion. His pained expression switched to a smirk, wondering whether he should consult Cohen before the Bailiff passed sentence on the swine.

He looked at the Ripper file spread out before him, re-reading the statement that the Professor and that trollop had given of the description of the murderer. The information didn't bother him but the thought of that Orlando Delbrotman (who names a child *Orlando* for Heaven's sake?) made his blood boil and his ulcer sliced through him like a burning knife. He hated the man, and he despised the two inspectors from the *great* Scotland Yard.

Those three had continually impeded his efforts in solving the case, and what's more had taken up more office space than he could afford. How could he and Barker conduct a case without continually falling over each other in the two rabbit holes that were left in his Police House? Well once this business was over, they could just get out and leave him alone. Greensworth massaged his temples wearily. His headaches were getting worse, and he was sure that the Professor was the cause of it all. Why did the man contradict him all the time? Did he possess a hidden agenda or was he just purely perverse?

His painful thoughts were interrupted by a knock at the door. He responded with a 'come' before sitting up straight in his chair, as if he had been busy working and not affected by pain.

'Sir?' Hugh Barker walked in.

'Yes?'

'The accused has been shifted to the interview room and the Professor and the inspectors have demanded to attend the interrogation.'

Greensworth's ulcer spat venom, and the superintendent grimaced in pain. 'Damn and blast it they just want to interfere.'

'They've got orders from Chief Inspector Godfrey ...'

'Yes, yes I realise that,' he snapped back. 'Co-operation indeed. They just want to rob me of my success.'

Barker shook his head. 'But you've caught the Ripper Sir, no one else can gainsay you on this, and we no longer have to employ that sailor for more drastic measures. Everything's been tied up neatly and smartly.'

Greensworth rose, walking to the door. 'Concerning that issue Barker, there's no need to contact Skinner yet, it'll just be a waste of time. Besides, I doubt we'll see the money you gave him returned so he may as well earn it.'

Hugh Barker gave him a questioning look, wondering if the superintendent was going to elaborate but Greensworth just smiled and left the room.

The Professor handed Douglas a fresh handkerchief while Wainwright emptied the contents of the medical bag onto the table.

'See, see,' sobbed Douglas. 'I have nothing in my bag that is incriminating.'

Brett picked up a comb, a crumpled program of *The Maiden's Dilemma*, and a cracked, worn brown leather purse. He opened the purse and spilled a few copper coins into his hand then placed them on the table. 'Nothing out of the ordinary here.'

Douglas nodded vehemently. 'You see I told you so.'

Brett leaned across the table. 'That may be but you're still going to have to account for yourself as Greensworth is not going to let you off the hook that easily.'

Douglas wailed miserably. 'But I'm innocent.' He looked up at the Professor. 'Oh my good Sir, you do believe me, don't you?'

The Professor gave him a pitying look. 'Yes Douglas but you're going to have to be very careful in regards to answering any questions that I or the detectives here *and* Greensworth may ask of you. Any slip could, I'm afraid, be fatal.'

Douglas went visibly pale so the Professor quickly added, 'and we mustn't let that happen, must we?'

Douglas felt as if he was going to swoon and contemplated passing out but was brought back from the brink when Greensworth and Barker erupted through the door. Wasting no time, Greensworth stalked straight up to the accused and produced the knife that Douglas had brandished in the tavern boudoir. He dangled the knife threateningly in front of the terrified man. 'Well, well, well, then. You look a little distraught I must say. Seems funny that you should be frightened of a weapon like this!'

The inspectors shared an anxious glance. They knew that Greensworth was itching for a fight, and anything could tip him over the edge but they were going to make damned sure that no harm would come to the defenceless Douglas.

'Were your victims afraid?' taunted Greensworth; his face a mixture of mock innocence and twisted curiosity. 'Did they weep and plead for mercy before you started carving them up?'

The Professor took a step forward, hovering protectively over Douglas. He wished the superintendent would stop harassing the poor actor, it was getting them nowhere. Hugh Barker glared at the Professor and moved closer to his superior displaying obvious support for him in direct opposition to the others.

'And you studying to be a doctor too, but you weren't allowed to practise medicine in the proper way because you failed, so you were going to make sure that you'd practise it by butchering whores who crossed your path!'

Douglas could not take his eyes off the knife; the taunts terrified and consumed him. 'No, no! I love women ...'

'Love to murder them? In cold blood? Love to tear their innards apart?'

'Greensworth, enough of this! This isn't helping!' growled the Professor.

'Why did you do it?!' spat the superintendent ignoring the alien. 'By what possible right did you think you could get away with it? You stinking piece of filth!'

Douglas howled in terror and anguish, shaking his head. 'No please!'

'You think you can elude justice! You'll hang for this, I swear! And you won't find peace until your neck snaps in two, and then you'll rot in the pits of Hell forever!'

Greensworth's frenzied mind burned like the fire in his belly, and he raised a hand to strike the actor who cowered in his seat. The detectives rushed forward shouting at him to stop the tirade but before any damage could be inflicted, the Professor grabbed hold of the superintendent's wrist, twisted the knife from his grasp and threw it on the table.

'I said enough!' The Professor's eyes flashed with an unearthly light and gradually Greensworth stopped his badgering and became calm.

Douglas sat trembling, then to his shame, felt a sickening sensation of wetness between his legs. The Professor kept staring into Greensworth's eyes whilst directing a question to the actor. 'Now Douglas, I want you to collect yourself then tell me about the knife. How did you happen to have it upon your person?'

Another wave of nausea swept over the actor and he couldn't speak. He felt embarrassed and disgusted by his inability to control his bladder and he shifted uncomfortably in the chair casting a defeated look at both detectives. Wainwright nodded his head in encouragement to the actor, not realising what had just happened; Brett did notice but chose to say nothing.

'Well you see … I,' began Douglas. He glanced at Barker who looked fit to explode at the audacity of the Professor ordering the superintendent to keep quiet. Greensworth however looked suitably calmed and the alien turned towards his assistant, after noticing Douglas's fearful expression.

'Well Mr Barker?' asked the Professor. His tone was laced with a warning. 'There's no point in screaming and arguing. We require simple questions to receive simple answers to gain the information we need. And we need it in a quiet uniform way. Is that not so Mr Greensworth?' He looked at the superintendent who bore a feverish if somewhat glazed expression.

'That is so,' he replied mildly.

Barker could not understand his superior's behaviour but hoped that perhaps he had something up his sleeve that would confound the overbearing Delbrotman.

'When you're ready Douglas,' prompted the alien.

Douglas quivered a moment more before sighing. 'Well you see I took that knife from the theatre. It's just an old prop from Julius Caesar and I took it as a souvenir.' He looked at the Professor and gave a sad smile. 'A great actor used it once, you know. The Great Herbert Beerbohm Tree.'

The Professor nodded in encouragement. 'Go on.'

'If you look at it closely the blade slides back into the handle thus ensuring the actor who portrays Caesar is safe from harm when he is murdered in the play.'

Brett picked up the knife, examined it, and noticed the oversized slot in the handle. He carefully placed a finger on the tip of the blade and it slid back up the hollow of the handle.

'But surely that knife must have a switch to hold the blade fast,' remarked Barker suspiciously.

Brett again examined the knife but shook his head. 'There's nothing here that suggests that.'

'The theatre does not possess props that could inflict real damage.' Douglas gasped at the notion.

'Then why try to kill that trollop of yours with it then?'

The Professor shot a warning glance at Barker.

'I was not trying to kill her!' replied Douglas desperately. 'I was pretending to kill myself knowing full well that it would never work. I was feeling melancholy at the time because my theatrical career was probably coming to an end.' He looked down despondently. 'I know I acted foolishly but I craved deep sympathy from the one woman who I can truly say means so much to me.'

Barker rolled his eyes as if he had just about heard everything; Greensworth was uncharacteristically silent.

'So you weren't trying to kill anyone,' concluded the Professor.

'Never,' was the vehement reply.

'But you were found within the locations of the murder victims,' argued Barker.

'Yes but only as an innocent bystander. It was just coincidence that I happened upon the poor souls.'

Barker walked over and leaned clenched fists on the table in front of Douglas. The actor cringed feeling intimidated. 'But you used to visit those whores.'

'Only poor Martha.' He dabbed a handkerchief to his eyes. 'I was quite fond of her.'

Brett held out a warning hand towards Greensworth's underling. 'Why don't you give the man some room. Go stand in the corner with your friend.'

Barker's expression turned black, and he stalked back towards Greensworth who was passively observing the proceedings.

The Professor sat down on the chair opposite Douglas. 'Please continue.'

He nodded feeling much more secure now that both Barker and Greensworth had moved further away. 'I cannot fathom why I am accused of such monstrous crimes. If all the evidence that you possess has come from me discovering the victims, then it cannot be enough. Others saw their poor bodies too.'

'That's not all,' retorted Barker from across the room. 'You carry a medical bag and previously you have passed yourself off as a doctor.'

Douglas shook his head. 'No, that is a lie. I never claimed such a thing. I admit that I did go to medical school ...'

'Then you do admit it,' Barker interrupted.

The Professor turned around and hissed at the man to be quiet. Barker clenched his jaw and gave a meaningful look towards his superior who ignored him and remained silent.

The Professor smiled kindly at Douglas. 'Tell me about your history in medicine.'

'There's really not much to tell,' he shrugged. 'My father was a doctor and he used to practice here in the East End, administering to the poor.'

The Professor nodded in encouragement.

'It was his dearest wish for me to follow in his footsteps but being young and hot headed as I was then, I repeatedly ignored his desire. I really wanted to be an actor of great calibre, perhaps Shakespearean, but I was either not good enough, or my family was not good enough.'

The Professor frowned. 'What do you mean?'

Douglas smiled bitterly. 'Perhaps my acting prowess was somewhat lacking but as soon as theatre companies discovered my roots, most doors were closed to me.'

Barker gave a twisted grin. 'That's because you're a *Jew*, isn't it?' He said the word as if it was a vile disease; the actor looked hurt and ready to weep.

The Professor raised both eyebrows. 'And that is a crime?'

Douglas sighed sadly. 'It is to many. For my family's beliefs, we were relegated to this end of London so my father could at least find employment to feed us.' The sadness in his eyes touched the Professor's alien soul. 'At least some of the people here did not mind being attended to by a Jew. It's better than dying I suppose.'

'You see my family name is Cohen, and my first name is Cyril. Douglas Forbes-Montague is only a half-hearted attempt at a professional, gentlemanly, yet theatrical name. Unfortunately, others discovered my true identity as they may have known me when I was a child, or perhaps they knew my father and his work.'

'So you decided to change your name and become an actor,' concluded the Professor. 'With your father's blessing?'

Douglas spluttered. 'Good Heavens no! He liked the theatre, but it was no career for his only son. He made me promise never to try and pursue my fancy but go to university just as he did.' He shrugged. 'I was unhappy but I did as he wished. Unfortunately, I soon discovered that I had neither the skill nor inclination for the task. When I had completed my first year, the money that my father had given me was almost gone. Then he became very ill and died shortly afterwards. I took the money that remained, left the university, changed my identity and moved to Whitechapel. I managed to audition and secure employment at The Ivory Palace, and as you can see, nothing has changed since that day.'

'What a marvellous tale,' said Barker sarcastically in response to what Douglas had just recounted.

Douglas gave him another hurt look. 'I speak the truth Sir, upon mine own father's grave.'

Barker sniggered. 'Oh you can dispense with the wordy Shakespearean claptrap. I know how the likes of you operate. Mr Greensworth and I have been observing you for so long that it seems laughable for you to attempt to seek such sympathy.'

Douglas's expression was a mixture of fear and puzzlement.

'What are you prattling on about?' demanded the Professor. 'He speaks the truth.'

Barker smiled cruelly and glanced at Greensworth for sup-port who determinately stared into space. 'So he promised his father he would become a doctor, and he studied for only a year. *Quite long enough,*' he stressed sarcastically, 'for him to gain enough skill in surgery. But then his father dies, and the money runs out. So what does he do? He scuttles like a rat back to his old haunts and takes out his miserable failed existence on the one thing that is abundant around here.' Barker paused for dramatic effect. 'Whores. They're easy to come by, and equally easy to get rid of. Who would care if a handful of 'em go missing and turn up in pieces.' He stalked over and growled, 'who indeed?'

'No! That's not so!' cried Douglas desperately, frantically looking at the PC and then at the alien.

Brett shook his head and tut tutted. 'And is that all you've got?'

Barker narrowed his eyes. 'I beg your pardon?'

'You heard. That he dropped out of university, and for that he goes around murdering women?'

'Just as the Professor said,' added Wainwright. 'You're trying to twist the truth into incriminating evidence. So what if he's a Jewish actor who once tried to be a doctor? That doesn't make him a murderer.'

The Professor reached into his coat pocket and produced a small fragment of paper. 'Pardon me for interrupting but could someone fetch a pen and some paper.'

Wainwright looked at him, frowning. 'What for?'

'Humour me if you will.'

'Oh this is becoming ridiculous,' blasted Barker. He swivelled around to face Greensworth. 'Sir I implore you to say something.'

'What?' Greensworth asked reasonably.

'*What,*' echoed Barker angrily. 'I don't understand Sir! What is wrong with you?'

'Oh do be quiet,' said the Professor with a pained expression on his face. 'You're giving both Mr Greensworth and I a headache.'

Barker, looking fit to explode was stumped for words.

Wainwright left the room, returning moments later with some paper, a pen and an inkwell and he placed them in front of the Professor.

'Now let's clear this thing up once and for all.'

Douglas looked hopeful and the detectives waited for the Professor to pull the proverbial rabbit out of his hat. The Professor placed a blank page before Douglas and handed him the pen. 'Now Douglas, or do you prefer Cyril?'

Douglas shrugged. 'I answer to both.'

'Very well. Now I want you to write on the paper what I dictate to you.'

The actor nodded and dipped the pen into the inkwell. The Professor then read out the contents of the note just loud enough for his ears alone. Douglas's expression turned from curiosity to one of horror.

'What are you trying to do to me?' he whispered fearfully.

The Professor made no reply but beckoned the inspectors to move closer, then invited Greensworth and Barker to do the same. Despite being extremely angry, Barker was curious to find out what Delbrotman was up to.

'Well?' he asked reproachfully.

The Professor handed his note to Brett and asked him to read it aloud.

'"*tonight and the morrow at The Whister's Inn. Leave coach, same time. J*"' He then returned the note the alien.

'Inspector, is that what Douglas wrote on the paper?'

The detective glanced at the page then nodded.

'Well then,' replied the Professor. 'That proves everything. Douglas cannot possibly be Jack the Ripper.'

'What are you talking about?' demanded a bewildered Barker. 'Where did you get such a note?'

'I happened upon it in my investigation, and I was going to divulge my discovery but I was somewhat sidetracked when you arrested Douglas.'

Barker looked at the handwriting of each note, which clearly showed that the penmanship of one was completely different to the other.

'He could merely be writing a different way on purpose.'

The alien sighed wearily. 'Oh do be reasonable. Now what hand did Douglas use to write that note?'

'The right,' replied Brett.

Wainwright clicked his fingers, instantly recalling the conversation they had had with Doctor Grantley. 'Jack the Ripper's left-handed. It can't be Douglas.'

'Exactly! You can tell that Douglas is not ambidextrous,' the Professor turned to Barker, 'that's being able to write with both hands.' Barker glowered at the man's condescending tone. 'Now have a look at his right hand.'

Douglas held out his hand and gave the Professor a puzzled look.

'The hand that writes is always larger than the other from greater use,' explained the alien. 'And what's more there is a tiny callous on his middle finger. Obviously, he writes often.' He looked expectantly at the actor.

'That's right I do, because when we are given scripts to memorise, we must record important information on them,' replied Douglas, always enthusiastic about his art, no matter the circumstances. 'You know the sort of thing: where we must move and be positioned at certain points in the script. And I have also tried my hand at writing plays, as it were.'

The Professor let out exuberant 'ha. There, you see? He can't possibly be the one we're looking for. And I think *some of us* owe him an apology.'

Possibly when Hell freezes over thought Barker angrily but Greensworth nodded in agreement with the Professor.

'He is perfectly correct, and on behalf of myself and Mr Barker, I do humbly ask for your forgiveness.'

Barker nearly passed out.

'Excellent,' approved the Professor. 'Now I think we should order Douglas a cab and return him to wherever he wishes to be taken.'

Douglas smiled giddily then passed out again, hitting his head on the table.

Diary Extract 1.5
Jack the Ripper is still at large but an innocent man has been saved from the gallows.

After administering smelling salts and attending to the bruise on Douglas's forehead, I hailed a cab to return him to The Ten Bells. He informed me that he wanted to allay Elsie's fears and inform Molly that all was well. I offered to find him something more suitable to wear than a long coat, but he would have none of it. I could hardly blame him for being in such a hurry. As I handed him his father's precious medical bag, I was struck with a feeling of such sympathy for his plight. He is a poor pathetic individual and unjustly hounded for his beliefs. Although accused of possessing medical knowledge, the true accusation is the fact he is Jewish. Who has the right to hate others for what they believe in? I cannot and will not understand it as there is nothing to understand. Narrow minded, ignorant fools spread a poison of bigotry then they in turn hound the innocent. I realise I am pontificating but I just cannot stand the injustices of this universe, and I will never be silent in my views.

After seeing Douglas safely off, I returned and checked on Greensworth. I dislike applying mind control on anyone but I must admit he was the exception. Unfortunately, his mind is highly unbalanced, and I do not know how long my control will last. Hopefully long enough for the inspectors and I to finish the case once and for all. Mr Barker on the other hand was ranting and raving about obstructing the course of justice etc etc, so to keep him quiet I placed a hypnotic field on his anger, and now he is as agreeable as Greensworth—for the moment.

I shall write later as the cab that the detectives and I share has arrived at our destination. It is time for them to see my ship. It is also time for them to learn that human beings are not the only species that exist in this universe.
Diary Extract End - 1.5

INTERLUDE

Norman Queltayler felt ill. Whenever he glanced through the port window of his quarters, he felt a sudden urge to rush to the bathroom and wait for his last meal to make an encore appearance. He abhorred the nauseous sensation of moving through hyperspace and heartily wished the mission was over.

No one on the *Dragonfly* suffered from hyperspace syndrome—the bilious feeling of being displaced—except him. In normal space and real time, he always felt terrific. He could go about his business, cataloguing plant samples collected from dozens of different planets quite happily, but when the ship made the jump to hyperspace—that was it; a constant urge to vomit. He supposed that seafarers on Earth hundreds of years ago felt much the same but you'd think that after the first few dozen missions he would have overcome the blasted syndrome by now.

He had visited the ship's doctor but the laser hypodermic he'd been given had done absolutely nothing to relieve the nausea, except manage to leave a burn mark on his forearm. The doctor had apparently been *doctoring* for only a few months and was of the aggressively new school where *no prescribed medicine was good medicine*. Norman had asked him why he seemed to be the only one who felt bilious whenever the ship entered hyperspace, to which the supercilious little upstart of a medico answered, 'well what do you think?'

'Well if I knew then I wouldn't be bloody well standing here asking you, would I?' Norman was furious.

The doctor shrugged then entered his pontificating mode whilst wandering up and down in front of Norman with his usual self-importance. 'Well in the olden days, say a few hundred years ago in the twentieth century, they used to administer tablets to people who suffered from air or sea sickness.'

'Great, give me one of those.'

The doctor looked shocked, then annoyed. 'Surely you jest Mr Queltayler. How primitive do you think the medical fraternity is now?'

So Norman stormed out of sickbay taking his nausea with him, in the fervent hope that the doctor would die very soon of some monstrous disease for which there was no cure. And even if a cure was found, his colleagues would frown upon bombarding the doctor's system with drugs, and when the fool asked if he was going to die, the others would say: *Well, what do you think?*

He stomped down the corridor making loud clanging noises with his boots on the metal floor and made a rude gesture at the surveillance camera on the wall.

'Mr Queltayler,' a voice called reprovingly. Norman spun around to see Commander Nile sauntering up the corridor, wearing a skintight grey singlet and a flowing pair of black trousers which accentuated her hourglass figure. He scowled at the woman while still managing a sidelong glance at her chest.

'Well, what do you want?'

Commander Nile tut tutted gently. 'Well, what do you want— *ma'am*. I am an officer you know.'

Norman burped feeling the bile rise in his throat. 'Look *ma'am* I'm suffering from hyperspace syndrome, and I don't feel well. I just want to go back to my quarters.'

Nile shook her head, affecting a look of concern. 'Poor Norman, perhaps a good workout in the gymnasium would take your mind off your troubles. I've had a terrific exercise regime designed for me. I'd be happy to arrange something for you.'

Norman looked at her as if she had just offered him a dose of poison; she chuckled. 'Dear, dear, I suppose that's out of the question then.' She slunk over to him, and he could smell the perspiration on her body and feel the breath from her lips teasing his senses. 'Perhaps I could do something else for you to take your mind off your troubles.'

Norman was amazed that such a high ranking and beautiful officer would make such an offer but the pessimistic side to his nature kicked in, and he knew there had to be a catch. The *catch* walked around the corner just as Nile brought her lips close to Norman's.

'What the hell's going on here?' demanded Captain Adam Laroque, his pasty face flushing with colour as his blood pressure rose. 'You, Commander Nile, Mr Queltayler, answer!'

Norman backed away and shook his head. 'Nothing Sir. Commander Nile here was just enquiring about my health.'

He gave the woman a dubious glance. 'Was she now?'

'He looked as if he was about to faint,' explained Nile with a winning smile. 'We can't have our ship's botanist collapsing now, can we?'

Laroque fought down the jealous urge to strike the woman. 'I suppose you were about to administer mouth to mouth?'

Nile ran her hand through her long chestnut brown hair. 'If I had to.'

'Yes I just bet you would.'

'Oh really Captain, surely if someone needs help … '

At this point Norman reminded them of his presence by vomiting on the floor.

Norman was back in his quarters, confined by Captain Laroque until further notice. Bloody cheek. Him and his high falutin' ways would be his downfall one of these days, he thought vemonously. Laroque had only risen to the station of captain so quickly because his father had every politician this side of the Venghasi Cluster in his pocket. Twenty-two years of age and already the captain of the *Dragonfly,* as well as head of the fleet in the ensuing invasion force. He supposed that was why Commander Eleanor Nile was either trying to please him or make him jealous. Perhaps she figured that getting a leg over Laroque was a way of getting a leg up the promotional ladder.

Norman sank down on his bed and stared at the metal rivets in the ceiling. Why had he been called up for this mission anyway? What the hell did they need a botanist for, when all they were going to do was blast that planet—what was it called again? Phymord—anyway? The politicians had demanded some kind of mineral that was abundant on the planet so they could turn it into fuel. They'd offered the Phymordan government about two-and a-bit credit discs and some pretty jewellery for the entire yield. Norman had remembered seeing the response on the News-Cast from the government officials who were appalled at the pitiful offer. The Phymordan President had said that although he had been willing to help the Earth colonies with their fuel needs in the beginning, he would not sell his planet's minerals for the miserly sum offered. This really pissed off the colonies and its politicians, so now the minerals were going to be taken by force.

Getting back to the question of why he was needed? Norman could only hazard a guess. Perhaps there would be some plant samples he could take, if the fleet left anything standing after the invasion. Or more likely he was simply bound by a contract, and like it or not, he had to go where he was sent. He didn't care that much anyway. Soon the *Dragonfly* would be coming out of hyperspace with the rest of the fleet. Then his nausea would go away, and he would just stay put until it was over.

Aurelia sat watching the News-Cast in her lounge when Kyeldsen came shuffling in with another little boy.

'Hello, who do we have here?'

'This is Arnuu,' replied Kyeldsen cheerfully. 'We've become friends now. Could I go over to his place and have lunch with him?'

Arnuu morphed into his natural state and smiled. 'He's really welcome. I'm glad he finally came out to play with us.'

Aurelia looked pleasantly surprised then noticed something strange on her son's face. 'Kyeldsen, what's that on your fore-head? Is that a bruise?'

Kyeldsen's heart skipped a beat, and he took a step backwards. 'No Mother.' Harnessing what little energy he stored, he managed to transform the blue mark back to its natural pale colour. Aurelia frowned, then shrugged. 'I must have been imagining things.'

Arnuu breathed a sigh of relief that the boy's mother could be so easily fooled. The last thing he wanted was to get into trouble for picking on her son.

She rubbed her chin thoughtfully. 'Well, I don't know whether I should let you go.'

'Oh please,' implored Kyeldsen. 'I'll be good.'

'It's not that ...'

He grinned at her. 'I'll even eat a Mol-Ener Bar before I leave.'

Aurelia laughed, pleasantly surprised. 'Goodness! This is new.' She gave Arnuu a dazzling smile. 'I think you'll have to come around here more often.'

'Does that mean I can go?'

'All right but be back before sunset, at least two segments before.'

Kyeldsen gave her a big hug. She placed an arm around her son, then ushered both children into the kitchen.

'Well that was certainly easy,' said Arnuu after Kyeldsen had finished his Mol-Ener Bar. They were walking back outside to find the other children.

Kyeldsen grimaced. 'I hate those bars. They taste like mine-waste.'

Arnuu cackled. 'Well if you can't even stomach one of those, how are you going to take seeing an execution you little *non*?'

Kyeldsen shot him a murderous look. 'You have no idea how strong I can be when I set my mind to it.'

Arnuu poked out his tongue; he did not like his playmate's ferocious tone, nor the strange feeling it gave him.

Den Taln Marg was handed a simple brown robe to wear while waiting in his cell. The guards had already attached a molecular inhibitor bracelet around his spindly wrist to keep him in his natural state, which meant the robe was far too big for him. Marg hated it but he hated his pathetic weakened, natural state more.

He refused to touch his final meal, successfully smearing the mushy contents across the bleak stone walls in a last act of defiance. The guards consciously ignored his behaviour as Den Taln Marg's miserable fate had been sealed segments ago. There was nothing more he could possibly do but wait for his termination.

Margh however, felt nothing but contempt for this world and its petty justice system and was extremely sorry that he had not killed more people when he'd had the opportunity. He considered the Phymordan ability to transform was a powerful weapon that could be used to exploit the universe but the feeble government and its puny citizens would have none of it. Fine. If they didn't want that power to be realised, then they deserved to die. He had taken care of that, and he felt neither fear nor regret when the guards returned to take him on his final journey.

Tox waited for Arnuu and Kyeldsen to return, burdened with an uneasy feeling. What if something went wrong when they tried to infiltrate the execution? What if they were caught? Would they be tried as minors by the justice system and sent to jail, just because Arnuu and the others were daring Kyeldsen to go? She didn't want to think about such consequences but the more she tried to shut out the awful possibilities, the more anxious she became.

'What's the matter with you?' complained Jogih, noting Tox's troubled expression. He had returned with a large sack slung over his muscular shoulders and once he dropped the bag on the ground, his brawny shape shimmered to reveal his natural state.

'Nothing,' snapped Tox. 'What could possibly be wrong?'

Jogih shrugged then opened the sack revealing several different sized costumes. 'You tell me. You look as if you don't want to come with us.'

Tox knelt and pulled out a loose white toga from the bag. 'I wish I didn't have to but I'm worried that you'll all get into trouble if I don't.'

Jogih snorted. 'My father is a court guard. If we're caught, he'll be able to get us out of trouble.'

'Didn't I hear you say to Arnuu that you were worried about doing this though?'

Jogih pulled out another white toga and slipped it over his head. 'It doesn't matter what I said. If Kyeldsen wants to be in our group then he has to do this and you, Arnuu and I have to make sure that he goes through with it.'

Tox sighed then put on her toga just as Arnuu and Kyeldsen came walking up the hill. Kyeldsen looked pale and tired, his form almost more see-translucent than normal and he immediately sat down on the ground, trying to catch his breath.

'The little *non* can't stand the pace,' stated Arnuu cruelly.

'Shut up,' retorted Tox, as she handed the boy a toga.

Kyeldsen took it giving her a puzzled look. 'What's this for?'

'A disguise,' replied Jogih before Tox could reply. 'Each person who attends an execution always wears a neutral white wrap over their natural state. My father says it's the law.'

Kyeldsen pulled the toga over his body and stood up. The neck hole sagged down to his belly and the hem dragged behind his painfully thin legs. Arnuu cackled loudly, pointing rudely at the boy. 'It's too big. He'll never be able to convince anyone that he's an adult.'

Kyeldsen growled his displeasure and tore it off. 'I won't wear it then! I don't care!'

'You have to,' commanded Jogih. 'What did I just say? We all must wear one.'

'I won't go then! I hate you. I hate you all!'

Arnuu picked up the discarded toga and pulled it over himself. It fitted perfectly. 'You're just afraid. You don't want to see how they execute criminals.'

'I'm not!' the boy spat, his face turning red with fury. He bent over the sack and began rummaging around in desperation. 'I'll find one that fits.' He cast a contemptuous glance at Arnuu. 'Only someone who's fat could have fitted into that one.'

Arnuu glowered and was about to say something equally nasty when Tox shook her head as if to say *please don't start this again*. So, he made a face at her instead then sulked until Kyeldsen was ready.

A line of black-robed Phymordans assembled in the Court-Chamber waiting for the signal to proceed. The chamber doors opened then a loud bell chimed in discord, and the group marched down a stone corridor; their steps synchronised with each further chime. They turned at a junction where six guards stood armed and waiting to take Den Taln Marg into their custody. Marg stood passively, scratching his arm that wore the molecular inhibitor.

'And about time too,' said Marg in mock reproof. 'We cannot allow the public to wait for my performance forever, you know.'

The guards ignored him, waiting for their superior. When a purple-robed Phymordan appeared from behind, they moved to one side allowing him to walk to the front of the procession.

'Ah,' exclaimed Marg, busily straightening his brown robe. 'I must look my best for the great Dissector.'

The Dissector gave him a pained look before replying. 'You are not charged to speak.'

'Dear me. I must apologise. Will I be punished for that do you think?'

The Dissector sighed gravely. 'Your foolish banter does nothing for your case.'

Marg's sarcastic expression turned venomous. 'What could I possibly do to make it worse? Would you dissect me first, then repair me, then dissect me again?'

One of the guards grabbed hold of Marg's spindly arm and dug his thick fingers into the flesh. 'Silence.'

The criminal sucked in his breath but refused to cry out. He would never give them the satisfaction.

The Dissector cocked his head. 'You can make some amends by dying honourably, you know.'

Marg's face turned white from the pain. Then the Dissector held up a hand. 'Release him.'

The guard took his hand away and Marg doubled over holding his injured arm.

'I do not take pleasure in another's pain,' explained the Dissector. Marg grunted contemptuously. 'But I know that you do.' The Dissector held out a hand and the chief guard handed him a small metal device. He activated a switch, and the molecular inhibitor beeped. 'That is to make certain you do not escape when we enter the amphitheatre.'

Marg looked suspiciously at the bracelet around his wrist.

'If you try to escape,' continued the Dissector calmly. 'It will send a signal to the neural network of your brain and burn out your mind.'

'Perhaps a welcome alternative to my execution,' murmured Marg thoughtfully.

The Phymordan slowly shook his head. 'The pain you will endure when you are executed will only last a few moments. The agony from destroying your mind would last several cycles.' He stepped forward menacingly. 'It would be a slow lingering death Den Taln Marg.'

A bright silver hovercraft flitted out of the clouds and came to settle on the ground beside the crystal spires of the city. The dust swirled beneath the base of the craft and a door slid open. A cheerful face on a round head attached to several mercury-coloured tentacles slithered out of the craft and winked at the four nervous children, waiting.

'Good afternoon Madam,' he nodded at Tox then smiled at the boys. 'Sirs.'

Tox cleared her throat. 'Yes, good afternoon. We wish to be taken to the Court ...'

'Ah,' he waved a tentacle as if reading their thoughts. 'I bet you're going to that execution then eh?' He shook his head. 'Nasty piece of work that Den Taln Marg. He deserves all he gets.'

Tox smiled weakly. 'Indeed.' She glanced at her friends for support. 'But we don't want to be late.'

The driver waggled several tentacles in excitement. 'Certainly not. I promise you we'll get you there, no trouble at all. With *Light Speed Taxis—*,' he patted the matte black logo in bold lettering across the side of the craft, 'we'll get you there on time.'

Tox frowned, wondering if the driver was the same one she had seen on a holo-advertisement for the taxi-company. He certainly looked the type.

'Well in you go then, strap yourselves in.' He helped the children into their seats then jumped into the driver side. He turned around and gave them a curious look. 'Pardon me for asking but you are over the legal age, aren't you?'

'Of course,' said Tox, somewhat nervously. 'We've seen many executions.'

'It's just our size, isn't it?' said Kyeldsen sadly. 'We don't look big enough to be adults.'

The driver shifted his tentacles uncomfortably. 'Well ...'

'It affects everyone in our family you know.' He pointed to Arnuu, Jogih and Tox. 'My brothers and sister and I have stunted growth syndrome.'

The driver looked embarrassed. 'Really? Why's that?'

'Our mother lived near the mines before we were born, and she inhaled too much mine-waste gas.' Kyeldsen leaned forward, dropping his voice. 'It stunted our growth in the incubation stage. But you wouldn't say anything, would you?' The boy gave a heart-felt sigh. 'It's very embarrassing.'

'Of course not. It's courageous of you to speak about it at all.'

Kyeldsen leaned back in his seat with a smug expression on his face; he had risen in Arnuu's and Jogih's estimation but Tox's guilt intensified.

The taxi driver entered his code into the hover craft's computer system, released the gravity lock then pulled on the wheel and the craft launched quickly into the sky.

'Beautiful day for an execution,' said the driver conversationally. 'I'd go myself but I've got a wife and two kids to feed so I've got to work today.'

Kyeldsen and his companions nodded politely while gazing through the windows at the birds-eye view of the outstretched land. To the east were the rocky hills and valleys of the Purple Mountains and to the west were the farming plains that looked like giant patchwork quilts made up of maturing vegetables. Looking over the shoulder of the driver in the front seat the children spotted the imposing building that was the Court-Chamber and the amphitheatre that stood beside it. They could already see hundreds of Phymordans looking like tiny dots milling around the gates. The hovercraft dipped and the driver engaged the gravity lock, bringing the taxi with a soft wump to the ground beside the amphitheatre entrance. The driver turned around and held out a tentacle. 'That'll be ten credits thanks.'

Jogih handed him a disc marked with a black strip and the driver fed it into the computer. After a few seconds the disc popped out with half the strip removed. 'Excellent,' approved the driver, handing the card back to Jogih. 'You're an honest family.'

'Honest?' Tox felt worse than before.

The driver nodded and lowered his voice as if concerned that someone else might hear him. 'Yes well, I shouldn't really be telling you this but since you were honest with me about your er, health ...'

Tox cringed.

'You may wonder why I appear to be a deca-tentacle life form?'

Tox shrugged and the others nodded, vaguely interested.

'Well, there's many a passenger that's tried to give me a fake credit disc then make a run for it before the computer tells me it's counterfeit. So, I decided I'd sprout a few extra arms so I could keep my front tentacles on the computer in front of me, while my back tentacles would be ready if I ever needed to grab anyone.' He demonstrated by gently seizing Jogih's arm. The boy still gasped in surprise. 'Anyway,' he continued cheerfully, 'enough of my chattering, out you get and enjoy yourselves!'

The children got out of the taxi and Jogih pocketed what was left of his credit disc. 'So much for this.'

Arnuu looked at him. 'What do you mean?'

'I got a twenty-credit disc from my father last birthing-cycle and this taxi ride just wiped half of it.'

The taxi driver fortunately missed Jogih's comment and waved cheerfully then closed the door to his craft and launched it back into the sky. Tox waved back then looked around trying to get her bearings, while the three boys stared goggle-eyed at the imposing stone gates of the amphitheatre. Kyeldsen looked in awe at the fine detail of historical etchings that had been carved into the stone; it told the story of the power struggles of the Ancients of Phymord when they had once been warriors.

The children wound their way through the citizens mingling in the doorway and Kyeldsen touched the edge of one gate. Instead of feeling hard and rough, it felt smooth and smelt of metal rather than rock. The others also touched the surface and gave one another puzzled looks, trying to work out what type of metal it was.

'What's this made of?' asked Arnuu.

'Denzium,' a rich, deep voice replied.

The children swivelled around fearing that their cover had just been exposed. A male standing as tall as Tox smiled at them pleasantly. 'Are you interested in mining materials, or just curious to know how the effect of the plane was achieved?'

Tox's mouth felt dry and she shook her head but Kyeldsen stepped forward electing to be spokesperson. 'My brother was just wondering how the surface can feel so smooth when it looks like rock.'

The man chuckled. 'A wonderful refining process is the answer. Raw Denzium when mined, looks like red clay, but once purified, it turns to sheets of virtually indestructible plasty-glass. Once the process is complete it can either be used in the construction of buildings or mixed with chemicals to serve aesthetic purposes.' He pointed at the massive stone structure. 'This entire amphitheatre is made of refined Denzium with a hybrid of chemicals to make it appear as if it had been created from stone a thousand cycles ago.' He grinned at Kyeldsen. 'I daresay when we are long gone it will puzzle future archaeologists as to its age.'

Kyeldsen smiled then Jogih and Arnuu smiled as well, though not quite understanding what this stranger was talking about.

'My name is Tomer,' continued the stranger, 'and I invite you all to sit with me. It is most gratifying to see others like myself willing to be seen in public, despite being handicapped.'

Tox managed to find her voice and squeaked, 'handicapped?'

Tomer nodded pleasantly. 'Stunted growth syndrome. I see each of you suffer from the disease as I do?'

Kyeldsen smirked, priding himself on such good fortune. 'Yes we do.' Turning around he introduced the others—giving false names—then allowed Tomer to usher them through the gates of the amphitheatre, and to their seating.

Captain Adam Laroque stepped onto the bridge of the *Dragonfly* and breathed a triumphant sigh. The imposing scanner at the far end of the command deck was displaying random patterns of light, indicating that the ship was still travelling in hyperspace; his crew was busy monitoring the progress of the flight and of the fleet in turn. Everything was going to plan, and it would only be a matter of minutes before the fleet would exit hyperspace and appear in the Phymordan Sector. His ship would then make planet-fall near the capital city, and he would enter the command for the force field to be activated. Once the *Dragonfly* was secure, he would give the order for the rest of the fleet to destroy what needed to be destroyed, then the mine would be his. Captain Adam Laroque would then become Admiral Adam Laroque at the tender age of twenty-two.

As he happily daydreamed about his power and promotion, Commander Nile stepped onto the bridge and gave him a winning smile. She had fashioned her chestnut brown hair into an old-style Earth braid, applied mascara and eyeliner to her deep blue eyes, and red lipstick to her full lips. Her navy-blue uniform was impeccably pressed: functional enough for the assignment the captain had set her, yet tight enough to accentuate her curvaceous figure. Laroque, instantly aroused, returned her smile.

'How long before we reach the sector, Captain?' she asked in honeyed tones.

Laroque cleared his throat before barking at one of his underlings seated at the navigation controls. 'ETA Bennett?'

Lieutenant Bennett, clearly annoyed at being addressed in such a fashion—since he was twenty years Laroque's senior, and been in several battles before *that* young puppy had even been weaned—swivelled around in his chair and gave him a blank look. If the captain couldn't even remember his rank, why should he answer his question at all? 'Pardon?'

Laroque narrowed his eyes, noting his patronising tone. 'I said ETA *Mr* Bennett.'

'He means estimated time of arrival,' said the young ensign at the navigation controls. Laroque gave the boy a look of annoyance and ordered him to return to his work.

'Oh, I see Captain,' replied Bennett, pretending to finally understand. 'Do you want the ET-*DOUBLE*-A-SAP?'

Laroque leaned towards Nile for help, clearly not understanding his lieutenant's little joke. The crew, however, secretly enjoyed it.

'He means do you want to know our time of arrival as soon as possible?' whispered Nile helpfully.

Laroque grunted and cleared his throat, graciously allowing Bennett his joke. 'As soon as possible Mr Bennett.'

The chief navigator nodded then swivelled back to the controls in front of him and entered in the command. 'Twenty-eight seconds Sir,' he confirmed.

Laroque licked his lips, tasting victory. He glanced at Nile who licked her lips in return.

Kyeldsen and the other children were given the honour of being seated in the front row of the amphitheatre with Tomer. He explained that the officials allowed the best seating for the handicapped. Tox felt more guilty than ever; Kyeldsen felt quite pleased; and Arnuu and Jogih, again failed to understand what the grown up was talking about.

'What does he mean?' whispered Arnuu to Tox.

'He means we have priority seating in the front row because we *suffer* from a disease.'

Kyeldsen looked at away with a haunted expression. 'We do suffer from it.'

The little girl gave him a searching look but he refused to make eye contact with her. Instead, Kyeldsen looked around the open theatre and watched as one by one all the seats were filled. When everyone was settled, a bell chimed, silencing the chatter. Immediately the voice of the President of Phymord was heard over the amphitheatre loudspeakers, relayed from his underground chamber in the heart of the city.

'Citizens of Phymord. It is my solemn duty to announce that His Excellency Lonsai le-Jut, the Dissector, shall execute the aggressor Den Taln Marg this day. May he die honourably to atone for his sins. Peace above all.'

Tox shivered and Arnuu and Jogih shared a nervous look; Kyeldsen however, seemed untroubled by what was about to happen.

On the platform before them a large, metal block was being covered with a black cloth by a court official. A second chime rang out then a pair of doors opened and a procession of black cloaked Phymordans walked slowly onto the stage. They stood flanking the doorway their arms crossed in front of them.

Tox felt as if she was going to faint but the boys seemed mesmerised by the strange proceedings. Tomer put a comforting hand on her shoulder.

'Is this your first execution?' he asked kindly.

'Yes.'

'Well if you begin to feel dizzy just turn your head away.'

Tox nodded nervously but despite her fear, turned her head towards the doors as Den Taln Marg appeared dressed in a brown robe flanked by two guards.

'Murderer!' shrieked a citizen, standing up.

'You killed my sister!' screeched another. 'I hope you die in agony as she did!'

Everyone started looking around and whispering. A court guard marched over to the two who had spoken and told them they would be evicted if they could not remain silent. Marg yawned, barely acknowledging his accusers.

The Dissector appeared from behind Marg and everyone in the amphitheatre collectively gasped. The purple robed figure walked slowly over to the block and bowed his head to the two guards. They bowed in return, then took hold of Marg's wrists and dragged him over to the block. Marg looked at his metal bracelet and suddenly thought that he should try and escape while he still had the chance but the Dissector had anticipated this and activated a switch on the control unit he held in his hand. Boiling pins and needles seared through Den Taln Marg's brain, and he cried out in agony. The Dissector de-activated the unit and Marg fell, panting.

'I warned you Marg.'

The criminal groaned. 'I thought you said it would only kill me if I tried to run away.'

'As long as you wear the bracelet it determines your thought processes. Even contemplating escape constitutes escape itself.'

Marg's body slumped as the guards hoisted him up onto the block then attached clamps to his spindly legs and arms.

He opened his mouth and gasped. 'Don't do this. Please!'

The Dissector clicked his fingers, and a guard ceremoniously handed him a silver knife; the blade shimmered in the sunlight.

Tox's heart started pumping wildly and she could feel the perspiration tickling her armpits. Jogih and Arnuu felt equally afraid but tried not to show it. Kyeldsen however sat transfixed.

'Den Taln Marg,' declared the Dissector. His voice carried and echoed throughout the entire amphitheatre. 'You no longer have the privilege of being whole. You must be displaced. You must never again be complete.'

Marg's eyes widened in horror as the blade was lowered towards his torso. His face registered fear and disbelief, then as the blinding agony of the Dissector's knife began its work, he screamed in terror.

Tox cried out in fear and buried her head in Tomer's shoulder; Jogih and Arnuu's innocence was taken from them and obliterated.

Kyeldsen stared in horrified fascination as Marg's bloodcurdling cries ceased. The Dissector quietly continued to slice through the criminal's body. After completing the incisions, he carefully lifted Den Taln Marg's organs from his body and placed them symmetrically beside the open cavity.

The audience sat transfixed in the eerie silence. Then the silence was broken by the unexpected sound of an explosion.

The *Dragonfly* had made planet-fall by early afternoon, Phymordan time. The surveillance screenings at the planet's spaceport some fifty kilometres away had not detected any ship pass through their atmosphere, as the *Dragonfly* was equipped with detection dampeners. This rendered them invisible to any form of exposure if the ship was no larger than 800 metres in diameter. Coupled with this the captain had ensured that the ship was cloaked, and all force fields were operational.

Norman Queltayler felt the soft wump of the ship touching ground and the familiar sensation of his room vibrating when the exhaust ports spewed out hot steam. His stomach was finally settling now that he was back in real space, and he contentedly pulled the blanket over himself, rolled over in bed and dropped off to sleep.

Captain Laroque hailed the commanders of the ten ships exiting hyperspace and instructed them to orbit the planet until he gave the order to fire. The crew who had been handpicked to accompany Commander Nile to carry out the ground battle were making certain that they each carried all necessary equipment for the offensive. They all wore protective anti-radiation and heat/cold sensitive suits and carried out checks on their personal force field (FF) activators.

Nile punched in a code on her wrist computer and the data sent to the men scrolled passed her eyes. 'Make certain your FF activators are in working order. I will not be held responsible if you are shot at and the assault punctures your suit and ultimately yourself. Understand?'

The men checked that their force fields were impenetrable, then confirmed with a 'Ma'am'.

'Weaponry,' Nile stated firmly.

The group attached phasers, timed explosives, and molecular scramblers to their waist belts. Nile walked up and down the line, nodding approvingly, clearly enjoying the power that she felt with thirty men under her. The notion amused her in more ways than one.

'Make sure the scramblers are calibrated correctly. If you fire at a shifter and you have not made the necessary calculations, the weapon will interfere with your personal force field then ultimately you will mutate until you resemble a jellified mess. Take it from me, it is not a pretty sight and I will not tolerate any casualties, if by some miracle you survive your own negligence.'

Captain Laroque walked briskly into the ready room and looked proudly at Nile and his men. 'Do not let me down,' he announced dramatically. 'The colonies are depending on you. I am depending on you.' He looked at Nile. 'When this offensive is declared a success, there will be rewards in promotion and wealth.'

Nile smiled and delicately removed a compact from her hip pocket and applied a touch more rouge to her cheeks. Her crew looked at her appreciatively then Laroque requested a private word with the commander. She followed him into the corridor where he tried to kiss her but she gently pushed him away.

'Must keep my mind on the task,' she whispered teasingly, and kissed the tip of his nose.

Laroque fought the urge to grab her again, instead wishing her and her team success. When the captain was no longer in sight, Nile cast a contemptuous glance in his direction. When the battle was won she would get promoted *and* get the hell off this stinking rust bucket and away from his stinking command—as well as other things. She grimaced at the memories then returned to the ready room where her crew had already donned safety helmets. She fitted hers over her head then activated the hull door. Bright sunshine spilled in through the hatchway.

Laroque returned to the bridge and flipped a switch on the panel before him. Ten faces appeared on the scanner, displaying the ten commanders of the fleet. 'I have despatched the ground offensive of thirty-one officers who are heading for the Presidential Palace in the city. Fire power is to be concentrated there before the ground offensive takes place. Commander Nile is waiting for these orders to be carried out before she starts her mission.'

The commanders nodded.

'Commander Darol.'

The middle-aged man on the screen looked directly at his captain. 'Yes Sir?'

'Take the *Vulture* to the co-ordinates I am now sending you and cover the mines. They must be protected from accidental damage. The rest of you.' He grinned cruelly and lifted his fist. 'Destroy it all.'

The amphitheatre rumbled with the vibrations of explosions and the crowd jumped up in fear and confusion. The Dissector looked up beyond the clouds to see a black spot growing larger by the second. A bright flash lit up the sky and a spear of light shot through the atmosphere and exploded the gates of the theatre. The Denzium compound shattered in a shower of tumbling glass and everyone started screaming.

'What's happening!' shrieked Tox above the confused and terrified cries.

'It's a ship!' replied Tomer, pointing to the sky. He could hardly believe what he was about to say. 'We're being attacked!'

There were people running everywhere in bewildered terror, knocking into each other, trying to flee from the holocaust. Another blast from the approaching black spot revealed as a fighter ship—exploded the walls of the amphitheatre destroying dozens of Phymordans with it. Their blackened, twisted bodies stood frozen in mid air then collapsed into dust.

Tomer grabbed hold of Tox's hand, and called after Arnuu, Jogih and Kyeldsen, trying to push them through the chaotic sea of people.

'I can't change!' squealed a woman, hopelessly. 'I want to fly away but I can't change!'

'It's fear,' another woman shouted. 'You must concentrate otherwise you're finished!'

The first woman cried out, toppling over as the frenzied crowd crushed her under its feet.

Tomer pushed the children through, receiving cuts and bruises from the crowd equally desperate to get away. They climbed over the fragments of the theatre but Kyeldsen tripped over gashing his arm on a jagged piece of Denzium. He cried out in pain and Tomer turned around, running back to him. He grabbed hold of the boy and dragged him out of the stampede that would have crushed them all a moment later.

'Are you all right?' he shouted to the boy, trying to examine the cut.

Kyeldsen brushed tears away from his eyes. 'I think so.'

'Here,' said Tomer. He tore off a piece of his toga and wound the material around the boy's arm to staunch the bleeding. 'We mustn't give in to fear.' he said firmly. 'We've all got to get away from here and the only way to do that is to concentrate and change into some sort of flying creature. It doesn't have to be elegant but we must have wings, it's our only hope.'

Tox grabbed hold of Arnuu's hand and looked up as the black ship that resembled an insect opened fire again. 'Look out!'

Tomer swivelled around and screamed, 'it's too late! Run!'

The group ran as a mixture of fear and adrenaline flooded their systems. Kyeldsen followed, trying to keep up but his weakened state was beginning to catch up with him and he flagged behind. Another explosion rocked the ground, and he slowed down, gasping for breath, realising that he had lost the others. Where were they? He turned around to see the insect ship dip over the amphitheatre finally destroying it completely, leaving nothing but a blackened hole. It then concentrated its firepower on the survivors below. Kyeldsen held his throbbing arm and started running back looking for his companions.

Dodging blasts and terrified Phymordans, he shouted their names until he was hoarse. He tried thinking rationally, retracing his steps to where he had been separated from them. He stumbled back, where the remains of the amphitheatre stood and saw four small forms scattered in the debris.

The taxi driver injected the accelerator to top speed, tearing across the sky, back to the amphitheatre. He had just narrowly missed being atomised by a fleet of fighters firing at the city. This was madness. Who were they? Why were they destroying everything? He set the scanner and checked for the location of the amphitheatre. The spot was still the same but on visual it was now a blackened, smoking heap. He could see from his readings that there were expired life forms scattered everywhere and he prayed that his four little friends whom he had seen only a short time ago were not among them.

An insect fighter high above jetted over him, sending him into a spiral spin. He grabbed hold of the instruments and dragged his craft back on course, cursing loudly. When he reached the ruined theatre, he throttled off and partially engaged the gravity lock, bringing him closer to the ground. He spotted a little pale form, kneeling beside four black sticks and landed close by. The driver threw open the door and jumped out.

'Hey!' he shouted. 'Are you all right?'

The little form wailed in anguish, beating his head with his hands. The taxi driver scuttled over on all ten tentacles and gasped at the sight. The little fellow was not surrounded by four black sticks but by four dead Phymordans. The shock and realisation of this had sunk in, returning him to his natural state.

'They're dead,' he cried over and over again.

The taxi driver grimaced and placed an arm around the child. 'I came back to look for you and your brothers and sister.'

Kyeldsen looked up at him, still clutching his throbbing arm. What's happening?'

'I don't know,' the driver replied desperately. 'Some sort of invasion force is trying to wipe us out. I've got to get you away from here.'

Kyeldsen nodded vaguely, dazed and in shock by what was happening.

'I'm so sorry for your family,' consoled the Phymordan. 'But you must come quickly. Who knows when they'll return here to see if there's any survivors.'

Kyeldsen allowed himself to be guided towards the taxi then his stomach flipped over in terror. 'My mother.' He gave the driver a desperate look. 'What about my mother?'

'Where does she live?'

'Near the Purple Mountains. About a nano-segment's walk from the city.'

The driver swallowed. 'We'd better get back. The city's under attack as well.'

Aurelia ran out into the confused hubbub, screaming her son's name. A series of fighters swooped over the houses nearby, sending them up in smoke. She ducked then tripped over, shielding her ears with both hands. Other Phymordans were calling out

228

desperately for their families and loved ones, each not knowing if the other was still alive. Why was the President not ordering a counterattack? *Peace above all* was the Phymordan way of life, but how could he sit in the Palace beneath the city and witness such devastation?

Her servo-bot came trundling out of the house after her shouting: 'alert, alert! Danger! Take cover! Alert, alert!'

Aurelia jumped up and felt a shadow swallow the sun. She looked up to see a large insect-like ship open a port in its metallic belly and fire. She screamed and ran back to the house; the servo-bot was atomised.

Kyeldsen sat staring anxiously through the window of the taxi, as the hovercraft tore back to the city. He forgot about his bleeding arm as his whole being was consumed with fear for his mother, together with a growing hatred toward the invaders—whoever they were.

Nile wandered through the destroyed city, exultant to the extreme. She had been very close to picking out one of her younger, handsome officers to *satisfy* her triumphant state but the stupid fool had forgotten to calibrate his scrambler just as her crew blasted open the President's quarters. True, he had jellified the Phymordan guards when they tried to intervene but he had also jellified himself as well. Now thanks to him her suit was a filthy mess with his remains splattered all over it. When the mission was over, she would have to requisition a new one.

It had been so incredibly easy. At first, she thought it had been too easy. How could the President allow his world to have absolutely no defences? She had asked him that nagging question before placing him under arrest. He had told her that hundreds of years before, Phymordans had been extremely aggressive, and delighted in warfare. They had fought with many species until they waged a chemical war with a neighbouring planet, destroying it completely and practically crippling Phymord in the process. From that day on, Phymord dispensed with every weapon and became entirely passive, concentrating on creating and preserving life; only disciplining aggressors as the last resort. The war that changed Phymord forever had lasted a mere twenty minutes.

So their pathetically, benign ways had cost them their planet anyway. It would not have come to this if they had given the colonies what they wanted, but they refused, so naturally the next step was to take whatever was needed by force.

The commander watched her ground force clamp a molecular inhibitor around the President's arm and march him back to the *Dragonfly*. Mission was almost complete.

Nile headed back to the ship, stepping over the jellified remains of Phymordans and city debris then suddenly looked up as a small hovercraft dipped and banked over the city then came to rest a short distance away. Commander Nile checked her phaser and started to run towards it.

'Quick! Open the door!' demanded Kyeldsen.

The taxi driver did as he was instructed and the little boy jumped out. He expected the driver to follow and turned around. 'Come on, help me!'

The driver's look was sad. 'I've got a wife and two kids to find first. Take care of yourself. I promise I'll be back as soon as I find them.'

Kyeldsen watched him close the door then launch back into the sky. A moment later the craft disappeared from view.

The little boy looked around in dazed disbelief at the ruined houses and smoking, blackened city. Everything he had ever known was gone forever. The city spires, the neighbouring homes, the people ... he turned around and ran towards his house but suddenly the forgotten pain from his injured arm reasserted itself and he doubled over in agony. He peeled back the stained cloth to examine the wound, but his head began to swim and his mind plunged into darkness.

Nile wandered over to where the hovercraft had landed, kicking at the dust where the craft had left indentations on the ground. She tapped the communicator on her wrist to inform Captain Laroque of her whereabouts but was sidetracked by the sight of a small form lying motionless. She walked over to it and noticed its arm was a bloody mess. Leaning over it, she was startled by a desperate cry up ahead. She turned to find a woman with long violet curls crying convulsively near a half-ruined house. Nile readied her phaser and fired a warning shot. The woman jumped back in fear, instantly returning her to her natural state.

'Who are you? What do you want?'

Nile regarded the specimen with detached curiosity. She undid her helmet and threw it on the ground, brushing stray strands of hair from her eyes. 'I am Commander Eleanor Nile of Earth Colony Delta VI. We are claiming this planet for the mine and its yield.'

Aurelia gave her a horrified look. 'You killed and destroyed everything. You killed my son.'

Nile tapped her chin thoughtfully. 'I'm not quite sure about that. Was he in the city at the time?'

Aurelia shrugged hopelessly, not fully understanding why she was even speaking with this unknown enemy. 'He was with a group of friends.'

Nile smiled sweetly and aimed her phaser at the woman. 'Well good for him.'

The fog in Kyeldsen's mind gradually dissipated and he managed to find his feet, albeit unsteadily, and walk the rest of the way home. The house was wrecked but his mother was still alive! He could see her. He could see her with another humanoid aiming something at her. He felt fear then the fear slowly festered into hatred.

'As much as I've enjoyed our little chat, I'm afraid I'm going to have to leave you now and return to my ship. The mission is nearly at Final Phase you see.' Commander Eleanor Nile smiled again and took out her lipstick. Aurelia watched in horrified fascination as this human smeared red colour across her mouth. Aurelia's eyes flickered to a sudden movement up ahead—it was her beloved son.

Nile dropped the lipstick, noticing where the other woman's eyes had strayed. She turned around to see an injured life form running towards her.

'Mother!' he called desperately.

Aurelia screamed, 'no! Get back! You'll be killed!'

Nile laughed at the tiny figure growling angrily, getting closer and closer. 'Let's see if this will take the wind out of your sails.' Nile replaced the phaser in her pocket and picked up her helmet, secured it on her head then grabbed the molecular scrambler. She turned towards Aurelia and fired.

Time stopped. Time started slowly. Fear gripped. Fear stopped. Fury set in.

Kyeldsen froze as waves of emotions swept over his senses as he witnessed his mother screaming in agony. Her spindly arms twisted around her while her body spun out of control, gradually melting away until she became a bubbling mess of nothing. He stood stock still, traumatised by the hideous display, while Commander Nile blew at the tip of the molecular scrambler as if she were playing a scene from an old Earth 2-D Western.

'Bulls eye,' she declared triumphantly, throwing back the visor of her helmet. She nonchalantly looked at the little shifter frozen to the spot. 'You'll take root if you stand there much longer.' Nile laughed at her own joke.

Kyeldsen could have sworn that he heard someone talking to him, but it must have been his imagination. This was all a dream. This was the sort of dream he had just after his father was killed in the mining accident. Kyeldsen hadn't actually witnessed the incident but in his dreams he had. He could still see his father burning alive in front of him as he plummeted to his death after saving a group of miners. This was just like that dream, but instead it was his mother who was burning. It was she who was leaving him to fend for himself. It was she who was twisting and melting. Bubbling and melting and twisting ...

Kyeldsen blinked twice and looked down at his injured arm. The blood had congealed but his skin felt tight and it still hurt. You couldn't feel the hurt in a dream. A single tear dripped down his cheek and he turned to see who was standing before him. When a Phymordan was gripped with fear, it prevented any transformation. But when a Phymordan was angered, a sudden burst of adrenaline would change him into a raging fury.

Commander Nile looked at the child and laughed. Such a weak little squirt with an annoyed expression across his shadowy face. She would delight in scrambling this piece of sludge.

The blood boiled in Kyeldsen until his every fibre wanted to hit out and destroy. He could feel the molecules in his body finally twisting and changing until he exploded into molten lava, spewing out hot flame in anger and desperation. Nile jumped back, clearly shocked and afraid at the display. She had not realised that this injured native could demonstrate such aggression, particularly after finding out that the Phymordans had long abandoned their aggression and warmongering.

She raced out of the way, trying to jam her visor back into place as the FF activator would be useless unless her suit was sealed. She finally managed to lock it in place as Kyeldsen's rage washed over her but the force field and suit protected her from the assault.

Kyeldsen growled but his strength dissipated rapidly and his molten form morphed back into its natural state. He collapsed on the ground and passed out.

Nile grinned at the shivering bundle and calibrated her scrambler, aiming it at the child.

Kyeldsen dreamed for a moment. He dreamed of the time when he had a virus that almost killed him. He could see his mother anxiously hovering close by, as the Elders shook their heads in despair.

'Is there nothing you can do?' Aurelia asked, tears prickling her eyes.

The Elders sighed and murmured to each other. 'If his fever does not break, then he will collapse into a coma then die.'

Nile pushed up the visor of her helmet once again, checking to ensure that the calibration was one hundred percent correct. She stood over the child and was about to relock the helmet when suddenly the shifter's eyes snapped open smiling cruelly at her. It then disappeared. Nile jumped back and swivelled around on the spot. What was it doing? Playing a game of cat and mouse? She started to perspire and she wiped the droplets away from her forehead. Strange. It wasn't that hot, was it? She quickly checked her wrist communicator for the status of her suit. It was functioning normally. Then why was she feeling so hot?

She walked a few steps and suddenly felt very tired. Why did she feel tired? No, it wasn't tiredness, it was something else. She felt ill. Her head felt hot, so hot that it felt like a ball of fire. She felt as if she was going to burst. She felt faint. Nile felt bile rising in her throat and she passed out.

Kyeldsen travelled through her bloodstream, observing and learning how the human body functioned. He travelled to the base of her neck, making certain that he did not disturb her spinal column or nervous system. When he was satisfied that Kyeldsen/Virus had raised her temperature to the point of driving her to lose consciousness, he morphed into pure thought. Kyeldsen felt a rush of air as he travelled across the blackened abyss that was the human's mind. The human was a female and her name was Eleanor Nile and she was a commander on a ship stationed close by called the *Dragonfly*. It was invisible to the naked eye but not to Kyeldsen anymore.

Kyeldsen saw memories floating through her sub-conscious, like books peeling back their leaves:

Eleanor was a child.

She lived on a planet settled by Earth called Delta VI. Her mother was a maintenance worker, employed to clean apartment domes of the rich and powerful. Her father was ... was a shadow. He had died when Eleanor was four years old and she had met him only once. Her mother had not been pair-bonded to him as he was a science officer and she a lowly cleaner. He had promised her mother that he would take care of her, but they were together for only one night, then never again.

Eleanor's mother had told her that he had gone away on a secret mission to the stars. Eleanor believed her mother until she was thirteen. The other children in her school teased her when they found out the truth about her parents. How did they find out? Eleanor discovered that they had stolen some DNA samples from the colony labs and matched them with samples from her father.

Kyeldsen felt a gust of hot air swirl around him and wondered how long this human would survive before the fever destroyed her mind forever. He certainly did not wish to be trapped in here when that eventuated, so he sped on more hastily through her remaining memories.

Eleanor's mother died when she was sixteen and Eleanor joined Fighter Command. Her beauty and talent allowed her to breeze through the training. She made certain that she slept with every official, politician, and flight officer in return for higher status. She had an affair with Grand Admiral Robert Laroque that lasted several months before he bought her a commission on the *Dragonfly*. The mission was to seize the mines of Phymord then destroy the planet in its entirety. When Grand Admiral Laroque placed his son in charge of the fleet, she soon began an affair with the son.

She was impure, ambitious and vain. Her beauty was accentuated with artificial colour to her eyes, lips and cheeks. She was a cold-blooded murderer who deserved to die. All those like her deserve to die.

Kyeldsen felt a lurch in her sub-consciousness so removed himself from her system, reappearing in his natural state, beside the prostrate woman just in time. Her face was red yet she was shivering, and she was murmuring unintelligibly. Kyeldsen sat wheezing and shuddering, watching the human, while wondering if he was ever going to be able to find the necessary energy to morph again. Nile cried out and her eyes snapped open. She turned her head towards the child, then the virus Kyeldsen had infected her with finally completed its task. Gingerly, Kyeldsen felt for the woman's pulse. There was none.

Kyeldsen sat beside the dead woman for several moments, unsure of what to do next. He hadn't realised that it was possible to morph into pure energy when he was so weak but he'd been possessed with such vicious loathing for the human that it suddenly felt completely natural to do so. Of course, after the event he felt like a gutted shell and almost decided to give in there and then, and die beside his mother's murderer ... his mother's murderer? How could he even contemplate such a thing? Everything felt like a horrible, bizarre dream, as if he were watching the events that were passing instead of experiencing them firsthand. He shifted his weight uncomfortably as the throbbing in his arm brought him rudely back to reality and he stared at Eleanor Nile and her horrid painted face. He hated her with every fibre of his being. He hated the humans who had destroyed his world and while he had been privy to the woman's thoughts, he decided to adopt an old Earth saying—an eye for an eye. As the humans obliterated everything he had ever known; he would in turn obliterate them. He tried standing up but his legs would not obey him and he toppled over, on top of the dead woman. He grimaced as his hand accidentally slipped into one of the belt pockets that were fixed around her hips. He curled his fingers curiously around the foreign object inside and pulled it out.

It was flat and rectangular, the size of his palm. A silver substance covered the object and when he pulled the silver back it revealed several small blocks of brown all connected together. It didn't look like a weapon but it was hard to tell, and he couldn't remember any of the dead woman's memories showing this material at any stage. He smelt the *brown* but its aroma was nothing like he had ever encountered before.

The twin suns in the sky warmed his weary body and an unexpected brown paste melted onto his hand from the brown block. He dropped the substance onto the ground with a start. Not thinking clearly, he licked his fingers to remove the substance and was pleasantly surprised at how sweet the brown tasted. He slowly picked up the brown in its silver jacket and nibbled at a corner. That too tasted sweet and he suddenly felt the energy returning to his exhausted body. With quick resolve he wolfed the remainder of the brown then returned his attention to what now needed to be done:

1. Morph into Eleanor Nile.
2. Find the *Dragonfly*.
3. Stow away on board until a suitable body could be copied then disposed of.
4. Wait until the fleet returns to Delta VI then find a way of destroying everything. *Particularly females who have horrid painted faces.*

Norman Queltayler rolled over in bed and breathed a contented sigh. He was feeling so much better now and was trying not to think about the time when the *Dragonfly* would have to make the return jump to hyperspace for the journey home. He would deal with that nausea when it came. He opened his bleary eyes, wondering how Laroque's band of merry *destructioneers* were progressing. They probably had the whole thing wrapped up by now as Phymord was about as equipped for war as his stomach was for hyperspace. Still, he supposed they would be back soon with the President in the brig, the planet levelled and therefore no possibility of him attempting any plant cataloguing at all. If there had been any plant life which survived Laroque's attack, it would have had to have been made from solid star alloy with a couple of hundred force fields clamped around it.

Norman smiled at the absurdity then leaned forward and swung his legs to the floor, while kneading the kinks in his neck. He was about to fix himself a drink from the food dispenser that sat beside his prized potted Oulian cactus when he heard a gentle tap at the door. He sniffed in annoyance at this disturbance before placing his palm against the sensor-pad beside the doorway. The metal door slid open and he expected to find someone waiting for him but the corridor was empty. He glanced both ways then closed the door.

Activating the food dispenser, he ordered himself a soda water and took a sip, only to hear another tap at the door. He placed the glass on his bedside table and sighed heavily. 'What is it now?' He again activated the door but again the corridor was empty. By the time the third tap came his blood pressure was on the rise and he stormed over and slammed his hand against the sensor-pad.

'If this is another prank, I'll report you to our beloved little Captain, you pisshead!'

Expecting to find one of the officers who routinely delighted in practical jokes standing there laughing his fool head off, he was surprised to see Commander Nile leaning against the doorway. She had a smile on her lips but her eyes looked haunted.

'Commander Nile? Are you all right?' It was a simple enough question but it took the woman a few moments to reply.

'I feel tired,' she eventually replied. 'I need rest and I need some brown. A lot more brown.'

Norman frowned, wondering what she was talking about. 'Then why don't you rest in your own quarters?'

Nile shook her head slowly.

Norman wondered if something that had happened out there had affected her mind. She took a step forward and held out her hand. 'May I come in?'

Norman glanced behind him, imagining the hullabaloo that would occur if Laroque, or anyone else for that matter found them together *alone*, in his quarters. 'Let me take you back to your room. Or perhaps sickbay if you're not feeling well.'

'I'm fine,' she snapped harshly. 'Just allow me to rest and give me some brown!'

Norman gave her a quizzical look. 'Brown? What are you talking about?'

She dug her fingers into her belt pocket and thrust some torn silver paper into his hand. 'Brown! Brown! I must have some now, before ... before I ...' Her eyes rolled back into her head and she fell forward. Norman grabbed hold of her and half carried, half dragged her over to his bunk and laid her down. He hurried over to the food dispenser and ordered three blocks of chocolate, then came back to the bed and handed them to the drowsy woman. He watched her tear open the wrappers and wolf them down.

He shook his head in disbelief. 'Jeez, you don't seem yourself.'

The woman's eyes snapped open, and she smiled. 'I'm not.'

Norman watched in growing horror as her figure dissolved into shimmering light then reform into a thin, pale silhouette. He shrieked and ran to the door but suddenly felt as if he could move no further and collapsed on the floor. Kyeldsen slid off the bed and adjusted the phaser that had belonged to Nile, from stun to kill.

'Why?' Norman managed to utter in terror.

'You killed my people,' replied Kyeldsen quietly. 'You destroyed my world.' He aimed the phaser at Norman's head. 'And you also killed my mother.'

Norman squeezed his eyes shut as he heard the weapon fire. In that split second before he died, he thought of Muriel Cottland, a girl he hadn't seen since they were both fourteen. Why he'd never drummed up the courage to kiss her he would never know.

Captain Adam Laroque entered the bridge and received a triumphant round of applause from his fellow officers. He smiled and held up both hands trying to stem the rousing reception, though clearly enjoying the attention.

'My fellow officers, we have Phymord, or what it will be known as from hence forth—Earth Colony Laroque I, in honour of my distinguished father.'

The officers nodded to each other in agreement and there were supportive murmurs throughout.

'We each of us fought long and hard and I know that all our families back on Delta VI will be proud of our success.' His face grew solemn, and he held up one hand to stay the applause. 'However, there are always casualties of war, and it is with great sadness that I must report the death of Commander Eleanor Nile.'

'We found her remains on the edge of the city upon our return and buried her with full honours. She is not however, beneath the earth of an alien planet but has now become part of Laroque I. May she live on in her deeds and her bravery.'

Laroque bowed his head, and the other officers followed for a minute's silence out of respect for her passing.

'And now,' he continued briskly, 'we return to Delta VI, leaving three of our ships in this sector, waiting for the arrival of our President to perform the official take-over ceremony. This planet will then be known throughout the cosmos that it is ours and ours alone.'

The thunderous applause that followed fuelled the twenty-two-year-old captain's ego to new extremes. In that moment he had quite forgotten about Nile.

Kyeldsen dragged the body of Norman Queltayler outside the ship and dumped it beneath the retro rockets just as the troops returned. He swiftly morphed into Norman then hurried back inside. He was physically exhausted, and he needed more chocolate but that would have to wait.

Laroque, euphoric from his latest triumph, was bragging about the devastation wrought to the planet to several of his men. As they walked along the main passageway, he spotted Norman and demanded to know why he was not in his quarters.

'I needed some air,' replied Kyeldsen/Norman hastily.

'Over your bout of hyperspace syndrome, eh?' Laroque grinned at his fellow officers, and they laughed.

Kyeldsen returned the smile, oblivious to the sarcastic tone in the captain's voice. 'Yes Sir.'

'Then back to your quarters.' He then turned around declaring. 'We return to Delta VI ASAP, OTD!' He reaffirmed the two terms once again, feeling as always, superior when he used abbreviations. Two of his officers turned to each other and silently mouthed 'OTD?' What did that mean? A third whose name was Bennett according to the nametag on the man's uniform, whispered that OTD meant *on the double*. The captain did not hear Bennett speak, nor did he hear himself being called an idiot by the same officer.

Returning to Norman's quarters, Kyeldsen waited for the command for the ship's departure. He did not have to wait long as the voice of the computer placidly instructed all personnel to strap themselves in for take-off.

Kyeldsen did as he was instructed as the ship's engines began to rumble, then he felt his body being pressed firmly into the back of the seat as the ship rapidly left the planet's surface. He peered through the window, watching his world disappear before his eyes. He would never see it again, that was certain. When the computer confirmed that take off was complete, Kyeldsen unstrapped himself from the chair and stepped out into the corridor, experimenting with walking using the two strong legs he now possessed. He saw other human officers wandering by, not even glancing in his direction. Good. Better to be inconspicuous. A young red-headed officer, however, did take notice of him and stopped for a quick chat.

'Oh Mr Queltayler.'

Kyeldsen stopped walking and turned around. 'Yes?'

'How goes the nausea?'

Kyeldsen frowned. 'I don't have any.'

The man smiled and nodded sagely, evidently pleased. 'You see? Most of the time, no medicine is good medicine.'

Kyeldsen gave him a quizzical look but remained silent. This was obviously a conversation that had begun with the real Norman. 'Agreed.' Kyeldsen hoped that was the correct response. Apparently it was, and the man continued on his way.

Kyeldsen kept walking, until he felt completely comfortable in his new body and found himself on the bridge. There were humans everywhere, manning control stations, checking computer read-outs or observing the star fields floating by on the giant view screen.

The captain barked out a command to one of the officers. 'How long before calculations are complete to make the jump to hyperspace?'

'Calculations complete, on your mark Sir,' the officer replied.

Kyeldsen could see that the captain enjoyed the feeling of power as he watched him flex his fingers then clench them into a fist. 'Engage!'

The officer activated the controls then suddenly the screen filled with strobing, flashing lights.

'Hyperspace jump complete,' confirmed the officer.

Kyeldsen wondered what was going to happen next.

It had been a full cycle since the ship had left real space and Kyeldsen was worried. His food dispenser had broken down and he had asked for someone from maintenance to come down and repair it but so far no one had. It was getting harder and harder to maintain Norman Queltayler's shape, and once he had accidentally shimmered out of form before he reached his quarters. Fortunately, there had been no one around to see this but it was only a matter of time before someone did, then his cover would be blown.

He resolved to sneak into someone else's quarters and activate their food dispenser and stock up on the brown he so desperately needed for energy; so he waited and watched the other officers until deciding that the best food dispenser would naturally be in the captain's cabin. When Laroque left his quarters for the daily meeting, Kyeldsen shed Norman's image then morphed into the captain. This had drained what little energy he had left, and he knew that the shape would not hold for long. He quickly found the cabin and placed his hand on the outside sensor-pad and opened the door. Looking around the spacious room, with its reclining chairs, double bed, and fully stocked dispenser, he let out a small whoop of joy and quickly activated the device, collecting the chocolate with both hands. He did not notice someone enter the room behind him; someone who had forgotten to retrieve his daily reports for the meeting. Kyeldsen's delight nosedived and he spun around to see who had discovered him.

Captain Adam Laroque's mouth went dry with fear. 'You! Who are you? What the hell's going on?' Laroque's fright turned to anger. 'You're a bloody shifter! You're under arrest!'

Kyeldsen shimmered in terror which returned him to his natural state. He dropped most of the chocolate and tried to get away but Laroque grabbed hold of his arm. He squealed and concentrated until his arm morphed onto his opposite side, leaving Laroque clutching at air, as Kyeldsen ran out of the cabin.

The captain slammed his hand on a red button situated on the wall then brought his wrist computer to his lips. An alarm boomed throughout the ship. 'This is Captain Laroque. We have an intruder on our ship, I repeat, an intruder. He is a shifter and can transform into anyone or anything. Ready your molecular scramblers for *alien-scan*, then if positive, fire at will!'

Kyeldsen fled. He couldn't go back to Norman's quarters because it was too close to the captain's; he tried frantically to morph himself into pure energy but his fear kept him trapped in his natural state. He could hear the reverberating sounds of heavy boots on the metal floor and buried himself in a recess in the wall, hoping the shadows would hide him, and breathed a sigh of relief when the officers ran passed.

Eating the last of the chocolate in his possession he willed himself to calm down, then transformed back into Norman. As he walked unsteadily away from the wall four officers accosted him.

'I hope you catch him,' he said weakly, hoping that the form would hold. Three of the officers nodded.

'If you see anything, let us know,' instructed the fourth. Kyeldsen nodded nervously attempting to smile. The officer looked at him suspiciously.

'By the way Norman, has your nausea cleared up now that we're in hyperspace?'

Kyeldsen could feel his face turning red as he tried to remember what the ship's doctor had said to him. 'Yes thank you.'

The four officers nodded then walked away. Then it suddenly dawned on the officer that the *real* Norman suffered from nausea *within* hyperspace; he set his molecular scrambler to scan and directed it towards Norman—it registered positive.

'He's a fake! I've got him! Fire!'

Kyeldsen ran as the officers furiously calibrated their weapons and opened fire. He bolted into the first room that he came to with the men in hot pursuit. He tore around the area, frantically searching for another way out of what appeared to be the engineering room. When he realised that there was only one way in and out, he stopped dead, wailing loudly.

'You killed my mother! You killed my friends! You destroyed everything! Now you want to finish it and kill me!'

The engineers looked up from their work mildly amused, unaware that the botanist was in fact Kyeldsen, trying desperately to hold onto his shape. So what was Norman raving about this time? He must have been at the Zhique-wine again. Strong stuff if you took too much and it was evident to the crew that he must have knocked back a few too many and was beginning to hallucinate.

Kyeldsen looked at their faces, tears blurring his vision. His eyes came to rest upon a young woman with blue paint around her eyes and red paint on her mouth. He saw in his mind's eye Nile with her painted face killing his mother. He resolved to never surrender and just as the officers fired their scramblers, he disappeared into the ether.

Kyeldsen felt sick as his mind and body warped and spun and stretched and retracted across the vortex. He wasn't sure whether he would survive morphing into energy, then jettisoning his form into hyperspace but so far, he was complete. Or as complete as the vortex would allow him to be.

He could see strange colours bend and twist around him and he felt as if the entire universe was crawling through his form. His form jerked suddenly, thrusting him into the fourth dimension and he knew for certain that he would not survive for long exposed to such drastic elements, and decided that he had to jump at the next available opportunity.

When his mind saw an opening, he tried dragging his form together but instead received an abstract blow to the head.

Travelling through the vortex in a teaching vessel, a lone traveller felt a strange lurch while dozing at his navigational controls. He decided to land and take stock of the situation before recording his events in his new diary.

Kyeldsen's being was stretched beyond breaking point and when he feared he would miss the chance to escape, his adrenaline kicked in and he clawed himself out of the vortex, landing in a heap on some moist green elements before passing out.

He breathed in and out several times before opening his eyes. The air smelled clear and fresh, but the sky looked all wrong. Shouldn't it be pink and gold and magenta? Why was it blue with great wads of grey? And why did the ground feel so cold beneath his body? He tried turning his head, but it felt too heavy. He then tried lifting his arms but they felt as if something were pinning them to the ground. He heard a strange clip clopping sound from somewhere close by and wondered if Arnuu was playing the game again.

Wait a segment. What game?

You know.

No I don't.

Yes you do. The game where everyone has to change into something else. And the last one to morph is out.

Oh that game. The one you play with Arnuu and Jogih and Tox and ...

Yes that's right.

But they're dead, aren't they? The humans came and murdered them all and destroyed your planet and killed your mother then tried to kill you.

Kyeldsen shuddered in agony. Was he going mad? But then he remembered. He remembered everything. The battle on Phymord. The *Dragonfly*. His escape to hyperspace then being crushed into Dimension-4. He tried shaking his head but it hurt too much. So that's where he was. He must have landed on Delta VI before the *Dragonfly* reached planet-fall. For a brief moment he felt at peace then suddenly he realised that something was terribly wrong. Dimension-4? What was that again? Time. It was the dimension of time, and he had been thrust through it. There was no telling where he was or when. He was a lost refugee in unknown territory.

He felt like crying then a very strange sensation made his toes wriggle. He could feel hot air and something cold and wet, and he sat up in terror as a large fur covered quadruped stood sniffing at him. It was dark brown and had big black eyes. Kyeldsen opened his mouth to scream and tried scrambling away. The quadruped snarled and started yelling at him in an unknown language.

'Woof! Woof, woof!'

Kyeldsen leapt out of the way, frantically looking for somewhere to hide. He saw several tall, thick grey stalks covered in vegetation and started climbing one to get away. The quadruped ran after him howling until another voice nearby started calling. Kyeldsen practically ran up the huge, strong stalk and eventually the quadruped lost interest and trotted over to a female who was wearing long grey clothing with a white sheet tied around her middle.

'Bad Alfred!' scolded the female. 'If the master caught you trying to run away like that he'd send you to Cook who'd make sausages out of you. Bad dog!'

Kyeldsen listened to the female's words and understood them. She was human. This was a human settled planet. But when was he? He looked around from his vantage point high in the tall stalk and saw a row of white buildings fenced with narrow metal poles surrounding the garden that hid him. He heard the clip clopping noise again and saw that the sound came from two large quadrupeds pulling a large black box on wheels. It stopped in front of one of the buildings and a door to the box opened. Out stepped a grey-haired human male dressed in black. Kyeldsen watched him close the door to the box and slowly climb the steps to his building.

Kyeldsen felt that this was his final chance. He had to exist somehow but he knew he could not do so in his vulnerable natural state. Summoning up his last reserves of power he shimmered and morphed into a large brown dog and ran over to the man on the steps.

'Hello Alfred!' the man said pleasantly. 'What are you doing over here? Doctor Burns would not be happy if he knew you were running around by yourself.'

Kyeldsen ignored him and started growling, baring sharp fangs. The man's smile faltered.

'Now Alfred, that isn't very nice, is it? I am going to put my bag inside and get Mrs Craven to take you straight back.' He inserted the key in the door while Kyeldsen started barking loudly.

'Down Alfred! Down!' the man yelled. He quickly turned the key and opened the door then tried slamming it shut but Kyeldsen was too quick and leapt at the man viciously, biting and clawing at his face. The man toppled to the floor, hitting his head with a jarring thump. Kyeldsen immediately stopped barking and checked the man's vital signs. The human was alive but unconscious. He turned around trying to find a place to hide then quickly morphed into the appearance of the man and dragged the prostrate figure through the first inner door that he saw. He looked around noticing a desk with papers tidily stacked, medical tomes and other publications in a book-case, and a further door behind the desk. He hurried over and opened it. Inside up against the far wall, stood a single bed. Kyeldsen thought he heard a woman's voice calling, so he frantically dragged the human through the doorway and lifted him onto the bed, before closing the door. His body melted away and reformed into its natural state. He took several deep breaths then concentrated with all his resolve and found him-self once again, inside the mind of a human. He decided that he had to become this male to survive.

The first thing that he discovered was that this human was a surgeon by the name of Andrew Laurence Grantley. The next thing he learnt that time was short, as the doctor was seriously ill.

▲

CHAPTER 12

PC Briggs was pleasantly surprised to find the superintendent and his assistant in such amiable moods, so much so that he secretly wondered if he had walked into the right place. What had brought on such a welcome change? There was no *Briggs, get out and do some work! You don't get paid to sit around doing nothing!* Or *Briggs, stop running after the detectives all the time. You work for me, not for them!* Instead, he was greeted politely, and *asked*, rather than being told to go back out onto the streets and report anything of interest. He was even informed that Greensworth had made a mistake in thinking that the actor, Douglas Forbes-Montague, was Jack the Ripper. Normally the superintendent would never have divulged such sensitive information to a lowly constable, particularly since he had been in error all this time—and freely admitted to being so.

So, an amazed PC Briggs left the Police House (after turning down the offer of a cup of coffee from Barker) and began his daily patrol. The streets were crammed with locals going about their business; not in the least bothered by a lone PC maintaining a casual eye on their comings and goings. He wondered if he should try striking up a conversation with someone just to see if he could manage to glean any new information that might be of use, when he noticed two women walking towards him. One, the Professor's young friend Molly, with her arm around the other who he recalled had assisted Molly the night the Professor had escorted her to the theatre. The woman, Elsie looked pale and exhausted, and she was leaning heavily on her friend for support. Molly gave the constable a hopeful look when she spotted him in the crowd, so Briggs made a point of stopping to greet them.

'Do yer know wot's 'appenin' with Douglas?' Molly's eyes were filled with concern. 'Is 'e awlright?'

Elsie brushed tears away from her swollen eyes. 'E's a gorner, isn't 'e?'

Molly gave her friend a worried look, Briggs however, smiled broadly, happy to be the bearer of good tidings. 'He's perfectly all right. Douglas has been cleared of all charges and was released a short time ago.'

'Wot!' exclaimed Molly, excitedly. She hugged her friend closely. 'See! I told yer the Professor'd get 'im off!'

Elsie's expression rapidly changed from confusion to shock then to delight. A fresh set of tears, this time of joy, poured down her cheeks as she realised what this meant; Douglas had been saved and maybe, just maybe things would turn out for the best. Perhaps there could even be a future for them together. She wiped her eyes and thanked the constable before giving the startled PC a huge hug.

'You're welcome,' Briggs replied, laughing despite feeling somewhat embarrassed at the outright display.

Elsie laughed too then her heart spun when she looked over the constable's shoulder at the sight before her. She gasped, 'Douglas.'

Briggs turned around to see the portly gent running towards them through the crowd. He held a bag in one hand and waved frantically with the other, calling out to Elsie. She rushed past the constable and fell into Douglas's arms, showering him with kisses. He cried with joy and Elsie burst into tears yet again.

'I thought yer were done for,' she wept.

'Me?' He laughed bravely. 'The theatre has not seen the last of Douglas Forbes-Montague II.' He kissed her gently on the forehead. 'And Elsie hasn't seen the last of her Cyril.'

Molly and Briggs watched the couple walk away arm in arm; an oddly comforting sight in a world where comfort was often a stranger.

It had been a very long night for the detectives and the Professor, so after allowing themselves a catnap for an hour in the cramped office, the inspectors paid a visit to the nearest barber shop before returning to the Police House. They had asked the alien if he wished to accompany them but he declined, stating that his growth was barely recognisable—which wasn't a lie. He simply omitted to mention that he was, in fact, incapable of growing a beard.

Once the inspectors returned clean shaven, the Professor poured them both a strong cup of coffee hoping that the caffeine would do its duty and keep them awake. He knew that they were still tired but they would have to put off sleep until a later stage. 'So gentlemen, now that Douglas is no longer a suspect it's time to turn our attentions to the real murderer.'

'The one who isn't a human,' stated Wainwright with a hint of irony; he took the cup from the alien's proffered hand.

The Professor smiled. 'That's right. And as I said to you before—from what both Billy and the paper boy reported what other explanation can there be?'

Wainwright felt a nagging suspicion that there should be one but for the life of him he couldn't think of any.

'Now the question is: which world is he from? And what brings him here?'

The detective shook his head in mild disbelief. 'I can't believe we're actually having this conversation. It's like we're talking about something as commonplace as what he eats for breakfast.'

The Professor laughed. 'After I've shown you my surprise I'll wager that you'll be willing to believe that even I'm not human.'

The detectives looked startled.

'But don't worry,' he continued ushering the stunned men out of the office. 'Unlike Jack the Ripper, I can assure you I'm quite harmless.'

The cab dropped the Professor, Wainwright and Brett near The Ten Bells and the two men followed the alien up the street and into the blind alley. There was a mound of hay rotting against one wall and a broken barrel lay upturned beside it; beyond that, in the corner, stood the Professor's ship invisible to the eye. The alien walked over to it whilst the detectives exchanged dubious looks: what on earth was he doing?

In response to the detectives' silent question, the Professor retrieved a metal cube from his breast pocket, turning it over to reveal a small circular indentation which he then pressed with his thumb. He stepped back and the air crackled and warped, then a metal door solidified out of thin air.

The detectives looked astonished but due to the alien's hypnotic support protecting their minds, they accepted the strange scene. The Professor gave a sigh of relief as he did not want his friends being distressed in any way.

The alien placed his hand on the surface of the door, and it slid open with a hum. He beckoned the inspectors to enter. 'This way.'

The two men shared a wary glance then Brett stepped over the threshold followed by his colleague. The Professor set the door out of phase once again, climbed inside and closed the door. 'This, gentlemen, is a lift.'

They were standing in a small room; the walls were made from mesh allowing coloured light to filter through and a touch-screen pad flashed awaiting command. The detectives looked around nervously; expectantly. The Professor stood in front of the pad and keyed in a sequence of codes before announcing, 'hold tight gentleman, we are going up.'

Instantly the detectives felt a jolt in their stomachs as the room began to rise, gradually picking up speed.

'What's happening?' Brett whispered.

'No need to concern yourselves,' assured the Professor. 'This lift is heading for the 85th floor—the top level.'

Brett and Wainwright looked at each other barely able to comprehend what the Professor had told them, and what they might see next.

A minute passed and the lift came to a gentle stop. A door opened and they found themselves in a brightly lit area housing strange machinery. 'Come along, you're quite safe.'

The detectives walked out of the lift and looked around. There were metal desks grouped in one corner of the room, and touch-sensitive pads lining two of the walls. Each desk had what appeared to be a note pad set into its surface, but on closer inspection was actually a blank screen. A lectern stood at the head of the room and there were two doors at opposite ends, which were closed.

Wainwright raised both arms then let them drop to his sides, clearly mystified. 'I don't understand. What is this place?'

The Professor frowned. How could the two detectives from the 19th century comprehend a spaceship from the future? 'This is my transport. But unlike a coach that travels from one location to another by road, this ship can travel from one world to another, in any time period.'

'How?' asked Brett, just as confused as his colleague.

The Professor rolled his eyes; how to explain *that* in simple terms? 'It mathematically opens a specific dimension to enter or exit the vortex.'

Brett frowned. 'It what?'

'It can disappear and reappear.'

Brett nodded. He could understand that. It was a bit like a magician doing a conjuring trick.

Wainwright shrugged, attempting to make sense of it all. 'But this room? What is it?'

'It is a classroom,' replied the alien. 'In fact, this entire ship is a teaching vessel.'

Wainwright gave him a blank look.

'It was custom built for educational purposes. I am a teacher and part of my duties were to take students on field trips to study different worlds, the stars and quantum phenomena. This is the room is where I taught theory.' The Professor walked over to one of the doors. 'The room in there is the student dormitory.' He opened the door, and the inspectors looked inside to see several beds. 'And if you would like to follow me,' the alien walked to the opposite door and opened it to reveal a circular room in darkness. He keyed a code on a wall panel and instantly the room was bathed in soft light.

'This is the observation deck where my students learn first hand what it is to be a quantum astronomer or an observer of the cosmos. By throwing back the shutters across the ceiling you come face to face with the knowledge that there is more to the universe than you could possibly imagine. But I won't be doing that today as we have much more important things to talk about; and as well as that I don't want to drive you completely out of your minds—viewing hyperspace for the first time isn't for everyone.'

Brett sighed. He was completely overwhelmed, having no idea what the Professor—the man he thought was from Scotland Yard—was talking about. The alien gave him an apologetic look, almost as if he had read the other's mind.

'Forgive me, allow me to clarify. Currently this entire ship exists in what is called hyperspace, outside what is normally understood as your three dimensions—length, breadth and height. That is why the ship is invisible to the naked eye.'

'However, using a special calibrator that acts like a key, enables me to bring the ship into real space. Hence the door that appeared in the alley.'

Both Wainright and Brett nodded politely, though neither understood what the Professor was talking about, except that he was a teacher. The alien however, blissfully continued his instruction.

'Your ocean-going vessels are powered by steam engines; this ship employs engines as well but they are called computers with quantum drive systems. To travel both through time and space takes an enormous amount of energy. This is supplied from the eighty five levels below, which house the many sections making up the quantum drive computer array.'

Brett wanted to laugh. He was listening to a language he could never hope to understand but at the same time he was beginning to accept what the Professor said.

Wainwright walked over and gave the alien a long searching look. 'I can barely believe what I am about to say but, you're not human. You look like us but you come from another world. That's right, isn't it?'

The alien nodded.

'You're not from Scotland Yard then?'

'No.' The Professor gave him an apologetic look. 'I was how-ever, telling the truth about wanting to help. But the only way was to allow you to think I had been sent from the Yard. I mean, think about it. Would you have believed me if I had told you that I was a visitor from another planet?'

Brett and Wainwright shared a smile.

'Of course you wouldn't,' replied the alien.

'So apart from solving crime on this world and being a teacher on your own world, what else do you do in your spare time?' Wainwright grinned but the Professor's expression darkened.

'I try to keep ahead of them.'

Wainwright frowned. 'Them? What do you mean?'

Because everyone thinks I shot Jackard Menz after I caught him tampering with his grad-scores on the university network. He was brilliant, could have been my finest student and gone on to do anything but he lacked direction; was lazy; and spent his time disrupting classes rather than working. When he failed his Dux Degree, he tried to tamper with his results, and I caught him in my office unlocking the codes in the system to change his scores. He begged me to turn a blind eye; he could not fail; he would pay handsomely; without a high pass mark, his family name would be disgraced.

I refused his pleas; he knew the penalty for failure. There was nothing I could do.

When I attempted to reset the correct scores in the system, he rushed at me and pressed a staser to my head. I managed to hit the alarm on the desk but as we struggled, the weapon went off and Menz collapsed, blood spurting from a wound in his chest. I attempted to staunch the bleeding but to no avail. Then the Wardens came rushing in and I tried to explain what had hap-pened; I told them about his attempted sabotage of his results, and his threats to kill me if I did not comply with his wishes. In trying to wrest the weapon away from him, it discharged. It was a terrible accident—nothing more.

Menz, blood bubbling from his lying mouth croaked 'he shot me in cold blood.'

The Wardens tried to arrest me but I managed to evade them by grabbing a data-hexagon from the desk and hurling it at the Head Warden. In the confusion I bolted for the docking bay, locking the door behind me.

I opened the first vessel I saw and escaped. I knew I could never return. Who would a Supreme Court believe? A teacher of no significant standing? Or the last words of the only son of the Ruling Class and University Admiralty?

The Professor sighed deeply, willing the image of Menz's last moments to recede into the recesses of his mind. He looked at Wainwright who was clearly confused as to why the alien had been silent. 'Forgive me, I ... '

'Are you all right?'

The Professor nodded grimly, touched however by the detective's gentle tone. 'I will be. And now to work, we have so much to do and there is not a moment to lose.'

The alien ushered the detectives back into the classroom then activated one of the touch-sensitive pads, searching for species within the universe that could change their shape. The detectives watched in curious fascination, as the alien tapped away at the coloured lights before hearing a grunt of frustration.

'There are just over nineteen hundred species that can change shape. That doesn't help us very much.'

The Professor moved to another keypad on the wall and keyed in another pattern. To the inspectors' surprise, a three-dimensional picture appeared out of thin air, hovering in the centre of the room. It looked like a cluster of stars at night.

'Right,' said the Professor confidently, 'I've tried to narrow the field by instructing the computer to search for shape shifting life forms that shimmer out of shape before solidifying; and who use organ extraction as a method of execution.'

Again, the computer sifted through the information on the 3D display searching different star systems. Wainwright and Brett walked over to the picture, marvelling at the sight. When the correct star system was found, the picture zeroed in on a planet, somewhat smaller and denser than Earth; it was surrounded by three other planets, smaller again. The Professor scrutinised the picture then adjusted something on the first keypad and a row of data scrolled down beside the picture of the planet. It was not in English so the Professor obligingly translated for his friends.

'This planet here,' he pointed to the hologram in question, 'is known as Phymord. The Phymordans have the ability to alter their appearance into tangible life forms like you or I …'

The detectives looked horrified.

' … or they can transform into intangible formations like radio waves, pure thought etc. Relative to 1888 they are known to be a warrior race and have invaded various neighbouring planets. One,' he pointed to the one closest to Phymord, 'took umbrage and declared war on them. Phymord then waged chemical warfare lasting roughly twenty minutes thus crippling their enemy and themselves in the process. It appears that after the war, the Phymordans biological make-up was damaged. They could still transform but if they experienced fear, the molecules within their bodies would instantly return them to their natural state.'

'Good God,' uttered Wainwright. He could hardly believe what the Professor was saying.

'After the war, a new President of Phymord took over office but refused to continue fighting as so many people had died. He made a solemn promise to turn his world around and eventually

Phymord became a passive nation, only punishing those who broke the law.' He looked at the detectives, his eyes glittering. 'Listen to this: the worst crime a Phymordan could commit was murder and his punishment was a ceremonial extraction of all vital organs.'

'Just like Jack the Ripper,' said Brett eagerly.

The Professor nodded.

'But if he is on our world. How did he get here?' asked Wainwright.

The Professor activated another datapad on the wall and further statistics spilled into the air. 'In five hundred year's time, Phymord will be attacked by an Earth colony and taken over. There will be no survivors except for the President who will be taken prisoner,' he looked up sadly, 'then publicly put on display before being executed.'

The detectives shared a horrified look.

'But,' the Professor continued, 'there were unofficial reports of *another* Phymord stowing away on one of the colonist's ships. The crew attempted to catch him but when apprehended he disappeared and never returned.'

'That's got to be him then,' cried Brett.

'Correct,' agreed the Professor. 'Now Phymordans have the ability to travel through dimensions thus travelling back and forth in time. But why 1888? Surely he would have wanted to find the colonist's planet, not Earth, five hundred years in his past.'

'Perhaps we better ask him that question when we find him,' suggested Wainwright tersely. 'So, assuming he will experience fear when caught, what should we look for when he transforms into his, what did you say? Natural state?'

'Good thinking.' The Professor activated the keypad again and a holo-picture of a small, pale shadowy figure with spindly arms and legs appeared before them. The detective jumped back in surprise, accidentally nudging a touch screen panel on the wall opposite; when the Professor turned to find out what he had done, it was too late.

'What happened?' demanded Wainwright frantically as the room began to vibrate.

The Professor hurried from one datapad to another, assessing the situation only to inform the detectives that it was no longer morning but half past six that night.

Brett looked appalled not wanting to believe it could be true. 'What!'

'I'm afraid Mr Wainwright accidentally activated the time displacement function and propelled us into the future, and no,' he waved a hand dismissively before Brett could protest, 'I cannot take us back as it is too dangerous.'

'So, what do we do?' demanded Brett, clearly annoyed at being unable to do anything.

The alien sighed. 'Well, I had not anticipated this loss of time however, we will just have to make the best of it.' He hastily ushered the detectives into the lift. 'The carriage driver will be at The Whistler's Inn right at this very time, waiting for Jack, just as the note said. You need to get over there as soon as possible and wait for me.' The lift came to a stop and the Professor activated the door allowing the detectives to exit the ship.

'What are you going to do?' asked Brett.

'I need to check on Doctor Grantley.'

▲

CHAPTER 13

Charlie Fry sneezed noisily, wiping the phlegm on one of his dirty sleeves. He had been waiting for Douglas for what seemed like ages and was beginning to wonder if the actor was ever going to appear. What the hell was he doing all this time? Banging some whore? Or worse still—knocking 'em off? He paced up and down in front of the tenement block, grumbling loudly. It was all Skinner's fault, making him hang around to keep an eye on things. But there was nothing to see, and if Douglas didn't make an appearance soon, he would just tell Skinner to *stick it* and then go buy himself a jug of ale and drink til his guts pickled! This idea seemed a much better alternative and he seriously contemplated leaving his post when without warning a prostitute galloped out of the building accidentally colliding with him. She glowered, interrupting his thoughts of ale. 'Watch yerself!'

Charlie glared at the ruddy complexion and bloated figure stuffed into an old red dress standing impatiently before him. His glare however rapidly melted to an oily grin when he recognised her trade. 'So sorry m'dear. I'm waitin' for a friend, see? And 'e 'asn't showed up yet so why don't we go upstairs and do some fancy jigglin'?' He rested a suggestive hand on her plump shoulder.

The whore rolled her eyes. How many times had she heard those *sweet* words before? 'Where's yer money?'

Charlie sniggered and produced a gold coin. The woman gave him an astonished look which rapidly turned to one of greed. She didn't care if he'd earnt it or stolen it, the point was: it would soon be hers! She reached for the coin but he held it back, so she grabbed him by the shirt-front and marched him inside the tenement and upstairs. They passed a drunk near the bottom of the stairs snoring blissfully, his dreams undisturbed.

When they reached her room she opened the door, pushed Charlie inside and banged it shut. Minutes later, Douglas whistling a merry tune, entered the building and opened his medical bag. He took out a loaf of bread carefully placing it next to the sleeping vagrant then stepped over him, heading for his room on the floor above.

Mrs Craven deposited the basket of firewood near the kitchen hearth, grumbling to herself. If it wasn't one thing it was another. First of all, the one night in the week she could call her own had been cancelled by her employer, and when she asked what she was needed for, Grantley informed her that she was to prepare a four-course dinner for two to be served in the dining room of the surgery. A four-course dinner with so little time to prepare? Granted she kept the larder well stocked but couldn't he have given her more warning? Then she made the terrible mistake of asking if *Mrs Grantley* would prefer duck or veal? The doctor gave her a surprised look then snapped that the dinner guest would not be his wife, and from where did she get such an absurd idea? Mrs Craven apologised, explaining she assumed he would be spending the evening with his wife, as it was their wedding anniversary.

'Anniversary? How do you know that?' His voice was indignant.

'You told me Sir, the very first day I was in your service, to always remind you when the day arrived, so you could arrange something special for Mrs Grantley.'

Doctor Grantley squeezed his eyes shut and sat down on the edge of his desk, massaging his temples. His eyes suddenly sprang open and he smiled. 'Oh yes, I remember now.'

Mrs Craven gave him a worried look, concerned that he had yet another headache. 'Are you feeling all right Sir?'

He swallowed then nodded. 'Quite well Mrs Craven, thank you.' He smiled again then stood up, patting her affectionately on the arm. 'You're always worrying about me, aren't you? But there's no need, it's just that I've been under a great deal of pressure lately.' He looked away, worry clouding his expression. 'A great deal.'

Mrs Craven decided to risk asking another question. 'The dinner then Sir? Who *will* be your dinner guest this evening?'

The surgeon hesitated then cleared his throat. 'A colleague of mine wishes to discuss new surgical procedures, amongst other things. So I thought it would be practical to invite him to dinner. I would like you to prepare the same volume of food for my guest that you would for me.'

Mrs Craven gave him a startled look imagining how much she would have to cook. 'That will take a good while Sir. I will have to start immediately as I'm due to visit my daughter, and I may run out of time.'

The doctor looked at her in annoyance. 'You will be handsomely paid as usual. I'm sure your daughter will understand.'

'I hope so Sir.' The housekeeper looked down almost afraid at Grantley's response.

'Circumstances change,' replied the doctor icily, noting the woman's less-than enthusiastic response. 'Mrs Grantley is in bed with a cold so I am working tonight. If I am working, then so must you. Any more questions?'

The housekeeper bit her lip, curtsied, and hurried out of his office, heading for the kitchen. Several hours later as she tossed more wood on the fire, she heard a knock at the door and opened it to find one of the gentlemen from Scotland Yard asking to come in.

'Good evening Mrs Craven,' greeted the Professor. 'I must apologise for this late hour but is Doctor Grantley here?'

Mrs Craven smiled and bade him enter. 'You're expected Sir.'

'I Am?'

'Yes Sir, if you will please follow me. I'm sorry that Doctor Grantley is not yet here but he was called again to Buckingham Palace.'

The Professor nodded. 'I see. How is the duke's ear?'

'Still enflamed I believe.'

Mrs Craven showed him into a small discreet dining room furnished with a leather sofa, drink's cabinet, and a dining table with seating for six. A fire crackled cheerfully in the grate, and the Professor absent-mindedly flexed his fingers towards the flames as Mrs Craven poured him a glass of whisky. He politely took the glass, sniffed at the strong substance then took a measured sip.

'So the doctor is expecting me?' He hoped *that* was a prompt to find out what was going on.

'Oh yes Sir. He said a gentleman was coming,' replied Mrs Craven. 'He informed me that a colleague was to dine with him this evening and that I was to prepare the dinner.' She frowned. 'He was referring to you Sir, wasn't he?'

The Professor smiled and with a twinkle in his eye, raised his glass to the woman. 'Oh yes.'

After Mrs Craven had excused herself and returned to the kitchen, the Professor swiftly placed his glass on the mantel piece and tiptoed out of the dining room and into the doctor's office. He hoped that there would be just enough time to have a good look around before Grantley returned or the real dinner guest arrived. Touching nothing in the office, he headed straight for the locked door behind the desk and peered through the keyhole. Nothing but darkness met his gaze. He reached into his pocket and taking out a metal clip, bent it out of shape then eased one end into the lock. After several tense moments, the mechanism clicked, and the door opened. He picked out the faint outline of drapes, so he crept over and slowly pulled them aside. The evening moonlight spilled in through the windows, and he turned around to see something for which he'd been preparing himself, since deducing that Jack the Ripper was an alien.

The Professor shivered, feeling the effects of the energy leakage from the frozen dimensional pocket before him. To anyone unfamiliar with such a sight, it would have seemed as if a strange, frozen mist had mysteriously localised over the bed. When the Professor approached, he could see a figure dressed in black shrouded within the mist, stretched out across the covers. He placed a finger on the surface of the mist, feeling the spark from where fluid time attempts to touch frozen time. The Professor sighed heavily and pulled the drapes back into place then left the room, re-locking the door. He walked through the hallway and into the kitchen, where Mrs Craven was busily stirring soup on the stove. She picked up the ladle, blew on it and took a sip, then quickly placed it back in the pot looking embarrassed at being caught sampling a taste. The Professor ignored her discomfiture and walked over, determined to find out some more facts if he could.

'Mrs Craven, remember when you told me that Doctor Grantley consumes a large volume of food?'

'Yes Sir.'

'Has he always eaten so much?'

She frowned. 'No, not always Sir.'

'When did his appetite begin to increase?'

'Just about the time of the incident with Alfred.' The housekeeper wondered at his sudden curiosity of her employer's habits.

The Professor narrowed his eyes. 'Incident?'

She shrugged wiping her hands on her apron. 'He said it wasn't anything really. He had just arrived at work and Doctor Burns's dog Alfred, came running over to him and attacked him for no good reason. Poor Doctor Grantley fought him off but received a nasty bite on his arm, and he also fell and hit his head.'

'Did he now?' The Professor looked away then narrowed his eyes thoughtfully. 'Had the dog ever attacked him before?'

The housekeeper shook her head. 'He was a dear old fellow. He wouldn't have hurt a mouse. I don't know what got into him that day.'

'And this was when Doctor Grantley began eating more than usual?'

The woman nodded and bit her lip nervously. 'It's all over that new medicine you see, I'm not supposed to speak to anyone about it. That's why I didn't mention it when you were here last.'

Not wishing to waste any more precious time, the Professor gazed into her eyes, instructing her mind that she must divulge any information she had to him. Her rapid response received a glowing smile from the alien. 'He said that after the attack he started taking experimental medication that could heal wounds quickly and boost energy levels but the side effects of the medicine gave him a voracious appetite.'

How extremely convenient, thought the Professor. He walked back through the doorway then hesitated before turning around. 'Where is the dog now by the way?'

'Doctor Burns had him destroyed.'

The coach driver pulled gently on the reins and the horses came to a stop outside the surgery. The doctor opened the coach door and stepped out into the street. Looking up at the driver, Grantley gestured for him to follow.

Once inside his office, the doctor carefully placed his medical bag on the table and opened the top drawer of his desk.

'Now you do remember my instructions, Mr Oder.' Grantley looked expectantly at the brute.

Arthur Oder's eyes narrowed and looked even more pig-like than usual. 'Eh?'

'About tonight,' prompted Grantley irritably. 'I assume you haven't forgotten my correspondence?'

'Y'wot?'

Grantley gave him a look of contempt. 'My note to you.'

Arthur absent-mindedly reached into his pocket, recalling how the stranger in the grey suit had chased him through the streets, and made him lose a fragment of the note that the doctor had given him. The other half was still safe in his pocket.

'Well answer me!' Grantley demanded loudly, silently voicing *you pathetic human*. When there was no response, Grantley pulled out a metal box and opened it to reveal several bundles of fifty-pound notes, neatly tied together. Arthur gazed at the money, magically finding his voice once again.

'While I was waitin' for yer at 'Er Majesty's, a man turned up an' started tryin' to talk to me.'

'Yes.' Grantley's tone was long and questioning.

Arthur looked away nervously. 'Well I sorta panicked 'cos I didn't like the look of 'im so I ran.'

Grantley nodded sagely. 'So that was why Her Majesty had to arrange for someone else to return me to my rooms?'

Arthur stared at the floor and mumbled in agreement.

'I see. You still have my note of instructions, don't you?'

The ruffian's expression betrayed fear and pleading. 'I didn't wan' 'im askin' anythin', see? But when I was runnin' I got knocked over an' part of the note got ripped from me 'and.'

Grantley looked coldly at him and snapped the box shut. 'So your pursuer, whom I deduce is that meddling Professor from Scotland Yard has put two and two together.'

Arthur was about to ask what adding two and two together would have to do with anything, when a gentle knock at the door plunged them both into silence.

'Doctor Grantley?' called the voice of Mrs Craven from behind the door. 'Is that you Sir?'

Grantley brought his forefinger to his lips warning Arthur not to speak, then hastened to open the door a crack. 'What do you want? I am extremely busy.'

Mrs Craven tried to look past the doctor into the room, but he barred the way so she saw nothing. 'I'm so sorry to tell you that your dinner guest left within minutes of you arriving.'

'Dinner guest?'

'Yes,' the housekeeper nodded. 'Professor Delbrotman begged you to forgive him for not waiting but he had pressing matters and will speak with you at the next available opportunity.'

Grantley's blood turned cold and he could sense the molecules in his body attempting to alter and return him to his natural state. He coughed clearing his throat, trying to dispel the fear. 'Thank you Mrs Craven.'

'But the dinner is all prepared. Shall I still serve it Sir?'

Grantley sucked in his breath. 'In the dining room. I shall be in presently.' He slammed the door shut in her face.

Returning his attention to his carriage driver, he reopened the metal box and removed the bundles of money. Arthur remained silent, eyes glued to the king's ransom. But it wasn't money that the doctor handed the driver, it was a tiny papier mâché box which Grantley instructed him to open.

Arthur lifted the lid and looked at the contents suspiciously. It appeared to be a square of chocolate. 'Wot's this for?'

'Insurance,' replied the doctor simply. 'If by some chance you are caught and accused of being,' his voice dropped sharply, 'Jack the Ripper, then you must eat this piece of chocolate.'

'Why?'

Grantley walked over to the driver, staring into his ugly face. 'It will ensure that you forget everything that you know about me. Therefore, if you are interrogated, then you won't be able to answer any of their questions.'

Arthur looked at the chocolate and gave the doctor a wary look, mindful of his employer's brutal methods. 'It won't kill me, will it?'

The doctor chuckled, amused at the man's distrust. 'Now why would I pay you good money only to have you killed?'

Arthur shrugged his shoulders before being handed a crisp new fifty-pound note. He snatched at it quickly. 'But if they did catch me an' I forgot who yer were, they still wouldn't believe I was telling' the truth, would they?'

Grantley closed the lid of the little box in the man's grubby hands. 'Professor Delbrotman has a powerful mind that knows when a man speaks the truth.' He smiled enigmatically. 'And remember—I will always be here to protect you.'

Annie Tuttle waddled over to the two inspectors and handed them each a glass of beer.

'Could I interest yers in a basin of stew, my dears?' she asked invitingly. 'My 'usband makes it best in the 'ole of England.'

Brett declined quickly, almost spilling the beer he held in his hand. The last thing he wanted was to eat anything cooked in this filthy place. 'We've already eaten,' he explained.

'I see,' she replied curtly. With a token air of disappointment, she waddled away pushing a drunken, prostrate figure draped over the counter onto the floor with a thud. There was a roar of laughter from the crowded tables as the drunk, oblivious to his rough handling, continued to snore happily curled up on the dirty floor.

Brett checked his fob watch again, pocketing it for the third time. 'I wonder what's keeping the Professor.'

Wainwright shook his head, then taking a sip of beer immediately spat it out. 'Shit! What the hell have they put in this?'

Brett laughed, then raised his eyebrows. 'God only knows. But the first rule of thumb is to never ever drink in public houses that smell worse than the local cesspit. The act of ordering a pint is only done to blend in.'

Wainwright grimaced, pushing his beer away; he made a mental note to remember that, should he ever have to visit another cheap establishment like The Whistler's Inn again.

Moments later, a handsome cab delivered the Professor to the inn, and he entered the tavern to be greeted with the usual revelry that a newcomer attracts. He nodded his head politely then looked around the crowded room to find the detectives seated at the bar. Turning down a local girl's cheeky offer who was annoyed at his rejection, he hurried over then proceeded to answer their questions.

'So the real Grantley, unconscious from the dog attack, has been locked up, and the false Grantley who is really a *Phaymord* …'

'Phymordan.'

Brett nodded. 'Yes right—is running around London performing ritual murder just as it was performed on his own world.'

'Summed up beautifully,' commended the Professor. 'And the real Grantley has been put in a frozen time pocket so his unconscious state will not deteriorate.'

'Do you believe that the Phymordan tried to murder Grantley?'

The Professor shook his head. 'I doubt that was his original intent. If he had, he would never have been able to fool the community, not to mention his family for so long.'

Wainwright looked puzzled. 'How so?'

'Well if the real Grantley had died, then our Phymordan friend would not have been able to transform himself into pure thought and absorb the memories and knowledge from the doctor's mind.' He paused nodding thoughtfully. 'His personality and knowledge had to be plucked in order to be convincing.'

Wainwright nodded, digesting the information. 'So what happens now?'

'We wait for his carriage to arrive then we arrest him and the driver.'

The Professor and the two detectives made their way towards the stables trying not to look too conspicuous. The stable hands ignored them, occasionally stopping to tell each other bawdy jokes before getting back to their mundane work. After about an hour of walking near the stables and commenting on the horses, the Professor was beginning to think that the coach wouldn't come but before voicing his concerns the carriage in question entered The Whistler's Inn stables and a solitary figure stepped down.

'Are yer horses to be stabled Sir?' asked one of the boys.

'No,' the figure replied. 'Just water them as I won' be stayin' long.'

The Professor and his companions crouched outside the stable wall and watched the man dressed in a long, black coat hurry to the door of the inn and disappear inside. Brett immediately wanted to rush after him but the Professor laid a restraining hand on his shoulder.

'What is it?' asked Wainwright, glancing at the two black horses harnessed to the carriage.

'I just want to check for some metaphorical fingerprints,' replied the alien enigmatically. The inspectors shared a puzzled look, wondering what *fingerprints* might be assuming it was a term fixed far in their future. They followed him inside the stable then witnessed the transformation of their alien friend from an intelligent, serious individual to an English buffoon. Brett smirked, wondering if the Professor had ever been a thespian on his home world.

'Good evening again,' the Professor declared expansively.

The stable boys looked up showing vague interest at the newcomer.

'Remember me? I was here just last night.'

'Oh yeah,' replied one of the young men, wiping his hands on his shirt. 'Still lookin' for that man yer wanted to talk to?'

The Professor beamed at him. 'Actually no. I just want to have a closer look at his horses.' He pointed at the black carriage.

The stable boy frowned suspiciously. 'Why?'

The Professor walked over to him and grinned again, this time inanely, recalling the magistrate he had bumped into the day before. 'I appreciate good stock. Comes from my time being spent on the Punjab, what?'

The boy nodded slowly unable to tear his eyes from the Professor's inane expression; an expression that was hypnotic. He only wanted to inspect the horses. It seemed perfectly natural to let him do so.

'Go ahead Sir.'

The Professor thanked him and shook the lad's hand.

'How do you do that?' asked Brett in wonder. 'One second he's suspicious, the next he's welcoming you with open arms.'

The Professor shrugged. 'It's a talent the people from my world have over other life forms—hypnotic suggestion. I don't like practising it as it holds people against their will but as we are in a hurry, needs must do.' He gave a small apologetic smile then turned his attention not to the horses, but to the carriage itself.

'What are we looking for?' asked Wainwright, scanning the coach as if willing evidence to magically appear.

The Professor circled the carriage before pausing at the side door. He ran his hand over a pale, faded mark on the wooden surface and tut tutted.

'What is it?' asked Brett.

'Look at this,' he declared barely above a whisper. The inspectors looked at the faded mark.

The alien regarded the two men curiously. 'What do you think it is?'

'At an educated guess, it looks like where the Royal Coat of Arms should be.' Brett ran his fingers across the surface. 'This carriage must belong to the Queen.'

'Then Grantley uses this when attending Buckingham Palace,' concluded Wainwright.

The Professor nodded. 'Come along. Let's catch the lackey first.'

As if on cue, Arthur Oder walked out of the inn wiping his mouth from the stew which had dripped down his chin and onto his coat. He hadn't seen the Professor abruptly duck behind the carriage followed by the detectives, neither did he take much notice of the stable boys who stopped what they were doing, sensing that something was about to happen. Arthur sniffed the air and walked over to the carriage bumping into the horses; they neighed their objection and he told them to shut up. He turned around wondering why the doctor was taking so long to arrive when suddenly he heard someone shout 'now!' before being knocked to the ground in a sudden attack. Arthur screamed in anger and surprise and tried scrabbling beneath the coach but was quickly pinned down by three determined individuals.

'Well done!' applauded the Professor to his friends.

Arthur screwed up his face recognising the toff's voice. 'Get yer bleedin' 'ands orf me!'

'Oh no,' replied Brett smugly. 'Not when we've finally got you where we want you.'

'I ain't dunn nuthin'!' He winced as Brett dug his knee into his back.

'Wot yer doin'?' demanded one of the stable boys.

The Professor glared at him. 'Making an arrest if it's any of your business.' He jumped up searching for something with which to bind the man's hands. A length of rope hung from a nail and he grabbed it, handing it to Wainwright.

'Good,' he glanced at Brett. 'Hold his wrists together.'

Brett sat on the brute making certain that he couldn't escape and once his hands were securely tied behind his back, they hauled him to his feet and dragged him out into the open.

'I'll get the coach ready,' said the Professor.

'Where yer takin' me!' bellowed Arthur, cursing his stupidity and the risks that Grantley made him take.

'To a nice snug cell,' replied Brett coldly. 'I'm sure the cockroaches will be pleased with some fellow company.'

Arthur spat in the inspector's face, earning the brute a blow to the head from Wainwright and as Brett brushed the gob of spit from his forehead, Wainwright grabbed a fistful of Arthur's greasy hair, yanked it back and snarled, 'I'll have your neck swinging from a long rope before you can say "Jolly Jack is Doctor Grantley", do you hear me, you miserable scum!'

Arthur heard the words echo in his tiny mind and a stab of fear raced through his heart. What could he do now? Would the doctor bail him out? He suddenly remembered the chocolate that would make him forget, stashed in his trouser pocket. When they locked him up, he would eat it then everything would be all right.

Charlie Fry buttoned up his fly and opened the door of the whore's room. After enjoying a sweaty interlude, he was rewarded with seeing Douglas leaving his room across the hallway and making his way down the stairs. Charlie quickly scuttled after him then rubbing both hands in excitement, ran in the opposite direction, heading for The Horse's Saddle.

In the corner of The Ten Bells, Molly sat despondently waiting for the Professor's return. Each time the door opened she looked up in hope, willing his smiling face to search out hers but was continually disappointed to see only the regulars enter. Oliver sat at the bar lazily puffing smoke rings from his lips, allowing the ash to flutter elegantly to the floor. He swivelled around on the stool and observed several prospective customers making gross advances to the uninterested girl. 'Ow's about it my pretty one? Yer look ripe for it t'night!' Her constant reply was to 'bugger orf. I ain't fer sale.'

Oliver slid off the stool and wound his way around the packed tables, finally reaching her spot at the back of the room. He leaned over the table menacingly, sucking on his cigar. 'An' just wot are yer playin' at?'

Molly frowned in annoyance at the intrusion, keeping her eyes on the door. 'I dunno wot yer mean.'

Oliver chuckled sarcastically. 'Don' give me that.' He leaned closer, blocking her view. 'Why aren't yer encouragin' company?'

Molly gave a slight shrug and scowled at his mean face. 'I'm waitin' for someone.'

'The Professor?'

'Thas right.'

Oliver gestured around the room. 'Well 'e ain't 'ere, is 'e? An' while yer remain under my protection, yer will take on other payin' customers until 'e graces us with 'is presence.'

Molly stared at the surface of the table stubbornly. 'I'm waitin' for the Professor an' I ain't goin' with anyone else.'

Oliver grabbed hold of her chin and twisted her face around to his. 'Yer will, yer little bitch or I'll 'ave a piece of yer meself!'

Molly's eyes filled with tears, and she gasped in pain as his fingernails dug cruelly into her flesh. His eyes bored into hers daring her to defy him, then suddenly he released her and slapped her harshly across the head; she whimpered and buried her head in her hands.

Oliver's expression was smug when the girl began to cry but he snarled when Backer tapped him on the shoulder with a meaty hand.

'Wot!'

'Oliver,' said Backer, trying to ignore the girl's sobs. 'Yer told me to tell yer, if 'e came back.'

Oliver frowned then saw a portly figure seating himself on a stool. 'Well, well, well then, if it ain't the great thespian 'imself.'

Puffing and panting from running all the way from Whitechapel, Charlie came bursting through the door of The Horse's Saddle, eager to tell Skinner who he had found. He glanced around but couldn't see the sailor as a cheering crowd had gathered blocking his view. He leapt up onto a table and watched as a burly brute of a man was banging Skinner's head repeatedly on the floor. How long Skinner had been taking punishment, Charlie didn't know but when the sailor lay still, the brute eased off and Skinner saw his chance. He kicked out and managed to push his assailant away, then flung himself on the thug and pummelled his face until blood burst from his nose. Charlie joined in with the others, clapping and cheering. It was always fun to watch a good fight and Skinner always put up a juicy one. He wondered who had started it and what it was about but then decided that he had better share his news otherwise Skinner would probably start on him next.

'Hey!' he shouted above the hubbub. 'Listen up!'

The crowd didn't respond.

Charlie jumped up and down on the table. 'It's about ol' Douglas!' A roar from the crowd drowned out his words, and a wharfie with a thick black beard and an incensed expression thought Charlie had just insulted him. He turned around and stabbed a finger at him. 'Did *you* call me an' ol' *arse*?'

Charlie gulped first then screeched out, 'no, no! I said I found Douglas! He came 'ome first an' now I think 'e's gone orf to The Ten Bells!' This vital piece of information finally seemed to do the trick, silencing the rowdy horde. He looked around self-consciously as everyone stared at him.

Instantly forgetting the fight, Skinner stood up, wiping the blood from his face. 'Right, good work Charlie.' He gave the brute a vicious grin. 'It's time to put yer fists to better use. We're gonna get 'im!'

The thug dragged himself up and stepped away from Skinner, dabbing gently at his nose with the back of his massive hand. The sailor was right, there would always be time for settling old scores once the Kipper was done away with.

'It's now or never gentleman.' The sailor jumped on top of a nearby table and looked pointedly at Charlie. The thief took the message and quietly got down, joining the other followers.

'We strike now when 'e least expects it, and we strike 'ard!'

Grunts of assent from the crowd prompted Skinner to greater heights of volubility in his mission to rid the world of murderers like Jack the Ripper.

'Ain't this wot we've been waitin' for?'

His followers nodded.

Skinner grinned viciously. 'We've got the muscle!'

'Yeah!'

'We got the weapons!'

'Yeah!'

Mrs Wickens, the proud owner of The Horse's Saddle drank a toast to each *yeah* and armed herself with a rolling pin.

'An' we've got the right, 'aven't we? It's down to us, the citizens of England to bring this scumbag to 'is knees! The Peelers do nothin' so we'll be the law!'

'Yes!' The men stabbed their fists into the air and Skinner soaked up the delicious feeling of absolute control. 'So wot we gonna do?'

'Get 'im!'

'Nail 'is arse to the ground!'

'Rip 'im apart, til there's nothin' left!'

Skinner punched his fist into the air. 'Thas right. We're gonna rip the Ripper.' He grinned smugly, pleased with how well the words sounded together. 'We're gonna rip the Ripper. Rip the Ripper!'

United, the sailor's mob began chanting the three words over and over again. Mrs Wickens and her serving girls dragged out the stash of clubs, knives and torches from behind the bar, and everyone scrambled for a weapon.

'Follow me!' screamed Skinner, drunk with the exhilaration of finding a perfect excuse to inflict grievous bodily harm on a new victim. The horde stormed out of the pub and lit the torches in the night sky, ceaselessly chanting: 'Rip the Ripper, rip the Ripper, rip the Ripper …'

CHAPTER 14

Doctor Grantley/Kyeldsen sat alone in the dining room of his surgery, devouring the last morsel of the apple pie that Mrs Craven had prepared for dessert. He had systematically worked his way through *two* four-course meals, as it was becoming increasingly difficult to maintain the molecules of his human form. The huge amounts of food he needed had already grown and he knew his housekeeper was becoming suspicious. That was the reason he lied to Mrs Craven about inviting a dinner guest. And that was also why he was beginning to wonder how he could maintain the charade for much longer. But what then? Could he risk allowing the real Grantley to die? That would certainly help relieve the energy drain he constantly suffered by keeping Grantley alive. But did he have the confidence to be Grantley forever, without the safety net of Grantley's buried memories? And how would he dispose of the real Grantley's body if he did allow him to die? The grandfather clock in the hallway struck the hour and he quickly dismissed such foolish thoughts; he could do this. He *would* do this. For his mother's sake and for Phymord, he would continue tearing apart every living whore if it killed him. And if in their death throws they wondered why he was doing this to them, he would call it a necessary act of revenge against Eleanor Nile's twisted, licentious and undeserving life.

Grantley snapped his medical bag shut then putting on his hat and coat, walked out of the surgery and into the street, waiting for a passing hansom. When a cab appeared, he hailed it and told the driver to take him to one street before The Whistler's Inn. Once the cab arrived at his destination, he walked the remainder of the way and entered the stable. The coach wasn't there which meant Arthur was late again. Grantley waited five minutes; then ten minutes; the ten rapidly turning into twenty. Just where was the imbecile? He hoped he hadn't gone off boozing again because if that was the case, then it would be the last thing he ever did. The minutes continued to tick by, and doubt started gnawing away at Grantley's irritation; this frightened him because doubt meant fear and fear meant transformation against his will.

'Scuse me Sir,' ventured one of the stable boys from within the shadows. Grantley snapped his head around in the direction of the voice. The distraction allowed him to bury his concerns.

'Is there summink we can do for yer?'

Grantley smiled coldly. 'No thank you.'

The stable boy came out from the shadows holding a pitchfork. 'Do yer wanna sit down?'

Grantley was not inclined to waste further precious energy by responding, so remained silent. Unfortunately, it only fuelled the boy's curiosity.

'Are yer p'raps after that fella? The one wearin' a fancy coat jus' like the one yer got on.'

Grantley narrowed his eyes suspiciously. 'Perhaps.'

The boy leaned on his pitchfork and gave the doctor a smirk. 'Funny that, the coat I mean. 'Spose 'e won't be needin' it much longer. Probably won't be needin' nothin' at all soon.'

Grantley loathed cryptic responses dipped in attempted humour, particularly when delivered by pathetic human flotsam, but he did need to know if the boy knew anything so he handed him a shilling. Instantly the boy's explanation was forthcoming.

'Well 'e was nabbed by these fellas. I fink they was Peelers or summink. Anyway 'e got taken away by 'em.'

Grantley felt his blood run cold. 'Were there three of them? One dressed in a grey suit?'

The boy nodded. 'Yeah, thas right. An' they drove orf in the coach that the poor bugger came in with.'

The doctor's expression turned thunderous, and he stormed out of the stable and back down the street. How could Arthur have been so stupid? What if he forgot to eat the chocolate? What if the Professor managed to drag any information out of him? Grantley growled in frustration before hailing another cab. The hansom came to a stop, and he seated himself inside, breathing furiously.

'Where to Guv'ner?'

Grantley didn't know. He knew that the time had finally arrived to face the Professor but it would have to be on his terms and his terms alone. He could never allow any being, human or otherwise to better him.

'Sir?' ventured the cabby, when his passenger didn't respond.

'Be quiet, I'm thinking!' Grantley closed his eyes and gently massaged his aching temples. What could he do to the Professor? Did he have an Archilles heel? Then what was it? Or perhaps *who* was it? Grantley smiled, recalling the night when he had attempted to kill a young whore but was prevented, when the bitch bit him. She had screamed for help and help came in the form of Professor Delbrotman. He remembered catching a glimpse of the man, with the harlot in tow. They seemed quite friendly too. Grantley's eyes snapped open and he breathed a triumphant sigh.

'Driver,' commanded the doctor. 'Take me to The Ten Bells on Commercial Street.' He shut the door with a bang and shimmered to form a new shape.

Elsie rolled over in bed, careful not to disturb the sleeping form of Douglas. He looked so calm and peaceful; there was not a trace of worry or concern across his countenance, and she hoped there never would be again. Thanks to the Professor, her Douglas was a free man. She smiled contentedly then realising the time, quietly got out of bed and got dressed, glancing at Douglas snoring gently. Sensing that he was being watched, Douglas stirred and opened his eyes.

'You're leaving already?'

'Ave to,' Elsie replied. 'Oliver don' like us girls bein' late.'

'Well he might just have to get used to it.' He gave her an enigmatic smile and Elsie wondered if it meant that somehow, Douglas would rescue her from Oliver's clutches.

She blew him a kiss as she left. 'I'll be waitin' for yer.'

Once Elsie had gone, Douglas threw back the covers and hunted around for his clothes. He was in dire need of fresh linen and a decent pair of trousers. As he dressed, he thought about when he first arrived at Elsie's lodgings after his release. He sat her down and explained how the Professor and his two colleagues had established his innocence. He also mentioned how Greensworth and Barker had been forced to back down. He did not, however, mention that in his terror he had lost control of his bladder when he was being questioned; that was far too embarrassing beyond words.

Looking around for his shoes he regretted his stupidity in frightening Elsie when he pretended to stab himself with the prop knife. When he apologised, she said, 'forget it. It doesn't matter. I'm just so glad you're safe.' They kissed and for the first time ever, she refused to take any payment from him.

After that, Douglas returned to his lodgings in Whitechapel to change, before hurrying to The Ten Bells, all the while blessing his darling Elsie.

Oliver was waiting as per usual for his girls to turn up for the evening's trade and was not impressed with Elsie being late. She had become a little too high handed recently, what with her sharp tongue and keeping things from him like that toff's dress. He wondered if he had been too soft with her, allowing her to get away with too much. That was his problem. He'd always been a sucker for a pretty face—even if it did belong to an old slut.

He struck a match, lighting a cigar as the door opened. He looked up with interest expecting it to be Elsie, however, it was Douglas whistling a merry tune. The actor closed the door behind him, then rubbed his hands enthusiastically, looking for a spare table. He spotted the pimp and grinned—as if everything was back to normal. This did nothing for Oliver's foul mood.

'I'm back,' grinned Douglas, oblivious to Oliver's sour look. He seated himself on a stool beside the pimp.

'So I see.' Oliver planted his cigar firmly between his teeth. 'So 'ow's about yer explainin' t'me wot the coppers were on about?'

Douglas brought a nervous finger to his lips and shushed him. 'Not so loud. I do not wish my ordeal to be known by everyone.'

Oliver glared and he stabbed a finger at Douglas' chest. 'They said that yer was the Kipper ...'

A group of card players at a nearby table looked up suspiciously at Douglas. The actor's cheeks burned and he gulped nervously. 'Please Oliver, I've been through enough. I do not wish to speak about it.'

'Then get out.'

The actor looked shocked. 'I beg your pardon?'

'You 'eard. There was too many of my girls, not to mention payin' customers wot saw yer bein' carted outta 'ere by the Peelers. If they think yer up to no good then they won't be 'appy.' He leaned forward and blew puffs of smoke into Douglas' face. 'An' if they're not 'appy then I'm not 'appy.'

'But I am innocent,' squeaked Douglas.

Oliver nodded. 'I believe yer Dougie 'cos I don't think yer got the backbone to gut a cockroach but if anyone 'ere suspects ya then they won't come back, an' that's bad for business.'

Douglas' chin trembled. 'But Oliver, even if everyone saw me being carried out, how would they know anything? Only you, Backer, Elsie and Molly heard the precise accusation from the constable's lips.'

That type of annoying, sensible logic was not going to get Douglas anywhere because Oliver always had to be right, (even when he was wrong) so he responded with a vicious glare then smugly thought of something much better to say. 'Well, I don' think the clientele would appreciate coppers runnin' in and outta 'ere when they feel like it. It don' do much for privacy, see?' He finished with a resolute nod of the head, pleased at *his* logic.

'But what about my Elsie?'

'*Your* Elsie? She's *my* Elsie. She belongs to *me* not *you*.'

Douglas's eyes filled with tears. 'Please understand Oliver, she's all I have.'

'Oh me 'eart bleeds for yer.'

Douglas remained silent for a moment attempting to control his trembling voice. 'Then that's it then?' He looked despairingly at the pimp. 'All I have been to this place and its people is worth nothing to you?'

'Piss orf.'

Douglas felt as if Oliver had just plunged a knife through his broken heart, but the pimp merely jerked a thumb towards the door, indicating that the actor was no longer welcome. His face crumpled as he slid off the stool, then he made his way to the door. Turning back, he took one last look around and waved to Molly whose head was still stinging from the blow she received from Oliver. She brushed a tear from her cheek and beckoned Douglas over but he shook his head and exited The Ten Bells forever.

After closing the door Douglas suddenly resolved to head back to Elsie's lodgings. If Oliver didn't want him around then he could go to hell, but he and *his* Elsie would find a way to be together—no matter what!

'Rip the Ripper, rip the Ripper, rip the Ripper ... '

... came the chant of dozens of wharfies, thugs and prostitutes who had joined Skinner's mob intent on mayhem and murder in their quest for revenge. Children on the streets ran from the horde, terrified of the ugly shouting and fearful for their lives. Ahead of the mob, Skinner, his club held triumphantly aloft was king of all he surveyed.

Douglas, on his way to find Elsie, heard the chanting.

'Rip the Ripper, rip the Ripper, rip the Ripper ... '

He frowned. What the deuce was going on? He could see the glow from the torches in the next street, and he could hear the pounding of footsteps together with the raised voices of the mob.

'Rip the Ripper, rip the Ripper, rip the Ripper ... '

In the darkness, Skinner led his mob, carrying their knives and clubs and hell bent on destruction. One street away Douglas heard the angry rumblings growing louder.

'Rip the Ripper, rip the Ripper, rip the Ripper ... '

As he turned the corner, he recognised that dreadful fellow, Skinner at the head of a large group of people coming towards him.

Douglas froze.

Skinner, his face contorted with hatred said just two words: 'Get 'im!!'

Arthur sat wedged between the two detectives inside the carriage as the Professor drove the horses, encouraging them to hurry. Brett kept a suspicious eye on the brute while Wainwright asked him the same question repeatedly.

'Why don't you just confess now? It'll be a lot easier on you if you do; you may even receive a lighter sentence.'

'I don' know nothin'. Yer can't pin anythin' on me.'

'Fine,' replied Brett curtly. 'Either way, you're going to get locked up, tried, then sentenced to be hanged.'

Arthur shot him a look of pure loathing, safe in the knowledge that Grantley would keep his promise and somehow get him out of the mess that he was in.

Outside, the voices belonging to Skinner's ranting mob drifted on the wind and the Professor leaned forward trying to catch the words. The sinking pit in his stomach told him that something terrible was about to occur. But from where was it coming? And more to the point, to whom were they referring?

Arriving at the Police House the Professor brought the carriage to a standstill and jumped down from the seat. He peered inside the window and saw a light shining from Greensworth's office; the superintendent was obviously still hard at work.

He opened the carriage door allowing Wainwright to alight first, then Arthur, then finally Brett.

'Lock him up, then fill Mr Greensworth in on what has occurred,' the Professor instructed sharply.

The alien's abrupt tone caused Brett to ask, 'is there something wrong?'

'Yes I believe so.'

Arthur grunted contemptuously.

Wainwright tightened his grip on the criminal's collar and asked, 'can we do anything to help?'

'Not directly but do either of you happened to carry a firearm?'

Both men nodded.

'I'll need to borrow one.'

'You can take my revolver but what do you need it for?' asked Brett.

'I don't know. Hopefully I won't need to use it but I don't like the sound of what I just heard. I need to find out what's going on. In the meantime, you take him,' he glanced at Arthur, 'inside and lock him up. I trust Mr Greensworth will still be in a reasonable state of mind so you shouldn't have anything to worry about there.' The Professor took the gun from Brett, slid it inside his jacket, then climbed back up on the driver's box and took hold of the reins. 'Oh, and one more thing.' He leaned over beckoning to his two friends. 'Take care to leave out anything about Grantley's *twin* when reporting your findings.'

The inspectors shared a knowing look and despite himself Arthur looked interested he would have liked to have known what the Professor meant as well. Did Doctor Grantley have a brother?

'Where will we be able to find you?' asked Brett.

The Professor sighed. 'I don't know. Look, I'll return as soon as possible.' He tugged at the reins and drove off.

Disturbed by the noise outside in the street, Greensworth came out of his office and opened the door to see a stranger flanked by the two detectives. He gave Brett and Wainwright a questioning look before brushing away beads of perspiration from his forehead.

'What's going on Mr Brett?'

The inspector pushed Arthur roughly across the threshold. 'We have some good news. We've caught the Ripper's little helper.'

Elsie headed for the tavern via the empty marketplace and the tenement blocks with their noisy inhabitants. She stopped to chat with some of Oliver's girls who were looking for customers, then bought a penny's worth of bread from a street vendor, before turning the corner into Commercial Street. Just as she reached The Ten Bells, a hansom cab pulled up near the tavern and Professor Delbrotman alighted. Swallowing the last of the bread, she called out to him waving frantically. 'Oh Professor, thank yer for what yer did for my Douglas.' She ran over to him, flung her arms around the startled man and planted a firm kiss on his lips.

He was filled with revulsion but hid his feelings with a weak smile while untangling himself from her grasp. Then he reached up and handed the driver a handful of coins. As he pocketed the fare, the driver had the oddest feeling that the passenger who alighted from his cab was not the same man who had originally stepped inside.

The cabby shrugged, pocketing the generous payment. If the toff was willing to pay double then what was it to him if he looked a bit different?

Elsie frowned. 'Are yer feelin' awlright love? Yer don't look yer usual 'appy self.'

The being who wore the Professor's face smiled. 'Please forgive me, my dear. I have been under so much pressure lately.'

'Course yer 'ave. Wot was I thinkin' eh? Well yer come in with me, an' I'm sure that Molly's got a table for us, an' when Douglas comes, we can all 'ave a nice quiet drink an' celebrate.'

The man frowned. 'Molly?' His frown however transformed into a smile when Elsie opened the door and a young girl with curly brown hair jumped up and rushed over to meet them. Of course, his eyes glittered triumphantly, how could he ever forget his little friend?

Molly gave him a bright smile, instantly forgetting the dull ache in her head, then taking the Professor by the hand, seated him at a spare table before hollering at the barman for a drink. Elsie followed close behind then sat down at the table beside them, impatiently waiting for Douglas to arrive.

'Your copper beer,' announced Backer lumbering over and handing the Professor a glass.

The alien looked at the drink in disgust and placed it firmly on the table with a bang.

'Thank you,' he replied curtly. Oblivious to his harsh tone, Backer returned to his place behind the bar and continued to spit polish the glassware.

'Constable Briggs told us wot 'appened with Douglas an' everythin': y'know, 'ow yer got 'im orf,' said Molly, attempting to start a conversation. She looked expectantly at the Professor, somewhat concerned by his cool manner.

'Indeed?' he replied simply. 'Well it's all in a day's work.'

Elsie scoffed. 'A day's work? Never. It's 'cos you're the best copper an' yer know when someone's innocent.' She patted his hand affectionately.

The Professor swiftly slid his hand away; he looked at all the whores and their drunken companions and a feeling of revulsion surged through him.

A filthy miscreant smoking a fat cigar wandered over and pushed up a chair beside him, turning his stomach.

'Well, well then,' declared Oliver expansively. 'My Molly's little protector 'as finally made an appearance.'

The Professor stared coldly at the man and remained silent.

Oliver shrugged. 'Not yer usual chirpy self then, eh?'

'Wot do yer want?' interrupted Elsie.

Oliver gave her a reptilian grin. 'Molly owes me some money, thas all.'

The Professor glanced at the girl's pale face, noting the fear she felt for this cigar-smoking brute, so he reached into his pocket and handed the pimp several coins. 'Does this satisfy your primitive needs?'

Oliver looked at the alien as if he'd just escaped from the lunatic asylum. 'Dear oh dear, we did get out of the wrong side of bed this mornin', didn't we?' He pocketed the money and stood up to walk away, before turning to Elsie with a smug expression on his face. 'By the way, just before yer managed to get yer arse in 'ere t'night, surprise, surprise, Dougie turned up an' I told 'im 'e ain't welcome 'ere no more, an' that means no more visitin' ya neither.'

'Wot? Why?' Elsie silently cursed herself for taking so long. If she'd been quicker about it then she would have gotten to see Douglas before it was too late. Why had she wasted so much time stopping to chat with the girls and buy that bloody bread?

Oliver's eyes flashed in anger. 'I don' 'ave to justify my reasons to *you*, madam! This is my business an' wot I says goes.' His face twisted into a sneer. 'If yer don't like it, then yer can pay me orf, an' yer free to go.'

Elsie looked away feeling sick at heart. How on earth could Douglas pay off that swine?

'I think it's time we left,' announced the Professor, abruptly taking Molly by the elbow in a firm grip. 'Come along my dear.' The girl gave him a confused look before casting an apologetic glance towards her friend.

'I'll be back later, Els',' she murmured before being marched outside.

'That was a bit mean to leave so quick. Wot about poor Elsie?'

'Don't concern yourself about Elsie, all will be well.' The Professor hailed a passing cab and ushered Molly towards it. He opened the carriage door and smiled at her. 'Hop in my dear. I have a surprise for you, and afterwards we'll try and sort something out for *poor Elsie*.'

Molly smiled and stepped inside. 'I knew yer 'ad somethin' on yer mind. Wot's me surprise?'

He stepped in after her and closed the door. 'You'll see.'

Douglas ran, his face red from exertion and his heart pounding. This was a nightmare. Why were they chasing him? How could they possibly think that he was *that* revolting murderer? And after everything that had happened to him the previous night, why now? He raced up the alley, accidentally colliding with a figure who was stumbling out of a nearby pub.

'Out of my way!' Douglas gasped frantically.

'Dougie?' uttered Joshua, confused. He turned and saw a wild mob running after the actor and spotted Skinner screaming and cursing with dozens of others behind him, brandishing fire torches and clubs. He stumbled out of the way as Douglas disappeared into the distance, with the mob hot on his heels.

Elsie sat alone, her eyes brimming with tears. What was she going to do now? How could Douglas ever possibly raise enough money to free her from Oliver? She sipped at the beer that the Professor had left, barely noticing when one of Oliver's regulars rushed through the door, eagerly looking around to tell someone his news.

'Ey!' Joshua exclaimed, rushing over to the bar. 'They're 'eadin' for the wharf; quick before it's all over!'

Oliver looked up in annoyance. 'Wot yer on about?'

'There's a lynch mob!'

Backer was confused. 'Wot?'

Joshua groaned in frustration at the block headed gorilla. 'A lynch mob! 'E's gonna be lynched!'

A sailor who was thumping on the piano stopped and turned around. 'Who?'

'Im! Yer know, the great actor!'

'Wot?' cried Elsie, her heart hammering in her chest.

Oliver looked incredulous, 'yer don't mean, Dougie?'

Joshua nodded. 'One and the same.'

Elsie dropped the glass she had been holding and flew to the door.

'Now wait a Goddam minute 'ere!' shouted Oliver.

Elsie wrenched the door open and heard the angry cries in the distance. She rushed out into the street followed by the regulars who took one look at each other and charged out after her.

Oliver looked on furiously as Backer tried to follow them. 'And where the bleedin' 'ell do yer think yer goin'?'

Backer stared at him blankly. 'To see Douglas get lynched.'

Oliver spat on the floor. 'Yer get paid to serve beer, not to bugger orf when yer feel like it.'

Backer faltered, looking around the empty room. 'But there's no one 'ere to serve now. Come on Oliver why don't we go see wot's goin' on, then maybe try to get 'em to come back for a victory drink afterwards.' Backer looked at the pimp hopefully, quite pleased with his clever suggestion.

Oliver grunted. 'I s'pose.' He marched passed the barman grumbling. 'But if this is a waste of my time, I'm 'oldin' *you* responsible!'

Backer shrugged and followed him out locking the door.

Kyeldsen stood in the dining room staring at the unconscious form of Molly stretched out across the sofa. Excellent. The ether had worked out exceptionally well leaving him with a perfectly intact hostage for later use. He turned away smugly before a wave of nausea hit him like a thunderclap and he staggered against the wall. He needed more energy, so he reached into his jacket pocket and took out a piece of chocolate and bit into it. The nausea receded as quickly as it had come, and he breathed a sigh of relief.

He walked over to the mirror hanging on the wall then focussed his concentration on the face that returned his stare until it shimmered and melted away, returning him to the appearance of Doctor Grantley. He felt pleased with the finished product, recalling only a short time ago when he had walked across the threshold of his office, leaving a confused Molly in the hallway after their return journey.

'Why are we 'ere?' she had called out.

'Doctor Grantley invited myself and a companion to dinner,' Kyeldsen had replied, as he poured ether onto a wad of bandages.

'Then where is 'e?' She glanced around nervously at the shadows that danced from the open doorway of the surgery. Kyeldsen/Professor walked out of the office with his hands behind his back.

'Doctor Grantley had to make a return visit to Buckingham Palace but gave me his key, and said we were to make ourselves comfortable while we await his return.'

The girl gave him a dubious look. 'An' yer don' mind me bein' 'ere with yer?'

Kyeldsen/Professor smiled cruelly. 'You are my young lady. Why should I be ashamed to be seen with you?'

The girl shrugged then hugged herself with her arms. 'I'm not really dressed for the part though, am I?'

Kyeldsen/Professor stepped forward slowly.

'I mean, yer changed ... into yer nice black suit an' all.'

He smiled once again in amusement; it wasn't merely his attire that had changed. 'My dear I have a surprise for you.'

She gave him a curious look but returned the smile. 'Wot is it?'

Kyeldsen/Professor's eyes glittered with excitement. 'You will get your surprise if you are a good girl and close your eyes. Come along now,' he gently chided. 'Close one then the other.'

Molly giggled nervously then obeyed. 'Awlright, I'm ready.'

'So am I.' The whisper was lost barely before it reached her ears as Kyeldsen struck like lightning, clamping a hand around her throat and stuffing the ether-soaked bandages over her nose and mouth. She gave a muffled squeal and struggled for a moment before slumping in his arms. Trying not to burn too much of his precious energy, he picked her up over his shoulder then dumped her on the sofa in the dining room. After gagging her and securely binding her hands and feet he knew it would only be a matter of time before the Professor sought him out. And when that occurred, he would cure him of his curiosity once and for all.

Arthur sat on the floor leaning against the same cell wall where Douglas had languished the night before. He pulled out the papier mâché' box that the doctor had given him and carefully opened the lid. Good; the chocolate was still pretty much in one piece. He heard voices from the room above and knew that it wouldn't be long before the Peelers would be at him for information about his boss and his fancy work. Well, they could stew in their own shit first before he was going to help them with anything! He grinned smugly and popped the chocolate into his mouth allowing the layers to melt across his tongue before sliding down his throat. He hoped that it would work quickly.

It did. It made him forget. It made him forget everything.

In fact, it even made his heart forget to keep beating too. Arthur's eyes almost shot out of their sockets, and he gasped clutching at his chest, as a fire burnt through every fibre of his being. The blood in his veins clogged and his brain felt fit to burst. Within a few short seconds Arthur Oder's eyes glazed over, and he slumped against the cell wall with the empty box beside his already stiffening fingers.

In that brief moment if Arthur had still been alive, he would have seen the two detectives unlock the door to his cell and walk towards him. He would have heard Brett yell at him and felt Wainwright nudge his leg. Instead, his body fell sideways; the inspectors rushed to loosen his collar, feeling for a pulse. There was none.

Brett called out to Greensworth, as Wainwright picked up the little box, sniffing at it. There was a tiny fragment of chocolate still inside; it had to be poison.

Wainwright showed his colleague the box.

'Perfect,' hissed Brett, 'we had the bastard and then he had to go and kill himself.'

'Don't forget about what the Professor said though,' whispered Wainwright. 'This one was merely the messenger. We still know who the real one is.'

Brett bent down again and examined the dead man's frozen look of horror. 'It must have been bloody powerful to work that quickly but why would he be so stupid as to take it willingly?'

'He probably didn't know.' Wainwright bent down beside his partner. 'I wouldn't put it passed his employer to cover his tracks by lying to him.'

Brett looked up as Greensworth entered the cell then upon realising that the prisoner was dead, quietly went back upstairs and returned with a notebook, and ink and pen. He began scribbling down notes for the coroner.

'Do you think his employer meant to get rid of him?'

Wainwright shrugged. 'Perhaps. Or maybe he was told it would drug him thereby rendering him useless to interrogation.'

Brett stood up nodding sagely. 'All a ploy to cover the killer's tracks.'

The three men remained in silent contemplation for a few moments, the only sound coming from Greensworth's pen. Brett was about to add something to his previous statement, when he was interrupted by the sound of dozens of footsteps and shouts echoing from the room above the cell. Greensworth stopped what he was writing then giving the detectives a startled look, bounded out of the cell with Brett and Wainwright hard on his heels.

'Sir!' gasped PC Briggs flanked by several other uniformed officers. 'We have a situation at the wharf-side!'

Greensworth gave him a grim look. 'What is it, Constable?'

'It's Jack the Ripper Sir. There's a mob chasing after a man and I swear they're gonna kill him.'

'Alert all officers available,' commanded Greensworth.

'We have Sir, they're on their way.'

The superintendent grabbed his baton then called to the detectives. 'Let's go.'

CHAPTER 15

The road had come to an end and Douglas realised that there was nowhere further to run, short of jumping off the pier. This prospect filled him with dread as he couldn't swim and he was sure Skinner and the mob would be only too glad to watch him flail about in the water, until he drowned. He frantically looked around searching for somewhere to conceal himself, then spotted a door to a factory up ahead. He ran over and twisted the doorknob but it wouldn't open so he banged on it loudly but no one came out.

He was panicking; he had to hide somewhere, so glancing over his shoulder, terrified that Skinner would appear any second, he hurried along nearly tripping over his own feet. His salvation came in the shape of shipping crates stacked up against a building, so he dashed over wedging himself between the crates, praying the mob would pass him by.

Within seconds Skinner stormed onto the wharf, then realising that he too could go no further held up a hand for everyone to stop. The chanting ceased and everyone came to a disorderly standstill, waiting for the sailor to tell them where to go next. Skinner looked around suspiciously, confident that Douglas had to be around here somewhere. He was probably hiding as it was hardly likely the killer would have shinned up the factory wall and legged it over the rooftop. Nor was it likely that he jumped into the water. To be certain, Skinner told the others to wait while he ran over and peered down the side of the wharf. The water lapped gently against the wooden posts but no one was hiding amongst them.

'Yer 'ere somewhere, I know yer are!' the sailor suddenly shouted. The mob looked around in all directions, itching to begin its lynching. 'Come out yer stinkin' bloody murdering coward!'

Douglas bit into his fist, trying not to whimper.

Skinner waved his torch threateningly in the air. 'I can smell yer, y'know! No one smells worse than a Jew!'

In agreement the mob shouted out cruel, taunting remarks and Douglas felt terror-stricken. Not only did they think he was Jack the Ripper but they also knew that he was Jewish. He briefly wondered which they thought was the worst.

Skinner swore. Why wouldn't Douglas for once be a man and take the bait and come out to face his fate? Well, if he wouldn't do it, then Skinner would make him! The sailor strode over to the building then sensing somebody watching him, turned towards the crates up ahead. Charlie came rushing over with several others in tow, wondering what the sailor was up to.

'E's here,' whispered Skinner.

'Where?' Charlie couldn't see him.

Skinner smiled. 'Burn the crates an' find out.'

Charlie was exultant and hurried over and thrust his torch at the nearest crate when suddenly a voice cried out in fear and surprise. The rest of the mob rushed over to witness Douglas come stumbling out from his hiding place, shaking off an angry rat biting at his leg.

Skinner grinned victoriously. 'Ladies and gentleman, may I introduce ya to the *late* Jack the bloody Ripper!'

He whooped in triumph then the mob screamed, charging at the actor. The rat took one look at the insane humans then scurried away leaving Douglas rooted to the spot, tears pouring down his cheeks. He closed his eyes and whispered, 'dear God.'

The mob descended, slashing and beating Douglas to the ground. Some of the thugs were injured in the confusion but no one minded as it was a small price to pay to rid themselves of this perverted killer once and for all. Skinner laughed maniacally, revelling in the carnage, and no one held back even when they saw Douglas's blood seeping into the ground and the fact that he was no longer putting up a struggle.

Elsie, Oliver's girls and the customers from The Ten Bells arrived at the wharf within minutes, witnessing dozens of thugs raining blows at something on the ground up ahead. Elsie screamed in anguish and tried to run over but was held back by one of the others.

'No! Ya'll only get yerself killed!' shouted Isabelle.

Elsie struggled in her friend's arms. 'No! It's Douglas! No!'

In that chaotic moment three gunshots rang out and everyone froze, wondering where the sound had come from. There was silence and everyone held their breath until out of the shadows, revolver in hand, the Professor appeared, walking towards the mob. When he realised who was lying on the ground, and what had been done, he fired another warning shot in the air. The mob flinched perceptibly, unsure of the Professor's intentions; they backed away leaving the bloody and battered remains that had once been Douglas, alone. The Professor walked over and felt for a pulse in vain; he then pointed the gun at the mob choking back emotion.

Elsie, unable to stand the unbearable silence any longer, cried out breaking free of Isabelle's grip and rushed over to the actor's body. She buried her head in his neck, caressing his broken face, begging him to wake up. The Professor gently rested a hand on her shoulder, and she turned to look at him.

'Why?' she choked. 'Why? He was my Douglas!' Trembling from head to foot she turned to face Skinner who was scowling at her. Her face twisted with rage. '*You* did this! Yer bloody murderer! Yer bastard, I'll kill yer for this! I'll kill all o'yers!' She raced over, trying to punch and kick at the sailor but the alien rushed to stop her, pulling her away. Skinner held up a fist, angered that she should try to hit him but a single look from the Professor holding the revolver made him think twice.

Elsie felt as if she was trapped in a ghastly nightmare, and she slumped like a rag doll against the Professor. If she could just wake up, Douglas would be waiting for her. He wasn't sprawled on the ground, dead. No, he couldn't be. He was alive and he loved her; and she loved him. She looked down at the face that was barely recognisable, and her stomach churned. She groaned, then collapsed on the ground and vomited. The Professor looked horrified, then Isabelle pushed passed him and bent down placing an arm around her stricken friend, trying to comfort her.

The alien looked at each member of Skinner's mob slowly shaking his head in disgust. 'What right do you think you have in taking the life of another? You people are an abomination!'

Skinner's face twisted into an ugly sneer; gun or no gun, he wasn't about to be spoken to like that. 'We don't 'ave to answer to *you*! We just caught ourselves Jack the bleedin' Ripper! Someone who never gave mercy to our women and someone wot the coppers ain't never been able to catch!' He stepped forward defiantly. 'Now that 'e's dead, 'e can bloody well rot in the pits of 'Ell forever!'

Skinner's bold reply bolstered the confidence of his followers, and they supported their leader with murmurs of assent.

The Professor's expression darkened with barely suppressed rage. 'You mindless creature, this man was not Jack the Ripper!'

Skinner responded to the alien by spitting on the ground then Charlie stepped forward, electing to explain just how wrong this gun-wielding toff was.

'Oh I think ya'll find 'e was,' replied Charlie with an authoritative air. 'That's 'cos 'e was a doctor ... *and* a Jew.'

The Professor heard one of the thugs whispering *bloody Jew* to his neighbour and it took every inch of willpower not to fire his gun at the brute. But then that would have been stooping to their level but what could he do or say to this monstrous collection of humans that would penetrate their malicious minds? He could have told them that they were a bunch of ignorant creatures, with no understanding or compassion. He could have demanded to know why they should hate Douglas so much just because of his faith. He could also have said that they were now, no better than the real Jack the Ripper. He could have said a million things but knew that it would have done no good. They wore their prejudices like a badge of honour; there was no getting through to them so instead of responding he merely murmured, 'your ancestors should never have climbed out of the primordial slime.'

He glared at these mindless aberrations, and he lowered the revolver when suddenly a cacophony of whistles blasted and a swarm of police officers, Brett and Wainwright amongst them, descended on the crowd. Skinner swore, yelling at everyone to scatter before being wrestled to the ground. The rest of Douglas's killers tried running away but in the confusion were caught one by one and slung into horse-drawn cages that arrived within seconds of the arrests.

The detectives raced over to the Professor, and he quickly explained what had happened before handing Brett back his gun. They were sickened at the sight of Douglas's remains and told the Professor that the real killer's lackey had just consumed poison and had died in the Police House cell. The Professor sighed not knowing what to do next. His indecisiveness lasted only for a moment however, when one of the police tried arresting Elsie and Isabelle.

'No Constable,' the alien intervened. 'These ladies have nothing to do with Douglas Forbes-Montague's murder. I do however, want you to arrange for the body to be taken to the morgue immediately. Go and find the superintendent, he will know what to do.'

The constable released the women and hurried off, just missing Oliver and Backer sneak passed and make a run for it. They had been observing the goings on from a safe distance and disappeared into the night before anyone realised they'd even been there.

Elsie kept staring at Douglas, not wanting to leave him. 'I don' want 'im takin' away. They'll bury 'im in a pauper's grave!'

'No they won't,' assured the Professor kindly. 'I'll make sure he has a proper burial.'

Elsie started crying again. 'I can't leave 'im!'

Isabelle looked on helplessly then suggested that she should come home with her; the Professor nodded approvingly.

'Now that's a good idea.' He looked into Elsie's red and swollen eyes and gently calmed her frantic mind. 'You need some rest, Isabelle will look after you.'

Elsie nodded slowly. 'Yes. But wot about Molly? Molly liked Douglas too. She'll want to know what happened to 'im. Is she 'ere?

The Professor frowned. 'I don't know where she is. I haven't seen her for several hours.'

'Wot yer mean?' asked Elsie, beginning to feel particularly sleepy. 'Yer two jus' left the tavern together.'

The Professor felt a sinking feeling in the pit of his stomach. 'I did what?' He gave the inspectors a startled look.

'Yeah,' insisted Isabelle, placing an arm around her friend's shoulder. 'I saw yers go too. Yer looked in a right 'urry, yer did.'

'In a hurry,' echoed the Professor, fearfully. He knew he hadn't seen Molly since Douglas's arrest. It must have been the Phymordan. But what would he have done with her? Would he have harmed her? He told Isabelle to look after Elsie until his return then called to the inspectors.

'We've got to go to Harley Street immediately.'

'Do you think he'll be there now?' asked Wainwright.

The Professor nodded. 'Why else go to the trouble of pretending to be me? I think, *I hope*, he is using Molly has bait, because the alternative is unthinkable.'

'Right,' said Brett, 'Let's go then. Shall we use his carriage? Where did you leave it?'

The Professor shook his head. 'No. We'll use my ship, it'll be quicker.'

The detectives shared a nervous look, then hurried after the alien just as Skinner was thrown into one of the horse-drawn cages.

'Mr Hugh *bloody* Barker,' the sailor spat as the superintendent's assistant locked the cage. 'This was all your doin'! *You* paid me to do the job; to chase the Kipper down! *You* owe me!'

Barker however had no recollection of Skinner's accusation due to the Professor's hypnotic influence and he shook his head. 'Save it for the judge; I'm told he likes a good laugh!'

Skinner looked outraged. 'Yer bastard, I'll get yer for this!'

Barker signalled the buggy drivers with their angry captives, swearing and cursing, to leave the area. Their next stop would be a cell in the Police House.

The Professor stepped out of the ship and looked around. He had safely landed in the kitchen of Grantley's surgery and no one, it seemed, was about. He gestured for the detectives to follow him, then allowing the door to remain linked to real space, he closed and locked it securely.

Bringing his finger to his lips, he tiptoed across the tiled floor and peered through the doorway. The hall was in darkness, and there was no sound of anything except for the ticking of the grandfather clock. He beckoned for Brett and Wainwright to follow him, and they padded across the carpet, constantly keeping an eye out for any movement in the shadows.

Everything seemed far too quiet for the Professor's liking but he knew he had to find Molly and kept edging further along until reaching the dining room and looked inside. He could have sworn he heard a muffled groan coming from within, so he turned to the detectives and jerked a thumb towards the room, alerting them that someone was in there. Readying themselves for whatever lay ahead, they cautiously entered behind the Professor who was leaning over the sofa, greatly relieved to find Molly still alive, though bound and gagged. Her eyes widened in surprise then horror as he pulled the gag from her lips. She gasped, about to scream so he clapped a hand over her mouth, hoping that no one had heard her.

'It's all right,' whispered the Professor. 'You're safe.'

Molly gave him a terrified look and cringed when he leaned closer.

'I know you think that I am the one who was cruel to you but it wasn't me. It was a criminal who is a master of disguise.'

'He's right,' whispered Brett. He smiled at her in encouragement. 'Remember us from the Police House when you came with the Professor?'

The frightened girl nodded.

'Well, we have discovered who Jack the Ripper is and just like the Professor said: he can disguise himself to look like anyone.'

The Professor removed his hand from her mouth, and she explained how the *other* Professor had kidnapped her and put her to sleep by forcing a strange smelling cloth over her face. The detectives and the alien shared a look of contempt for the barbaric act on an unsuspecting girl.

As the Professor untied her bonds and helped her to sit up, she asked, 'so who is the Kipper?'

Before anyone could reply, there was a flash of light from the hallway causing Molly and the detectives to automatically shield their eyes from the glare. The Professor blinked several times then ducked as a bullet whizzed passed his ear, imbedding itself harmlessly in the wall above the mantelpiece. Molly screamed and the detectives whipped out their revolvers, aiming them towards the door.

'Put down your weapon,' the Professor called out. 'We want to speak to you but we can't do that while you're shooting at us.'

When there was no response, the Professor slowly moved forward with his hands in the air. 'As you can see, I am unarmed and I'm sure you would not wish to harm an unarmed individual.'

'Oh really?' came the reply from the hall.

Brett and Wainwright hissed at the Professor to get down as a figure appeared in the doorway, pointing a pistol at the group.

'Let me to introduce myself, my name ...'

'We know you're not Grantley,' Brett interrupted, his gun trained on the figure.

'No I am not,' the creature sneered.' He smiled condescendingly at the Professor. 'So you finally managed to discover who I am—or rather who I am not. May I ask how?'

'The usual methods,' replied the Professor guardedly; he wasn't about to elaborate.

'Well before I was so rudely interrupted,' Kyeldsen/Grantley glared at Brett, 'you of course know me as Doctor Andrew Grantley, surgeon to Her Majesty the Queen, and those humans who can afford my expert services.'

The detectives were staggered by the creature's arrogance.

'My true identity is Kyeldsen.'

'Formerly of the planet known as Phymord,' completed the Professor.

Kyeldsen nodded approvingly. 'Very good. You have been doing your homework.'

The Professor sighed. 'So why are you here disrupting this time period?'

'Ah,' Kyeldsen's eyes twinkled. 'I promise all will be revealed if your human companions will drop their weapons.'

Brett snorted. 'Forget it.'

Kyeldsen nodded. 'Very well.' He turned to the Professor and cocked his gun. 'Then I shall shoot Professor Delbrotman.'

Assuming a bluff, the inspectors kept their guns poised; Kyeldsen shrugged, then fired his pistol.

▲

CHAPTER 16

The Professor staggered, clutching his forearm as blood seeped through the torn hole of his jacket.

'That should be a lesson to you gentlemen,' warned Kyeldsen. 'Now slide your guns across the floor to me. You should never assume someone is bluffing.'

Molly wept silently as Brett examined the Professor's wound. 'It's not serious.'

'It's a mere scratch,' dismissed Kyeldsen. 'Haven't you any backbone?'

The Professor glared; it may have been mere a scratch but it certainly didn't feel like one. 'This has gone far enough.'

Kyeldsen laughed, his finger resting comfortably on the trigger of the revolver. 'Far enough? My dear Professor, I've barely even begun!' He walked into the room and gestured with his gun towards the door. 'Now if you'll be so kind as to put your hands in the air and walk slowly into my surgery. And please don't try anything foolish; you know I won't hesitate to shoot.'

Reluctantly they did as they were instructed, then Kyeldsen opened the inner door to the office, revealing the real Doctor Grantley stretched out on a bed surrounded in mist.

'We know that he is the real doctor,' stated the Professor. 'It is, I have to admit, a rather novel way of keeping him alive.'

Kyeldsen shrugged. 'I had no other choice.'

'What did you do to him?' demanded Brett, bewildered at the prostrate figure within the strange mist.

'Nothing.' Kyeldsen seemed insulted by the notion. 'I merely changed into a dog and attacked him, hoping to render him unconscious, unfortunately the shock was too much and he suffered a brain aneurysm.'

Wainwright frowned. 'What's that?'

Kyeldsen gave him a withering look; humans could be so ignorant. 'It's a blood clot on the brain and it would have proved fatal, however, I froze him in a time pocket in order to keep him alive. He is perpetually moments from death.'

'To ensure your convincing portrayal of Grantley by plucking his living memories,' concluded the Professor.

Kyeldsen beamed triumphantly. 'Precisely.' His expression turned ominous. 'And oh the things that I discovered about the good doctor ... '

'Wot things?' Molly sniffed, brushing a tear away from her eye. She was frightened and confused and huddled towards the Professor hoping that he would explain what was going on. 'I don' understand any of this.'

Kyeldsen looked dismayed. 'Dear me, you mean you didn't tell her? Then please allow me the honour to demonstrate, *my dear*.' The form of Grantley shimmered out of shape and transformed into Kyeldsen's natural state. Molly's eyes widened in terror; she screamed in horror, then passed out.

Although the inspectors had previously seen a holographic representation of a Phymordan in its natural form, witnessing an actual demonstration left them visibly shaken. The Professor in the meantime was checking Molly's vital signs, fearful for her mental state. Kyeldsen, now wearing Grantley's clothes that hung awkwardly on his small frame, yawned nonchalantly as he observed the Professor with Molly.

As the Professor gently brushed his fingers across the girl's forehead, he shot a piercing glare at the diminutive figure struggling to keep his gun trained on them. Kyeldsen's spindly arms wavered, evidence of his weak state.

'How can you be so brutal?' The Professor stood up, towering over the tiny alien. 'Do you realise that she may be mentally scarred for life?'

Kyeldsen pouted. 'Like all of her kind, she's a scarred human, why should I care?' The Phymordan closed his eyes and concentrated, then a moment later transformed back into Grantley; he breathed deeply several times clearly weakened by the act.

The Professor grunted thoughtfully. 'That seemed to take a lot out of you.'

Kyeldsen gulped nervously.

'I mean you must obviously require a tremendous amount of energy to sustain your shape and the real doctor's existence.'

Kyeldsen flexed his human shaped fingers around the gun. 'I manage.' He shivered under the penetrating gaze of the Professor then looked away, his nerves overcoming his confidence.

'But there's more to you, isn't there?' the Professor mused, glimpsing something peculiar in Kyeldsen's unhappy mind.

Brett stood looking robotically from Kyeldsen to the Professor. He was starting to feel as if he couldn't take much more of this and wondered if his partner felt the same. He put a hand to his head and groaned.

The Professor, recognising the signs realised that the hypnotic suggestion was wearing off, due to witnessing Kyeldsen's transformation. He knew he couldn't move otherwise Kyeldsen might shoot again so he addressed them both. 'Forgive me Mr Brett and Mr Wainwright, I don't mean to be cryptic. Please allow me to explain.' The detectives looked at the Professor and he sent them another hypnotic suggestion to support their minds. 'What I meant was that this Phymordan is not only a murderer but merely a child; perhaps equivalent to a ten-year-old human being.'

The detectives were in control again and looked at Kyeldsen with disgust. Wainwright shook his head in disbelief. 'How could anyone, much less a child manage to do what he did?'

Kyeldsen's expression was venomous, furious that the Professor had worked out that he was not fully grown. 'I was forced to grow up in a matter of moments when my world was destroyed, and my mother was murdered by a human whore. *I* was forced to learn to survive and take matters into *my* own hands!'

The Professor nodded grimly. 'Oh I see.'

'Oh you see, do you? You don't see anything!' Kyeldsen was outraged. 'How could you possibly know what it is like to lose everything?'

The Professor's expression clouded. 'I do know.'

Kyeldsen grunted contemptuously and a tense moment passed before he regained control. 'So how did you realise that I'm not an adult?'

'It is quite evident from your diminutive size in your natural state.'

The Phymordan grunted irritably.

'You're obviously not in good health either,' continued the Professor, 'otherwise you would have transformed into something by now that could at the very least immobilise us, instead of depending on that firearm to keep us in check.' He waved a disparaging hand towards the gun.

Kyeldsen felt a surge of fear and his molecules ached to return him to his natural state. 'Take care, Professor

Delbrotman lest I shoot you again, and this time I promise I won't be so careful.'

'That's why you have to eat so much isn't it?' challenged the Professor, ignoring the boy's threat. 'You need an ever-increasing amount of energy to maintain your shape and to keep Grantley alive but it's never enough, is it? There just isn't enough food to maintain you permanently, and the more energy you burn, the weaker you become!'

'Shut up! Shut up!!' Beads of perspiration dripped from Kyeldsen's forehead and he shimmered out of shape before re-solidifying.

The Professor tut tutted. 'Take care. You must try and keep your emotions in check.'

The inspectors shared a conspiratorial glance—there just might be a chance that they could overpower this rapidly weakening creature if they could just grasp the right moment.

Kyeldsen took out a handkerchief and dabbed at his forehead, desperately trying to stay in control. He would not allow these creatures to get the better of him. He *would* maintain his present shape. Taking a deep breath, and half wishing for a Mol-Ener Bar, he turned to the Professor. 'You must be curious to know why I must kill, because there is a reason; a very logical reason in fact.'

'Revenge?'

Kyeldsen smiled bitterly. 'Do you have any idea what the humans did to my world?'

The Professor nodded grimly. 'We know that Phymord was invaded and colonised by humans, but there was an unofficial account of a Phymordan who escaped from a human ship.'

'That was me. I was trapped, so I morphed into energy and transported myself into the vortex but was dragged into the unpredictable fourth dimension and ended up here. My initial plan was to wait until the colony ship returned to Delta VI and exact my revenge but circumstances changed so I had to change with them.'

The Professor listened intently to Kyeldsen then suddenly recalled something that had been bothering him since arriving in this time-period. Could it have been purely coincidence that he had felt a tremor in the vortex at the exact same time that Kyeldsen had been propelled into the fourth dimension? An unprotected life form in the vortex would have sent noticeable ripples through the current. What if Kyeldsen had accidentally collided or at the very least been buffeted by his ship?

Kyeldsen gave him a triumphant look, almost as if he could read the other's thoughts. The Professor quickly shut off his mind to the intrusion, but it was too late, Kyeldsen had glimpsed something of interest.

'Yes Professor Delbrotman,' he replied. 'The tremor you detected was when I was attempting to exit Dimension-4. I knew I could not withstand the elements of the vortex for long, so I attempted to escape, only to be struck by an abstract foreign body. I tried again, this time, successfully, and found myself thrust into this time period on Earth. A rather drastic way to travel, don't you think? I'm sure you journey in much more comfortable surroundings.'

The Professor narrowed his eyes, not at all happy where this conversation was heading. 'I take it you are aware that I am not human.'

'I knew that from the first,' replied Kyeldsen simply. 'When the three of you came to me for help, I looked into your minds when I demonstrated that Jack the Ripper was left-handed, remember?'

'When you cut your finger?' prompted Wainwright.

Kyeldsen looked at the detective. 'I saw merely human thoughts within *Messrs* Brett and Wainwright's minds but detected a powerful alien presence within yours, Professor Delbrotman. Well, you could naturally understand my fear and apprehension, so assuming you would not expect anything, I sent you what I call an hypnotic veil that would at least temporarily confound clear thinking on your part.'

It took a moment for the implication of Kyeldsen's words to sink in and the Professor felt shock and indignation in equal measure, partly because the ploy had worked thereby preventing him from thinking clearly and acting quickly; and partly because a mere child had managed to control him without him knowing it, dealing a hefty blow to his ego. 'So that's why I frequently felt a barrier each time I was getting closer to the truth. How dare you interfere with my mind! Hypnosis is not a tool to be used in such a fashion!'

Kyeldsen stuck out his tongue rudely. It looked bizarre and outlandish coming from the adult face of Grantley and the Professor's expression turned thunderous at being bested.

'You have no right, no right at all … '

'Gentlemen, please.' Brett stepped forward, mindful of the situation growing tenser by the moment and not at all pleased with how this strange creature was tightening his grip on the firearm. 'My partner and I are trying to understand what has been going on here, and I would appreciate it if we could return to the matter at hand.' He looked at the child intently, trying to ignore the weapon that was now being aimed in his direction. 'You were saying about why you murdered those women?'

Kyeldsen sneered at the inspector. 'Quite right Mr Brett. Allow me to elaborate.' He cleared his throat theatrically. 'When people committed murder on my planet, they were executed by organ extraction.'

'The same method you used to murder those women,' completed Brett. 'We know that. But what we don't know is why.'

Kyeldsen raised both eyebrows in mock approval. 'Well, you see a whore killed my mother and so I decided to kill every human on Delta VI using Phymordan execution but because I was thrust into this world in this century, I was unable to carry out my initial plan. Instead, I targeted any whore within my grasp and exacted my revenge explaining to them while I carefully dissected their steaming organs from their filthy bodies, that they not only deserved to be dead but they deserved never to be whole again. They had to remain a hollow void for eternity, because that's what Phymordan execution means and that's what I felt when my mother was taken from me.' He giggled viciously, his voice dropping to a whisper. 'Funnily enough they never contradicted my explanation. I daresay they must have agreed with me.'

Wainwright clenched his fists, sick to his stomach and Brett swore under his breath, appalled by the child's twisted sense of humour. The Professor stared accusingly at the alien.

'It's impossible to condemn me, you know.'

Brett raised an eyebrow. 'Really?'

Kyeldsen nodded and giggled maniacally. 'You see I do whole heartedly admit that I did it, and yet at the same time it wasn't actually me.'

The Professor scowled. 'Well since you're playing at being Grantley, I suppose you're going to tell us that you're willing to lay the entire blame on his shoulders.'

Kyeldsen gave him a surprised look. 'You're closer to the truth than you realise, Professor Delbrotman. But why shouldn't I blame him? After all, he had begun the task of ridding this world of whores before I ever set foot on this planet.'

The Professor registered shock then suspicion. 'I beg your pardon?'

Kyeldsen smiled triumphantly, thrilled that he had left the best part for last, and that the fools standing before him had never suspected anything. 'I speak the truth. You see even if I had never come to this miserable world, Grantley would have killed as many painted females as he could by dissection.' He laughed. 'Isn't it simply amazing? I mean what are the odds that a human doctor such as he would decide to execute whores precisely in the same manner as myself.' He chuckled. 'Hard to believe, isn't it?'

Brett ran his fingers through his hair in astonishment, trying to come to grips with the shocking implications. 'Are you trying to tell us that Doctor Grantley, I mean the *real* Doctor Grantley had begun murdering prostitutes before you even arrived?'

Kyeldsen nodded enthusiastically. 'Oh yes, but he'd only managed to murder the first, what was her name? Oh yes, I remember, Martha Turner.'

Wainwright looked horrified. 'So what you're saying is regardless of whether you had come here or not, there would still have been a murderer known as Jack the Ripper.'

'Precisely.'

A few moments of silence prevailed as the shock sunk in, with the realisation that the real Doctor Grantley was also Jack the Ripper.

'I have to say that I was just as surprised as you are when I first found out.'

The Professor shook his head in disbelief. 'But why was the real Grantley committing murder?'

Kyeldsen waved the gun playfully. 'Oh that's easy. He was fast approaching the age of retirement and hated the very thought of it. Imagine, a fine, prestigious surgeon being told to stop practising and hand the reins over to another who would also be physician to the Royal Family.'

'Must have been a giant blow to the ego,' the Professor said quietly.

'Exactly,' agreed Kyeldsen.

'After receiving such unhappy news before debating whether to tell his wife, he returned home in the early hours of the morning after attending to an emergency. His feelings on the subject were particularly bitter that his career was almost over, despite his excellence in experience and skill.'

'He noticed a carriage outside his neighbour's house and thought it rather odd at such an early hour, until he saw the front door open and a whore emerge on the arm of his neighbour. Grantley saw him kissing her, then watched as she was bundled into the carriage before it drove away. The neighbour spied him watching then called him over and tapped the side of his nose.

'"*Sorry you had to see that, old boy,*" said Mr Flaxter. "*The wife's been away y'see, and since she and I don't often, well, you know,' he waggled his eyebrows suggestively, "I thought a spot of fun wouldn't go astray. Eh?*" He laughed rudely and dug his elbow into Grantley.

'"*Quite,*" replied Grantley, with a promise to forget what he had just witnessed, then he unlocked his front door and stepped inside. Just as he was about to go upstairs, a frightful image clawed its way up from deep within his subconscious, and suddenly he was five years old again, waiting for his mother to return from visiting her sister. He thought he heard her laughing in the stables and ran over only to discover his father with his trousers pulled down lying on top of a strange woman with her skirts bunched up. He watched them for a few moments as they writhed together on a pile of straw, until the woman's eyes snapped open, and she gasped and pointed at him. Grantley's father rolled away, dragged his trousers up and charged over to take hold of the terrified child.

'"*What did you see?*" he demanded, shaking the boy violently. "*Answer!*"

'The young Grantley shook his head. "*Nothing Father, nothing.*"'

"*You had better not have seen anything, and you will not breathe a word of this to your mother when she returns, or I will send you to the workhouse. Do you understand?*"

'The child bit back tears and ran off. He had seen the painted face of the whore with her powder and lip-rouge and an immediate hatred for her swelled within him.'

'The memory passed, and he was back in the present heading up the stairs to his bedroom. But in that wild moment, his mind twisted and he was determined to show the world that he had lost none of his medical skills and decided to exact his revenge on every whore who crossed his path because of that buried memory.'

The Professor gave a heavy sigh and massaged the bridge of his nose. What an unhappy situation for the real Grantley as well as the fake, and yet at the same time he could forgive neither for their barbarism and callous disregard for the innocent. They could not go unpunished but he knew that history had never discovered who Jack the Ripper was, so the next series of events would have to be handled with extreme care.

'You can now see how I was justified. It was my revenge, and it was also Grantley's revenge therefore I am fulfilling both our wishes.'

There was dead silence.

'So,' announced Kyeldsen, 'the story ends.'

The Professor placed both hands behind his back, momentarily forgetting the wound on his arm; he winced. 'Does it indeed?'

The child shrugged. 'You know everything, so there is nothing more to say except for this,' he trained the gun on the Professor, 'I want your ship. And there's no point telling me you don't have one because I've seen it in your mind, and I also know that it can travel through the all-important Dimension-4. Give it to me now.'

'What?' The Professor gave him an incredulous look.

'Well I'm not about to stay here if I can get back to my planet *before* the humans invade. With your ship I can save my mother.'

'Out of the question.'

Kyeldsen smiled frostily. 'I don't really think that you are in a position to deny me anything.'

The Professor gave him a contemptuous look. 'I really couldn't care what you think but I am not tampering with future history and that is final.'

Kyeldsen cocked the gun. 'Well what if I shoot you instead?'

'Then you would have no one to operate the ship.'

'So you will take me back then?'

'No.'

Kyeldsen growled, a deep guttural groan, and turned the gun on Wainwright and fired but a warning from Brett saved his partner, who instinctively ducked behind the desk. The bullet missed him by mere inches and the noise caused Molly to stir in her troubled unconscious state. Kyeldsen then trained the gun on Brett, however, the inspector had anticipated this and threw himself under the desk beside his colleague.

'Enough!' shouted the Professor angrily. 'I will have no more bloodshed, do you understand?'

'Then take me back.'

Scowling, the Professor reluctantly agreed, then Kyeldsen marched all three out of the surgery and into the kitchen. He looked at the metal door standing in the middle of the room and turned up his nose, unimpressed.

'Is this it?'

'Appearances are so very often deceiving,' replied the Professor pointedly.

Kyeldsen smirked. 'True.' He ran his hand over the door's surface and felt a strange, pulsating sensation emanating from within. For the first time since landing on Earth, Kyeldsen saw his way clear. He would return before the invasion and save his mother.

He looked directly at the Professor. 'Open it.' As the Professor walked slowly towards the door, Kyeldsen trained one of the revolvers taken from the inspectors at the Professor, while keeping guard on the other two with his pistol.

'Well let me pass,' scowled the Professor.' If you want me to open it, I need to get to it.'

Kyeldsen looked suspiciously at him but took a step back. As the Professor rested his hand on the surface, he glanced towards the door leading to a courtyard and shouted. 'Mrs Craven, look out!'

Kyeldsen turned, alarmed that the housekeeper had apparently returned. Seizing the opportunity, the Professor, lunged at the boy while he was distracted.

'You liar!' shrieked the child, realising that the Professor had been bluffing and that there was no one there.

In the confusion, Kyeldsen dropped one of the guns and Brett quickly scooped it up while Wainwright leapt forward and wrestled with the boy. Kyeldsen growled and spat then closed his eyes, concentrating all his frustration and hate, until it transformed him into a raging fire. The Professor and Wainwright backed away in surprise from the boiling heat, as Kyeldsen's flaming face danced with maniacal rage.

'I will burn you all to death!'

Brett frantically flung himself at the back door and opened it. Spying a mop and bucket just outside, he grabbed the bucket and emptied its contents onto the flames. This caused Kyeldsen to return to his natural state. He shrieked in surprise and collapsed on the floor, shivering in the dirty water.

He closed his eyes and willed himself to return to Grantley but couldn't muster the energy to do so. He looked miserably at the burning embers of the doctor's clothing. The Professor, meanwhile, spying one of the guns close by, dived over trying to kick it away from Kyeldsen's path but the Phymordan snatched hold of it first and squealed in pain as the hot metal burnt his fingers. He aimed it at the Professor then uttered, 'who will win the game?'

A shot rang out and the Professor jumped backwards, fearing that he had been wounded a second time, however, it was Kyeldsen who had been shot. As he collapsed, a luminous, golden foam spurted from the hole in his chest. The Professor turned to face Brett who had shot the Phymordan.

'I'm sorry,' the inspector said. 'He would have killed you this time.'

The Professor frowned and bent down to the child, feeling for a pulse. There was none. Kyeldsen was dead.

✧ ✧ ✧

Within the inner office of the surgery, a cocoon of lightning wrapped itself around the mist surrounding the real Grantley and it imploded soundlessly. Time started and the blood clot ruptured, killing the doctor instantly.

✧ ✧ ✧

Dozing in front of the fire, Charlotte Grantley, wearing her dressing gown and wrapped in a blanket wondered if Andrew was ever going to return home. She was rather annoyed that he seemed to have forgotten about their wedding anniversary; there hadn't even been flowers sent as an apology.

The grandfather clock in the drawing room chimed 3 am as she sat in her husband's chair whilst the fire dwindled to a few dying embers. She was startled when she heard a thunderous knocking at the front door. She threw off the blanket and ran towards the door almost colliding with one of the maids who had heard the noise and had reached the entrance before her mistress. When the girl opened the door, two men could be seen silhouetted against her candle. They identified themselves as detectives from Scotland Yard and needed to speak to the lady of the house.

Charlotte Grantley, standing just behind the maid, made sure that her dressing gown was properly buttoned and invited them in.

'You may go Mary,' her mistress ordered, 'and now gentlemen, what brings you here at this ungodly hour?'

'Mrs Grantley,' said the fair-haired man, I am Detective Inspector Jonathan Brett, and this is my colleague Detective Inspector Sydney Wainwright. You may wish to sit down as I'm afraid we have some bad news.'

Charlotte swallowed and nervously began fiddling with her collar.

Wainwright stepped forward. 'It concerns your husband Doctor Andrew Grantley. I'm afraid he took a bad turn earlier this evening ... '

Diary Extract 1.6
It's all over. Jack the Ripper—or should I say Jack the Rippers—are now dead.

After Kyeldsen's death, the detectives helped me carry the real body of Doctor Grantley into the kitchen and we laid him on the floor. I said that the only way to explain what had happened that night was to invent a story whereby we had decided to visit the doctor to ask him some further questions regarding the case. Upon entering the surgery, we had found him sprawled across the kitchen floor, beside a smashed lamp that had started a fire. We quickly extinguished the flames deducing that he had entered the kitchen, fell ill, then collapsed and died, dropping the burning lamp.

The detectives felt very uneasy about providing false evidence to the coroner but I explained in no uncertain terms that the truth would have to be hidden forever. Firstly, no one would believe such a wild tale about an alien masquerading as the doctor and secondly, it would not be politic to openly accuse the real Grantley as there was not a shred of evidence that supported the facts, and it could be highly embarrassing to Scotland Yard and the Queen of England as well. And finally, history never discovered the Ripper's true identity and history must remain fixed.
Brett and Wainwright reluctantly agreed, then said that they would contact the coroner then inform Grantley's wife of the incident. In the meantime, I proceeded to hide any evidence that the coroner didn't need to know about. I placed a large vase in front of the bullet hole above the mantel piece in the dining room and pushed a framed picture to one side covering the other holes in the surgery. I then wrapped Kyeldsen's body in a blanket and placed him inside

my ship then went to look in on Molly. She was still unconscious, so I very carefully informed her injured mind that it had really been me that had taken her to Harley Street to have dinner with the doctor. I had not tried to harm her, nor had she seen nor heard anything to do with Kyeldsen, particularly his transformation. As I wasn't completely confident that my suggestion would work well enough, as insurance, I told her mind that anything out of the ordinary that she thought she saw, had all taken place in a bad dream. I then carried her into my ship.

After attending to the graze on my arm and changing into a fresh coat, I landed within Whitechapel and carried Molly into her lodgings. By coincidence, Isabelle lived in the same tenement block, and she came out to greet me, asking if Molly was ill. I told her that she'd had too much to drink that night then asked if she would mind keeping an eye on the girl. She readily agreed and said lightly, 'course I will, love.' Isabelle was already looking after Elsie who was still sleeping, which was the best thing for her, so I excused myself and said that I would return for both women shortly.

I returned to my ship uncertain what to do next. I knew that I should not be interfering in their lives, yet I felt wrong leaving Elsie and Molly to the mercies of Oliver after everything they'd been through. But what could I do? To take them with me was out of the question. And if I had just given them money to start a new life, somehow, I knew Oliver would find a way to get at them, and the money.

I programmed my ship to return me to the blind alley where I first arrived, then hurried to The Ten Bells and peered through the window. Everything looked unusually quiet and empty, so I banged on the door but got no response. I shouted that it was only me and to open the door to which a voice answered: 'go away!' I recognised Oliver's growl, so I politely explained that I was not going to arrest him but I had a business proposition for him. The door opened and he looked suspiciously at me, so I stepped closely (trying not to breathe in his foul breath) and concentrated on his mind. I needn't have tried so hard, his mind was as easy to penetrate as an eggshell, and I instructed his subconscious that he had generously allowed Molly and Elsie to leave with me and that at no time in the future would he ever attempt to seek them out. I then left him standing on the threshold and returned to my ship then went back to the morgue to wait for the detectives.

Sometime later Grantley's widow was brought in to identify the doctor's remains and when that unhappy task was complete, I spoke to Brett and Wainwright, asking their opinion on what should be done about Elsie and Molly. They both agreed that it was right for the women to leave their hellish existence, then Wainwright suggested the perfect solution. He told me that his cousin was a minister of religion who assisted people who had been traumatised by various means such as drug addiction or forced into prostitution. The Reverend Henry Wainwright had a parish in London and if I wished, the detective would investigate to see if Elsie and Molly could be assisted in some way. I readily agreed, relieved that perhaps their lives could be turned around.

By this time, it was early light, and I remembered my promise to Elsie concerning Douglas's burial, so telling the detectives that I would catch up with them I then proceeded to arrange for his funeral. I was told that he could be buried later that day so returned to Isabelle's lodgings to find Molly and Elsie awake. Elsie had told her what had happened to Douglas, and they were both consoling each other. Isabelle said goodbye as she had to return to The Ten Bells, then I explained that I had arranged for Douglas's funeral and had also spoken to Oliver concerning both women. They asked what I meant by that, and I told them that after I had spoken with him, he and I agreed that they no longer worked for him. They were dumbstruck then started crying again, wondering how they were going to make a living working alone. I then explained about the minister, and they cautiously agreed to meet him.

After Douglas's simple ceremony Elsie asked to return to his lodgings as she wanted to have some of his things to remember him by. Unfortunately, news travels fast and his meagre belongings had already been ransacked; one carrot-haired old hag was still rifling through his wardrobe when I walked in, and I ordered her out unless she wanted to be arrested on the spot. She cursed loudly then ran out of the room, clutching several pieces of paper. One leaf fluttered to the floor and Elsie picked it up. It contained several lines from the play 'The Maiden's Dilemma'. Elsie placed it on the wooden slats of the bed (that was all that was left; the bedding and mattress had long gone) then pushed the bed frame away and pulled at a loose wooden floorboard revealing some medical books and a bible wrapped in a shawl. She gratefully took the contents, together with the sheet of paper and we left.

The next morning Wainwright took the girls and I to visit his cousin, and we explained their unhappy situation. He and his wife very kindly talked to Elsie and Molly for a long time. Afterwards the women agreed that it would be nice to stay a while and assist where they could in the church. The Reverend Henry Wainwright, some years older than his cousin but equally kind and intelligent, said that they could stay as long as they wished and perhaps in time to come, could both find a situation as a maid hopefully bettering themselves. The prospect made both Elsie and Molly afraid yet at the same time excited.

I was however, concerned about the possibility that they would somehow slip back into their old ways and feel bound to return to prostitution and so voiced my concern to the minister but he said that he and his wife would never let them return. Besides, there were a number of women who lived with them in a group of small houses, supplied by the church and maintained by donations from generous benefactors. These women were in the process of recovery and this in turn would support and aid Elsie and Molly. I told the minister that I would help them collect what little belongings they had, then return shortly. Elsie and

Molly both hugged me when I escorted them back home and I promised to visit soon.

I returned to the Police House to find the detectives in something of a quandary. They knew that the case was closed; the problem was, no one else knew that and so they were forced to go through the motions of continuing their investigation as if nothing had happened. I told them that it wouldn't be long before Scotland Yard asked for their return then said my goodbyes.

I left Earth, then jettisoned the body of Kyeldsen into the Solar System's sun, wondering what to do next. I decided to reprogram the ship to return me to a secluded location, close to Scotland Yard exactly one month after the time I had spent in the East End. On entering Scotland Yard, I asked an officer at the front desk if the two detectives had returned. Luckily, they had, just the previous week and we shook hands upon seeing each other again. I asked them if they had been disciplined in any way after supposedly failing to catch the Ripper. Fortunately, nothing had happened to them on an individual working level, however, there had been such a public uproar that the Home Secretary and the London Police Commissioner were forced to resign, and Scotland Yard left severely embarrassed. The Chief Inspector had understood about the difficulties of the case and not laid blame on Wainwright and Brett but there always had to be scape goats and they were in the form of the other two men.

Brett then told me that Greensworth had tried to hang himself and been promptly packed off to a hospital for the insane. I knew it would have only been a matter of time before his mind completely snapped; in fact, I was surprised that my hypnotic suggestion managed to last for so long. I then asked about Hugh Barker and was told that the new superintendent did not allow Barker the same freedom that his predecessor afforded him. That was certainly welcome news!

Wainwright showed me some newspaper clippings concerning the mob that had killed Douglas. Everyone involved had been tried then hung, except for a thief known as Charlie Fry. Apparently, a prison guard had been alerted to a fight breaking out in one of the cells and when he opened it up, he found the sailor Skinner, throttling the life out of the man. Since the sailor had already been condemned to death, it didn't matter to him to take one more life.

The detectives and I went to see Molly and Elsie and the change in them was remarkable. Helen Wainwright said they were learning to cook and attend to the church gardens; this gave them a sense of worth and they looked forward to a happier future which was most heartening. I said my goodbyes promising to visit again then said my final farewells to the detectives. We shook hands again and wished each other well.

So, I am now, once again, alone in this ship and have decided to leave the navigational controls on automatic pilot as manually controlling them can be rather tiresome after a while.

As I have no new data-hexagon I have decided to retain this diary for later use. In any case it is rather cathartic to put 'pen to paper'.
Diary Extract End 1.6

158 timing measurements had passed since the dismantling of the homing device. After this phase elapsed, the secondary device hidden beneath the main engine sent out a signal, asking the first why it was not responding. When no response was received, the secondary device became the primary and it automatically sent out a distress signal that the vessel was still in progress and that the occupant was still alive. When this message was received, an alert was sent out. The murderer of Jackard Menz had finally been traced and would be apprehended in 38 timing segments ... 37 timing segments ... 36 timing segments ...